Trekachaw

B.R. FLORES

TREKACHAW
Copyright © 2019 B.R. Flores

SWR Press
P.O. Box 6235
Oceanside, CA

SWR PRESS

Book design by GKS Creative, Nashville

FIRST EDITION

978-1-7331623-0-2 (print)
978-1-7331623-1-9 (ebook)

TXu 2-036-726

Library of Congress Cataloging-in-Publication Data has been applied for.

I dedicate this book to my caring, loving,
and supportive husband, Steve.
You encouraged me from the beginning
and never tired of listening to my ideas.

prologue

Jupiter nearly ripped Azha into particles as he passed through her massive red cyclone. Narrowly escaping death, he flew to one of her moons and discovered shelter in a cave deep beneath the icy crust of Europa. The cave glowed orange with a warm, soothing atmosphere that provided him a sense of well-being and a hideout. Azha was grateful he had eluded the grotesque Gystfin, knowing that had he not, his fate would have been an agonizing death. This powerful Beast was relentless in his quest to fulfill his revenge by destroying those who betrayed him, and to prove his worthiness amongst the alien's intent on the conquest of Earth and those who protect her. For now, Azha waited far from the war, not knowing if all was lost. As the days passed, hints of color in his stripes became brighter across his chest and legs. This was a good sign, giving Azha hope that soon he could leave the cave and continue his journey home...

As Azha recovered his strength, on a planet light years away, a meeting was taking place, a meeting that, had they known about it, would have astounded the warriors on both sides of the battle. For while blood was being shed, lives lost, and conflict raged, a cabal had formed. Worlds would suffer by the cabals' rapacious betrayal of those who entrusted them with power that was pivotal in the war.

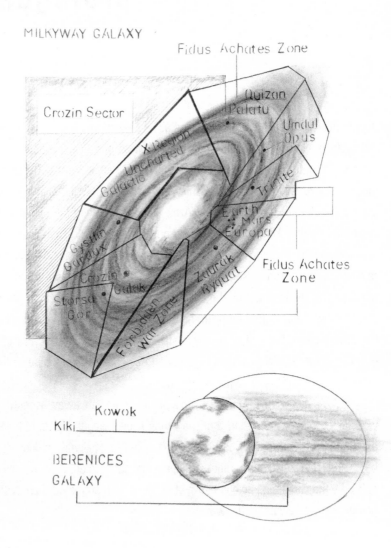

MILKYWAY GALAXY

Fidus Achates Zone

Crozin Sector

Quizan
Palatu

Umdul
Opus

X Region
Uncharted
Galactia

Trinite

Earth
Mars
Europa

Gysttin
Gordux

Fidus Achates
Zone

Crozin

Zaurak
Ryquat

Gdaka

Storsa
Gor

Forbidden
War Zone

Kowok

Kiki

BERENICES
GALAXY

one

PRO TEMPORE EARTH

*Call it destiny, good fortune, or perhaps bad luck.
Whatever you call it, the fate of this ordinary man was the beginning.*

LIFE has a way of throwing us curve balls, of changing things up when we least expect it, and of challenging all our best-laid plans. But in his wildest dreams, he would not — could not — have predicted what was in store for him.

Cole had inherited his father's tall, muscular physique and his mother's olive skin and thick, brown hair. He was strikingly handsome, charismatic, and impossible to ignore. During his years at the University, Cole rightfully earned his reputation as a player. That is, until he laid eyes on the stunning brunette that was to become his wife. To everyone's surprise, once the two became a couple, Cole distanced himself from his old girlfriends and frat boy lifestyle. Soon after graduation he took an oath to protect and serve with his brothers in blue at the local police department.

A year later, Cole was fresh off probation and on top of the world. His wedding was in two short days, and tonight was his last graveyard shift. During briefing, all eyes and harmless groom jokes were exhausted on the rookie. Sergeant Swartwood conveyed his congratulations, then reminded patrol to cover Cole's beat if a late call was dispatched to keep the groom out of hot water. But problems were highly unlikely as his beat covered an area of the county inhabited only by an occasional farmer.

Like most July nights, the air was hot and humid making him sweaty and uncomfortable. Cole was already regretting not taking the night off. Having five hours left until the end of his shift, he needed to think of something to keep himself awake. Checking out the musty, old, abandoned winery was as good a diversion as any.

For generations, the local teenagers had hung out there, especially during school break. Heading south, Cole drove to a junction where he turned onto a remote dirt road. For miles, he followed the path of the headlights leading him far away from the sleeping city. Rolling to a stop, he blacked-out the headlights and parked his cruiser in front of the winery, listening for any sounds. During the past couple of weeks, patrol had arrested groups of underage kids drinking alcohol and smoking dope. By now he would have heard them and seen glimpses of shadows as they scattered into the trees. Cole searched the forest with the floodlight, finding the perimeter surprisingly quiet. He aimed the spotlight towards the main entrance and noticed the door was slightly ajar. It wasn't that way last week, or perhaps he hadn't noticed. Most likely, kids had broken into the winery out of curiosity or to hide from the police. Either way, he'd check it out. Besides, it had been at least a decade since he'd explored the winding hallways and mysterious dusty dungeons. Sipping the last drop of warm coffee, Cole crunched up the cup and tossed it on the passenger-side floorboard. At least he could get out and stretch his legs. He grabbed his flashlight from the charger and stepped out softly, careful not to make any noise from the dry brush beneath his feet.

Not a sound was heard in the still of the night; even the crickets were asleep. Keeping an eye out for any threats, Cole quietly closed the car door. The moonlight lit the rocky path leading to the entrance where spider-web curtains blocked his way. Evidently, the door had not been left ajar; it was merely shadows of the night playing tricks on him. Pulling on the rusty handle did not budge it. Cole propped his foot on the side of the doorframe and pulled harder. This time, the creaky hinges gave way a few inches. He peeked through the crack and couldn't see anything but pitch black. Shining his flashlight through didn't do much. Satisfied that no one could have broken into the building from that door, Cole wondered if continuing was worth his curiosity. Another hot coffee sounded good, but he'd already had four cups and was wired. Checking out the winery gave him something to do until the end of shift.

Cole was familiar with the maze of winding hallways and low rock ceilings as well as the concealed, narrow, stone staircase that led to isolated, underground cellars where barrels had been stored for decades. As an adventurous youth, he'd spent many hot, summer days inside the winery with his buddies. Drawn in by those childhood memories, Cole yanked the door open enough to squeeze his body through, then searched the area with his flashlight to get his bearings. From there he continued onward into the passages where, most likely, his radio would not transmit.

The last time he'd snuck into the winery was on Frank's fifteenth birthday. They'd constructed a booby-trap over the doorway of the last cellar beneath the winery to catch anyone who dared invade the secret hideout they called C.F. Dungeon. Remarkably, nothing had changed in all those years. Every room was crammed with rickety furniture and smelly wine barrels was the same. Before calling it a night, Cole wanted to find their secret dungeon to see if anyone had tripped the booby-trap. Checking his watch and realizing he had less than an hour before daylight, he picked up the pace. Cole navigated the narrow winding hallways leading to the concealed stone staircase.

There it was. He hesitated at the top to shine his flashlight down the stairwell. At best, he could see the first three steps into the abyss. As a boy the ceiling seemed much higher and the stairs not as steep. He reached above to touch the cold rocks with this hand. It couldn't have been more than six feet. Cole shined his light down the stairwell and tested the first step, then another, and another. The ceiling gradually dropped, forcing him to duck his head lower and lower until he reached the bottom. Pausing on the last step, Cole had second thoughts about going any further. Checking his watch again, he saw it was almost the end of shift. Another couple of minutes wouldn't matter, he was so close.

Directly ahead was a large stone chamber that felt eerily different than he'd remembered. Something felt wrong, perhaps a hunch or a sixth sense telling him to turn around. He told himself not to be such a wimp but couldn't stop the feeling in the pit of his stomach. This was ridiculous. Scary monsters who go bump in the night were concocted to frighten little boys, not a police officer. Even so, he remained perfectly still until the feeling passed. Placing one foot in front of the other, Cole moved forward through the chamber into the musty hallway leading to the last cellar room.

A faint light was glowing from the cracks of the partially opened door. Cole attempted to radio dispatch, giving his location, but his portable did not transmit. Someone had found their secret dungeon and was hiding inside, and Cole intended to find out whom.

"Police Department, come out with your hands up."

He waited for a response... nothing but a flickering light.

"Police department, I know you're in there. Come out with your hands up."

Someone was moving around and had dimmed their light from white to yellow. Cold sweat dripped from Cole's forehead as he removed his gun from its holster and stepped behind the door, using it for cover.

"Police department, show yourself."

He pushed the heavy door half-way open with his foot. The creak of hinges echoed off the walls, drowning out the pounding of his heart. Cole peeked inside and saw no one, yet the cellar was lit with a soft, yellow glow. He lowered his gun and shuffled sideways until he was in the center of the room. The cellar flashed into a silver light then dulled to a greyish-blue. Cole switched off his flashlight and placed it on top of a dusty wine barrel, and re-holstered his gun. A calm, hypnotic wave swept over his body and his mind was filled with visions of sparkling, silver oceans and a horizon on fire. Terrified and transfixed, he forced himself to relax, fearing any movement could interfere with his vivid hallucination. He was at peace, floating above the silver ocean in an unfamiliar world. The blue light dimmed to a dark grey and the visions began to fade. His legs felt numb and heavy, so heavy they were impossible to move.

A jolt awoke Cole from his trance into a grim reality of excruciating pain. He was burning up inside and jerking violently out of control. Something was tearing him apart, separating his very soul from his flesh.

"Stop! Help! Down here!" screamed Cole. But no one could hear his screams beneath the old winery. Defeated and wrenched with nausea, Cole stopped struggling and surrendered himself.

He watched his hands and arms vanish before his eyes, leaving a silver hue in their place.

SEEING THROUGH BLURRY EYES, Cole focused on the outline of the rock ceiling. His head was spinning, and his body ached when he moved. Cole closed his eyes wondering if it was morning yet and how he'd ended up on the floor. Whatever happened was over, and he was in no shape to do anything about it. Right now, he needed to move and get the hell out of there. Rolling over onto his side to stand up was easier said than done. Every muscle ached and he couldn't think clearly. He decided to lay flat on his back until his head quit spinning. Besides, the cool dirt felt good against his skin. Cole looked down. *I'm naked, why am I naked? Someone must have undressed me and stolen my uniform? What sick person would do that? What else did they do to me?*

Cole concentrated on trying to remember anything after he'd parked his cruiser, but his mind was blank. He must have been drugged, but how? He needed to shake it off and call for help. Where was his portable radio?

Sluggishly, he rolled his head to the side and stopped. His brain hurt so badly he felt like it was going to explode. But turning his head had been worth it. The flashlight was still on top of the wine barrel. Slowly, he turned his head in the opposite direction. From there, he could see the open doorway and beyond into the dark hallway. Cole closed his eyes to brush the loose dirt off his face. Squinting, he thought he saw something and rubbed his eyes to focus on whatever it was. *What is that?* A huge, deformed hand with long fingers was in front of his face. Cole ducked and slapped the hand away. *Damn that hurt.* He'd slapped his own hand? This was crazy. His mind had to be playing tricks on him. Maybe he was in a coma and all this was nothing more than a bad dream. At least that made sense. Odds were, he'd been injured and was recovering in a safe hospital bed somewhere hallucinating on morphine. That had to be it. Sooner or later he'd wake up and this would all go away. Cole raised his head and cringed. A huge reptilian thing was sprawled out on top of him. Mustering all his strength to get away, he wobbled to his feet, then collapsed onto his back. Cole stared up at the ceiling and screamed for help. A bellowing roar came out of his mouth. It was petrifying. Terrified to move, he lay perfectly still while searching the cellar with his eyes. He spotted a pile of rumpled clothes on the ground, just out of reach. Moving as little as possible, he stretched out and grabbed the nearest piece. At first, he didn't recognize his own police shirt. It was scorched and torn, with most of the buttons and his badge missing. He reached out and grabbed another blue rag that could've been his slacks, or what was left of them. The waist band was riddled with small burn holes and the legs were shredded. His cellphone had been blown apart and was in several pieces on the floor. Mentally and physically exhausted, Cole gave himself permission to rest for a few minutes. Instead, he drifted into a restless slumber.

Falling, falling, the devil was chasing him to suck out his soul... The world was spinning, and Gystfins were waiting to take his head.

He sat up just before smashing onto jagged rocks. Awakening from that nightmare did not change the nightmare he was in. Perhaps now he was strong enough to escape the cellar. Completely convinced that he was either crazy or dead, Cole decided to make the best of an awful situation. His throbbing head and most of his body aches were almost gone. What worried him was the voice in his head that was getting louder and the strange thoughts he couldn't control.

Whatever Cole had turned into to was quite amazing when he wasn't scared to death. The new body must have been seven feet long, and it was extremely muscular. Twisting from side to side, Cole admired the beautiful orange stripes that ran in the same direction where his ribs had been. They were luminescent and perfect, as if painted on meticulously. The same stripes continued down the torso, the length of the legs and across the top of his feet. *No way!* Realizing there were missing body parts – parts that meant a lot to him, Cole groped every inch of himself searching for a penis. Nothing. There was nothing but smooth surfaces with no openings. *That's impossible, how am I supposed to go to the bathroom? This is insane, I must be on drugs.*

Now Cole was positive he had died, and this was his punishment for being rude to so many people when he was younger. Such a joker, thinking he was funny. Could this be his punishment? But for what? He'd never done anything that bad enough to deserve this. Screw it, he'd put an end to this right here, right now. All he had to do was find his gun and kill whatever this was. Cole crawled on his hands and knees over to the wine barrel and grabbed the rim to help pull himself up. There it was, wedged between the rock wall and a rickety old crate. Every step to salvation was worth the pain. Resting his back against the wall he slid down next to his gun. The voice inside his head was begging him to stop. Cole picked up the gun and held it in his hand. There was the voice in his head again. Maybe it was his subconscious telling him to stay alive. He looked down at his legs and closed his eyes. He was a demon. Cole placed the muzzle against his temple and squeezed the trigger. His head flinched but the gun didn't fire. He struggled to rack-it, but the slide wouldn't budge. Holding it close to his face in the dark, Cole could see the barrel and slide were warped, as if melted. Enraged he smashed the gun against the rock wall, shattering it into pieces, and screamed at the voice in his head to stop. Cole felt the surge of his orange stripes flash into a blinding purple. Scared to move, he sat still until they faded back to orange. He felt a wave of relief, glad the gun hadn't fired. What he wanted more than anything was to go home. He'd be missed at the end of shift. All he had to do was wait.

And wait he did, long hours turned into insufferable days. Where were his brothers in blue? Why hadn't they searched the winery? If he waited to be rescued, he'd rot in this ghastly dungeon. Cole told himself to face the facts. His perfect life was over, and he was on his own. Fed up, he grabbed his uniform slacks. But why bother, he had nothing to hide. Amused over his absurd predicament changed the stripes on his body from orange to green. Cole was beginning to understand that his emotions influenced the color of his stripes. It was time to leave the cellar and face the world. He was starving but not hungry for food. Something else was necessary to keep him alive. Maybe he should listen to that nagging voice inside his head telling him to find a Target or Targus? Checking his six, the only thing useful was his flashlight. With that in hand, he headed for the door, stark-naked.

Walking down the narrow staircase was bad enough in his Human body; now it was going to be a real challenge. Even before he took the first step, Cole smacked his head on the stone ceiling, scraping his forehead. Dazed, he stumbled backwards, then shook it off. This time he crawled up the narrow staircase on all fours. At the top he peeked around the corner into a pitch-black hallway. It was a good thing he'd brought the flashlight. But the shaft seemed much smaller in his hand, and the toggle was difficult to flip. After flipping it on and off several times, Cole banged the head between his hands trying to fix the problem. *And still no light.* Okay, if he shook it hard enough, maybe the stupid thing would work. Cole shook the flashlight so vigorously back and forth that he accidently hit it against the rock-wall, sending it flying out of his hand. He heard the flashlight hit the ground followed by a, 'clunk roll-roll-roll clunk roll- roll- roll clunk', over and over as it slowly rolled down each step of the steep staircase. Eventually and annoyingly, it came to rest on the dirt floor far below.

Infuriated by the difficulty of crawling up the staircase and the loss of his flashlight, Cole's temper flared. The area lit up bright purple, revealing every corner and crevice along the rocky hallway. Indeed, this new body had its perks. When he calmed himself, his stripes changed to orange then faded away into the dark. Cole concentrated, willing his stripes to intensify again, and he began to glow brighter and brighter, lighting up the winding hallway leading to the main entrance. Excited to be finally free of the winery, Cole pushed on the door just enough to peek out. Opening the door a tad more, he checked the gravel road where he'd parked the patrol car. His cruiser was gone, and no one was in sight. That same nagging voice in his head was warning him not to step outside. This was nuts. Going back into the winery was not an option, and somehow, he knew the sun would satisfy his hunger. Cole brushed off his fears and pushed the door wide open into the glorious sunshine. A blanket of warmth covered his weak body, rejuvenating his strength. He stretched out his arms and slowly turned in a circle, absorbing the sun's life force. Outside the winery his stripes were a stunning green that boldly stood out against his luminous tan skin. Cole surrendered his fears and mistrust to the voice inside his head. An instant sense of wellbeing and self-awareness gave him the direction he was searching for. From now on, he would embrace the mutation as a gift, not a curse. No longer in control, he felt himself fly onto the clay roof of the old winery to explore Earth through reborn eyes. Tiny details were vivid, and his head was filled with amazing sounds. Songs from colorful birds perched high above in a majestic oak tree were soothing, although listening to them was creating a rift between the voice promising salvation and the need to preserve his Human soul. Before he could protest, the voice took control of his body and he stretched out on the rooftop. Distracted, he began to fantasize about all the possibilities as he soaked up the sun's rays. He could have stayed there forever, but he owed his family an explanation. Cole stepped off the roof, landing softly on the ground to begin the trek towards his Human home. Once again, the voice warned him of dangers and to use caution as he neared populated areas. Wishing he could skip the whole confession, he questioned why and how he was going to explain any of it to a Human. Off to one side of the wooded trail, an inviting boulder with a flat ridge beckoned him. This felt like home. He'd stretch-out and soak up more sunlight until night fell.

THE SUN HAD SET, THE MOON was full, and it was time to fulfill his commitment. Navigating the streets in the moonlight was easy, avoiding Humans was tricky. Nothing had changed, yet he felt different about everything. Ginger had been the love of his life, but he did not feel that way now. Regardless, she deserved to know why he was not coming home.

Cole was confused. While part of him realized – and accepted – that his life was to be different now, he stood in his backyard feeling homesick. How could he so easily give this life away? He wished the voice in his head would let him think and stop telling him what to do. Faint odors of an outdoor grill with sizzling ribs brought back precious memories. He imagined kicking back on a lounge chair, sipping a cold beer, while Ginger prepared the fixings. Watching her set the table with plates and glasses always relaxed him after a long day.

Resisting the nagging voice in his head, Cole fought off a disturbing sadness as he spied on Ginger and his mother through the kitchen window. A couple of steps closer would suffice to eavesdrop. It worked. His keen ears picked up every word. Ginger and his mom were in a heated argument over whether he was dead or missing. Cole crouched beneath the window trying to guess how many days he had been in the winery. Two, maybe three days tops? Listening to them bicker with one another gave him the justification to leave without an explanation. Somewhere out there was home, not here and not Earth.

The yard grew brighter and brighter. His emotions were out of control. Ginger and his mom stopped arguing mid-sentence and shuffled closer to the window. They leaned forward to peer out into the mysterious glowing backyard and screamed, horrified by the creature crouched beneath the window. Cole sprung-up, stepped-back, and covered his ears to muffle their shrieks. This was his moment of clarity. All he could think of was fleeing this exasperating planet plagued by irrational Humans. Instinctively his body transformed into pure energy and streaked across the sky until he unconsciously willed himself to stop. Weightless and free, he floated far above the magnificent blue orb, Earth in all her glory. Finding peace in space, Cole was confident that he no longer required air, gravity, or his weak, Human-half. Somewhere hidden within this spectacular universe was home. He closed his eyes trying to remember where his planet was concealed amongst the infinite galaxies and their stars. Distracting him were useless cryptic images of Earth and ages forever gone. These memories were blocking his instincts to navigate home and were consuming energy he could no longer afford to waste. If he were to survive, the voice in his head was his only chance. Floating in space gave him time to reflect and ponder his limited options. Leaving Earth and traveling deep into the cosmos with no clear direction was unavoidable, even if it meant his demise. The next star on his journey was many light years away, but active planets could provide an alternative energy. Mars was an excellent place to begin. She was convenient and uninhabited. In less than a blink of an eye he found himself floating above the small red planet and looking back at Earth. Considering why he cared to look back was dangerous. Adding to his confusion was the knowledge that Mars had once been a fertile planet, one that tragically died many years ago. How he knew didn't matter. What did matter was the knowledge that beneath his feet a cold iron-core guarded tragic stories of a distant holocaust. He felt profound sorrow. Taking a moment to appreciate her beauty, Cole marveled at the rocky terrain with sheer, red stained cliffs shadowed by the distant sun. Nonetheless, she was no longer capable of providing an energy source. Her atmosphere was thin and arid except for random patches of frozen water. Gazing up at the glittering stars made Cole feel even more lost. Where was his planet and where to begin? One tiny star cried out to him. Cole turned into energy and sped past Neptune, leaving Earth's solar system into the Orion Belt.

On and on he traveled into the void. Time and space became irrelevant and impossible to decipher. Cole had underestimated the distance and was growing weak and afraid. Returning to Earth was no longer an option; he'd gone too far. Without an energy source he would eventually vanish into oblivion. To conserve strength, he became dormant, sailing on the waves of black matter for the long trek. What was once a brilliant light streaking across the Milky Way Galaxy dimmed to an insignificant glow in an endless prison of night.

two

FORLORN EARTH

FRANK grew impatient, angrier, and more discouraged the longer the case dragged on. His only salvation was to comfort Cole's grieving family and protect them from the media invasion. The mysterious missing Police Officer story and Cole's photograph had been broadcast on every news channel across the nation. Adding to the madness, an endless stream of reporters had bombarded the small city. After weeks of searching day and night with zero leads, the Police Department declared Cole officially missing. The media moved on to current breaking news, and the assisting agencies were sent home. Cole's case was considered cold and officially closed pending further evidence. Frank was positive that his friend had succumbed to a heinous murder. Someday his bones would surface, ending the mystery and providing closure for his suffering family.

Soon after Cole's disappearance, Frank and Judy learned of Ginger's pregnancy. Together with Cole's mother they supported her during the funeral and with the birth of Cole's baby boy. People moved on, along with any hope of finding Cole. But Ginger never gave up. In her heart she believed the strange creature in the backyard was somehow connected to Cole's disappearance. Cole's mom, Beverly, feared the authorities would simply dismiss their preposterous monster encounter. No doubt, most of their friends would consider them temporarily insane from grief, or worse, they'd be accused of fabricating a crazy story for attention. Eventually Beverly refused to discuss the incident even with Ginger.

As the months passed, Cole's mother grew bitter and withdrew from everyone and everything. Day after day, she spent most of her time sitting at the kitchen table staring out the window at nothing. When the day was over, Ginger would tuck the old woman into bed and kiss her forehead goodnight. In the morning, Beverly would wait for Ginger to awaken before she'd get out of bed. Her old eyes were always sad and swollen from crying the night before. Each day she'd shuffle out of her bedroom and find herself sitting at the table to begin the vicious cycle all over again.

FOR GINGER, COLE'S DISAPPEARANCE SEEMED like yesterday. Everyone had a suggestion about how she should move on with her life, and they weren't shy about expressing them. Friends were unanimous that Beverly should be moved to a care facility, adding that it was not only for her sake, but for Ginger's too. Apparently, this would allow Ginger the freedom to date. As far as Ginger was concerned, everyone should mind their own business. Getting into a romantic relationship was not practical with a young child, and she wasn't ready. Nonetheless, Frank's wife, Judy, had other plans, and she was not taking *no* for an answer. She'd arranged a dinner for the three of them and a blind date for Ginger at a restaurant downtown. Frank begrudgingly agreed, believing the date was more for his wife than for Ginger.

The man Judy had chosen for Ginger was her new boss. Andrew was an accomplished bio-engineer and professor who had recently accepted a position at the local government research facility. Supposedly, he was in the final stages of closing escrow on one of the most prestigious homes in the area.

Full of trepidation, Ginger slowly prepared to meet Andrew. The commitment was not going away, no matter how much she dragged her feet. Feeling sick to her stomach as she traveled to the restaurant, she continued to drive. No more excuses. Although, with any luck all the parking spaces would be full. She knew she was being childish wanting any excuse to turn around and go home. There were plenty of empty spaces. Sitting in the parking lot wasn't going to change anything either, except make her late. She might as well go in, if nothing else, give it a shot.

three

IN ABSENTIA

"One must evolve to endure"

A light blinked, then another and another. Was it possible in this cold relentless void he felt warmth? Cole rotated in space to absorb the magnificent Targus Sun. Against all odds, he'd found his minuscule solar system hidden amongst billions of stars...

What an incredible journey. All the same, he was grateful that it was almost over. Cole yearned to feel Palatu's breeze and vibrant atmosphere against his body. For a hundred and thirty-five years she had been his life force and sanctuary. Through it all, visions of sparkling, silver oceans had kept him sane. Home. He could see Palatu in the distance. From this moment on, he swore to himself never to leave her again.

Cole forgave himself for taking the Human's soul the moment he morphed into body form above Palatu. Silver oceans sparkled, and the warm, red, volcanic ground felt good between his toes. A deep absorption of carbon dioxide and vapor penetrated his brilliant skin, making him feel whole again. In all his grandeur, Cole's regal silhouette appeared divine against the kaleidoscope sky. Wanting to revel in being home for as long as he could, Cole laid on the ground to look up at the Targus Sun through the forest's canopy of yellow leaves. Earth and his Human life were nothing more than fading memories of a dream; however, though it drew him in, his life on Palatu was fragmented and confusing at best.

Falling asleep wasn't what he'd planned, but apparently his body needed rest. Upon awakening, he felt stronger, mentally sharper, and fully energized. It was time to face his past, regardless of what that meant. Cole strolled towards his village enjoying the warm breeze and colorful tropical trees. The jagged volcanic cliffs beyond the forest were covered in aqua flowers with bright red leaves. In the distance, layers of volcanic mountains were erupting, sending showers of magma fireworks into the sky.

While part of him was at home and at peace, his Human-half buried deep within his soul was screaming to be heard. This part of him was of the Earth, and it wanted to go home.

four

QUIZAN AXIS

WITH their race in danger of extinction, several years before Cole's journey to Earth, a small rebellious group of Quizans had secretly explored the possibility of a merge with an alien species. After thoughtful consideration, Humans were by far the best candidate. Never in their wildest dreams could they have imagined just how incredible the hybrid would be. Cole was stronger, faster, acute, and fearless. Be that as it may, for thousands of years a Quizan merging with an alien species was strictly forbidden. Besides, no one believed a Quizan could survive the long journey, or that a Human merge was truly feasible. But there he stood, living proof that they were wrong. Nonetheless, his blatant disregard for the King's Rules meant severe punishment for him and his close friends and diminution of his wife's status in the clan's hierarchy. This he could not allow. Rodia's family was of old Cavern descent, dating back millions of years. Though he was eager to see his wife, his fears heightened the closer he got to home.

Cole froze. His keen ears caught the faint sound of something approaching. He was right. A group of Quizan males came into to view around the bend. Clueless, they came closer and closer,

making such a ruckus the Ayaks flew out the trees. At last, one of
them looked up and screamed. The other four stopped so abruptly
they fell over each other into a Quizan pile. Shrieking hysterically,
they pushed and shoved each other, then flashed into red energy
as they disappeared into the forest. Shocked by their reaction,
Cole also flashed into red energy and shot up into space. He was
now looking down at Palatu.

That did not go as planned.

Cole descended to search for the frightened Quizans. Calling
out, he hoped they were still hiding amongst the trees, "I'm Azha
from Cavern Village. Do not fear me."

Thinking aloud Azha smiled, *"Azha? Yes, my name is Azha."*

All five Quizans peeked out from behind trees, curious to see
if Azha was the strange creature standing before them. One of his
oldest friends shouted, "Alien, what's your wife's name?"

"Belton, it's me Azha. I found Humans."

He could not recall his wife's name. The crazy thing was, he
had known it just moments before.

"I heard you alien. Prove you're Azha and tell me your wife's
name?" Belton demanded.

Dumbfounded, he tried to remember. *Ro... Rod... Roddie. Yes,
yes. Rodia, that's her name.*

"My wife's name is Rodia," he shouted back.

Belton jumped out from behind a tree, "Azha, is that really you?"

Azha's stripes turned green as he spun in circles. "Yes, Belton.
I merged with a Human called Cole."

One after the other the little Quizans ran towards him, *"Azha's
returned to save us all!"* they shouted.

Shoving one another aside, they climbed up Azha's legs and
hung onto his large fingers. They were all talking at the same

time, making it impossible to understand a single word they were saying.

"I promise to answer all your questions, but right now I want to see Rodia," laughed Azha.

"Yes, yes, come, follow us," they shouted in delight.

All agreed it was a joyous day to celebrate as they pulled and sometimes pushed Azha on the path towards Cavern Village.

AZHA WAS A GIANT COMPARED to his frail friends, and Cavern Village looked primitive compared to the Villages he'd seen on Earth. Given a choice, he would have spent more time in the forest adjusting to his new role, whatever that may be. But good or bad, it was too late to turn around. Belton had scurried ahead and was shouting for all to hear.

"Azha found Humans and returned powerful to save us all. Behold, Azha is here."

Quizans ran cheering from their caves to join the booming celebration in the center of the courtyard. Rodia pushed and shoved her way through the crowd until she laid eyes on the stranger who claimed to be her husband. This cruel imposter was not Azha. Heartbroken, Rodia fell to her knees in grief and began sobbing. Watching her restored his determination to save his clan. How arrogant of him to judge the village so harshly. Azha leaned over casting a shadow on his little Quizan wife.

"Rodia, don't cry. It's me."

She heard a hint of Azha in the creature's voice. Perhaps the imposter was telling the truth. Was it possible Azha had merged with a Human and found his way home? If so, he'd be the bravest

Quizan that ever lived. Rodia stared at the ground and wiped the tears from her face. "You scare me."

"I don't want to scare you, I just want to go home."

Rodia raised her head to look at the giant, "Me, too."

Azha took Rodia's hand, and together they pushed through the mob of cheering Quizans, relieved that his journey was finally over.

Several uneventful days later his homecoming was interrupted by King Myosis who had heard about the merge and was livid. He made a spectacle of himself as he stormed across the courtyard towards Azha's cavern with four Leaders by his side. Streams of curious Quizans trailed behind to watch the show. Rodia and Azha heard the commotion, looked outside, and saw they were about to face the King's wrath. Azha stood in the doorway and Rodia turned into energy. King Myosis and the four Leaders stomped past Azha without a word as they barged into his cavern.

"How dare you defile yourself with a Human. Breaking my rules is blasphemy and will not be tolerated," the King blustered. Raging on, he waved his arms theatrically to enhance his verbal thrashing. Azha was not afraid of the King, but he refused to speak or defend himself until the old tyrant was spent. Red faced, King Myosis mocked, "Has your Human-half made you dim? Say something!"

When his insults did not get the reaction he wanted, the King turned purple and his cheeks puffed out. Fuming, he blubbered something about how he was going to make an example out of Azha. The King's behavior was ludicrous, and Azha couldn't help himself from smiling at the old fool.

"Myosis, look outside. The whole village is listening and stretching their necks to get a glimpse of the show you're putting on. You need to stop acting like a dumb-dilly-wad."

King Myosis's mouth dropped wide open and he went ballistic. Screaming, he began stomping his feet and finger-waving, "I am not a dumb-dilly-wad. You're a grotesque abomination. Leave this village and never return. That goes for Rodia, too."

The King jumped up and poked Azha in the chest with his crooked finger. Azha's stripes flashed bright purple. Enough was enough. It took all his restraint not to back-hand the old fool. Azha clenched his fists and roared with the sound of thunder until the cave walls shook. King Myosis and the Leaders dropped to their knees and crawled into a corner. Terrified, they hunkered down, sheltering themselves from crumbling rocks and dirt falling from the ceiling. Long after the dust had settled, King Myosis and the Leaders remained huddled together. Looking down upon them, Azha thought, *'What cowards, fools, and bullies. How was I ever afraid?'*

Coming to the realization that Azha was not going to crush him, King Myosis scrambled to his feet and brushed himself off. "It's best you leave Palatu and return to Earth. Clearly, you do not belong here. Our enemies will punish all of us for your selfish rebellion. Go now and you might be able to save Cavern Village from their wrath."

Azha hissed and his yellow-eyes narrowed as he moved dangerously close to the old King. "I'm not going anywhere. Do not threaten me again or you'll feel my wrath. Now get out of my cavern while you still can."

Avoiding eye contact, King Myosis and the Leaders scampered out the cave without another word. Half-way across the courtyard Myosis found his courage again and shouted back, "How dare you threaten me. Wait until the next tribal meeting. I'll punish you, *you,* ugly abomination."

Rodia flickered out of a rock crevice directly above the doorway where she had hidden to watch the entire fiasco. The King was a vengeful tyrant who never forgave or forgot. She worried the King would make good on his threat and command the village to banish her and Azha at the next meeting. Seeking support, Rodia morphed into body form and ran to Belton's cavern where she found him sunning in the dirt outside his doorway. With a curt slap to his forehead, she demanded he wake up. Belton swatted her hand.

"Go away."

Rodia circled him a couple of times, then kicked him in the leg and jumped back.

"Get up, Azha's in trouble. How could you sleep through all the noise? We need your help."

Belton sat up groggy, "Is Azha hurt?"

Trying not to cry, Rodia shook her head no.

"Azha defied the King. He's going to command the village to cast us out at the next tribal meeting."

Belton stumbled to his feet. "We won't let that happen."

five

HUNTED TO EXTINCTION

QUIZANS were highly intelligent and extremely passive. Since Palatu did not have indigenous predators, the frail Quizans thrived and lived a peaceful existence unaware of the bloody crusades taking place within the same Galaxy. Ongoing galactic wars had depleted resources on planets near the front lines, resulting in planets far away being claimed and stripped of their precious raw materials.

Despite the vastness of space, a Ryquat research ship discovered Palatu. Therefore, according to them they had exclusive mining rights. It wasn't long before the Ryquats and another species called the Gystfins formed a coalition to occupy Palatu and construct enormous mining camps designed to strip the planet. The Ryquats supplied the technology and the thickheaded, brawny Gystfins received a percentage for their manual labor.

Upon arrival almost a decade ago, the Gystfins hunted the frail Quizans simply for the thrill of killing. The Quizans' only defense was to flee and hide from them. During one of their many brutal attacks, a Gystfin bit off a Quizan's head and discovered something extraordinary. When he inhaled the grey mist that floated from the Quizan's neck, he felt a warm rush. After the high, he was able to breathe the hostile atmosphere and fly without the aid of an apparatus. This discovery triggered mass-executions across the planet. Hunting raids became more frequent and lasted much longer, forcing the Quizans to hide from their adversaries underground for days, sometimes even weeks. Often the Quizans preferred to die underground rather than surfacing only to have their heads bitten off. Additionally, the young adult Quizans who'd lost their mates were not reproducing. Bonding rituals were sacred and allowed only one mate through their expected three hundred years of life. Becoming prey to the Gystfins destroyed their sense of freedom and their way of life. No longer could they roam the forests or swim in the oceans without the threat of being hunted and killed by unthinkable acts of torture. Loved ones who dared to venture outside the village confines seldom returned. Clustered together, they grew accustomed to absorbing the sun close to home, if not directly outside their cavern doorways.

Faced with a dismal future, a few brave, rebellious Quizans banded together to secretly discuss retaliation against the alien hunters and the tyrant King Myosis. In truth, they were scared, spiritually defeated, and weak. Azha's return lifted their spirits and gave them the courage to believe now was the optimal time to fight back. If they failed to stop the onslaught, the Quizans species would be hunted to extinction.

WITH LESS THAN AN HOUR before the tribal meeting, Belton rallied four Quizans willing to openly support Azha. In unison, they knocked on his door eager to share their master plan to thwart the

King's Rule. Thankful for their support, Azha and Rodia invited them in. Belton introduced them by recounting their stories...

"Duro and Choan are the last surviving Quizans from a coastal tribe located near the Equate-Ocean region of Palatu. During the last moon eclipse, they witnessed a single Ryquat slaughter their Silwat tribe in less than two weeks. These two eluded the Ryquat by hiding underground while the glutinous Beast gorged himself on grey-death energy until he lay bloated on the beach, unable to fly. Still, they barely escaped death from lack of sun-energy waiting for the disgusting Ryquat to leave. When the Ryquat finally flew away, they searched the village for survivors. Every cupola pod was empty, the sandy beach was barren, and the trees were no longer filled with bustling friends and kindred. Despite all their efforts, they did not find a single Quizan alive. To this day, they mourn the loss of their beloved family and their Silwat Tribe."

Belton did not know the whole story...

Indeed, Choan and Duro were the last known Silwats. What kept them alive was one purpose, and one purpose alone: revenge. They were determined to kill the vicious Ryquat. If they were to survive this atrocity, Cavern Village was their best chance. Afraid of an imminent attack, they buzzed from tree to tree trying to conceal themselves. Even though traveling this way was slow and exhausting, they arrived several weeks later unscathed to tell the story of the merciless Ryquat's massacre.

Having nowhere else to go and tired of hiding, they pleaded for asylum and acceptance into the Cavern Clan, even knowing that King Myosis loathed Silwats. On many occasions, the self-serving King had voiced his dislike for their tribe, referring to them as, *'Savages that took joy in aggressive acts.'* Myosis and his Leaders demanded loyalty and obedience from Duro and Choan before they'd consider them worthy members of the lower echelon. Tired and defeated, they willingly accepted their status and the label of radical Silwat outsiders.

Zith was the youngest and last surviving son of King Myosis. Azha focused his attention on the prince. "Correct me if I'm wrong, but aren't you Myosis's son?"

Glaring at Azha's insolence, Zith refused to answer the question. Azha squatted down coming face to face with the young prince, and asked him, "Can we trust you?"

Zith's stripes glowed red. "Do not question either my ability or fortitude."

Azha grunted, tilted his head sideways, and slowly leaned back. Frowning, he studied Zith and chose his next words carefully. Tension filled the cavern as everyone fidgeted uncomfortably waiting to see the outcome. Belton's loud tapping of his foot on the dirt floor sent little puffs of dust into the air. The young prince floated to his feet and crossed his arms over his chest.

"If I must explain myself, I do not agree with my father's cynicism or his greed. My two older brothers died cowards, unwilling to speak out, even in their own defense. They turned into energy and hid underground, leaving their wives and quieys to be slaughtered by the Gystfins. Not long ago, a Ryquat murdered them for their grey-death energy. A Quizan overheard two Gystfins boasting how they'd taken turns pissing on their royal slimy little heads and grumbling about a Ryquat who took them without paying. One of the Gystfins imitated the Ryquat saying, *'I will eat the royal grey-death energy and let you know if it's better.'* I'll never understand why they didn't just turn into energy and fly away. I would rather die fighting than to live like this any longer." Zith's shoulders slumped and he sat down, "Besides, what kind of King will I be if I choose not to fight?"

It was settled, Prince Zith would join the war.

Vopar's family were victims of a vicious attack while walking in the forest near the village. His younger brother survived because the Gystfins were too busy sucking out his father's and sister's grey-death energy to notice that he'd escaped. Vopar's face twisted in anguish.

"We found Vious hiding in the forest almost dead. Both of his legs were shredded, leaving him permanently crippled. When I told King Myosis, he dismissed me by saying they shouldn't have been in the forest and then ordered me out of his cavern."

Vopar's reason for joining... *Revenge.*

Azha listened patiently to their stories, trying to determine who was trustworthy. They boasted of unrealistic schemes to kill their enemies and dethrone the King. Even though he respected their moxie and determination, he strongly doubted their capabilities. Likewise, he wasn't that much better off. What little he knew about fighting was inherited from his Human-half. At best, those memories were cryptic and confusing.

Thinking out loud, Azha caught himself mid-sentence, "Aren't you the same Quizans who turned into red energy and hid...?"

"Aren't you the one who did the same thing and shot up into space?" Belton countered.

Looking at each other they laughed and agreed their boasting was fun, but not realistic.

TODAY WAS THE FIRST DAY in many years the King felt the necessity to gather the entire clan in one place. Gathering of smaller numbers had been used for many years to avoid mass murders in a single attack. Even so, he couldn't resist the opportunity to disgrace Azha in front of the entire village.

The King was not disappointed. Azha's transformation frightened most of the clan as he entered the hall, causing some to shuffle backwards, while others turned into energy. Worried sick, Rodia hid her fear and walked proudly alongside her husband, telling those she passed not to fear the giant. The hum of curious Quizans quickly grew into furious debates by those eager to judge the half-Human. Trying not to think about the King's threat to exile them from the Caverns forever, Rodia masked her emotions and fought to control her colors.

Towering above the small Quizans provided Azha with an unobstructed view of the caustic King squatted on his sacred ledge. The King glared back, making his intentions clear. The old tyrant revered power and took pleasure in reigning with an iron fist. King Myosis rose from his ledge and pointed his long, thin finger at Azha. It was obvious the old tyrant was about to preach a well-rehearsed sermon.

"Behold this abomination before you. He dared to defy my rule and merged with a Human. Therefore, as King, I cast him out along with anyone who follows this mutant."

Shifting as one, the crowd turned away from the King with all eyes fixed on the half-Human giant standing alongside the back wall.

Azha's voice thundered in response, "Yes, look at me. I'm stronger, faster, I can defeat our enemies. I risked my life to merge with a Human. Listen to this old fool and you'll all die."

The crowd buzzed softly, discussing whether the merge was right or wrong. Soon, the debate turned into a loud roar of heated discussions.

Suddenly, explosions shook the ground and dirt crumbled from the ceiling. A barrage of Gystfins stormed outside the entrance trumpeting their barbaric attack. Red energy lights scattered in chaos darting about the cavern, leaving Azha standing alone. One familiar death shrill sent Azha sprinting outside where he desperately searched for Rodia. He had to look twice before he believed what he was seeing. In the center of the courtyard, a paunchy Gystfin was crouched over Rodia's mangled body. He was crushing her hips with its crusty knees and had both of her arms stretched out above her head. The Beast smugly opened his massive jaw and glanced sideways at Azha revealing large mustard-stained fangs. Snot dripped from his muzzle, and thick saliva drooled from his mouth onto Rodia's nearly lifeless face. Her blue energy had not transformed yet, giving him seconds to stop the Beast from biting off her head. Azha sprinted across the courtyard and slammed into the Gystfin, sending them both tumbling over the dusty terrain. The Beast appeared dumbfounded, showing signs of weakness as he sprang to his feet. Posturing, he stomped his large matted feet on the ground then shook his body, sending a shower of urine from his thick spotted fur. Azha ran to Rodia and gently cradled her in his arms. Her glazed eyes were open, but she could not hear him, nor could she speak. Azha screamed for help before the Gystfin attacked again. Belton morphed from red energy into his Quizan body with his arms stretched out, *"Give her to me. I'll hide her in your cavern."*

Azha fell to his knees and carefully placed Rodia into Belton's arms. He spun to face the Gystfin, hungry for revenge. The stripes on his body flashed purple and his yellow eyes narrowed with thin, bloodshot veins. He streaked towards the reeling Beast and rammed himself into its thick, calloused chest. The impact launched the dazed Gystfin high into air, cracking several of his ribs. Landing on the ground with a loud thud, the Beast lay flat on his back. Saliva poured from his mouth, and his fangs chattered in desperation. Unable to sit up, the Beast rolled in the dirt, moaning in pain. The stench of feces smeared across the Gystfin's stomach and down his haunches permeated the air. In a last-ditch effort, he grabbed Azha's leg and hung on with all his might. Azha stomped the Beast until he let go and then looked into his eyes to see if he was alive. The Beast groaned, and his eyes opened. His paunchy body jerked back and forth across the ground as he howled in pain. Azha kicked the Gystfin in the face, shattering several fangs, then stomped on the Gystfin's chest until he stopped moving. Seeing that he was finally dead did not satisfy Azha's need for revenge. He straddled the Gystfin's chest and tore flesh from its broad ugly face until he ripped out its eyes from their deep sockets.

A BLINDING PAIN SNAPPED AZHA out of his frenzy. His shoulders were on fire from sharp claws and long fangs buried deep within his flesh. Azha flipped over into a front-roll, sending the Gystfin tumbling across the courtyard. Shaking off the pain, Azha scrambled to his feet and prepared himself for another attack. Lying on the ground was a sturdy branch. In his mind he pictured Cole's Police Baton and picked it up. The younger, disheveled Gystfin jumped up and down pounding his chest, then bolted towards him shrieking. Just before the Beast was within reach, Azha stepped aside and swung the branch. A wail was proof that Azha had hit his mark. The Gystfin stumbled backwards, holding his forehead where a fountain of green blood gushed through his claws. Defeated and fleeing for his life, the Gystfin rose above the ground to fly away. Azha grasped a handful of crusty hide and slammed him onto the ground. The Gystfin crawled on his stomach through the blood-soaked dirt away from the alien slayer. Celebrating his victory, Azha walked alongside the Gystfin watching him suffer. This gave him time to ponder all the glorious ways he could kill the filthy Beast. Azha's thunderous roar told those who were watching the end was near. He flipped the snarling Gystfin over and choked him until his eyes were lifeless. Confidence filled Azha. Now, more than ever, he appreciated his Human warrior half.

THE COURTYARD REEKED with the stench of death. Quizans slowly crept forward, curious to behold the slain Gystfins. Aghast, they loitered in silence, not sure about what they had just witnessed. Azha snapped out of his rage and ran frantically towards his cavern, screaming for Belton, but no one was there. He heard a faint call in the distance and ran outside. His friend was waving his arms, motioning for him come quickly. Azha ran towards Belton's cavern, terrified at what he might find and in denial of what he already knew. Halfway there, weak-kneed and shaking, he stopped and bent over. Everything seemed to be moving in slow motion. In his mind, he pictured the last time he held her, and he heard Cole's voice praying deep within his soul. Concentrating on placing one foot in front of the other, Azha focused on her being alive. That is, until he entered Belton's cavern. His brilliant stripes turned from red to pasty beige, sickened by what he saw before him. Rodia's eyes were closed and she appeared lifeless, lying on a narrow ledge at the far end of the cavern. He rushed to her side. This was beyond what he could reason with or accept. Afraid to move her, he touched his wife's shoulder and gently ran his fingers down her arm. The setting Targus Sun glistened rays of light into the furthest corners of the cavern and across her face. While Azha waited for any signs of life, Rodia's body faded before his eyes into gray-death energy. With her last will... she floated to her brave husband. Azha closed his eyes and welcomed her into his soul; this would be last time he'd feel warmth and love from his wife, Rodia.

six

MALUM

"Those who take time to find themselves have nothing to lose"

AZHA could not fathom another second at the Caverns without Rodia. Floating in space seemed to be an inviting escape. He turned into energy and flew through the trees, leaving Palatu behind, along with unnecessary and unwanted attention. He'd risked everything, and she died anyway. Grief-stricken and blood-thirsty, Azha looked down upon Palatu and vowed to destroy every Gystfin and Ryquat.

A flickering light spiraled in space several times before stopping, "May I float with you?" Belton asked.

Azha sighed. "I can't imagine my life without Rodia."

"No one else knows you're here. Would you prefer that I keep your secret?" Belton asked.

"Yes. You can stay," Azha said appreciative.

Azha needed to believe in something, anything, to make sense of all this death and misery. If not, then what?

"Belton do you believe I should go back to Earth? Azha asked.

"Don't go. You were right, we'll all die if we do nothing. The King forbids us to defend ourselves. His way is to submit if captured so others may escape. He's wrong. Without you, I fear we have no chance."

Hearing Belton gave Azha purpose. He'd return to Palatu and begin training immediately. Maybe, just maybe he could save the Quizans.

The entire Village reeked from the stench coming from the Gystfin's oozing carcasses left under the sun to rot. A cluster of Quizans circled the Beasts, complaining about the noxious smell and blaming each other for not doing something about it. Azha snuck up behind them and scolded, "Why hasn't anyone buried these nasty Gystfins?"

Several Quizans darted away, and others bounced off the ground. Puzzled by the question, one lively Quizan spoke-up, "What do you mean bury them? What is bury?" he asked.

Azha recalled this to be a Human practice not known to Quizans, so patience would be prudent.

Up close the Gystfins were even more disgusting. Their stench was seeping into Azha's stripes, making him gag. Walking away he told the group to rendezvous at his cave. The dizzy Quizans were gagging worse than Azha, and their stripes were a sickly blue color. Azha wondered how long they would've stayed by the carcasses if he had not told them to leave? If this was any indication, instructing the Quizans on how to bury something was going to require an incredible amount of patience. Once everyone settled in, Azha began.

"First you dig a very deep hole in the ground, approximately two ola's will do. After that, throw the carcasses into the hole. All the dirt that came out of the hole, goes back into the hole. That's

how you do it. Cover the nasty Gystfins with dirt and they won't
stink anymore... Got it?"

The Quizans rolled their eyes like he was crazy.

"What shall we make this hole with?" Several asked in unison.

Azha couldn't believe the question. Frustrated he threw his
arms up in the air.

"If this happened on Earth, Humans would have skinned,
cooked, and eaten the Gystfins by now," said Azha frustrated.

Everyone's mouth dropped open in shock and their faces
scrunched-up in disgust. Digging a hole was not going to happen.
Azha quickly figured out another way to dispose of the two rotting
carcasses.

Sternly and with less patience he began... *lesson two.*

"*OK.* Don't dig a hole. I want all of you to help drag the carcasses far away from the village. After that, find a deep ditch.
Once you've found the deep ditch, drag the carcasses over to the
ditch and throw them in it. Next, I want all of you to collect a
bunch of *damn frickin rocks.* Throw the rocks into the ditch until
the Gystfins are completely covered. Is there any part of this you
do not understand?" Azha snapped.

Unbelievably, the same Quizan asked, "Where do we collect
damn, frickin rocks?"

Azha slapped his forehead and shouted, "What? Geez, put
the damn rotting things in the ditch and cover them up with rocks,
any rocks."

Everyone agreed this was a splendid idea, and then the arguing
commenced about who was going to drag the stinky Gystfins out
of the village. Clearly, no one wanted to touch the nasty things.
Azha interrupted their bickering and ordered the whiners to get
out of his cavern. 'Ugh!'

Grudgingly, the group dragged their feet back over to the Gystfins with Azha following, just in case one of them lost their way. Keeping a safe distance from the stench, Azha got a better look at the nasty Beasts. They reminded him of earth's hyenas, except these animals were much larger and their hides were crusty with gross scabs. Repositioning himself upwind, he got close enough to kick the largest Gystfin over onto its back. His shoulders were broad, and his arms were long and muscular. What was entirely different were his hands. With three fingers and a short thumb, they looked like paws. Azha squeezed the pad and its six-inch claws extended-out like a cat's. Its face was broad and ugly with a wide muzzle baring long, baboon-like yellow fangs. Azha racked his brain wondering why he couldn't remember Gystfins. Having to compare the Beast to Earth's creatures was confusing.

Not a single Quizan had dared to touch either Gystfin. They were far too busy complaining and debating who should drag them. The same Quizan who asked the meaning of bury and inquired about the rocks asked Azha if he would help drag the very heavy Gystfins out of the village. This was a perfect opportunity for a quid-pro-quo. He'd ask the vocal little Quizan how Gystfins fly. Somewhere deep within his consciousness he knew the answer. But ever since the merge, he'd suffered from indiscriminate memory loss.

Frowning the Quizan asked, "What, don't you know?"

Embarrassed, Azha admitted that he'd forgotten many things from both past lives.

"Do you know who I am?" Asked the Quizan.

Azha shook his head no.

"I'm Roon, your friend before you bonded with Rodia. We're from the esteemed Kismet Ebb Tribe. Our beautiful tropical village is located on the opposite side of the red volcano, where waves of silver ocean spray the molten rocks."

So, I wasn't hallucinating in the old winery. Roon's description triggered a flood of precious lost memories of his village, his family, and of his old friend Roon. Even so, Azha still couldn't recall the answer to his original question. Roon's bright green stripes faded to a dull tan.

"Gystfins hunt us for their pleasure and our grey-death energy. Remember?" Roon asked.

"Sort of, but if you could fill in the missing parts for me I'd appreciate it," said Azha.

"When they first invaded Palatu, several Quizans were captured alive for food and taken to their ship. As soon as we were exposed to the oxygen, we died. After that, they tried eating us before we faded. That's when they discovered our grey-death energy. A Gystfin accidently inhaled some of it when he bit off a Quizan's head. He was immediately stronger, could fly, and was able to breathe our atmosphere without wearing that bulky second skin. Worse than Gystfins *are the Ryquats.* They always hunt alone, slaughtering hundreds in a single rampage, sometimes an entire village."

Desperate to remember, Azha closed his eyes, trying to picture a Ryquat monster. That ended abruptly when Prince Zith belted out his revelation, "*I know of a deep ditch. The dragging shall begin.*"

The motley crew of Quizans tripped over each other as they shuffled back and forth, circling the carcasses while acting as if they were extremely busy and working very hard. Neither Gystfin had been moved an inch. The constant bickering and complaining between grunts and groans were driving Azha crazy. Out of patience, he bent over and grabbed one leg from each Gystfin. With a yank, he straightened out their disfigured, bloated bodies and began dragging the Beasts through the dirt. Zith walked briskly in front of the group, guiding them to his special ditch.

Along the way the bickering continued; in fact, it got worse. Azha asked, then pleaded with the group to stop complaining. However, his efforts to silence them were completely ineffective. Teaching Quizans discipline and how to fight was going to be challenging, perhaps impossible.

None too soon for Azha, they arrived at Zith's *'special ditch.'* He had to insist they move their celebration dance aside so that he could shove the rancid Gystfins over the edge. Everyone watched as they tumbled down the rocky ledges before hitting the bottom with a loud thud. Mid-air, Azha noticed out of the corner of his eye several Quizans quietly and briskly walking away towards the village. Startling them with a sharp tongue, Azha barked, "*Stop*, get back over here and finish this. No one leaves until the ditch is full of rocks."

Completely out of patience, Azha asked Roon to walk with him back to the village. Prince Zith gladly volunteered to supervise the all-important burying detail.

"Begin the search for *damn, frickin rocks*. There'll be no glory for those who dawdle," Zith shouted in a Kingly command.

Azha couldn't help but smile, "Numero uno, I will return to check on the Rookies," as he and Roon walked away.

Roon scratched his head, "What do numero uno and Rookie mean?"

"Shit, I don't know. It just came out of my mouth," Azha said confused. In the distance, Roon and Azha could hear Zith yelling at the lazy Quizans. However, drowning out Zith were the Quizans, whining and bickering with each other about who was gathering the most '*frickin rocks.*'

The walk home was peaceful, allowing Azha the opportunity to think about how he was going to begin Quizan training and if their enemies had weaknesses. If there was a ship close by, it would make sense to sabotage that first. Roon was inquisitive about everything. He'd know if a Gystfin ship was orbiting Palatu. When asked, Roon perked up, confessing that despite the King's rule, he often explored space and that he knew where the ship was located. Azha proposed that when Belton was free from the Gystfin detail, the three of them investigate the ship together. Roon's stripes turned bright green as he spun around giddy.

EARLY NEXT MORNING, COLORFUL SLEEPING Quizans covered the courtyard. This was a good sign. For the first time in many years the clan felt safe enough to leisurely soak up energy from the Targus Sun without feeling threatened. Azha came across Belton and his wife catnapping on the ground near a small mesa. Without making a sound, Azha crouched down to whisper in his ear, "*Shhhh. . .* don't wake up Freya. Roon knows where a Gystfin ship is orbiting. Do you want to go with us?" Azha asked.

Belton gently picked up his sleepy wife's floppy arm and removed it from his shoulder. Quietly, he motioned that he most definitely wanted to go. The trio flew into the horizon in search of the mysterious Gystfin ship.

It wasn't long before Roon and Belton fell behind. Azha laughed aloud as he soared, spiraling them with each pass.

"Why is Azha laughing?" Roon asked.

Belton thought to himself, '*How would I know?*'

Roon continued to pester Belton. "What does a Human look like?"

"Um, I've heard they're ugly and they bond while in body form, not in energy like us."

Roon gasped, "That's not possible."

Miffed, Belton urged Roon to *go ask* Azha if he wanted to know any more 'things' about Humans.

From a distance, the Gystfin's ship appeared to be a shadow cast by Palatu. They were virtually on top of it before noticing the reflection of its contour against the moon's rocky surface. From the starboard side, the black ship was so thin it almost disappeared. As they flew towards the bow of the ship it expanded into an enormous flat sphere resembling a disc. Without Roon's guidance, Azha would never have found it.

Belton and Roon flickered about while Azha scouted the mysterious vessel up close. The hull was smooth with few portals, no windows, and a massive Isosceles platform that was barely visible. The ship was either abandoned or maintained by a skeleton crew. Azha hovered above a tiny vent, signaling Roon and Belton to turn into energy and follow closely behind.

INFILTRATING THE OMINOUS SPACESHIP WAS the adventure of a lifetime for the little Quizans. Azha was determined to destroy it, return to Palatu, and kill every marooned Gystfin on the planet. Belton and Roon quickly wandered off and were buzzing around a colorful circuit panel. Before he could rein them in, they accidentally activated a motion sensor and were darting about desperate to get Azha's attention. Bright lights switched on in a succession of components, illuminating tiers, decks, and endless rows of corridors throughout the vast ship. Their cover was blown, but at least now they could get a good look at the ship's interior.

The cargo bay they were in was stacked with containers as far as the eye could see. Flying through a myriad of bulkheads and corridors, Azha was awestruck at just how big the ship was. Catacombs were separated by hundreds of tiers that were divided into thousands of decks. Each deck housed what seemed to be an infinite number of massive cargo bays. Azha was reconsidering his original plan of destroying the ship to navigating it to Earth. All he had to do was figure out how to fly it. The ship would advance the Human species' understanding of space travel by decades, if not centuries. *Certainly, this grand token would be penance for his sinful abduction of Cole's body.* If not, so be it. He had no other options at the time. The journey to Earth had completely drained him of his life energy force. Even so, Azha struggled with his self-serving justifications to survive.

Azha morphed into body form. The air was refreshing and familiar oxygen. How strange that Gystfins breathed oxygen like Humans? Unlike him, Belton and Roon could not. They had to remain in energy or die from the toxic air. Azha was positive they welcomed the excuse to remain in energy while exploring the ship.

For hours, they searched tier after tier for the bridge and were no closer than when they'd started. Azha stumbled upon a schematic wall of neon screens located at the end of a long corridor. The screens were divided into three sections, and each section appeared to be a series of trajectory charts. Confused by it all, he stared at the wall trying to decipher the alien technology. Staring at it any longer wasn't going to make any difference; it made no sense. Fed up, he decided to search an area displayed in bold red. Before leaving, he memorized most of the complex symbols, routes, and grids.

Azha's instinct paid off. The bridge was located on the upper tier highlighted in red. If there were Gystfins on board, this is where they would be. Warning Belton and Roon to stay put, Azha did a quick search and cleared the tier of any Gystfins.

Walking onto the bridge was invigorating and brought Azha one step closer to commandeering the ship. It was grand, high-tech and sleek, not at all what he'd envisioned. Next step was to understand the alien symbols and logos on the control panels. To his surprise, these were self-explanatory and not all that complicated.

Belton and Roon were amazed at Azha. Being a part of this grand adventure with him was well worth the risk. Azha pushed several emblems, causing the massive ship to hum and the lights in the control center to switch on and blink intermittently. The dormant ship shook, and the entire bridge began to dance with a synchronized, spectacular neon performance. All around them they could feel the magnificent craft pulsate as if she had awoken from a deep sleep.

Flickering and afraid, Belton and Roon flew onto a low metal shelf next to Azha. A little concerned, but mostly humored, he squatted down to look at them, "Don't be afraid, we'll leave soon," smiled Azha.

Curious, he touched several more logos to see what would happen. A powerful surge jolted the spaceship forward. Since Azha had no idea what he had done, or how to stop the massive craft he thought to himself, 'Here goes...' and pressed down on another red symbol. The ship lunged forward and spiraled into a downward pitch. Azha catapulted up, hitting the ceiling, and then slammed down onto the floor. Unable to grab onto anything, he slid across the deck until he smashed into a metal wall. Belton and Roon helplessly shot through several walls and out the bulkhead into space. Dumbfounded, they watched as the Gystfin spaceship disappeared into the unknown. Powerless and bewildered, they decided it would be best to stay where they fell out of the ship and wait for Azha.

After many days of floating in space, Roon whimpered, *"What if Azha's lost?"* Even though Belton was trying desperately not to cry, his voice cracked, "What if he can't find energy? What if he faded away? What if a monster ate him?" Together they faithfully hovered in cold dark space awaiting their wayward hero.

FROM FAR AWAY A TINY light streaked towards them, growing brighter and brighter. It was Azha; he wasn't dead! They celebrated by sending sparks into space, signaling their location. Their hero ascended next to them with a big smile on his face, then closed his eyes and stretched out to soak up the distant Targus Sun.

Roon bawled and Belton babbled, demanding an explanation, "What happened? Where's the Gystfin's ship? Say something!"

"Not now, let me rest and then I'll tell you all about it," yawned Azha.

Several hours later, Roon was annoyingly bobbing his head in Azha's' direction while mouthing at Belton to ask more questions. Being silenced like that was irritating and rude. Azha should have been willing to divulge a few more details before taking a nap. Several more hours passed before Azha awoke.

"I tried to stop the ship for days. So, I gave up and flew out of it," Azha said acting as if he didn't care.

In unison Belton and Roon snapped, *"What? That's it?"* while shrugging their shoulders with doubtful gestures. Azha was in good spirits and chose to ignore their exaggerated antics by rolling over and not watching them. With that out of the way, it was as good a time as ever to head home. Besides, he was eager to begin the Quizan soldier training. Gloating to himself, he'd give anything to watch the Gystfins when they discovered their cargo ship missing.

RETURNING TO CAVERN VILLAGE WAS confusing. Everyone acted as if nothing had happened. They had spent several weeks lying in the sun all day, and Azha was beyond irritated. Quizans were complacent fools who never really intended to become soldiers. Training to fight the Gystfins should have started the day he returned, and instead the Quizans had continued their inactivity. This cavalier behavior was intolerable, and Zith needed to do something about it. Azha could feel his stripes turning red as he stormed across the village. Those unfortunate Quizans caught in his irate path turned into energy or ran to get out of his way before Azha purposely stepped on them. Zith ran to his doorway where he watched Azha stomp his way towards his cavern. By the time the overgrown oaf had barged past him, most of the village was traumatized. Having had his fill of cruel tyrants, Prince Zith jumped up and drop-kicked Azha in the shinbone.

"Owww, crap that stung. Why'd you do that?" roared Azha.

"I kicked you because you're yelling and stomping on everyone. Why would you do that?" Snapped Zith.

"For a good reason. Training should've started weeks ago," shouted Azha.

"Did it ever occur to you that everyone was waiting for you to be ready? Not one Quizan wanted to rush your mourning for Rodia. You're scary enough without doing that to them. You should apologize to everyone out there. And what is a crap?" asked Zith.

Azha bit his lip, "Um, that's difficult to explain. Huh, Human words meant to imply annoyance. Sometimes I think like a Human when I'm angry. I'll try not to act that way anymore," promised Azha.

Azha had assumed the worst of the loyal little Quizans. Zith's admonition made him realize he needed to be a tolerant leader that led by respect, not fear. Zith patted Azha's shin, then hop-skipped out of his cavern into the center of the courtyard.

"Hear me Quizans. Azha is sorry for his actions. He promised to restrain his violent Human-half from now on. Meet me tonight at Cavern Hall. I want everyone to consider whether we will, or will not, support Azha in the war against our enemies. If we Vox Populi to support Azha, we will be violating King Myosis's rules. So, think about your decision and come prepared."

Later that same day, King Myosis marched into his son's cavern demanding that he cancel the mutinous gathering. Sometime between his ranting threats and demands, Myosis realized that Azha was crouched on a ledge glaring at him. Clearly, he had interrupted their scheming to organize a rebellion to dethrone him. Myosis continued his rant waving his finger in the air. Moving a couple of steps closer to the door, the old tyrant forbid Zith from having any further contact with the abomination in the room. Yelling louder while shuffling a few more steps towards the door, Myosis ordered Azha to stop putting foolish ideas of war into his son's head.

Zith knelt before his father. "Forgive my defiance, but you're wrong not to fight. Quizans will cease to exist if we do nothing but submit and hide."

Azha's stripes were purple and his eyes glowed yellow as he stepped off the ledge towards the old Quizan. King Myosis stumbled backwards, "Can't you see you'll be the one who'll destroy us?" He then turned to his son. "If you do this, I'll ban you from the tribe and condemn your legacy."

Wiping tears from his face the young prince reached out to his father, but Myosis slapped his hand away. "Choose," demanded Myosis.

The young prince glanced over at Azha and then back up at his father. "I love you Papay, forgive me."

Hearing that, King Myosis bellowed, *"You are no longer my son or a prince. Leader Noyac is loyal to me. He'll heir when I ascend."*

THE SUN WAS SETTING, AND nightfall was around the corner. Most of the clan were waiting inside Cavern Hall. Many of them had already agreed that Azha was their best hope for survival. Young Prince Zith walked in and sat down on the same high ledge held by his father for over two-hundred years. The crowd parted, allowing Azha to pass as he positioned himself beneath the King's ledge. Full of promise, Zith stood up and clapped his hands, *"Silence, I would like to introduce our savior, Azha."*

"Thank you, King Zith. The rumors you've heard are true. My Human's name was Cole. On Earth, Cole was a fierce police warrior who protected his species. Join me tomorrow morning in the court-yard and I'll teach you how to be a warrior. Together we can fight the Gystfins. I can see by your faces, you have questions."

Several hands shot up into the air and chaotic chatter filled the hall. Azha pointed to a Quizan, granting him the first question. The crowd separated leaving him trembling and standing alone to face the giant.

"Are you more Quizan, or Human?" He mumbled.

"Neither, but my merge with the Human has made me stronger and wiser."

Zith pointed to another Quizan who was bouncing up and down.
"Will you return to Earth, or will you stay with us on Palatu?"
Ever since Rodia's death, Azha wasn't sure how he felt. For
now, he must say what they wanted to hear.

"Palatu is my home," Azha said with confidence.

"How do you plan on killing a Ryquat?" Choan asked.

"Good question. Those willing to fight, will learn tomorrow,"
replied Azha.

Zith floated above the crowd, "I am Zith, son of King Myosis.
I command from now, until the end of time, Quizans that merge
with a Human shall be called, Trekachaw."

Zith ascended and bowed before Azha, *"See his yellow eyes as
our guiding light, for he is our deliverance through this dark night."*

Dancing Quizans sang homage to Azha, as they spun in circles.
Faster and faster they whirled, sending sparks of light onto the black
cave walls. Heartbroken, Azha refused to dance without Rodia. She
was his last anchor connecting him to his Quizan-half. Accepting
this allowed him to embrace the strength and intelligence of his
Human-half, yet he loathed those random thoughts of brutality,
power, and lust. Looking around he no longer recognized himself
as one of them and was becoming a stranger in his own world.

The celebration continued throughout the night with whim-
sical acts of slaying their enemies. Watching the naive Quizans
pretend to conquer the enemy worried Azha. His arrogance may
have triggered an unrealistic confidence. Tired, Azha graciously
thanked everyone and begged his farewell. Walking home was
lonely without Rodia by his side. At times like this, he missed her
so much his body ached.

That night, Azha lay awake thinking about the Gystfin spaceship and how he had lied to Belton and Roon. In truth the ship

was not difficult to navigate; he'd simply lost track of time day-dreaming about his life on Earth. For hours, he had stared out a portal window trying to imagine what Ginger was doing at that very moment. Surely the oxygen affected his mind. Once, he even considered leaving Palatu and flying the ship to Earth, knowing full-well Humans were not the answer. On the other hand, neither were Quizans.

Azha recalled how startled he felt when he saw a silhouette of a man walking on the bridge. When he moved, the silhouette moved, when he stopped, it stopped. The silhouette in the mir-rored wall was Cole. Stark naked he turned sideways to examine the once familiar body. Intrigued, he wondered why that part had been so important. Cole had many pet-names, but mostly he called it... *Johnson.* Whoever Johnson was, he must have been very important to Cole. Azha closed his eyes wondering if the oxygen had caused him to hallucinate. Peeking out from one eye, Cole was gone. Had his mind played a sadistic trick, or for a fleeting moment was he Cole? Afraid to look at the mirror again, Azha concentrated on programming the ship to its new destination, Europa, one of Saturn's moons. Someday he'd return to Earth and use the Gystfin ship to transport Humans safely to Palatu. Azha wanted to believe, had to believe, Humans would welcome the chance to merge with a Quizan.

With his destination set and confirmed, it was time to leave. Azha turned into energy and allowed the massive ship to pass through him. Of two minds, he floated in space watching his space-ship disappear into the void.

seven

ANTE BELLUM

AWAKE and restless, Azha waited for the first hint of dawn to search for a suitable training site. He stepped outside into the dark and, lo-and-behold, hundreds of Quizans filled the courtyard eager to start training. Choan, Duro, Zith, Belton, and Roon volunteered to be training leaders. That was encouraging; it felt good to be busy and have a purpose. Azha waved his hand, directing the crowd over to a flat, open area at the north side of the village.

"Choan, Duro and Roon, you'll be Sergeants. Your first assignment: split the Quizans into three groups. Each group has a title, Squad #1, Squad #2, and Squad #3. Choose your squads wisely and share the stronger Quizans amongst you."

In short order, three squads were assembled with far less confusion than expected.

"The rest of you are called soldiers. Training will continue until everyone is combat-ready. If some of you take longer than others, that's okay. What I want and expect from all of you is your best effort. As you already know, our enemies are much stronger, and they have advanced weapons. To prevail, you must be faster and wiser. If possible, fight in numbers and at a safe distance. I will show you how to defend yourselves, ambush, distract, and kill the arrogant aliens. Zith has sent messengers to neighboring villages inviting them to join our training and crusade," said Azha.

Azha pointed at Belton. "He is called Lieutenant and has authority over the Sergeants. I'm called Captain and will not answer to anyone other than Zith."

Azha held a rock up and called out to his Sergeants, "Have your squads collect rocks about this size. Stack the rocks into three separate pyramid piles. We will need a lot of rocks, so get started."

Roon leaned over and whispered to the other Sergeants, "That size rock is called a *damn, frickin rock.* Bet you didn't know that?"

The sergeants were pleased, "Oooh... so that's what it means. Do you know what a pyramid pile is?"

"No, I'll ask." Roon ran over to Azha and whispered, *"What's a pyramid pile?"*

"Its rocks stacked on top of each other until the pile comes to a point at the top," advised Azha.

"Oooh, like that volcano over there, except smaller?"

"Yeah, exactly." Roon mumbled something as he ran away.

In no time, three large piles of hand-size rocks were perfectly stacked, and the Sergeants were eager to begin the next task. Not sure how to proceed, Azha figured the best instructors to imitate were his Police Academy Training Officers. He marched in front of the three squads, clicked his heels together, snapped a quarter-turn, and faced the future cavern soldiers. "Attention!"

Everyone looked confused and a few turned in sharp little circles.

"No, stop. Watch what I do," he shouted.

Azha started over, giving a detailed demonstration.

"When I shout *'Attention'*...stand up straight with your arms to your side. Cup your hands inward, like this." Giving them a few moments to prepare, Azha shouted, *"ATTENTION."*

Some were looking down at their hands and trying to cup them, while others were looking back and forth watching those who were attempting the hand-cupping example. Azha threw his hands up into the air.

Speaking louder he continued, "Everyone stop what you're doing and look at me. We'll practice *attention* later. Right now, you need to learn how to work as a team. Being prepared could make the difference between life and death, so train as if your life depends on it. First lesson is to throw a rock at a target. Everyone will take turns until you hit the target perfectly every time."

Azha set up a series of rocks spaced evenly apart on an open ledge. Aware of Cole's excellent baseball skills, Azha felt confident that he could hit his mark. From the top of the pile he handpicked a nice round rock, then stood sideways and tossed it up and down in his hand while staring intensely at his mark. With precision, he threw it hard and fast, knocking the target off the ledge. The Quizans let out *oohs* and *ahh's*.

"Now, *that's* how I want you to throw a rock," boasted Azha. "Everyone takes a turn until they're gone, then reset the rocks and start over. Rotate until your Sergeant tells you to stop," he instructed.

Azha was flabbergasted at just how badly the Quizans threw rocks. Half the time they couldn't even hit the ledge. More than a couple of times, they pinged each other. Rock training was going to take a very long time. Even so, they practiced relentlessly day after day until they mastered the fine art of throwing a rock accurately.

In the end, not one soldier complained or quit. Given free will, they were moxie little creatures.

Early morning on the 26th day of training, Lt. Belton requested Azha's presence for damn, frickin rock evaluations. Rock skills were competitive, making the demonstration nerve-racking for the new soldiers. After several grueling hours, the sergeants and soldiers passed with flying colors. To celebrate their success, Azha announced that every soldier would receive one Gystfin fang. Honored, yet curious about the extraordinary awards, Sgt. Choan asked Roon, "How'd Azha get Gystfin fangs, or should I ask?"

Roon was more than happy to share. "A couple of days ago, we snuck back where the Gystfins are buried. It took us all morning to remove the damn, frickin rocks. They were disgusting, kind of gooey, and stunk even worse than before. We bashed their jaws into pieces, well, Azha did most of it. Anyway, did you know a Gystfin has over two hundred fangs? Afterwards, Azha said we earned some *R & R* — that means fun time. Anyway, we flew to the ocean. I've missed swimming in the ocean. Do you want to know what the best part was? Azha made me the official Range Master of Damn, Frickin Rocks. Yep, I'm the only Range Master. Anyway, did you know Gystfin stink goes away when you swim in the ocean?"

"Ah... no I didn't," said Choan.

Zith pushed his way between Roon and Choan with a stern look on his face and hushed them, "Shhh, everyone can hear you."

Choan gave Roon the stink-eye, "Roon was the one talking, not me."

"Doesn't matter, race you to the Hall," Zith challenged.

Zith yelled at the spectators to clear a path as they slid through the doorway into the crowded Cavern Hall. Azha waited for the room to calm and began the presentation by giving one large fang to Lt. Belton and Zith. The remaining fangs were neatly displayed on the training ledge for all to admire. Walking in single-file, every sergeant and soldier selected their very own trophy. However, unlike past practice, there were no celebrations planned for that night. Phase-two training was scheduled at the crack of dawn.

AZHA AWOKE LONG BEFORE ANYONE else. Convincing himself that others would want an early start too, he visited one cave after the other to rouse his Sergeants and Zith. Grudgingly and half-asleep, they sat in the moonlight listening to Azha's master plan. Just after day break, Zith led five soldiers into the forest to search for long, sturdy sticks and green vines, while Belton and Choan's squads flew to the top of a volcano in search of flat, black rocks.

By mid-morning, the squads were assembled for phase two training. Each soldier received one stick, one long vine and two volcanic rocks. Finding a comfortable spot to sit down on, Azha waited for the soldiers to stop talking. Spear Class was officially in session.

"Can everyone see and hear me?" Asked Azha. "Good, watch how I strike two rocks together to chip off small pieces. Do it until it looks like this." Azha held up an example of a sharpened spearhead.

Bang, whack, bang, crack, thwack, chip, bang, it sounded as if everyone was working on a chain-gang. Entertained by it all, Azha covered his ears and watched as the Quizans created their first spearheads.

The rest of the afternoon dragged on, waiting for each of the soldiers to complete their first spearhead. Upon inspection, Azha

made sure to compliment their excellent work. Next, he demon-
strated how to wedge the spearhead into a slit at the end of a stick
and then wind a long green vine repeatedly around the shaft. By
the end of the day, the soldiers had produced strong, sharp spears
with razor-sharp tips that could pierce the thick leathery bark of
a Sopa tree. Training the soldiers how to throw the spears accurately required little time due to their proficient rock throwing skills.
Azha was pleased to discover that a soldier on Sgt. Choan's squad
had created a weaved tote-bag for carrying extra spears. Eager
to share his creation, he worked tirelessly into the night helping
other soldiers create their own bags. Azha was impressed by the
beautiful design, and that the bags were functional with straps
that draped comfortably over the shoulder making it possible to
carry heavy loads.

The soldiers were as ready as they were going to get. It was
time to be the hunter, not the hunted. But all was not perfect.
The entire village had rallied in favor of the training, except King
Myosis and his seven Leaders. Despite the King's best efforts, he
had failed to de-rail their spirit or allegiance. Traditionally a King's
reign among the clan was sacred and replaced by death alone. As
far as Myosis was concerned, the entire village were mutinous
radicals, including his ungrateful son.

SGT. ROON'S SQUAD #3 WERE given the first assignment. Their
orders were to scout the immediate area for Gystfins or Ryquats.
If any were found, they'd covertly stage at a safe distance to
observe. A scout would return to the village and report the location
along with any intel. Wide-eyed and enthusiastic, Squad #3 bid

their farewells and disappeared into the trees. The two remaining squads were given the prestigious *Roon R & R* break. Pleased with themselves, they took turns congratulating each other for their successful graduation. Azha stopped counting after about the fifth round of congratulations. Sgt. Duro had just lay down to take his break when a red-streak of energy broke through the trees. Mid-air, the scout morphed into body form, flying so fast that he crashed into a couple of soldiers on the ground before coming to an abrupt stop. Dizzy, he stumbled to his feet and limped through the courtyard spitting out gibberish while frantically waving his arms. Azha tried to calm the hysterical scout to no avail. At best, he understood every other word.

"Gystfins by Ayak nesting volcano. Breaking, smashing, horrible bites, huge one laughing."

"*Stop!* How many Gystfins are there?" Azha asked.

"Two, no three... I don't know."

Azha's stripes flashed bright purple. "Belton you're with me. Zith, Choan, Duro, meet us at the Ayak Volcano and bring as many rocks and spears as your squads can carry, and *hurry.*"

Belton handed his spears to Choan and dropped his heavy tote. Being unable to bring his weapons while in energy form was an unavoidable disadvantage for Belton. Be that as it may, Azha was the Quizan's only hope for survival. Together, they turned into red energy and streaked into the forest.

In the blink of an eye, they located Sgt. Roon's squad deep within the Ayak Forest. The soldiers were perched on sturdy limbs high above the Gystfin's camp. Only a keen eye could spot the angry, red soldiers perfectly camouflaged amongst the colorful tropical leaves. Dozens of dead Ayak birds were ripped apart and strewn across the campsite. Most likely they were victims of the

Beasts' sadism. The Gystfins had redirected their wrath upon a handful of unlucky Quizans. Azha crouched on the limb next to Belton and Roon.

"Tell your soldiers to kill the Gystfins within throwing range and watch the tree-line for any new ones."

Roon raised his fist into the air signaling his soldiers to attack. Azha streaked towards the largest Gystfin who was violently shaking and punching a female Quizan in the chest. This was his barbaric way of checking to see if there was any life left in her. Unaware of the threat above, he curled his large, ugly lips and bared dingy fangs as he positioned himself to bite off her head. Azha pounced on top of the Beast's shoulders, and in one swift motion he grabbed hold of its head and wrenched it until he heard the *snap*. The Gystfin dropped the Quizan and slumped to the ground, dead.

Azha caught a glimpse of a young Gystfin running alongside the dense tree line where soldiers were waiting for a kill. Before the Beast could swerve, a wave of spears rained down and impaled him. Shrieking in agony, the Gystfin crawled several yards, but there was nowhere to hide. The Gystfin moaned and looked up into the trees. He took one last breath before the second wave of spears ended his life.

A third Gystfin howled a cry of revenge. Small branches and leaves exploded as he flew into the trees. Mid-air he veered and stabbed his long claws through a soldier's chest. The soldier tried with all his might to cling to the limb. His tote of rocks and spears fell to ground as he was lifted into the air. Watching them fall, he knew death was near.

The other soldiers screamed, "Turn into energy, turn into energy." But it was too late, he could not hear them and his cries for Azha to save him were drowned out. The Beast opened his wide jaws and bit off the soldier's head. He sucked out the grey-death energy from the neck and then shoved the head into his mouth. With pleasure, he chewed with his mouth wide open as he rolled the soldier's head around with his tongue for all to see. The gruesome crunching sounds that echoed throughout the trees warned the others. Wanting to see the soldiers' reactions, he turned in a circle before spitting out what was left of the mutilated head. Laughing out loud, he repositioned himself on a tree limb to gloat, then urinated on the head lying on the ground beneath him.

Before the Gystfin could kill another soldier, Azha grabbed a spear off the ground and landed on the same limb behind him. The Beast was too busy making vile gestures to notice until he felt a sharp slap to the back of his head. Shrieking in anger, he glanced over his shoulder and saw the Trekachaw. Azha smugly grinned at him, then stabbed his spear into the Gystfin's ear with such force the tip pierced the top of his head. For a fleeting moment, the Gystfin looked at Azha in shock, then fell forward crashing from limb to limb until he hit the ground with a thump. Choan called out to Azha, "Over here. Where do you want us?"

The arriving squads looked worn-out carrying the heavy load of weapons. Azha pointed towards a clearing. "Leave everything over there and have your soldiers take cover in the trees until I know it's safe. Find Roon, he'll fill you in. Where's Zith?" Azha yelled.

"He stayed behind because King Myosis was threatening us."

"Is Zith in danger?" Azha yelled.

"I don't know, maybe?"

Azha floated to the ground thinking it was over, but he was wrong. Four more Gystfins broke though the tree line, shrieking their attack as they ran towards the injured Quizans. A wave of spears impaled two of the Beasts, killing them instantly. The other two split up, running in opposite directions. One Beast engaged in a cat and mouse game with the soldiers, while the other charged at Azha, spitting profanities and baring his snapping fangs. *Steady, steady...* he waited until the Beast was within arm's length. Azha jumped sideways and shoved the spear into its mouth, shattering several long fangs. The Gystfin bit down on the shaft and shook his head, desperate to break it. Azha held on tight and shoved the razor-sharp tip through its throat and out the back of its neck. Blood spewed from the Gystfin's nose and mouth. Another dead Gystfin. He let go and watched the Gystfin's body slowly slump forward onto the shaft. Freakishly, the shaft propped its bulky, limp body in an upright position.

The last Gystfin howled, "Azha!" and stomped the ground while searching the trees with red, crazed eyes. Froth spewed from his mouth as he flew into the trees searching for a kill. Unable to find a soldier in body form, he jumped from limb to limb chasing clouds of buzzing red lights. They taunted him relentlessly, driving him further into a blind madness. The fur down his spine spiked straight up, and he swatted frantically at the swarm of red lights circling his head. Desperate to catch his prey, he'd lost track of the Trekachaw who was following close behind. Jumping to a lower limb thick with leaves, the Beast pivoted, thinking he was going to catch a soldier. Instead, he came nose to nose with death. Panic-stricken, his eyes darted back and forth looking for an escape. He seemed confused, and then a look of defeat swept across his face. Azha rose above, giving a clear sign for the soldiers to attack. A wave of spears whistled in flight as they rained down. It was too late to run, and the last Gystfin fell to the ground, face down.

Azha roared and the trees shook. Looking up, he watched the soldiers' red energy circle above.

They had done well, but at what cost? Their innocence was gone forever. They'd hunted as a ruthless pack and killed without remorse. Roon sat on the battle-stained ground holding the dead soldier's mutilated head tight against his chest.

Azha leaned over. "Who was the soldier?"

Not more than a couple of feet away, the headless soldier's translucent body was draped across the chest of the youngest slain Gystfin.

Roon pointed at the body crying, *"Aeon Devotio, Aeon Devotio, Aeon Devotio."*

"Is that his name, Aeon Devotio?" Azha asked.

"No, no, no!" Roon wailed as he rocked back and forth.

A wounded soldier kicked the carcass of the younger Beast as he limped over to Azha.

"The soldier was Roon's brother-in law. *Aeon Devotio* means he's been cursed with eternal damnation because the Gystfin sucked out his death energy."

Azha placed his hand on top of Roon's head to comfort his friend; he had no words to lessen Roon's grief. The best he could do was walk away and leave him to mourn.

He had saved five Quizans from certain death; however, two of them had been tortured so heinously they were beyond recognition. Their bodies were riddled with deep puncture wounds and contorted from so many broken bones. Suffering in excruciating pain, they crawled across the ground begging for someone, anyone, to put them out of their misery. Though everyone wanted to help end their suffering, they could not bring themselves to honor the injured Quizans' dying wishes. Watching them suffer made it seem as if it took forever before death finally came and freed their gray-death energy to ascend. They were finally at peace.

Azha recognized the three remaining Quizans. Atue was his childhood playmate. After leaving Kismet Ebb to bond with Rodia, he never returned home. Years passed and for one reason or the other Azha always found a good excuse to avoid visiting his parents or Atue. Deep down, he was afraid of rekindling old feelings for his first love, Phera. Azha watched his severely injured, old friend pick himself up off the ground. In obvious pain and unsteady on his feet, Atue hobbled over to several soldiers and was thanking them profusely for saving his son. More than once he'd glanced sideways, frightened by the towering alien that everyone was calling Azha. Clearly, his old friend was afraid and trying to keep his distance. With the help of two soldiers, Atue made his way over to his terror-stricken son who was mumbling gibberish and dragging himself across the blood-stained ground. Delusional, or perhaps in shock, he was still searching for a place to hide from the Gystfins. Atue fell to his knees and embraced his son, "Etios, it's me, Papay."

The boy's legs had been twisted with such force that his feet faced the wrong direction and his tiny body was covered with bite marks. How he survived the attack was beyond comprehension. Azha respectfully kept his distance, giving Atue the privacy to comfort his son.

And then there was Phera, the third survivor. As quieys they were best friends, and later she blossomed into his first love. Be that as it may, when Azha was created, his parents negotiated a bonding troth with a prominent echelon family from Cavern Village. He had been promised to Rodia, not Phera. For years, Azha protested profusely, believing he could dodge the troth if he complained enough. However, tradition ruled. Fifty years later, Phera was as beautiful as the day he'd left Kismet Ebb. But everything was different now. He was a Trekachaw, not the Quizan she remembered. Azha called out to her, "Phera, do you know who I am?"

Boldly she walked over and squeezed his hand, "Of course, I do. Come, we need to talk."

She led him away from the carnage and sadness into the secluded forest. Memories of his childhood flooded his mind, making him dizzy. Gently she tugged on his hand. "Sit with me."

It was as if time stood still and he was young again. Her voice was soothing and for the first time since Rodia's death, he felt good.

"What I'm about to tell you is very bad. The female you tried to save, was your sister Azine. She wanted you to know how much she loved you and how proud she was of you. You saved her from *Aeon Devotio.*"

Finding it difficult to talk, his words were strained. "Are you sure she was Azine?"

Wiping tears from her face, Phera nodded *yes.* "Azha, our village was attacked by Gystfins. Five older Quizans gave their lives as a distraction so we could escape into the forest. Everyone hid underground until we began dying. One after the other villagers surfaced, only to be slaughtered. Can you help us?" Phera cried.

"I can do more than help. Follow me," said Azha.

Azha kissed Phera's forehead and they flew back to the campsite.

Azha rallied his Sergeants, "Phera just told me Kismet Ebb is being attack by Gystfins. Sgt. Roon, you and Choan's squad will accompany me to Kismet Ebb. Sgt. Duro, you and Belton escort the injured Quizans back to the Caverns and set up a defensive perimeter just like the one here. Phera, do you want to go with me or Duro?"

With no hesitation she responded, "*You.*"

Looking confused, Azha cursed, "Damn, I can't remember where Kismet Ebb is. My Human-half has clouded my memory."

Sgt. Roon spoke up, "No worries, I'll lead the way."

Choan and the soldiers gathered loose spears lying on the ground and pulled-out those embedded in the dead Gystfins. Even though Kismet Ebb was less than a mile away, their trek would take precious time carrying the heavy load of weapons. For Sgt. Roon and Azha, the flight would take a split-second.

PERCHED ON A TREETOP HIGH above the heart of Kismet Ebb Village, Azha could see an energized blue net that blanketed the entire area and far beyond into the forest. Until now, Azha had been baffled by how Gystfins were able to trap Quizans underground, but seeing the net answered his questions.

A faint light rising from beneath the ground caught his eye. It was a Quizan weak from starvation. Roon and Azha cringed as they watched him being violently stunned by the net. The jolt instantly paralyzed the young Quizan, forcing him to morph into body-form. Several Gystfins wearing black gear from the waist down ran through the luminous blue-net and grabbed the limp Quizan by one leg.

They dragged him out to an open area where two more Gystfins were waiting. They pulled the Quizan's legs in opposite directions and roared with laughter at his screams of pain until his hips snapped and his suffering no longer entertained them. After a fight over who was to get the Quizan's head, the winner ran away with the limp body. The other three waited for the next light to rise from the ground.

Somewhere close by, there had to be a power source for the blue net. The only obvious anomaly was a dense beam radiating from a small space shuttle docked on the opposite side of the village.

Azha nudged Roon and pointed at the shuttle. "Turn into energy and follow me."

Terrified, Roon wanted to flee, but Azha had asked, so he obeyed. They circled outside the village for several miles searching for any more Gystfins. Satisfied there where none, Azha covertly returned, flying through the thick trees with Roon following close behind. While they were away, several more starving Quizans had ascended from beneath the ground and were trapped underneath the blue net. They cried for each other and for themselves, for they knew it wouldn't be long until the Gystfins came for them, too.

Waiting was a luxury that Azha could no longer afford. How many more would die if he did nothing? Taking one last look around, he hovered above the shuttle and flickered a signal at Roon to get ready. Simultaneously, they streaked through the hull into an unknown danger. Inside, they found a Gystfin slumped over in a chair with his eyes half-open. The Beast inhaled and then blew out a rumbling snore, blowing spatter and foul breath across the cockpit. Azha morphed into body form and grabbed a handful of matted fur from both sides of its head. The Beast awoke, startled at first then irritated and arguing how he was not sleeping. Still foggy, he tried to turn his head to see who was holding him and realized whoever it was, would not let go. Shrieking and snapping his fangs, the Beast pushed himself away from the schematic screen and tried to stand up. When that didn't work, he kicked the chair out from underneath him and dropped to his knees trying to escape.

Azha spoke into his ear, "I'm half-Quizan, think about that before I kill you."

The Gystfin begged for mercy and screamed for help, but no one heard him.

"You do not deserve my mercy." Azha tightened his grip and wrenched its head until he heard the crunch.

Azha snapped his fingers motioning for Roon to look out the portal window. "Can you see any Gystfins out there?"

Standing on his tiptoes Roon was barely able to peek out the bottom edge of the window.

"I see a bunch of them laughing and pretending to kill us. Why do they enjoy killing us so much?"

Azha snatched the Gystfin off the floor and flung him across the cockpit. The carcass slammed into the hatch and slumped into a ball blocking the door.

"I don't know. But I enjoy killing them," Azha admitted.

Giving the cockpit a quick once-over, Azha sat down in the navigation chair searching for a weapons systems indicator.

"Roon, push down the lever on the door. Make damn sure it's locked."

The shuttle did not appear to be engaged, nor was it like anything he'd seen before. A raised, circuit board attached to an adjacent bulkhead had two lights on... one green, the other red. Azha stood up and yanked the circuit board off its bracket. Success. The beam disappeared, and the magnetic blue net vanished.

Roon squeaked and squatted on the floor, *"No. Oh no, they're running this way. A bunch of them."*

Several rotund Gystfins barged up the ramp and tried to open the hatch. Grumbling and cursing, they kicked the door a couple of times, and then there was silence. Sounds of heavy footsteps were followed by pounding on the door with a heavy object. When that failed, they demanded the door be opened.

Azha yelled back, *"Not happening, assholes."*

A few of the controls were like those in the Gystfin's cargo ship. Several rotating levers and icons formed a specific pattern beneath the largest port-window. The icons identified what appeared to be variations of a weapons system. Choosing a rotating lever with an icon that resembled a laser beam made the most sense. Azha rubbed his hands together, repositioned himself in the chair, and then squeezed the handle. A high-pitched whine pierced his ears and a complex, transparent electronic screen dropped down from the ceiling. The screen revealed chaos and a burning village. Roon peeked out the portal and gasped, *"Azha, look what you've done!"*

Trees and pods were on fire from the laser blast, and there had to be a dozen Gystfins strewn across the village sliced into cauterized, smoldering pieces. Roon was jumping up and down like a pogo stick shouting, *"I see soldiers, I see soldiers."*

Soldiers had climbed into trees with their totes full of rocks and spears waiting to ambush the Gystfins. On the ground, hordes of disheveled and injured Gystfins ran amok, fleeing the torched village into the trees. They didn't get far; from above, waves of spears and rocks rained down upon them. Many fell to their deaths, some crawled into the shelter of the trees, while others ran and never looked back.

CHOAN STOOD AT THE EDGE of the forest fearing they were too late. The thought had crossed his mind that Azha and Roon had died and their bodies had vanished before he and the other soldiers arrived. Sgt. Choan and two soldiers vigilantly crept up the shuttle ramp. Slow and steady they made their way to the top where noises could be heard from within. The exterior latch began to rotate. Choan shouted, *"Get off!"* and the hatch door flung open. Nose-diving off the ramp, they each landed with a belly-flop on the ground, then scrambled to their feet expecting to fight. To their surprise, a dead Gystfin was flung out the hatch door, bounced a couple of times down the ramp, then rolled, coming to rest at Choan's feet. At the top of the ramp stood Roon with a big smile on his face. Sgt. Choan dropped his spear as he sprinted up the ramp.

"I thought you were dead. Where's Azha?"

Rolling his eyes towards the inside of the shuttle, Roon stepped aside. "In here. Didn't you see him throw the Gystfin out?"

Azha swiveled in his chair to greet Choan, but instead of saying 'hello' or 'how are you', he chuckled and whistled a stupid noise.

Roon snickered, "Wow, is he green. Those stripes are bright."

Not one bit amused, Choan's stripes flashed to red. "Not funny. I was glad you weren't dead...not so much anymore."

"Grow a thick skin. Do you know where Phera is?" Azha asked.

Choan's face twisted, wondering if he had been chastised or if it was the Human side of Azha being Human. "She's safe, I left her with soldiers not far from here."

From the doorway of the shuttle, they watched a myriad of Quizan lights rise from beneath the ground. Barely alive, they morphed into body form to absorb rays from the Targus Sun.

Today was a victorious day considering the alternative. Over twelve-hundred Kismet Ebb Quizans had survived the Gystfin attack. Nonetheless, not everyone walked away unscathed. Numerous soldiers and Quizans had minor injuries, some were extensive, and a few had critical wounds. But a hundred and fifty-eight losses were far less than expected. To honor the fallen, the debriefing was postponed until morning.

THE COVER OF NIGHT BESTOWED promise of independence and gave them time to mourn their sacrifices. Camp was bustling with idle talk, and soldiers boasted of courageous acts. Phera stood alone in the shadows, searching for Azha. Countless nights she'd dreamt of the moment when Azha pleaded with her to bond. Young and foolishly stubborn, it was her fault he left. If she'd listened to him, they would've been together all this time. Never again would she make the same mistake.

There he was. She could see him in the light of the red moon walking across the courtyard with a group of soldiers. She waited for him to be alone, only to discover that hordes of idolizing soldiers surrounded Azha wherever he went. Frustrated, she gave up being discreet and said, "Azha, over here. Can we talk?"

And then, out of nowhere, Choan rudely cut right in front of her. "Azha, Roon and I want to go over some new training ideas with you."

Miffed, Phera spoke up, "*Azha,* may I speak with you in private?"

"*Yes,*" Azha winked at Phera and gave Choan a nod. "I'll meet you and Roon later. Phera, let's get out of here to talk."

Phera scowled at the gossiping groupies standing around them. Glaring back at them, she made sure no one followed.

"Would you like to stay with me at the copula tree pod tonight?" Phera asked.

"Yes," Azha whispered making sure no one could hear.

Merging with a Human had significantly altered his sexual appetite. He often found himself thinking about bonding with no logical justification. Random gratifying acts of bonding often flashed in his mind during the day, regularly at night, and a couple of times while he was fighting Gystfins. None of this made any sense. Even more disturbing than that, he often thought about random perverted acts with Rodia. Afterwards he felt guilty and ashamed, yet liked the feeling. That is, until her death would resurface, giving rise to excruciating sorrow. Twisted sexual memories of his Human wife seemed to be the bizarre antidote for his dark depression. This behavior was not normal for a Quizan. Maybe Cole was a perverted deviant. Right now, he was having a tough time controlling his lust. Phera wanted him, her invitation was unmistakable. He'd put aside his guilt, bond tonight, and feel better tomorrow. Surely that brash thinking had to be Human.

Strolling hand in hand down the steep winding path to the cupola tree pod brought back many wonderful memories. As a quirky youth, Azha had a notorious reputation for being fearless and rebellious. He often challenged his parents and explored outside the sanctions of Kismet Ebb. Phera was his best friend and accomplice growing up. They believed that someday their families would accept their devotion to one another and allow them to Owari. But that day never came. The pre-arranged Owari ceremony between Azha and a female called Rodia was non-negotiable by both families. Azha retaliated by sneaking into Phera's cupola pod the night before he was to leave Kismet Ebb in a last-ditch effort to sabotage the ceremony. All night long he pleaded with Phera to bond with him in silver energy. If they created a newborn quiey, the family from Cavern Village would ostracize Azha, ergo putting the kibosh on the bonding commitment. Azha's flawless plan failed when Phera refused to bond. To defy tradition would be unforgiveable, causing dishonor to her parents and future generations. Her fear of harsh consequences was greater than her desire to be with Azha.

That morning Azha left her side and snuck back into his cupola pod where he awaited his future. No sooner had he left, when Phera regretted her decision and crept out, concealing herself behind a tree where she spied on the ceremony. A group of elders escorted Azha, and his manany and papay from their cupola pod to the center of the courtyard. She watched him desperately search the area until he spotted her. Staring at each other, she felt his humiliation and sadness; but what haunted her was the disappointment on his face.

Azha hugged his rejoicing parents good-bye and flew through the dense tree line at the edge of the sleepy village without looking back. Mortified, Phera flew to the ocean cupola pod wishing she had a second chance and wondered if Azha felt as lost and empty as she did. Many agonizing nights passed before she felt strong enough to face the village, her controlling parents, and her life without him. Over the years, she rejected with her sharp tongue, a variety of qualified suitors. Clearly, her choice was to be alone.

They had walked far enough into the forest that sounds from the celebration had faded away. Ahead was a clearing where they could see the moon's reflection on the glistening ocean. This was a good place to talk.

"Do you know what happened to your parents?" Phera asked.

"I figured they were dead, or you would have told me where they were by now."

"I'm sorry. Almost two years ago, thirty Quizans were captured solely for their grey-death energy. At first, we thought a few of them had escaped. Later we learned the Gystfins let them escape so they could hunt them. We thought the Gystfins were going to leave Kismet Ebb after that, but they stayed. Your papay and manany couldn't stay underground any longer. When they surfaced, the Gystfins killed them. I heard it was quick and they ascended."

So much guilt. Not once in fifty years did he try to visit his aging manany or papay. Foolish resentment towards his parents and his passion for Phera always justified his decision never to return. Allowing his admiration for her to rekindle would be disrespectful to Rodia. She was a good wife and deserved his undivided love.

Phera's voice rattled his thoughts. "The cupola pod is not far from here."

Walking next to her made him feel at home, but that was a farce. She was different, more direct and mature. He was nervous and overthinking everything. The night was young, and tomorrow's challenges would come soon enough.

The cupola pod seemed so different from the last time he'd seen it. Thick, twisted branches had grown over most of it, making the pod appear to be part of a tree. Standing perfectly still, he listened to the familiar sounds of the night while gazing up at Palatu's hypnotic twin moons. Colorful beams lit the forest and glittered across the wide leaves as they moved gracefully with the wind. Azha pulled Phera close. His body burned inside, wanting her more now than ever before.

"Phera, I'm afraid I'll lose control if I don't bond soon. As a Trekachaw I have not bonded. What if I hurt you?"

She giggled and sashayed away knowing her teasing was maddening. He watched her body fade into white energy and disappear through the doorway. Following her lead, he flew into the small, glowing room and floated seductively close without touching her. Phera's white energy turned to silver and his into red. Azha bolted outside and flashed back into body form shocked and confused.

"*What, what are you doing? You want to bond in silver and create a quiey?*"

Phera flashed into body form. "*Yes Azha, I want a quiey. I've never bonded.*"

"I'm sorry Phera, you took me by surprise. I don't know if it's even possible."

"Azha, imagine the quiey we could create."

Phera faded into silver as she circled Azha, rubbing her essence seductively up and down his leg while coaxing him into the Pod. *Rodia never did that.* He felt primal, erotic; at that moment, nothing else mattered. Azha flashed into energy and merged with Phera, creating one brilliant, silver light. Euphoria was theirs with no end and no beginning.

Ravished, Phera separated from Azha and then patiently waited for a spark of new life. Nothing; her beautiful silver light was fading, and the time had passed for any viable quiey to form. Exhausted, she morphed into body form and curled up on the floor. Azha lay down next to her. If others judged, screw them. Without Phera, his Human-half would die of loneliness. As he pulled her closer, she sighed and closed her eyes.

Azha tried not to move. There was something outside. He sat up slowly not to awaken Phera. Uncertain, he concentrated on adjusting his sleepy eyes to the darkness. Staring out into the abyss, he focused beyond the doorway of the cupola pod. The noise was probably nothing, most likely his mind playing tricks. The balmy night was soothing, and he could smell sweet fragrances of the forest. Listening to the gentle ocean washing onto the red sand relaxed his mind.

The Targus Sun peeked across the skyline into the pod. Dawn was ending his bliss, and time was running out to think of a good excuse to postpone the meeting. So be it... Azha kissed Phera's cheek and whispered in her ear that he'd return before nightfall.

Phera lay awake for hours thinking about the night before. Bonding was nothing like she'd imagined all those years. On occasion, she would eavesdrop on a group of females who liked to gossip about each other's bonding experiences. All the females agreed how the males were lazy when it came to bonding. It didn't sound as if any of them were too pleased. So far, she didn't find that to be the case with Azha. Shaking off the fog in her head, she stood up, stretched her arms, and walked to the sandy beach to soak up the Targus Sun.

UPON AZHA'S RETURN TO KISMET EBB, Roon and Choan had already assembled the Cavern Soldiers and Kismet Quizans inside the Odeum Pod. First thing on the agenda was the recruitment of new soldiers. Azha clapped his hands together to get everyone's attention and then got right to the point.

"If you're a single adult, line up on this side. Everyone else move to the other side."

The crowd clumsily bumped into one another as they shuffled to their assigned sides of the pod.

"Everyone on this side will train with the soldiers. Everyone on that side, do what you can to help."

Only a few protested the recruitment. Azha recognized them to be the same Leaders that had stormed into his cavern with Myosis. Though not surprised by their attitude, Azha questioned their opposition.

"Explain yourselves," Azha ordered sharply.

A low grumble grew amongst the Quizans waiting to hear their answer. One Leader stepped forward, then paused to gain everyone's undivided attention before raising his fists at Azha.

"Quizans do not kill. We should stand by our creed," he yelled.

Out of patience and tired of their antagonism Azha thundered, "This has nothing to do with your beliefs. You're a coward."

Azha called out to Roon, "If they refuse to train, let them be the first to die the next time the Gystfins attack."

Cheers rang out in support of Azha. "Let them die if they won't fight."

Ignoring the rival Leaders who were still screaming at the crowd to be quiet, Azha dispersed the chanting group outside into the center of the village.

"The soldiers need your help to build strong spears like the one I'm holding. Band with us and learn how we defeated our enemies," shouted Azha.

The Kismet Ebb Quizans embraced Azha's offer, thus abandoning their ancient rituals and stringent traditions. And so, it began, a new future for a once-doomed tribe. All they needed was the right leader. That leader was *Azha.*

Night was falling, and the tribe was drained. Squad selection and inspecting the supplies gathered had taken most of the first day. Azha met with Roon and Choan to confide in them where he would be if needed. Trying to keep the location a secret, Azha covered his mouth and spoke so softly that he was impossible to understand.

Roon blurted out, "What, with who, where?"

"Geez, be quiet. At the ocean pod with Phera," whispered Azha.

Both snickered but assured him that they'd '*keep his secret.*' Exasperated, Azha thanked them for their discretion and streaked toward the ocean before they could humor themselves with any additional remarks.

THE DAY WAS GROWING SHORT along with Phera's patience. For entertainment she practiced morphing in and out of pure white energy, but it was getting late and she couldn't help but worry. As the moons appeared on the horizon, Phera felt herself giving in to her fears. She was having second thoughts about staying at the pod any longer when she saw his light streaking towards her.

Once again, morning came far too soon for Azha. Even so, he needed something to distract him from Cole's attitude. Lying awake, he sensed the Human's reluctance at merging with Phera. For Azha, this was another marvelous gift inherited from the Human... the ability to bond often. Asking for forgiveness, Azha hoped that someday Cole would understand and accept that being a Trekachaw was inevitable and extraordinary.

eight

VIS-À-VIS RYQUAT

"GOOD & EVIL ARE DETERMINED BY OPINION"

Fundamental hierarchy inherited by Kings and Leaders was being replaced by a rebellious society. Azha was the catalyst, giving rise to the end of sacred traditions followed for millions of years.

AZHA devoted the upcoming days inside the cockpit of the shuttle learning how to operate the complex schematics, but his nights were promised to Phera. Now that he had a better understanding of the technology, it would be foolish not to hide it from the Gystfins. During his fly-by reconnaissance searching for their camps, he spotted a secluded cave near the Village. The more he thought about it, the more he liked it. That is, if he could find it again. Azha walked down the ramp, confident that he could hide the shuttle where no one could ever find it. He'd ask Roon to go with him for company. It seemed the little Quizan was always in good spirits and incredibly entertaining.

Azha found him talking to a group of soldiers about the art of *'how to vine-wrap a spearhead.'*

Amused, he watched Roon exaggerate the winding technique, acting as if it was very complicated. Choan, on the other hand, was sitting stone-faced, explaining how to distinguish a good frickin rock from a bad frickin rock. If nothing else, the soldiers were on the same page when discussing a throwing rock. One after the other, everyone stopped what they were doing to look up at Azha.

"Sorry to interrupt. Do you and Choan want to go with me to find a cave?" Azha asked.

Choan shook his head *no.* "Unless you need me?"

"Nope, Roon's enough," Azha said dryly happy that Choan didn't want to go. More often than not, he was in a foul mood. Roon scrambled to his feet and ran in an awkward little dance towards the shuttle chirping, *"Yes, yes, yes,* I get to go with Azha." He slid to a stop at the base of the shuttle and hollered, *"Hurry up."*

Azha strolled up the ramp taking his sweet time alongside Roon, *who was non-stop hopping his way to the top.* Laughing to himself, Azha sat down snug in the pilot's seat and engaged the navigation systems. The shuttle hummed and rose off the ground hovering above Kismet Ebb.

Looking over his shoulder Azha warned, "Sit down and don't turn into energy my little friend. We wouldn't want you to fall out of the ship again."

Sharing yet another adventure, they flew above the forest to the mysterious cave near Cavern Village.

Finding the cave again was difficult. The easy part was landing the small craft on a mesa just outside the entrance. Excited, Azha disengaged the power in haste while Roon struggled to unlock the heavy door latch. Looking around, Azha was pleased to see that the sheer, volcanic cliffs concealed any presence or access to the cave. As they walked into its enormous mouth, a cold breeze brushed against their skin, sending chills up their spines. Inside, they took turns shouting, then listening to their voices echo off the towering rock walls. In awe, they gazed up at the spectacular maze of volcanic tubes that created a labyrinthine of beauty. They took a few moments to adjust their eyes. The polished rock floors seemed to be infinite with hidden secrets that disappeared into darkness beyond the light of the entrance. *The cave was perfect.*

"Roon stay here. Help guide the shuttle through the opening."

Nodding his head up and down nervously, Roon was proud that Azha trusted him with such an important task.

Standing alone in the gigantic cave was scary. *What if a Gystfin or Ryquat were lurking about?* How long had it been since Azha left? Roon had counted the volcanic tubes at least twenty times trying to keep his mind from imagining the worst. Staring at the entrance, he thought about turning into energy. But he needed to stay strong for Azha. Roon heard a hum coming from somewhere, getting louder and louder all around him. It was the shuttle hovering above the entrance. He scurried out of the cave, feeling his stripes turning from red to green. Looking up, he could see Azha waving from the cockpit widow for him to help guide the shuttle past the entrance. Bouncing back into the cave, Roon watched Azha dock the craft in the shadows behind a crag. All was good. Roon and Azha left the cave confident the shuttle was safe.

Azha flew back to the village with a bad feeling in his gut. He wished he could shake it off, but the feeling only got worse. The Gystfins had not returned to claim their shuttle, making Azha wonder why. Come to think of it, not one Gystfin had been spotted since the attack on Kismet Ebb.

WHETHER OR NOT THEY WANTED to admit it, everyone was a bit sad training was over. The Cavern and Kismet Ebb soldiers had become close comrades. Graduation was being held that evening in the Great Cupola Pod to honor the new soldiers and those in command. Upon Azha's arrival, all knelt to the floor and no one spoke until the great Trekachaw asked them to rise. Liberty had been a long time coming, but now it was official. Towering above them all, Azha watched the gentle Quizans dance into the night, knowing their celebration would be short-lived. The Gystfins' reign of terror was far from over.

Early next morning, family and friends gathered around Phera to congratulate her and Azha on their informal Owari. In the center of the village, Cavern Sergeants were shouting orders to the soldiers who were bustling in preparation to depart. For one last hurrah, they circled in formation above Kismet Ebb Village before disappearing into the forest, homeward bound.

Then, out of nowhere, stood a Ryquat.

Azha froze, then slowly reached out to grab Phera's hand. He pulled her back as he stepped forward to shield her from the monster. Afraid that talking out loud would provoke the Ryquat, he whispered through his teeth, "Phera go, tell everyone to hide underground... soldiers too. If I die, gather everyone who is willing and travel to Earth. More Quizans must merge to survive."

Azha tried not to show fear, but he could not control his trembling. Phera's fingers slipped from Azha's hand and she shuffled backwards taking one small step at a time. Unable to control his stripes, they flashed red, but he dared not flinch until Phera was safe. Though scared to death, Phera foolishly hesitated and gazed up at the sleek, black monster. The Ryquat vanished before Azha's eyes and Phera let out a blood-curdling scream behind him. He spun around praying that she was still alive.

The monster had reappeared between them and was pointing his finger at Phera while glaring back at him. Slowly, the monster raised his arm towards the sky, forcing Phera to float up. It was as if she was attached to an invisible restraint under his control. Desperate to escape she struggled, making whatever was holding her squeeze tighter and cause more pain. Her body stiffened, and she grimaced in agony, unable to cry out.

The Ryquat's eyes glowed red and he had no expression, no emotions, nothing that Azha could read. The monster made a fist forcing Phera's spine to arch backwards into a contorted, gruesome position. Phera was dying, and Azha didn't know how to stop the Ryquat. Defeated, Azha dropped to his knees.

"I beg you, do not kill her."

The vile Ryquat lowered its arm allowing Phera's body to descend until her feet touched the ground. Azha looked upon death's face and glaring back at him was pure evil.

"Rise Trekachaw."

Phera was unable to move, but for now she wasn't his target. Believing this was his one and only chance, Azha stood up gradually, trying not to agitate the Ryquat. Did he hear the Ryquat correctly? Had he said, *rise Trekachaw?* If so, maybe there was a chance for him to concede and save the village.

"I am Azha, we call you Ryquat. Her name is Phera. If you want to kill, choose me. I give myself willingly."

The Ryquat scoffed, "If I wished to kill you or your female, you'd already be dead."

He opened his fist and allowed Phera to go free. Azha heard correctly. The monster could speak Quizan.

"I do not want your female, I want you. The Quizans in the trees will not have long after we're gone. Gystfins are waiting to attack this village."

Phera screamed, *"Take me."*

The shiny black Ryquat cocked his head and his red eyes glared. Clearly, he was irritated at her brazen defiance. "If the female challenges me again, I will not be so gracious."

Azha yelled, *"Go Phera, you're going to get us both killed."*

Phera ran, hating herself for leaving Azha alone to die. Azha kept an eye on her until he could no longer see her. With Phera safe, Azha tested the Ryquat's resolve. "Now what?"

The Ryquat relaxed his stance and his demeanor completely changed. "Don't be so eager to die. I am Victis from planet Zaurak. You, on the other hand, are unfamiliar to me. However, I've been observing you for some time now and find you intriguing. My assignment was to investigate a rumor of an indigenous species being hunted to extinction and to sterilize you upon contact. That would have been a shame. You are quite impressive. Your abilities are nothing like I've ever seen or heard of. Did you really coalesce with a Human? You are worthy of further observation. I choose not to sterilize you… not until I know more. Maybe never," the Ryquat laughed.

Azha hoped the Ryquat's twisted laugh meant the same thing as a Human's joke told in poor taste. Taking a big risk, Azha boldly suggested the Ryquat leave Palatu. It appeared as if the alien may have grinned.

"No, I won't leave. You will answer my questions, or I'll sterilize you. I watched you spacejack the only Gystfin Cargo Ship within thirty light-years of here, so don't deny it. What I want to know is where you concealed it? Oh, and the Gystfin shuttle you hid in the cave, we're flying it to my battleship."

Azha agreed, considering the alternative. He was thankful to be alive and to have the village and Phera in one piece. Ryquat Victis abruptly ended the conversation, "It's time to go, Trekachaw."

The Ryquat closely shadowed Azha on the way to the cave. Landing inside, Azha thought of different ways to kill the Ryquat. But since he didn't know the alien's weaknesses, he'd have to wait. Grudgingly, he escorted the arrogant alien behind the crag and forfeited his shuttle.

On the flight up to the battleship, Azha found himself feeling disturbingly relaxed and intrigued by Victis. That is, until they were together for a while. The Ryquat never stopped talking. Long winded and loud, he explained everything at least three times. Boasting even louder, he elaborated on how a Gystfin Commander demanded a conflux to bellyache about a new species called Trekachaw. Making weird facial expressions, Victis parroted the Commander, '*The Trekachaw should be exterminated by Ryquats before its powers become too strong.*' He rambled on how the Commander accused the Trekachaw of murdering hundreds of Gystfins with no provocation. Smiling he paused, "We both know that's not true." Victis took a deep breath and pointed out a portal window, "Behold, my battleship. Isn't she magnificent?"

Indeed, the massive ship was spectacular, stretching as far as the eye could see. Nothing in the Universe could be more intimidating than this iron predator. Fascinated, Azha watched an entire section of the ship's hull disappear seconds before Victis flew the tiny craft onto a raised docking platform. Like magic, the side of the battleship re-appeared. Victis flipped several switches, then ran his hand across a circuit board causing the shuttle to power down. Without missing a beat, he disconnected the harness strap, pushed his chair back and stood up from the navigation station.

"Feels good to be back on board. Can't wait to get out of this suit."

What? He assumed Ryquats were impervious evil with red eyes and black as a raven. It never dawned on him that the Ryquat was wearing a spacesuit. An unexpected blast of oxygen filled the shuttle and what came next rattled Azha even more. Victis pulled a tag from the side of his head and peeled back a portion of his skin. Underneath was a second face, *a Human face.* The Ryquat felt around under his chin until he found another longer tag that concealed a small plastic device with a blinking beam of light. He aimed the device toward his body, then placed his right thumb over the light. In an instant, the spacesuit liquefied and was sucked-up into the device. Standing before Azha was a lean, muscular, *stark-naked Human.*

Was Victis the Ryquat a Human? Whatever he was stomped briskly down the ramp, then across a platform to a row of metal lockers adjacent to plastic benches and open showers. Azha peeked out the hatch door and looked back and forth across the docking bay to see if anyone else was there. As far as he could tell, there were no other Ryquats. Victis continued to rant and joke about something while opening a locker. Without taking a breath between stories, he pulled out a uniform, shoes, and a blue duffel bag. *Then, he slammed shut the locker-door and disappeared behind a shower curtain.* His constant chatter bounced off the open girders, creating an amplified echo, "Every single time… this water is as cold as a Crozin."

After that, Azha couldn't understand a thing he was saying. Victis alternated between mumbling loudly or singing in the shower. *Either way, he sounded terrible.*

The sweet oxygen inside the ship reminded him of Cole's life. Thoughts flooded his mind with vivid, Human memories and cherished, forgotten dreams. He missed Earth with all her imperfections and his simple life. Azha fought to suppress those emotions and concentrated on resisting his rebellious Human-half. Of course, none of this mattered if the Ryquat decided to kill him. Azha peeked out the door to see if there were any more Ryquats. The coast was clear... now was as good as time as any to move. Covertly he zigzagged down the ramp and froze at the bottom for a second, then tiptoed over to the showers and sat down on a bench.

Victis sang, "Can you hear me now?"

"Yes, I can hear you. Are you the only Ryquat on this ship?" Azha asked.

Victis paused... blew his nose at least five or six times in the shower and then crowed, "Do you really think I'm the only Ryquat on this enormous battleship?"

Azha mumbled, *"What a jack-ass,"* wishing he could take it back the moment he said it. "Did you hear me?"

"Yesss." In a drawn-out snide voice.

"Do you know what a jack-ass is?" asked Azha.

Victis stepped out from behind the curtain, dripping-wet with a towel wrapped around his waist.

"Ah, yes, foul mouth Trekachaw. I know what jack-ass means. I'll give you this one. Check your mouth or you'll regret it, agreed?"

Azha agreed. Victis began singing off-tune again while vigorously drying off with a towel. He stopped singing and tossed the towel on the shower floor. He opened his duffel bag and dug through it as he explained, "There's one hundred and thirty-three Ryquats on board. Now, I have a question. Do you remember being Human?"

Ryquat Victis was nothing like Azha had envisioned, and he felt comfortable on the ship. Maybe too comfortable. That could be a huge mistake.

"Yes and no. When I'm on Palatu, I'm more Quizan. It seems when I absorb oxygen, I'm more Human. Being on your ship and around you even more so."

"Well, that could explain why you smell. On Palatu you didn't have body odor, here you're starting to stink like a Crozin. Just so there's no misunderstanding, that's not a compliment. If you don't want to take an old-fashioned shower, over there's a Yeager. It's that box thing next to the showers. Step inside and push the blue button. You'll feel a burst of warm steam. After a red light goes off, you're clean. Either one will do the trick, I'll wait for you."

"No thank you. All I need to do is turn into energy, then morph back into body form to clean myself," replied Azha.

"Do it. You stink," Victis said disgusted.

Azha flashed into energy and back into body form. Victis rudely invaded his space to perform a sniff test.

"That worked. Might want to do that more often up here," suggested Victis.

"Since you're being so judgmental, pick up your towel. On Earth we call people like you, slobs," countered Azha.

"On my ship and Zaurak we have robots for that. But then, you wouldn't know this because you're primitive. See those things flying towards us? That's one of many robots we have on ship, so don't break it."

Victis changed the conversation asking about a Human merge. He teasingly admitted how he followed Azha to the Gystfins cargo ship. Not being able to get a word in edge wise, Azha began talking over him, "You've been watching me?"

"Of course. I've been observing and evaluating your abilities and intelligence. Why were you staring at your reflection on the navigation deck?" Victis asked.

"How long have you been watching me?" Azha questioned stunned by his bluntness.

"For a while. Since before you killed the first Gystfin," replied Victis.

Outraged, Azha insisted, "What else did you *watch* me do?"

"Well, I observed you and Phera at the cupola pod having a lot of Quizan energy sex. You must have inherited that ability from the Human. If you fight as good as you *Fu...* Excuse me, I try not to use profanity," replied Victis.

Disgusted, Azha closed his eyes. But Victis didn't notice. Most likely he didn't care. Victis continued to ramble on about how genetically a Trekachaw and Quizan could not create a new life. However, a male and female Trekachaw could.

Victis proudly confessed, "I have confirmed my theory. One night while you and Phera were sleeping in the cupola pod, I removed your DNA for testing. You heard me and sat up. I thought for sure you saw me. Lucky for you, you didn't look behind you. If you had, I probably would've been forced to kill you and Phera."

Victis just kept on talking while Azha sat in silence.

"I think more Quizans should coalesce with Humans... consider the possibilities. My test results confirmed you'll live a minimum of five-hundred earth years. Maybe longer, who knows."

Azha stripes were red with the tips turning purple.

"Victis, please stop talking," demanded Azha.

Even though he dreaded whatever else the brash pervert might spew, Azha asked another question. "Why did you kill thousands of Quizans?"

Victis stopped talking. Perhaps that question was the wrong one to ask. For all he knew the Ryquat was going to kill him right now, right here. Should've kept his mouth shut.

Victis finished dressing himself without saying a word and sat down on the bench opposite Azha. The Ryquat seemed uncomfortable. This time, Victis spoke in earnest and with compassion, thus revealing yet another side of the complicated alien.

"You deserve an explanation. I've never killed or harmed a Quizan. It all started about ten years ago when one Ryquat Captain was assigned to Palatu. He reported the Quizan loss was minimal and how Gystfins benefited from the grey-death energy. Production increased, costs were significantly reduced, and life support apparatuses were eliminated, which minimized the use of crude naphtha accelerants. In fact, his reports claimed the Gystfins were reducing a severely over-populated planet of Quizans. My mission was to investigate a rumor that Gystfins were hunting an indigenous species to extinction. If so, I was to replace the Captain and oversee the ongoing mining operations. During my initial investigation, I discovered a worst-case scenario. The Captain was addicted to grey-death energy and needed frequent doses to maintain a functional level. If not, his withdrawals were excruciatingly painful. He was immediately detained and transported to Zaurak. Last I heard, he's in a care facility still suffering from painful withdrawals and may have irreversible brain damage."

Azha snarled, "You condoned Gystfins killing Quizans because they were more productive after sucking out our grey-death energy?"

"Before, yes. Now, no. Viceroy Ryquats agreed with the Gystfins that the benefits outweighed Quizan loss."

Azha was infuriated by the narcissistic Ryquats. They condoned the slaughter of innocent Quizans with no shame, and for what... *Rocks?* Victis was just as guilty as the vicious Gystfins and bad Ryquats.

"Why are your stripes bright purple?" Victis stood up and stepped backwards over the bench to have a barrier between him and Azha.

'Does he realize how damn offensive he is to me? Hmm, he's afraid without that suit. I could kill him and escape. If I did, the Ryquats would seek revenge.'

Azha caught himself hissing and moving towards Victis, "My wife, Rodia, was killed by a Gystfin. She was innocent, kind, and giving. Do you have any idea the pain and suffering you've caused?"

Ready to pounce, Azha's eyes glowed yellow and his stripes blazed purple. Victis glanced in the direction of his suit.

"Azha sit down. I'm sorry about Rodia and for all the Quizans, but I had nothing to do with that. Any other Ryquat would have sterilized you at the Gystfins request, but I chose not to. Of course, I understand why you're angry, and you have every right to hate us. Think about what I can offer before you do something you'll regret. Calm down and we will talk about the future, not the past. I will try to protect you and the Quizans from now on."

Considering the consequences if he did what he wanted to do, Azha sat down on the bench. Victis sat on the bench after Azha's stripes faded from purple, to red, then to orange.

"Not to change the subject, but I find your stripes intriguing. I'm pretty sure red or purple means you're angry or ready to fight. What do the other colors mean?" Victis asked.

With what just happened, Azha couldn't believe the Ryquat's flippant question. Maybe he could trade information with the dumb-shit.

"I'll tell you what my colors mean if I can return to Palatu," replied Azha.

Curious to hear what the Trekachaw had to say, Victis would've agreed to almost anything.

"You're right, red is anger, or it can mean fear. Purple is rage or attack. Quizans have the same emotional colors, though somewhat less vibrant than mine. Right now, I am orange because I've calmed myself. When my stripes are green, I'm happy or excited. Phera told me when I sleep my stripes are yellow."

"She's right, your stripes are yellow when you sleep." Victis interrupted.

Azha's eyes narrowed, "Promise not to spy on me anymore."

Victis extended his arm out, "Fair enough, let's shake on it. I'll never spy on you again assuming we stay friendly."

If memory served, this was a Human tradition performed to solidify a peace offering. Silly as it may have seemed, he reached out and shook Victis's hand.

"If you're finished, I'll continue," said Azha.

"Please do," replied Victis.

"Pale or tan is sad or worried. Dark blue means ill, sick, or gravely injured, and grey is dying or dead. White is the most common color while flying or when we bond. Humans would call white bonding casual sex. Silver is the creation of a new baby quiey, or when I merged with Cole. That's it, can I go now?"

"Hold on to your shoes, why are you so eager to leave? Allow me to give you a tour of my battleship. Besides, I need to slam down a Mito drink. Unlike you Azha, I need food to fuel my body, and it'll give us a chance to talk some more before we go."

Azha smiled and smugly replied, "Victis, I am well-aware of those frailties."

Then it dawned on him, '*Before we go? What? Did he say shoes, hold on to your shoes? That makes no sense. No, no, no*'.

Azha chased after Victis, who was moving quickly towards a door. As he reached out for the door-handle, Azha blocked his hand.

"Victis, we made a deal. I want to leave now."

"Like I said, I need a Mito. Come on Azha, move. Walk with me to the galley."

Grunting and groaning Victis shoved Azha aside and opened the door. Beyond the doorway Azha saw a long, white hallway that lead to unknown dangers. Azha trailed behind feeling his stripes turning from orange to a reddish orange. Enough with blindly following the Ryquat. He'd turn into energy and return to Palatu. For no reason, Victis stopped and punched him in the arm. "Why are you getting angry?

Azha thought about punching him back but feared he would damage the Ryquat.

"What do you mean, *we'll go*? You're not going with me," Azha protested. *The Quizans would be terrified of the Ryquat.*

"I am, and you will introduce me to the Quizan tribes," Victis advised in a sharp tone.

Azha followed Victis into the galley where six Ryquats were seated on a narrow bench eating food. He had a flashback of Cole taking code-7 with a bunch of cop buddies on Earth. Being here was uncomfortable and allowing Cole to give rise to such strong emotions was dangerous.

The Ryquats sat staring at him, and he could not stop staring back. Victis had finished his Mito drink and was watching Azha stare at the crewmen. To break it up, Victis slammed the Mito bottle down on the table and announced that he was ready to go. *No sleep, but ready to go.* The Ryquats jumped up and stood at attention.

"Sgt. Bruce, advise Akio to stay in orbit. I'll be available on the planet. As you were, finish your lunch," ordered Victis.

It would have been impressive, if Azha had not been irritated at how fast Victis was able to wind his way back to the docking bay. If he'd slow down they could have a conversation.

"Wait-up, we need to talk," yelled Azha.

Down the ramp and through a door he disappeared. By the time Azha caught up, Victis was already undressing.

"Hey Azha, I named my spacesuit Vexy. *Guess why?* Vexy was my second wife's name. Should've never married her, *big mistake.* I loved my first wife. Married Vexy out of lust. Anyway, the suit's official name is 'Vita Brevis', which means *life is short* in Latin. In other words, Ryquats would die in space without them. Every suit is custom-fitted and designed for specific needs. Mine is the newest with all the gadgets. As I was saying, my second wife *sucked the life* out of me. *Oops, I didn't mean literally, matter of speech that's all.*" Victis snickered under his breath thinking he was funny.

Azha was exhausted from listening to Victis ramble on about nothing. *Does he ever shut-up? Couldn't get one-word in. Too late. He's suited-up, ready for his big introduction on Palatu. I'll talk to him in the shuttle on the way down. It'll give me a chance to explain what a big mistake this is.*

Azha briskly walked away, headed for the shuttle.

Victis whistled and pointed to a small portal. "Where are you going? We're flying."

Azha was out of options. "Victis this isn't going to work. They're terrified of Ryquats. Somehow, I need to convince the Quizans that you won't kill them. Until I do, you can't show yourself. And one more thing, on Palatu I'm in charge."

Victis appeared evil in his shiny black spacesuit. Convincing the Quizans to trust him was going to be a hard sale. The Ryquat stiffened and his cheerful demeanor changed.

"For now, I agree. But you will never be my equal, nor will you ever be in *charge*. Do not test me Azha. My kindness can easily turn.

nine

PASSIM

"Question your decision if you made a mistake, then your intent. Either way, accept responsibility."

FEELING free at last, Palatu was a welcome sight from space. Azha landed on a large, tree limb at the edge of Kismet Ebb to wait for Victis. Soon after, Victis swooped in next to him. This location was a perfect spot to conceal Victis, and they were high enough to observe the entire village.

Something was terribly wrong. Everything was too quiet and there were no Quizans in sight. Three Gystfins came stumbling out the doorway of the Great Cupola Pod carrying two half-dead Quizans by their feet. Azha's stripes flashed purple and he crouched ready to attack. Victis grabbed Azha by his arm and pointed, *"Stop, look in the courtyard."*

Gystfin after Gystfin, in what seemed to be a never-ending row of Gystfins were walking out of the Great Cupola Pod. The Beasts dragged their captives across the ground to a boulder located in the center of the village. Taking turns, they swung the screaming

Quizans in circles by their feet until they were unconscious. As a final act of either revenge or pleasure, they flung the frail creatures into the air smashing them into the jagged boulder, putting an end to the torture and their lives.

Azha was devastated. Most of the dying Quizans were the soldiers trained to defend the village. He counted sixty-one Gystfins desecrating everything in their path. So far, he had not seen Phera. She may have been savagely murdered while he was on the damn Ryquat's battleship. If he could start over, he would. Being a Trekachaw was not worth this. Rodia would still be alive, along with all the dead soldiers who had trusted him.

Victis had disobeyed and violated direct orders. Blatant interference with the Gystfins' mining contracts would not be tolerated by the Ryquat Viceroys. His next decision would jeopardize the ores necessary to fuel the battleships and could sway the ongoing war against the Crozins. *Perplexed, he decided to go with his gut.*

"I'll kill the Gystfins, but once we start this, we can't stop," Victis said in earnest.

Wanting them all dead, Azha asked, "How?"

Victis touched a device on his arm, "*Lock-in...* Silence... *Confirmed, stand-by for area sterilization, one klik.* Do exactly what I say, nothing more, nothing less."

Azha gave a quick nod, "I hear you."

"Fine, I'll fly into the village and contact the Gystfin's Kogbor. I need to find out if there are other ships. After I leave, sterilization will begin. Stay here, you'll be outside of the biological disintegration zone."

Victis grinned optimistically, "If I get in trouble, I'll yell *Vexy.* That's our secret code for you to help me, understood?"

Not waiting for Azha's answer, Victis dove off the tree limb and glided into the center of the courtyard.

The Gystfins scattered, leaving a wide berth around the Ryquat. One crusty, old Gystfin stood his ground. The old Beast grabbed an injured Quizan by the neck and dragged him through the dirt towards Victis.

"You go, Victis of Zaurak," he shouted.

"Explain Kogbor, why kill Quizans for no purpose? Let's agree to end our differences and continue to honor Viceroy and Fidus Achates contract."

"No, Victis of Zaurak. Agree no honor, all lies. Bring me Trekachaw, agree to bite off head," he snarled.

Kogbor roared, providing a wave of Gystfins the courage to attack. Triumphantly, he held the Quizan high above his head for all to see. Howling and spreading his legs apart was the Gystfin's way of showing he had no fear or respect for the Ryquat.

A thin, blue beam sliced through the air. Kogbor shrieked in agony, staring down at his severed arm lying in the dirt beneath him. The Quizan was gone and the Ryquat had disappeared. Hordes of Gystfins lost their courage and were scattering in every direction. Victis flew onto the tree limb and carefully laid the little Quizan into Azha's arms. *"No matter what, stay here," said Victis.*

Only time would tell if Victis made the right choice. But right now, he had to eliminate the Gystfins before they had a chance to report the incident or request reinforcement.

The black Ryquat appeared relentless as he swooped over the Gystfins' heads into the Great Cupola Pod. The pod was empty except for grey-death souls circling above his head. Outside, Kogbor was screaming in agony and shouting orders to the chaotic Gystfins, *"Kill the Ryquat, kill the Ryquat."*

Victis flew out of the pod and slapped the top of Kogbor's head to further provoke him. On the far side of the village, Victis spotted a shuttle docked on top of a mesa. Taking a second pass overhead, Victis saw Gystfins still sucking out grey-death energy from the severed necks of dead Quizans, even while Kogbor continued to scream at them to stop. He thought about killing them, but he was too late to save the Quizans and besides, the Gystfins would all be dead soon enough. Victis flew out of the village and landed in the tree next to Azha.

"There's a shuttle docked on a mesa directly across the court-yard. Can you fly it to my ship?

"No problem," Azha assured.

You've got fifteen minutes." Victis shot up into space and disappeared.

Azha carefully laid the Quizan's small, broken body between the intertwined forks of two branches.

"Are you strong enough to turn into energy?"

With all his might, the little Quizan lifted his head and nodded, 'Yes.'

"Fly with me to a shuttle across the courtyard. Stay in energy for as long as you can," said Azha.

"If I die my name is Pax. Thank the Ryquat for saving me," he cried.

Azha turned into a bright red light and waited for Pax as he struggled to turn into a dull greyish-blue glow. Most likely, Pax would vanish before reaching the shuttle. They flew across the village just above the Gystfins running amok on the ground. Pax followed, fading more and more into the final stages of grey-death energy.

How much time had passed since Victis left? Guessing five, maybe six minutes tops, Azha drifted through the metal wall into the cockpit. Two Gystfin were sitting in front of the navigation console preparing for take-off. Kogbor was curled up on a bench moaning in agony with his severed arm clutched against his chest, oblivious to the threat floating above him. Azha morphed into body form and snatched Kogbor's arm away from him. Before the other two could react, Azha swung the bloody arm, striking Kogbor across his face. His eyes rolled back and in slow motion he slumped forward falling onto the deck. Azha spun around to fight the other two Gystfins, but they were gone. Time had to be running out. Azha grabbed Kogbor and his severed arm and threw them down the ramp. Several Gystfins jumped sideways to avoid the tumbling carcass. Azha stood in the open doorway and hissed, making certain they saw him before he closed the hatch. Seeing their dead Kogbor, the Gystfins ran away.

Pax morphed into body form and collapsed. He was on the brink of death and could no longer speak. A blissful *Aeon Devotio* was beckoning his soul to submit and join the others. Azha knew direct sunlight was the Quizan's only hope for survival. With a flip of a switch, the shuttle was ready for take-off. Looking one last time through the portal window for Phera, Azha engaged the craft and flew towards the Targus Sun.

Far above, Victis watched the battleship monitor waiting for any sign of the shuttle. There she was, a dot in space. He breathed a sigh of relief.

Azha disengaged the shuttle and drifted silently in space. On the floor behind him, Pax was dying. Azha ran to open the hatch and gently scooped the dying Quizan into his arms. He carried the limp body to the sunny side of the shuttle's exterior hull and lay down next to him. The Targus rays were intense and felt good against the black, metal hull. For a fleeting moment Azha found peace amongst the chaos and self-doubt. No matter what, he would stay with Pax until his grey-death energy left his body. Azha closed his eyes, dreaming of his other life on Earth. Every day, vivid new memories were surfacing. Torn between now and then, he admitted to himself how much he missed being a police officer and the love he felt for his Human wife.

THUMP, his dreams were interrupted by something colliding with the hull. Sitting next to him was Victis, busy staring down at Palatu. Little by little, Victis stretched out one of his legs towards Azha. Trying to ignore the Ryquat was impossible. He deliberately scooted on his butt until he was close enough to touch Azha's head with his foot.

"Knock it off. Damn, you're irritating," said Azha.

Victis laughed, "Come on, sit up if you want to watch Kismet Ebb sterilized."

Azha sat up just in time to see a blinding light shoot out from the Ryquat Battleship. The beam narrowed into a steady, blue stream of pulsating light radiating down upon the planet. Mesmerized, they sat together watching the thin, blue light. The beam abruptly vanished, and the mighty Ryquat Battleship rolled, then pitched starboard until it was level. Seeing it in motion would make one believe the ship was alive as it rolled in space until its bow faced the sun, and then by choice became dormant once again.

Azha looked over at Victis, "What is sterilization?"

Though Victis rationalized the cost of war, the answer remained undeniably devastating.

"I had no choice. If even one Gystfin were to survive and report the sterilization to their Dux Ducis the Ryquats would forfeit Palatu's raw materials contract. We, the Ryquats, and several other species have been at war with the Crozins and their allies for thousands of years. Without us, the Crozins would have destroyed Earth long before Humans inhabited her. We protect many planets in the Fidus Achates territory. Now that you understand why the raw materials are so important, tell me where you hid the Gystfins' cargo ship?"

"First, tell me what sterilization means."

"Alright. The pulsating laser you watched, eradicates molecules unique to animals."

A wave of dread washed over Azha. "Were the Quizans underground sterilized?"

Victis punched Azha in the arm. "No, I wouldn't do that. Don't worry, the Quizans underground were perfectly safe. One of these days, sooner than later, we need to talk about genealogy. You should understand the progenitor of Humans and Ryquats and consider joining the Fidus Achates. Now it's your turn. Where's the Gystfin cargo ship?"

Pax forced his swollen eyes open. His stripes were yellow, and he was showing signs of healing. Slowly and painfully, he rolled onto his side trying to eavesdrop on their conversation. Several attempts to talk had failed. He was too hoarse from the bruises left by the Gystfin choking him. Azha caught a glimpse of Pax moving from the corner of his eye.

"Look at you. You're one tough Quizan."

Clearing his throat, Pax whispered in a raspy voice, "Thanks to you and the Ryquat."

Victis was waiting for an answer regarding the cargo ship's location. Azha wasn't ready to let go of his only ace. Victis was not the enemy, but neither was he completely trustworthy. Before the Ryquat had the chance to ask again, Azha punched him in the arm hard enough to know the pain would distract him.

"BAKA UNKO!" as he bent over, vigorously rubbing his arm.

"Hey, not so hard. Are you guys ready to go? I'm hungry."

Trying not to show his pain, Victis stood up and stretched out his sore arm. Pax and Azha turned into energy and floated though the hull. He envied them being able to do that. If only he could be a Trekachaw. For now, he'd take the long way around and enter through the hatch.

Everything was as good as it could be considering that he'd gone rogue. Victis navigated the Gystfin shuttle onto the docking platform and released a blast of oxygen into the cockpit. Pax flashed into energy, a little blue and woozy from the poison oxygen.

"Damn it Victis, Quizans can't absorb oxygen while in body form... *Are you trying to kill him?"*

"Of course not," Victis glared at Azha. "Sorry little buddy, I forgot. Stay in energy while you're on my ship. Give me a minute to get out of my Vexy suit, then follow me. My crew designed a chamber just for you."

Pax floated above, with Azha trailing behind Victis as they navigated through the winding corridors of the ship. At the end of a secluded hallway, they passed through a series of doors into a chamber that resembled a Palatu cave.

"Don't morph yet Pax, the chamber is oxygen-based," said Victis.

Victis exited the chamber and digitally code-locked the door. After a few adjustments, he waved *a thumbs-up* at Pax and Azha through a large plate window. Pax materialized in his new home, grinning from ear-to-ear. Azha left the chamber confident that Pax was in the safest place possible. Outside, Victis was nowhere to be found. Searching from room to room and down long corridors, Azha wondered where everyone had gone. He enjoyed exploring the ship on his own, but after a while he grew frustrated shouting out to whomever, *"Is anyone in here? I'm trying to find Victis. Hello, can anyone hear me?"* A familiar, pleasant odor guided Azha to the ship's galley where Victis sat eating a large stack of pancakes and an enormous fried egg.

"Where'd you go? I've been looking all over the ship for you. What if I just left without telling you?"

Victis stopped eating and placed his fork down on the table. "Have a seat, we need to discuss a couple of things."

Azha pulled out a chair and sat down on the edge.

"Pax can remain on ship for as long as he wants to. You can wait for me or return to Palatu, but I'm dead tired. After I finish breakfast, I'm going to sleep for at least eight hours. When I wake up, if you're not here, I'll rendezvous with you at Kismet Ebb."

A couple of fidgety Ryquats sat across the table watching Azha's every move. The moment Victis finished talking, one of the Ryquats jumped to his feet.

"Pleased to meet you Trekachaw. My name is Jacet. Captain, do you still want me to inject a Linguistic Chip?"

Victis pushed his chair back, "Yes, thank you for reminding me. Azha do you want one? The chip translates languages, making it possible for you to understand and communicate with different species within the Orion Belt. Jacet can inject the chip in your arm before you leave."

Quizan physiology provided an immunity from most diseases, infections, and contagions. Health care facilities and providers were nonexistent. Sticking a foreign object inside your arm was disgusting and terrifying... to say the least. Exacerbating his fear, Cole hated needles.

"Will it hurt? What happens if I turn to energy?"

Victis was too tired to be amused, "Azha it doesn't hurt. It's an itty-bitty microchip injected into your forearm. And how would I know what happens when you're in energy? Do you want the chip or not? Give him your arm, you big *Chovo.*"

"Chovo? What's a Chovo?" Azha asked.

"A large bird that lays big eggs. Think of a cross between a vulture, an ostrich, and a chicken. Now, give Jacet your arm."

Azha's stripes turned bright red as he grudgingly stuck out his arm. Jacet's hands were shaking when he picked up the small black case and he dropped it twice. Azha pulled his arm back and gave Victis a dirty look. Eventually Jacet was able to remove a silver device that resembled a ballpoint pen from the case.

"I apologize for being nervous. I'd appreciate it if you didn't hurt me."

Azha nodded.

Jacet placed the end of the device gently on Azha's forearm slightly above the wrist and asked, "Ready?"

Victis badgered, "Just do it."

Jacet closed his eyes and pushed down the top with his index finger to inject the Linguistic Chip. Victis leaned over to inspect the injection site.

"See Chovo, it didn't hurt. Turn into energy, let's see what happens."

Azha flashed. There it was, a micro black energy dot floating amongst his energy. He flickered and bounced trying to dislodge the chip, but it held fast. Enough with Victis and his Ryquats, Azha floated up and streaked out of the battleship towards Palatu.

KISMET EBB WAS BARREN OF life. Even the hardy Gruts were gone, and they could survive anything. Phera had to be hiding somewhere. She was too smart to have been captured. Azha vaguely remembered an underground lava cave where Quizans would hide when threatened. If memory served, it was not far from the surface and could easily accommodate eight-hundred Quizans. If not there, a few cold caves were occasionally used, but they were much smaller and deep within the planet's core. Confident, he began his search.

The lava cave was as grand as he remembered. It echoed hollow phantoms that bounced off the empty rock walls into the abyss. Disappointment came quickly; not a single Quizan was waiting to be rescued and there were no clues to follow. This was bad. Where would they have gone? Shaken by even the thought of the alternative, Azha streaked through molten rock into the nearest small, cold cave far beneath the planet. At last, he found a small group of Quizans huddled together in the dark. Though terrified, they were very much alive. Azha guided twenty-nine grateful Quizans from their looming grave to the surface. Weak from starvation, they collapsed upon the ground to absorb the Targus sun. Phera was not among the rescued.

A wise, old Quizan tugged at Azha's arm to get his attention. He told the legend of a secret, deep fissure beneath the floor of the lava cave. Ancient myths warned never to move the *blue-slate stone* that covered the entrance. Trespassers would enter an underworld of barren land and a sea of flames; evil monsters would rise, escaping from the hidden depths and infect Palatu with deadly plagues. Elders passed on the legend to scare young Quizans and Quieys from exploring the labyrinth of dangerous fissures.

Years ago, Phera along with several other adventurous young Quizans, had followed one of the fissures to a small grotto deep within the planet. What they learned was there were no monsters or deadly plagues, thus exposing the legend to be nothing more than a superstitious myth. The old Quizan squeezed Azha's hand, "Find the blue stone and follow the largest fissure. Phera could be hiding there."

Just as the wise old Quizan had described, Azha found the blue-slate stone and followed the fissure for miles beneath the surface to a small, cold, damp cave. From a crevice within a crumbling wall, three faint lights glowed. One light danced and circled him. At last, he'd found her. Phera had beaten the odds.

Over nine-hundred Kismet Ebb Quizans had died. A mere thirty-two survived, and Pax was the only soldier. Phera forgave Azha, but he was ashamed and exasperated. He should never have trained the Quizans to fight. And Victis, with all his power, should have sterilized the Gystfins long before they attacked the village a second time. His eyes burned and tears streamed down his face; regrets, so many regrets. How arrogant of him expecting peaceful Quizans to do what was unnatural and impossible.

Since there was nothing left of Kismet Ebb except for bad memories and the threat of another attack, Azha insisted they seek refuge at Cavern Village. While waiting for the weaker ones to absorb enough energy, Azha instructed them to cluster together and fly directly beneath him. This would be the best way to defend the small group. Next time, Azha would be ready with or without Ryquat Victis.

VICTIS AWOKE FROM HIS SLUMBER unaware of the devastation at Kismet Ebb. He flew over the ocean and landed in a tree high above the Village. Azha appeared shaken and was talking to a group of Quizans in the center of the courtyard. Believing he would be greeted with open arms Victis called out, "Azha, up here. Are you ready to introduce me?"

The Quizans flashed into red-energy and clustered into a tight ball behind Azha's leg.

"Go away, you're too late to do anything except scare the shit out of everyone left."

Victis flew out of the tree landing in front of Azha. "Where's the rest of the tribe. Why are you so red?"

"I'm red, because I'm mad at myself, but even angrier at you. These few lights you see behind me, are what's left of the tribe."

Victis walked in a circle with his hands clasped together on top of his head trying to think of something to say.

"This shouldn't have happened. Why weren't they underground? I told Phera the Gystfins were going to attack."

Azha lashed out, "This was my home, I grew up here. My lineage dates back millions of years before you or the Humans. *Everyone's dead. My family, my village annihilated by vulgar Beasts. And for what?* Quizans can't fight these monsters. Look at them. Teach me how to use Ryquat weapons if you want to save us."

Azha thought he heard a faint voice crying for help and stopped talking. Following the voice, he discovered a shivering Quizan hiding inside the trunk of a hollowed-out Jackoe tree. Apparently, when Victis abruptly appeared the little guy was unable to remain in energy. Scared to death of the Ryquat, he crawled on his hands and knees through the mud to the safest place he could find.

"Please don't leave me in here."

Azha was careful not to show his shock. The Quizans body was caked with thick mud. Most likely the mud masked the true severity of his gruesome puncture wounds. There was something very familiar about him, something about his voice or how he spoke.

"Do I know you?" asked Azha.

"I'm Atue, I tried to fight them."

The shivering little Quizan was a friend and another brave soldier who had survived.

"What happened, why didn't the Quizans hide in the Lava Cave?"

Atue kept shifting his eyes towards the evil Ryquat called Victis. Azha tried to reassure his old friend that Victis was a good Ryquat who was helping them defeat the Gystfins, but the fear on his face did not diminish. Azha reached into the tree trunk and gently pulled Atue out. Now being able to see his entire body, Azha cringed at his gruesome injuries. He dreaded having to move the broken little Quizan, knowing there was no good way of carrying him without causing more pain. As careful as one could be, Azha carried Atue slowly over to the other Quizans and laid him on the ground. Atue's face was gaunt as he spoke of the nightmare to Azha with a sadness that even Victis found difficult to hear.

"When this Ryquat captured you, Phera warned everyone to hide in the Lava Cave. All the soldiers hid in trees to ambush the Gystfins with our frickin rocks and spears. I've never seen so many Gystfins. They were in a killing frenzy. Somehow, they knew about the Lava Cave and had poisoned it with oxygen. The blue net was everywhere and trapped everyone escaping from the cave. We threw our spears and frickin rocks, but that barely slowed them down. They flew into the trees and trapped us with small blue nets that I've never seen before. We tried to escape in energy, but it was too late. We were paralyzed in body form. I was one of the first soldiers to fall out the trees. Playing dead kept me alive, but I'll never forget hearing them laugh as they piled bodies on top of me. One after the other, their grey-death energy ascended and their bodies vanished. I could feel the Gystfins getting closer and closer as they ripped and chewed apart the last few bodies sheltering me. I was able to turn into energy and float underground just before they pulled the last soldier off. I deserted everyone to save myself," Atue said ashamed.

Azha listened in disbelief. How was it possible the Gystfins knew about the Lava Cave? All Quizans knew it was a matter of life or death to keep it a secret.

"Atue, there was nothing you could've done. What happened then?"

"I found a small crevice just under the surface. Before I faded, I re-surfaced over there next to a pod. Everyone had either ascended and vanished, or their bodies were sucked dry. I didn't see any Gystfins, but you know that doesn't mean anything. They could've been anywhere waiting for more of us to ascend. I flew to the Lava Cave thinking whoever had survived would be there, but it was still poisoned. I resurfaced to absorb the sun, then flew to the smaller cave where you found us. Lucky for me, Phera told me about the cave years ago. All of us were afraid the Gystfins were waiting for stragglers, so we decided to stay underground for as long as we could."

"Are you able to turn into energy?"

"No, not yet."

Victis didn't hesitate to volunteer, "I'll stay with him."

Atue's face dropped and he shook his head *no* at Azha.

"Don't look at me like that, the Ryquat will protect you better than I can."

Grateful for the offering, Azha stood up and thanked Victis, knowing the sooner they left Kismet Ebb, the better. Thirty-one frightened Quizans flew beneath the Trekachaw to their new home.

THE CAVERNS WAS A WELCOME sight. The village was alive with bustling Quizans running to greet the Kismets with open arms. Released from his obligation, Azha escorted Phera to his favorite sunning spot at the top of a warm, flat mesa. As soon as Belton, Roon, and Zith spotted Azha, they ran to the base of the mesa and began talking loudly. Finding it impossible to ignore the fidgety trio, Azha whispered to Phera that he would be right back.

"Did the Gystfins attack while we were gone?" Victis asked.

"Yes! In fact, they attacked us twice. Our soldiers killed nine of the nasty Beasts. Everyone helped drag them to a ditch and cover them up with stink rocks. Roon came up with that name, *Stink Rocks*. Good name wouldn't you say?" Zith said.

Roon pushed Belton aside so hard, both stumbled and fell to the ground. "Move Belton. Azha, I stole a Gystfin shuttle," Belton picked himself up off the ground and pushed Roon back. "Dumb-dilly-wad," snapped Belton. Even though it was not presented very well, this was great news. From now on, other tribes would receive extensive training before being left on their own to defend themselves.

Zith shoved Roon aside, "*Roon move.* Azha, I need you, Belton, Choan, Duro, Vopar and Roon to meet me in Cavern Hall."

WITH NO WARNING, VICTIS SWOOPED in from above and landed in the middle of the village with Atue by his side. *Chaos erupted, with Quizans flashing into red energy and zig-zagging everywhere for cover.* For a moment the village was silent, then spears rained down on Victis from all directions giving him a split second to shield Atue with his body until the melee ceased.

Atue screamed, "STOP, Stop, STOP!" to no avail. The second wave of attack came with a hailstorm of rocks being thrown from the trees and a crossfire of boulders exploding across the ground. Victis dropped to one knee and pulled Atue beneath him in a desperate attempt to shelter his new friend from the deadly barrage.

"I'm Azha's friend! Stop throwing those things! You're only going to hurt Atue, not me!"

His screams fell on deaf ears, for no one trusted what the Ryquat had to say. Azha overheard the commotion and ran from the hall shouting, "Stand down, stand down, the Ryquat is my friend."

Hundreds of camouflaged soldiers on the ground appeared out of nowhere and the tree limbs bowed from clusters of angry soldiers staring down at the Ryquat. Standing next to Victis, Azha shouted to the trees and across the village for all to hear.

"Forgive me, I failed to announce my friend's arrival. Join me at Cavern Hall where I'll formally introduce Captain Victis. This powerful Ryquat saved Atue from an agonizing death. Let's show Victis our gratitude and welcome him to our village."

Looking out into the crowd, he was not surprised by their angry faces. In defiance, they blocked the narrow path leading to the hall. Azha gave them several warnings to step aside before shoving past them to allow Victis access. This was the first time a Quizan had come this close to a Ryquat and lived to talk about it.

Zith, Belton, Roon, Duro and Vopar were still determined to fight the Ryquat at the hall entrance. Azha was losing his patience and worried about how much Victis was willing to tolerate.

"Zith, accept his gracious offer, and command others to do the same," demanded Azha.

Zith frowned, "Why would you trust a Ryquat?"

"Because Palatu will cease to exist without him and I will die fighting the Gystfins.

Zith started to say something, then caught himself and reluctantly stepped back to allow them entry. A hostile crowd hissed to voice their hatred. Victis was showing an incredible amount of tolerance for their defiance. In doing so, Azha saw yet another side of Victis, giving rise to a profound respect and admiration for the alien. He was beginning to realize that he knew very little about the Universe and even less about what his enemies were capable of. If he had a future, perhaps he was meant to be with Victis.

"Stop this hissing, unless you want me to leave Palatu. Then you can try to defend yourselves without us," warned Azha.

"No, do not forsake us. I accept this Ryquat," Zith cried out.

"Quizans, without this good Ryquat, you will die, and I will die trying to defend you. The bad Ryquat is no longer here, he's being punished on his planet. Trust me, Victis is King of a mighty battleship."

Azha motioned to Victis that he had the floor.

The hall was silent, and a grim new reality loomed over the crowd knowing that what Azha said was the awful truth. Victis saw fear on the Quizans' faces and felt sorry for them. Maybe he should feel guilty for not stopping the carnage sooner.

"Thank you for allowing me this opportunity. I'm sorry for what the Bad Ryquat did to you. But I am not like him. I will do my best to protect Palatu," vowed Victis.

Zith stepped forward, "I accept the Good Ryquat's offer."

As a pledge of goodwill, Victis reached out to shake the hand of Zith. Apparently, his unusual movement startled Zith, causing him to fall backwards onto the floor. Soldiers rushed to defend their King by surrounding him with their spears pointed at the Ryquat.

"Stop! or I swear the next Quizan who hisses or points another spear at the Ryquat will feel my Human wrath. I don't care who it is."

Azha grabbed Victis's hand to demonstrate '*how to shake hands*' while explaining that it was an act of friendship and nothing more. The young King ordered the soldiers to lower their spears and then scrambled to his feet. Grudgingly, they obeyed. A low rumbling of hostile bickering continued to inflame the mob's attitude.

One small red light flickered above and landed in front of Victis. It was Atue. He would do everything in his power to defend Victis. The crowd gasped, shocked by his seeming betrayal, then screamed in protest. Atue screamed back just as loud.

"This Ryquat saved my life at Kismet Ebb. He volunteered to stay with me when I was too weak to turn into energy. The second Azha was gone, five Gystfins flew into the village wanting to bite my head off. They circled Victis trying to grab me, but he killed all of them to save me. I saw what he did. A Ryquat could easily kill everyone here and no one could stop him . . . *Not even Azha.*

Zith humbly apologized to Victis before addressing the angry mob.

"Atue and Azha speak wisely. Do not judge Victis by the bad Ryquat's hatred. Honor this Ryquat and be grateful to have such a powerful protector."

The young King whispered, "Tell me, good Ryquat, are there any other bad Ryquats we need to worry about?"

"Not if it is up to me," Victis reassured.

Ending the crowd's cold silence, Belton cheered, "Let's celebrate our victories with our new friend. Twenty-two Gystfins died and not one soldier injured."

Choan chimed in boasting, "I led the attacks on the Gystfins. I told the soldiers to stay in the trees. Did the sneaky Beasts surprise us with their blue nets? No, this time we surprised them. What then you ask? Well, Duro pretended to be injured and the Gystfins chased him. We threw spears and broke their heads with rocks. I watched them suffer, just like they made us suffer. Together we dragged them to the fissures and pushed them in. One by one they fell, disappearing forever."

Belton shouted out, "Does anyone want to hear what I did?"

"Belton, Belton, Belton," the crowd roared. "Okay, Okay, Roon and I flew into their shuttle. Guess what we found? Yes, an ugly Gystfin. He was ranting to a voice about how we were revolting. Sounded like the other voice was furious and refused to believe that we had the courage to fight."

Victis shouted, "What were they saying?"

"I didn't understand all of it, but the Gystfin looked scared and was staring out the window. I think he was explaining what was happening to the voice. The voice spoke Gystfin but sounded different."

Victis eyed Azha, "Belton, how long ago did this happen?"

"A while ago."

Choan jumped up and down waving his arm, "My turn, the Gystfin is alive. We threw frickin rocks at the shuttle and broke it."

Belton chuckled, "Yeah we did. He screams and growls a whole lot. Every time the nasty Beast looks out the window, he shows his fangs at us. We fly into the shuttle when he's sleeping and wake him up. That drives him crazy."

Azha sensed Victis was uneasy. "Take me to him," Victis said lowering his brow.

Why was this Gystfin so important to Victis? Belton and a trail of soldiers led them to where the shuttle was docked beneath the trees.

Sure enough, the exterior was riddled with dents caused by the frickin rocks. Dozens of soldiers were perched on limbs waiting to kill the Beast if he dared step foot out of the shuttle. Wasting no time, Victis jumped onto the hull and peered through the cockpit window.

"Tell your soldiers, I want this Gystfin alive," he said with his jaw clenched.

Terrified, the Gystfin locked eyes with the Ryquat and moved away from the portal window.

Victis yelled, "Open the door!"

The Gystfin aggressively shook his head.

Azha volunteered, "Let me fly in, I'll throw his ass out the door."

Victis jumped off the hull, "No, open the hatch and let me in." Then whispered, "When I'm finished, kill him."

Azha flashed into red energy and streaked through the hull. The Gystfin snarled and swung a metal plate at him. Thinking the Gystfin *pathetic,* Azha simply floated out of the hull and then floated back through on the opposite side. Again, the Gystfin tried to swat Azha with the metal plate. This time, Azha morphed into body form and jerked it away from him. His linguistic chip worked perfectly. Azha understood every foul word that spewed from his drooling mouth. Azha reached down to open the hatch and the Gystfin lunged forward. Azha pushed him aside yelling for him to get back.

"No, Ryquat kill me."

Feeling no mercy for the Gystfin, Azha opened the hatch.

Victis stormed up the ramp and slammed the hatch closed behind him. The Gystfin stiffened and stumbled backwards to the far end of the cockpit.

"Too late Ryquat, warned Crozins. Cargo ship coming. You..."

Victis grabbed the Beast by his throat and slammed him against the cockpit wall.

"Lie to me and you'll die a slow painful death. Tell me the truth and I'll let you go. No one will ever know."

Choking on his words the Beast gurgled, "Ryquat lies."

He stuck his thick wagging tongue out as far as he could to lick Victis's face. With a flick of a wrist, Victis sliced off the Gystfin's crusty ear. The Beast grabbed the side of his head screeching in pain. Victis stomped the bloody ear into the floor with his boot, then kicked it across the floor. "Next thing I'll cut off is your balls. I'll give you one more chance to talk."

The Gystfin twisted his body sideways shielding his testicles the best he could. "What you want Ryquat?"

"How many days has it been since you contacted the Crozins and the cargo ship? And when will they arrive?"

"Five days, Crozins here two weeks, Cargo ship three weeks. Crozins know you're alone. Take everything Ryquat, battleship too."

Victis ignored the comments and let go of his throat. "How many shuttles and Gystfins are on Palatu?"

"Four hundred, two shuttles. Why sterilize Gystfins at Kismet Ebb?"

Victis did not answer, "How many Gystfins need grey-death energy, and are there weapons on Palatu?"

The Beast snorted and grinned to display his razor-sharp, stained fangs. "We eat death energy. Palatu's boring. Pleasure hunting slimy parasites."

While blubbering about his cruel and unjustified treatment, the Gystfin bent over to search for his bloody ear on the deck floor. Victis ordered him to sit down and shoved him backwards. The Gystfin cried out in anger, "Where's my cargo ship, Ryquat?"

Azha smirked, "I took your cargo ship, right out from underneath you. Should've paid more attention to your ship instead of hunting defenseless Quizans."

The Gystfin's fangs chattered, "What are you? Why fight for slimy parasites?"

Victis interrupted, "Azha, don't answer that. Do you have any questions regarding the mission?"

"Yes. Who are the *Crozins and why are they helping the Gystfins?*"

The Gystfin straightened up in his chair, "Crozins' reward is good profit. Raw materials superior, no cull extracted. You get nothing, Ryquat."

Victis came face to face with the Gystfin. "Fine by me, you've done all the labor. Since our contract is void, I'll take the ship and materials for nothing."

The Beast hissed and curled his upper lip to suck out the thick snot dripping from his nostrils. Victis warned that if he spit, he would die. You could see the Gystfin thinking about it and if it was worth dying over, but then he swallowed.

"Crozins destroy your battleship and Palatu. Payback for sterilizing Gystfins. Ryquat lie, promise to kill Trekachaw."

In defiance, the Gystfin gyrated his hips forward, spraying dark yellow urine across the cabin. Howling with laughter, he bolted past Victis to where his severed ear was lying on the floor. Seeing that it was disfigured beyond saving, the Gystfin kicked his bloody ear into the air, deliberately hitting Victis in the chest with it. The Ryquat did not flinch.

"Crozins promise new profit. Fidus Achates territory planets, Earth and Mars," boasted the Gystfin.

Azha questioned, "Why Mars and Earth?"

Victis glared at the filthy arrogant Gystfin, "Because Ryquats came from Mars and they know we protect Earth."

Having heard enough, Victis raised his hand into the air. The Gystfin screeched knowing what was about to happen. With a flick of Victis' wrist, a thin blue beam cut off the Beast's thick head.

"We're out of time. Azha, where'd you hide the cargo ship?"

Azha was already half-way down the ramp carrying the Gystfin's head and dragging the foul-smelling carcass. Skunks on earth smelled better than a Gystfin. At the bottom of the ramp he dropped the head and let go of the body.

"Soldiers, wherever you're dumping the carcasses, take this one there," shouted Azha.

Right away the soldiers began to bicker amongst themselves, "It's your turn. No, it's not. You do it. I can't do it by myself!"

Victis was at the top of the ramp waiting for an answer. Without the Ryquat, Palatu, Earth, and Mars would be doomed.

"The cargo ship is orbiting Europa, one of Saturn's moons."

Victis nodded his head, "Not bad, Trekachaw. Europa was smart. No one would've ever thought to look for her there."

ten

SEMPER PARATUS

"UNDERSTANDING IS THE GIFT OF KNOWLEDGE"

THE cargo ship full of raw materials was pivotal in the war against the Crozins. Now that Azha had revealed its location, the sooner he could secure it, the better. A Ryquat battleship could easily reach Europa in less than ten hours, whereas, a Gystfin's cargo ship could take several days. Another problem: the ship was the size of a small moon and required a skeleton crew of sixty. Victis could spare fifty-five bodies without compromising his battleship. All options considered, recruiting and training Quizans was the only logical solution.

In the eleventh hour, Victis requested a village meeting at Cavern Hall to pitch his proposal. As expected, the mammoth cavern and its passages filled with curious spectators until there was no more room. Clustered outside the threshold, Quizans stretched their necks to see and strained their ears to hear what was being announced. Zith, Victis, and Azha positioned themselves on the Kings Ledge and waited for the crowd to quiet. Eventually the loud buzzing became a soft hum and they began to hush each other. Not until then did the Ryquat begin to speak.

"A mighty war is coming. The Gystfins and their allies are determined to exterminate you and destroy your planet. I will protect and fight alongside you, but right now I need five volunteers to go with us to Europa. Who will join me?"

Most looked terrified, some were somber, and others began to weep. No one dared to speak, and no one volunteered. Angered by the pathetic silence and by their unwillingness to commit, Azha demanded,

"Five volunteers are all he's asking for. Someone step up. This Ryquat is trying to save us. I'm ashamed to be half-Quizan. He should've let you all die."

One hand at the back of the hall raised above the sea of heads, then another, and another until six volunteers had raised their hands. Roon, Duro, Choan, Atue, Vopar, and Vious made their way through the crowd to the bottom of the Kings Ledge. Victis clapped his hands, *"Thank you... Thank you."*

Vopar valiantly lifted his crippled brother up, "Good Ryquat Victis, my brother Vious and I volunteer. Vious cannot walk, but he is smart and brave and can turn into energy. We will be loyal and do anything you ask."

Victis stepped off the ledge next to Vopar and Vious. "I am honored to accept you and your brave brother."

Frustrated and embarrassed by the lack of volunteers, Azha shouted at the crowd to get out. Zith and Belton lingered behind asking for a moment to explain their reasons for not volunteering and profusely apologized, begging for forgiveness.

Zith feared what his father might do if given the opportunity to regain his position as King. Belton could not bring himself to abandon his wife and young quieys. Victis accepted their apologies and reassured them they would serve the war best by holding down the fort. Belton was relieved to hold down a fort but didn't know what it meant. "What's a fort?"

Azha held in a smirk, "It's another word for village. Take care of the village while we're gone."

King Zith and Belton chimed, *"We will hold down the fort."*

The thought of Palatu being the epicenter of a galactic war unnerved Azha. In hindsight, perhaps King Myosis was wise not to fight. One thing was certain, there was no going back now. Victis snapped Azha out of his doom and gloom by shouting into his ear, *"Palatu to Azha, are you on lunch?"*

"What? Where on earth did you get your one-liners?"

Victis smiled, "I get them from watching shows and movies broadcast from Earth. Why heck cowboy, half the Ryquats are named after famous actors, celebrities and legends."

Azha's jaw dropped, and he found himself listening to Victis spout gibberish for the next ten minutes about his favorite TV shows and movies. Some sounded familiar, but not how he remembered them. Victis let out a yackety, yackety, yack and punched Azha in the arm. "See stump, that's funny."

'Aha!' So, that's why Victis thought it so hilarious to punch him in the arm. "Do you realize you're not quoting any of them correctly?"

"I don't care Azha, spoil spit. Anyway, it's time to go."

Six buzzing, nervous Quizans were waiting for Azha to brief them and begin their adventure.

"Follow me to the Ryquat battleship. Once we're inside, remain in energy until I say so. Victis modified a chamber where you can morph into body form. That's the only place. The rest of the ship has oxygen."

Needless to say, Victis was excited to board the Gystfin shuttle and engage lift-off. Hearing noise from the hull, he twisted his chair clockwise to stand up, flung the hatch door open and stomped down the ramp. A quick visual inspection of the exterior hull revealed several rocks lodged in the solar vents. Pulling with all his might, he jimmied out several of the rocks and kicked free a few more. Upon another inspection, it appeared the vents were clear of debris.

"Good job jamming the ship," Victis said, praising the Quizans soldiers as he tossed several rocks down to them.

One last look, and all was good. Victis ran back up the ramp and slammed the hatch door behind him. The shuttle sputtered, engaged, then hummed, rising above the trees. There it hovered for a second, then in a flash was gone.

Victis arrived long before Azha and the flock of slow Quizans. Liquefying his space suit never felt so good. Nearly colliding with several crewmen, he ran naked down the ramp to his locker, threw on a jumpsuit and then sprinted through the hallways to the Quizan chamber to check on Pax. Congregating in the corridor were a bunch of curious crewmen. Victis hollered at them to scram, knowing the shy creature would be terrified of so many Ryquats. He peered through the window of the guest quarters searching for his little buddy, but the room was empty. He knocked on the door and waited, he knocked on the door again... then banged on the glass.

Where was Pax? It would be prudent to inform him that six additional Quizans were en route to share the habitat. Most likely he'd turned into energy and fled the area to avoid all the crewmen. And now, despite ordering them all to leave, an obstinate crewman was tapping on his shoulder. Irritated to the point of boiling, he refused to respond or acknowledge the crewman. But, being subtle wasn't working. Gritting his teeth, he firmly advised, "Unless it's important... go away."

A strange baritone voice spoke, "Turn around."

"You'd better have something important," Victis said, turning around. Towering over him was a *new Trekachaw.* How was this possible? Was Pax a Trekachaw? Victis choked on his words, *"Pax, what have you done?"*

"I merged."

His transformation was incredible, he was magnificent. Now there were two Trekachaws. But with whom had Pax merged?

"Captain allow me to explain."

A flood of questions entered Victis's mind. But it was too late. Six dancing white lights floated through a wall into the corridor where they displayed a spectacular show of spinning lights before entering their new home. He watched through the window as they morphed into body form, all the while cursing under his breath, "Unko, unko, unko."

Pax had no idea what *unko* meant, but it sounded as if Victis was very upset. Before the last crewman disappeared around the corner, the new Trekachaw asked him what it meant.

"Unko means *shit* in Japanese." Red-faced Victis scowled, "Go, wait for me in the lounge."

Pax couldn't have taken more than two steps when Victis yelled, "Stop. Who'd you merge with?"

"Jacet."

Victis could feel his blood pressure rise and his face twist. Never had he felt this rattled or angry towards a crewman. *"Unko, unko, unko."* Trying to calm himself, he paced back and forth asking, "Jacet, Pax, *shit,* do you remember how to be a doctor?"

"Yes, I remember everything, nothing has changed. With your permission, I'd rather be called Pax."

"Why not Jacet? Fine, Pax it is," Victis said with a curt nod.

Victis yelled at a crewman who had made a big mistake of walking around the corner to find out if the Gystfins' campsite communications station had been destroyed yet. While yelling at the crewman he noticed another energy light following Pax down the corridor towards the lounge. Running as fast as he could after them he shouted, "Pax, wait up."

The light spun in circles, then streaked back and forth before morphing into Azha damn near on top of him. Caught off guard and still trying to process the ramifications of his reckless decision to bring a Quizan on board, Victis immediately became defensive.

"I did not approve this merge, nor was I advised of it."

Azha's poker-face seemed to be starring past him. Shifting his eyes slightly he warned no louder than a whisper, "Victis, look at the Chamber."

All six Quizans had their faces pressed up against the window watching the show.

Victis grumbled something unintelligible under his breath and his brow was dripping with sweat.

On the other hand, Azha was so excited he caught himself doing a little Quizan dance and glowing green.

"I couldn't get up off the floor after my merge with Cole. How'd you recuperate so fast? Come to think of it, the only source of energy in the winery was my flashlight. The batteries must have saved my life. Without them I would've vanished in that cold dark cellar."

Pax shrugged his shoulders, "For me it was easy, Jacet asked me. Remember he's the one who injected your chip. We talked about it, I flew out and merged with him over there, next to the door."

"Can you remember everything about your Ryquat and Quizan life?" Azha asked.

He whispered, "Most of it, but don't tell the Captain. I told him I could remember everything," admitted Pax.

"Don't worry, I won't. In time, little things will jog the rest of your memory. I'm glad you merged, it was lonely being the only Trekachaw."

Azha raised his voice, "Victis, nice to know it's possible to create more Trekachaws."

A crewman peeked around the corner distracting Victis from sharing a few choice words, "Captain I have an update on your request."

"Now... would be good," Victis snapped.

The Gystfins communications were destroyed."

Victis let out a sigh of relief, "With any luck, no one knows what I've done."

Inquisitive crewmen had returned and were blocking both ends of the corridor again.

"Ready your stations, we've got two hours before we're en route to Europa," ordered Victis.

Even with that said, several continued to linger asking if they could volunteer to become Trekachaws. Victis barked, "No, there will be no more Trekachaws. Go to your stations."

Azha interrupted, "Why not?"

"Because I said so. Why would you ask?"

"Why wouldn't you? Think about it, the merge would solve the oxygen problem on both ships. Trekachaws are superior and far more efficient than Quizans or Ryquats. Logically, we're exactly what you need to win the war." Azha poked Victis, "Don't be such a *Chovo*, Ryquat."

'Why not?' was indeed an excellent question. He had violated a long list of laws punishable by imprisonment or death. With nothing to lose, he might as well.

"You do have valid points. However, any crewman who merges will remain under my command until the end of their enlistment. Make sure the Quizans understand what that means. We're running out of time. Do whatever is necessary quickly," warned Victis.

Pax jumped in, "Perfect, I can ask the Quizans and I know of at least fifty crewmen who'd volunteer."

Questioning his decision, Victis walked away muttering, "Meet me in the in main lounge after you have the volunteers. This had better work."

Azha and Pax flashed into energy, opting for a short cut through the walls into the guest quarters. When they morphed back into body form, Pax posed to show off his new physique to inspire volunteers.

"There's Ryquats agog to become a Trekachaw like me. Who's ready?"

Roon raised his hand, "What's agog?"

Azha was just as baffled and waiting for an explanation along with the other Quizans.

"Agog? You don't know what it means? It's a common word. You know, ready and willing. Being enthusiastic about something."

After a meeting of the minds, Roon, Choan, Duro, Atue, Vopar, and Vious agreed to the merge if they got to choose their Ryquat and that agog was not a common word. Azha instructed Pax to wait a couple of minutes before escorting the Quizans to the lounge. In the meantime, he'd brief the Ryquats and have them ready for selection.

To speed things up, Victis announced ship-wide that all personnel interested in becoming a Trekachaw should respond immediately to the main lounge. Pax must have impressed the crew. It seemed as if everyone on board had tried to squeeze into the lounge. With the merges good to go, Azha flew in and morphed into body form, giving Victis a thumbs-up.

Victis cleared his throat, "To begin, don't ask any questions until I'm finished. It is imperative that you do exactly as I instruct. When the Quizans enter the lounge, stand perfectly still and don't say anything. If you're selected, a Quizan will float over your head. Once they've made their choice, everyone else leave the lounge quietly. Are my instructions clear?"

A crewman shouted, "Captain, I heard Trekachaws can live five hundred years. Which sounds great to me, but I've also heard that Trekachaws are sterile?"

Irritated by the crewman's narcissism, Victis had second thoughts about continuing the merges.

"Crewman, leave the room. You're excused from the process. For the rest of you, pay close attention. If you merge, you will no longer exist as an individual. You will become a new species with memories from both past lives. Trekachaws can live to be five hundred years old and yes, your method of sex will completely change. I've heard their way is better. You will be the birth of a new species capable of doing unimaginable things. Look at what Azha and Pax can do. This is a rare opportunity if you choose to embrace it. We need to evolve if we're going to win the war. If you have any doubts there's the door, excuse yourself now."

More than half the crewmen quietly worked their way through the remaining crowd and exited the lounge. Azha had lost interest in the controversy and was focused on a group of female crewmen standing near the back of the room. When he motioned for them to come forward, Victis gave a subtle jab with his elbow and a *'what's up look?'* Azha leaned over, "May I select one of them to merge with Phera?"

Overhearing the not-so-subtle request, they unanimously vowed their commitment to merge. Victis rolled his eyes and smirked.

And so, it began, with six white lights drifting through the wall. They swarmed in sparkling circles searching above the Ryquat's heads until they found their host. One lone light flickered above Victis's head awaiting his transformation. Victis gazed up at the sparkling light, wishing he could accept the Quizans offer to become a powerful Trekachaw. Taking every ounce of self-control, he resisted temptation.

"I am deeply honored by your gracious invitation, although I must decline. If I were to accept your offer, the Ryquat Counsel would rescind my position as Ship Commander. Perhaps someday I can join with another. Unfortunately, not with you today."

The light flickered red and circled above many heads before selecting another Ryquat.

Disappointed crewmen trudged out of the lounge, protesting in a low grumble about the unfair selection process. Victis demanded silence, warning them of insubordination. Watching the drama play out, Azha laughed to himself at how much they reminded him of Humans. He waited until Victis closed the door after the last malcontent exited the lounge.

"Shall we begin? When I point at you, tell me your name and ship assignment. You go first," said Azha.

"My name is Einstein, Chief Engineer."

"Victis, is this merge acceptable?"

"Affirmative." Victis gave a subtle nod.

"Einstein, the Quizan floating above you is called *Atue.* Do you truly understand what you're about to do?"

Sweat dripped down the side of Einstein's face and he bit his lip before looking up at the sparkling light.

"Amen...I 'm ready."

Atue sparkled from white into pure silver energy as he ascended into the top of the Ryquat's head. Einstein felt the alien's energy all around him and stiffened to keep himself from running. Unable to get enough air, his breathing became fast and labored until he took his last breath and fear was all that remained. The silver light disappeared into the top of Einstein's head, as life faded from his eyes and his rigid body turned into silver glitter consuming his flesh. Shining brighter and brighter he radiated into lightning bolts, forcing those watching to look away or close their burning eyes.

The silver light faded into the darkness revealing the miracle lying upon floor. Neither Atue or Einstein existed any longer. Joined as one, they awoke to begin their life as a mighty Trekachaw. Mesmerized by what they had witnessed, a profound peace of mind embraced the beholders. Azha recognized the confusion on the new Trekachaw's face and sat on the floor next to him.

"Do you know what happened?" Azha asked.

"No." Atue rubbed his eyes and then struggled to sit up. "Just a little dizzy, give me a minute."

He grabbed a nearby chair by its leg and dragged it to his side. As Atue pulled himself up to sit in the chair, he pushed Azha's hand away making it clear that he wanted to stand on his own accord. Within a couple of minutes, he had regained full function of his body and mind. Witnessing his recovery was incredible. The new Trekachaw smiled and stretched out his long arms, "I feel invincible."

Simon threw his hands up into the air and yelled, "Over here, I'm next in line."

Azha wasted no time, "Tell me about yourself."

"My name is Simon and I'm the Science Officer."

"Simon, the Quizan that chose you is called Roon. The rest of you listen up. Time grows short, so I want the remaining introductions completed before anyone else merges. Once that's out of the way, you'll all merge at the same time. *Agreed?*"

The Quizans flickered and the crewmen consented with a 'Roger that'. Next in line... Ryquat Washington assigned to Galaxy Security Ops. His merge with Duro, approved.

Eric volunteered, "I'm also G.S.O."

Victis gave a yes nod, approving Vopar's merge.

Dillon shouted-out, "G.S.O."

Azha glanced over at Victis who was already nodding his head in approval.

Until now, the introductions had gone off without a hitch, however the next one could be a quandary for the Ryquat.

"Dillon... the Quizan that selected you is called Vious. You need to know that he's unable to walk from a Gystfin attack. With that said, if you change your mind, I'll understand."

Dillon looked up at the sparkling light, "Could our merge give Vious a chance to walk again?"

"I don't know," Azha responded honestly. "But you must be sure about this, not only for yourself, but for his sake, too."

Dillon smiled, "It was just a question. If we can't walk, then we'll fly. Let's do this."

Last, but not least, there was Bruce, Sergeant of the Galaxy Security Operations Unit. Years ago, upon Victis's promotion to the elite status of Commander, he'd handpicked Bruce. There was no question about this merge; Bruce would stay loyal to him and the mission. Before continuing, Azha felt compelled to ask Victis about his decision to decline Choan's offer.

"Are you absolutely positive that you don't want to merge? This might be your only chance, and you were his first choice."

Victis could not hide his disappointment, "Azha I can't. As much as I would like to, I can't."

"Okay, but I think you're making a mistake. If you're sure, we need to leave. We'll be blinded by all the merges."

"I'm sure, let's go," replied Victis.

Azha nudged Victis towards the door. They exited the lounge and shouted at the crewmen standing in the corridor to evacuate the area. The battleship exploded into silver, creating a blast of light so bright the Quizans and Gystfins on Palatu could see her shine in space.

Far sooner than expected, the lounge door swung open and five magnificent Trekachaws stepped out into the corridor. They were beautiful and intimidating, with sleek muscular bodies adorned with bold colorful stripes. Envious crewmen in the hallway pressed themselves against the walls to allow a wide berth for the towering aliens to pass. All eyes were fixed, and heads turned as they walked to the end of the corridor to where Victis and Azha awaited. As a sign of respect, Choan knelt before Victis.

"Stand up Bruce, I'm not a King and you are not a Quizan," ordered Victis.

Azha noticed that Vious was missing, "Choan get up, where's Vious?"

The expression on Choan's face said it all, but he needed to hear it. "Answer my question."

"Vious did not recover. He asked to be alone," replied Choan.

"And so, you just left him? What do you mean, he didn't recover?"

Azha sprinted down the corridor towards the lounge.

The door was locked, and the window blinds were closed, making it impossible to see in. Azha banged on the door fearing the worst. "Vious unlock the door, or I'll fly in."

From within, a dismal voice replied. "Wait, give me a minute."

Azha heard Vious dragging himself across the floor and the doorknob being unlocked. After a few moments, Azha heard him scooting away from the door. Then there was silence. It seemed like a life-time before Vious spoke again.

"You can come in now. Lock the door behind you, I don't want anyone else in here."

Azha cracked the door open and peeked inside, dreading what he was about to see.

Vious was sitting on the floor punching both his legs over and over with his fists.

"I can feel them tingling when I do this."

"Stop hitting yourself. Have you tried to walk yet?" Azha asked.

Vious winced, admitting he had not because he was afraid to fall. Azha bent down and wrapped his arms around Vious's chest to lift him off the floor into a chair.

"You'll be fine, it's just going to take you a little longer."

They talked for a while about how strange it felt to be a Trekachaw, but mostly it gave Vious a chance to recover. Not asking for permission, Azha pulled Vious out of the chair, forcing him to stand. At first, he was shocked, then irritated, and then came a big smile that swept across his face. Vious caught his balance and steadied himself on Azha's arm. He was standing on his own for the first time in a nearly a decade. Excited to test his new legs, he asked Azha to let go of him. One baby step in front of the other he eased across the lounge to the other side. The young Trekachaw worked his way around the lounge until he no longer stumbled.

"Look at me Azha, can you believe it? Look at what a Ryquat did for me," he smiled.

Vious walked over to the door and paused, *'Thank you Dillon, I can never repay you.'*

Ready to begin his new life, Vious unlocked the door.

eleven

EX TEMPORE

"THEY SAY... FOR EVERY BEGINNING, THERE'S AN END."

IT was difficult for Azha to explain, even to himself, but now that he wasn't the only Trekachaw, he felt an enormous burden had been lifted. With less than an hour remaining, he asked Roon, Choan, and Victis to join him in a quick trip to Palatu. Even though Victis wanted to join them, he opted to rendezvous after briefing the officers and crew personnel.

Flying alongside his kindred Trekachaws, Azha felt empowered, for they were his equals and worthy of his sacrifice. It was a shame that Victis missed their first trip to Palatu; he should have been with them. Within seconds, Cavern Village was visible beneath them, revealing carnage and pandemonium. Quizan soldiers were chucking rocks and throwing spears at three hideous Gystfins moving incredibly fast. The Beasts were like Gystfins yet different, unusually large with well-defined bold purple stripes across their backs. Wishing there was more time to prepare Roon and Choan, Azha gave them some last-minute advice.

"You have the strength to easily kill a Gystfin. Do not hesitate and show no mercy, for they won't."

Azha roared, trumpeting their attack, and the three dove into the center of the melee. Roon had no Ryquat combat training and was hesitant despite Azha's warning; that cost him. A Gystfin slammed him into a tree, burying his fangs deep into his arm. On the contrary, Choan was swift and landed on top of a Gystfin's head, knocking him flat to the ground. He showed no hesitation or mercy for the vile Beast. Trying to free himself, the Gystfin flipped over screeching in pain and stood up with Choan coiled around his head. The crazed Beast ran across the courtyard ramming his head full force into a boulder. Choan flashed into energy and watched as the Gystfin fell to ground then scramble to his feet as if he didn't feel anything. Choan morphed back into body form, coiled around the Gystfin's head, and jammed his thumbs into its black eyes.

Azha threw a rock at the Gystfin holding Roon to distract him and then snatched a spear off the ground. As Azha ran towards Choan, he knew his choice could cost Roon his life. Before the Beast could free himself of Choan, Azha stabbed him in the chest, pushing the shaft downward until the spear penetrated out its lower back. A normal Gystfin should've died, but this one continued to fight.

Showing no signs of slowing down, the Gystfin curled into a bizarre ball and reached over its shoulder to grab Choan. Azha yanked the spear out and stabbed the Beast relentlessly, over and over as fast as he could. Shrieking in pain, the Gystfin shuddered and slumped to his knees.

Roon screamed for help. Azha and Choan glanced away for an instant and when they looked back, the Gystfin was gone. They caught a glimpse of his red-light streaking into the forest.

The largest Gystfin had Roon's arms pinned back, while another had its fangs buried deep in Roon's upper thigh. Realizing that he was going to die, Roon began to fight back. Unable to move his arms, he wrapped his legs around the Gystfin's head and squeezed with all his might. The Beast growled, spitting frothy blood and clamped down even harder. When Roon cried out in pain, the Gystfin went into a frenzy shaking his head to rip Roon's thigh into shreds. Choan flashed purple and slammed into the Gystfin holding Roon's arms, sending them both tumbling across the dusty courtyard. The Beast screeched and clawed the ground in a feeble attempt to free himself from the Trekachaw's grip. Perhaps this aberrant Beast was not capable of turning into energy like the other one, or fear clouded his mind causing him to forget. Either way, the unmistakable loud snap was heard when Choan yanked the Beast's head backwards and stomped on his lower spine. Its black bulgy eyes rolled upwards to solid white and its muscles convulsed as it flopped on the ground thrashing back and forth in the red dirt until his body wrapped freakishly around the base of a tree.

Azha thought he had choked the life out of the third Gystfin, but the Beast flashed into pure energy and disappeared into the forest. Shocked by what happened, they looked at each other in silence. If they hadn't seen them with their own eyes, they would have never believed it...Gystfins freakishly strong and capable of turning into energy.

Roon survived the attack. He was riddled with deep puncture wounds and slashes from the Gystfin's razor-sharp claws. As a Quizan his training consisted of rocks and spears, whereas his Ryquat-half was a science officer. Being forced to fight left his spirit as shredded as his body. Nonetheless, the tough new Trekachaw was determined get up and walk. One step and his leg collapsed beneath him and the world grew dark. When he awoke, Azha was yelling at him to stay down and Quizan soldiers were dropping from the trees screaming frantically for Azha to help Belton and Zith. They were last seen running into Cavern Hall along with several soldiers who were fighting an enormous Gystfin. Choan and Azha streaked into the cavern and almost morphed on top of a mutilated body sprawled across the floor. Azha looked twice before he recognized the body to be Belton. Above, countless spirits of grey-death energy circled the ceiling, giving testimony to brave soldiers who had died trying to protect their young King.

Lurking in the shadows of the cavern a grotesque, mutant Gystfin grunted to get their attention. He stepped out from the shadows and tightened his grip on Zith's neck to prevent him from speaking. Azha moved forward and the Beast violently shook the small body as if he were a rag doll. Azha stepped back slowly shifting his eyes towards Choan, "Stay here, I'll circle around behind him."

Slow and steady Azha circled the Beast, keeping enough distance between them not to provoke an attack on Zith, yet close enough to distract him.

The Gystfin snarled displaying fangs and hissed, *"See what you have done. I am King Myosis."*

Azha froze in disbelief. Then the unthinkable happened. Myosis shoved his son's head into his drooling mouth and bit down severing his head, then flung what was left of Zith's body across the cavern.

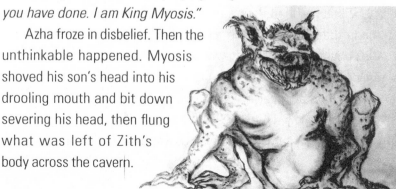

Choan and Azha streaked towards Myosis, but they were too late. The monster spit out Zith's head and disappeared through the rock wall. The noble, young King's grey-death energy rose from his body and floated over to his severed head. Azha fell to his knees and cried out that he was sorry. Zith slowly circled him to show a final act of loyalty and then faded away forever.

VICTIS GUESSED IT HAD BEEN twenty minutes since Azha and the other two departed ship. By now they were probably ready to leave Palatu. If nothing else, he'd have company flying back. What he thought was going to be a last-minute farewell became another unforeseeable crisis. Landing dead center in the courtyard, he saw a huge, purple-striped Gystfin lying face down in the dirt and Roon cut to shreds leaning against a stump. Dozens of Quizan soldiers perched in the trees were looking down at him. At least this time they weren't throwing rocks and spears. Obviously, something happened, but whatever it was seemed to be over. From across the village he heard a mournful sound that sent chills down his spine. Roon sat up and howled, joining the eerie cries of despair. For the first time, Victis was afraid of what he'd helped create.

"Help me," asked Roon. "Azha and Choan are in Cavern Hall howling death calls."

Victis grabbed Roon's arm and pulled him up. Together they made their way to Cavern Hall. Azha looked dazed, and Choan was bright purple with rage. Roon limped over to the closest ledge inside the cave and sat down to rest.

"What happened? Say something," asked Victis.

"Myosis killed Zith," wailed Choan.

The old bastard merged with a Gystfin and killed his only living son."

Victis was stunned. Roon gasped and began to howl. Belton moved ever so slightly. His eyelids fluttered, and his fingers flinched. Azha scrambled to his feet and ran to his friend.

Belton moaned, "Did we save Zith?"

Azha carefully rolled Belton's disfigured body from his side over onto his back. "No. I am sorry."

Belton had failed to protect their young King. Life was fading and soon he would join the others he so dearly missed. "Listen, before I die."

"You're not going to die. I won't let you," Azha said trying to keep his voice from shaking.

Azha carried his friend out of the dark cave to the top of a mesa, where he gently laid him down to soak up the glorious Targus Sun.

"Rest, then I'll listen. Fight for me. Please don't die." Azha felt numb as he sat down next to Belton.

"Azha now, it's important. King Myosis and the Leaders you rescued from Kismet Ebb tried to take back the realm from Zith. The soldiers and clan united, defending Zith's position as King. Myosis and the Leaders left the village furious, threatening us with retaliation. We believed he was just an old Quizan showing his stripes and would later calm down. They foraged the forest searching for Gystfins to merge with, without sanction. A soldier who was tracking them saw Myosis and seven Leaders fly out of the trees in silver energy and disappear into the Gystfin's heads. The tracker returned to the village to warn us, but it didn't matter. We didn't have a chance. They were big and powerful, fast like you."

Belton's throat felt like it was on fire, but he knew what he had to say was crucial.

"Azha... Azha, Myosis killed my wife and my quieys. I watched them die horribly. Myosis killed Freya..."

His voice cracked, and he began to weep.

"He bit her head off and made my quieys watch when he sucked out her grey energy. Thing is, Myosis couldn't absorb her energy and spit her out. That made him crazy, so he screamed at the Leaders to chew my quieys heads off slowly. They took turns throwing them back and forth, catching them with their claws. I can hear their screams, begging me to save them. I can't live without them."

Heartbroken, Belton closed his eyes. "There's more. They found Atue's quiey hiding in the back of my cave and dragged him outside. They kicked him so hard I could hear his tiny bones snapping. He tried crawling away, but Myosis stomped his head over and over into the dirt until there was nothing left."

Azha placed his hand on Belton's shoulder, "There was nothing you could've done. None of this was your fault."

Belton opened his eyes and his voice sounded urgent, "Tell Victis I overheard them talking about Leaders on his battleship. I think the Gystfins know your plans."

"You did good, Belton. I must leave you to tell Victis what you said. While I'm gone don't die on me. We need you."

As Azha flew to Cavern Hall, he couldn't shake seeing Zith's head being bit off. Distracted, he nearly collided with an injured soldier who was entering the cavern at the same time. Intimidated by the angry Trekachaw, the soldier squeaked when he tried to speak.

"*Not now soldier,*" Azha snapped.

"Belton told me Myosis has Leaders on your battleship spying on us."

"Did he say for how long?" Azha shook his head *No.*

Victis touched his wrist and sent a coded message, "*Vitta Belli Sotto.*"

"What does that mean?" Azha asked.

"Search the ship for intruders and prepare for battle. Choan, you and Roon stay on Palatu in case they return. Azha, we'll fly back."

TRAITOR MYOSIS AND HIS LEADERS wasted no time between Cavern Village and Victis' battleship to continue their rampage. Many had died and countless more were injured before the crewmen realized the mutant Gystfins had invaded the battleship. Atue, Duro, Vopar, Pax, and Vious were unaware of the attack until they heard screams for help. A crewman claimed there were huge Gystfins killing everyone in their path.

The five Trekachaws ran through corridors searching for any sign of the Gystfins. What they found was a path of mutilated bodies and bloody crewmen pointing in the direction of the bridge.

"They're taking over the ship."

The Trekachaws flashed into red energy and streaked through the walls onto the bridge. The flight crew had been ripped into pieces and strewn across the deck. Traitor Myosis and three Leaders froze, and their eyes were locked on the Trekachaws. It appeared as if they had rolled in the crewmen's blood with chunks of tissue stuck to their fur. In less than a heartbeat, Vopar and Vious grabbed the nearest Leader and broke his neck. Myosis and the other two Leaders vanished through the bulkhead, escaping into space. In a flash of red energy, the five Trekachaws followed in pursuit.

VICTIS EXPEDITED THE DOCKING PROTOCOL AND was securing the shuttle inside a lower hangar. Azha had already accessed the bridge. Despite transmitting a multitude of messages, Victis's crewmen had not answered a single transmission. At that moment, he wished he had accepted Choan's offer to merge. Fearing the worst, he sprinted towards the bridge, terrified at what he was going to find. Red emergency lights were blinking, and alarms were blaring alerts throughout the ship. The battleship floor dropped out from beneath him and he plummeted several feet. Grabbing onto the wall hand-rail, he pulled himself up and began to run again. The battleship repeatedly pitched forward out of control, making it difficult to keep his balance. Everything seemed to be in slow motion, and he grew increasingly nauseated at the carnage he witnessed while running through the bloody corridors. His fears had come true.

On the bridge, engineers were in a panic trying to stabilize the compromised circuits and damaged navigation flight controls. Azha was shouting at the traumatized Ryquats to remove bloody appendages from the instrument and flight control panels. Blood had seeped into the circuits and was causing them to short-out and catch on fire. The battleship was out of control, spinning headlong into the Targus Sun.

Victis was able to pull himself towards the bridge by hanging onto rails and taking one step at a time. At the doorway he waited until the ship pitched forward and let go. He slid across the floor towards the console and caught himself on the edge of a cabinet. Waiting a few seconds for the floor to level, he crawled over to the main terminal display-interface. Numerous relay terminals were cracked, with exposed and disconnected circuits. Victis screamed at Azha from across the bridge to help him remove a metal door beneath the main terminal. The massive ship began to spin so fast that everything not bolted down spun in the air, creating a tornado of thick debris. Unable to cross the bridge in body form, Azha turned into energy and flew through flying objects towards Victis. The moment he morphed into body form, a metal crate crashed into his shoulder knocking one of his hands off the cabinet he was clinging to. Before he could duck, several smaller projectiles left their sting on the side of his head. Azha dragged himself under the console desk just in time to avoid being struck by a dead crewman spinning in the air. Akio spiraled out of reach, screaming at Azha to catch him the next time he circled. His suit was bloody and in shreds, but he'd survived the Gystfin attack. Akio disappeared in the thick spinning debris and never circled Azha a second time. Together, Azha and Victis pried the metal door open and watched it rip from its hinges and spiral upward, joining the circling debris. Victis pulled out several circuit boards and reconnected numerous loose wires from the terminal. The main display interface panel lit-up and the spiraling battleship gradually stabilized into a steady vibration. Coughing from the black smoke that filled his burning lungs, Victis called out the best he could, "If you can you hear me, say something."

An Engineer yelled back, "Over here, Captain. We're *OK*. But I think most of the navigation crew are dead. We're from operations and engineering. What were those things?"

Akio yelled from across the bridge, "Captain, one other navigation crewman made it. The Trekachaws showed up just in time, or we'd be dead."

"Good to hear your voice, Akio. Do you need a medic?"

"Yes, both of us do."

Victis didn't answer the Engineer's question. He thought it best to let things calm down. Right now, he needed to check the ships' calibration, geomagnetic latitude, and the condition of the solar intake systems.

PAX STREAKED PAST PALATU ON his way back to the battleship. Somewhere deep in space, he remembered the ship had one physician, and that physician was him. For Atue, Duro, Vopar, and Vious, nothing in the Universe could deter them from the pursuit.

Directly ahead were the dense hostile gases of the vast Helix Nebula. If desperate enough, Traitor Myosis might find cover there to escape. Being somewhat faster, Vious and Duro sped off leaving Vopar and Atue behind in a last-ditch effort to catch the aberrant Gystfins and put an end to their bloodshed.

BACK ON THE SHIP, VICTIS was regretting the merge of his Chief Engineer and Atue. More than half of his engineers were reassigned to replace the dead bridge navigators. None of the engineers had enough experience to supervise the flight deck technicians, and the battleship was in dire need of extensive repairs. In addition, the weapon systems were at a minimum and the main terminal was fried. At best, to get the ship up to speed would take precious pivotal days. Myosis made a difficult situation into an impossible one, and the cargo ship orbiting Europa was no longer a viable option. After evaluating his limited options, Victis decided to contact the Umduls for assistance. With any luck, one of their ships would be within a couple of light years of Palatu.

...The Umduls were prominent members of the Fidus Achates Territory and close Ryquat allies. Throughout the galaxy, they had a reputation of being formidable warriors and respected spacecraft engineers. For thousands of years, the Ryquats provided avian-nautical blue prints and raw materials to the Umduls. In return, the Umduls provided the Ryquats with reliable high-tech battleships, cargo ships, transports, and shuttles.

Since there was nothing else Azha could do and the ship was stabilized for the time being, now was a good time to search for Phera and check on Belton's recovery. Victis agreed and requested that he and Roon swap places as soon as possible. But of course, nothing was ever that simple. Victis shoved a couple of syringe pens in Azha's hand, along with a verbal to-do list.

"Find out if Roon and Choan can understand Gystfins. If they can't, inject them with a linguistic chip. I'm assuming theirs fell out during the merge," said Victis.

Azha held the syringes in his hand as if they were a couple of hot potatoes.

"You know what this means, I'll be forced to fly in body form to Palatu. It'll take me forever to get there. Anyway, why ask me? I don't know how to inject a linguistic chip," replied Azha.

Exasperated Victis snatched one of the pens out of Azha's hand then placed the tip against his forearm.

"It's not that difficult Azha. Push down on the top just like an ink pen on Earth."

Fair enough, it was simple. Eager to find Phera, Azha accepted the task and flew as fast he could to Palatu in body form.

IT FELT GOOD TO BE home. Belton was basking on a mesa, appearing much better, and from across the village he noticed Choan and Roon towering over a group of soldiers. Azha waved to get their attention and walked towards them.

"It's good to be back. Belton looks much better. Have you seen Phera?"

Roon stared down at his feet, "We've been searching for her and Deneb ever since the Gystfins' left. A soldier said he saw them fly into the forest during the attack."

"So why aren't you looking for them? They could be hurt. Damn it Roon, what's wrong with you?"

"We have been looking, everywhere," Roon snapped.

Azha was worried sick that Phera was dead and taking his frustrations out on Roon.

"Sorry, I'm sure you have. Has anyone searched Kismet Ebb yet?" Azha asked.

"No, I'm sorry, it's haunted and burned."

With Roon, a returned apology could snow ball. It was best to leave that temptation alone and get on with the chip task Victis wanted. Azha opened his hand revealing the linguistic pens.

"These things inject what's called linguistic chips. If you can't understand Gystfins, Victis told me to inject one into your arm. Who's first? Stick out your arm."

Choan stepped back, "*No*, I'm not sticking out my arm."

Azha bragged, "I did it. Your Ryquat-half should remember these things. Look, mine is barely noticeable. The chip makes it possible to understand and communicate with aliens. When you merged with Bruce your chip probably fell out. Roon, you go first. Victis wants you back on the ship immediately."

Mulling it over, the chip did seem vaguely familiar. Besides, they figured any advantage regarding the Gystfins was worth a little pain. They stretched their arms out and closed their eyes anticipating the stick.

"You can put your arms down now. Geez, what a couple of quieys," mocked Azha.

For a fleeting moment, Roon considered disobeying the Captain's order. He preferred to stay on Palatu. But his Ryquat-half refused to entertain insubordination. Not only was Simon the Chief Science Officer, he was devoted to the Captain and their mission. So be it, the Ryquat won. Off to the battleship he streaked without a second thought.

twelve

EARTH

IN her heart, Judy always knew Frank had a thing for Ginger. Judy's desperate attempt to fix Ginger up with Andrew had back-fired horribly. He was a huge disappointment. For Ginger, he was a good excuse to give-up dating all together. On the flip side, Frank couldn't pass up the opportunity to follow his heart now that Ginger was a widow. For him, marriage with Judy was agonizing. It didn't take long before Frank and Judy found themselves routinely arguing over Ginger. The bickering dragged on for months until Frank made it painfully clear that he wanted out. His betrayal confirmed Judy's suspicions and justified her bitterness. In the end, she grew tired of being angry and agreed to a divorce. Frank gladly gave up the house, the new car, and his ten-year marriage. In return, he was free to pursue Ginger.

After a year of courtship and another year of living together, Ginger finally accepted his proposal. On the surface, their mar-riage appeared happy. But in truth, Ginger worked hard at pre-tending to be happy, especially around friends, family, and Cole Jr. If not in love, she was content, and he was an excellent father to her son.

Her precious memories of Cole were beginning to fade and there were days when she could no longer see his face in her mind. As soon as she could sneak away to the bedroom, she'd remove the second shoe box stacked on the top shelf inside the closet and open it ever so slowly to smell what was left of Cole's scent. Inside, one of his shirts was folded neatly with the last photo taken of him. Fighting back tears, she'd quietly place his photo back into the box and return her memories to the closet.

One joy in her life was watching her little boy grow into a perfect mini Cole. He had the same smile, the same walk, and his eyes were the same as the eyes she missed so much. She found herself taking solace in looking forward to special days such as birthdays, holidays, and those moments when she could accept the here and now. Today was going to be one of those days.

Waking up early, she jumped out of bed to begin the preparations for Cole Jr.'s birthday party. If everything went according to plan, the party would begin at noon. Last minute, she saw Frank helping Cole Jr. stick five, twisted, blue candles into his racecar cake. They were inseparable. Wherever Frank was you were sure to find his little shadow. One thing for certain, Frank never forgot or missed anything when it came to Cole Jr. Today was no exception. He'd make sure Cole Jr.'s birthday party was a grand-slam. The doorbell rang, and Grandma Beverly greeted the first of many little friends at the front door. For hours, the house was filled with laughter, games, giggles, and tummies full of cake. By the end of the day, sleepy eyes were ready to go home.

For some reason that night seemed especially difficult. Ginger had learned how to cleverly mask her depression from Frank. She didn't want to hurt him. He was a devoted, kind husband who lived to please her. But no matter how much she tried to fight it, she often laid awake at night wishing Cole was next to her. At times, her pain was so devastating she'd quietly sneak out of bed and find herself yet again in front of the kitchen window. On the inside, she was angry and screaming that life had cheated her. On the outside, she sat motionless with tears streaming down her face.

thirteen

VAE VICTIS

...Ryquats despised Crozins; they considered them a vile, ugly species. Likewise, and for good reasons, that same sentiment was felt by most Galaxy inhabitants. Crozins walk upright on three-toed hooves, but often run slumped over using their forearms to gain speed. Their faces are long and narrow with a split nose that can separate. Even from a distance they were easy to recognize by an oversized skull that hung freakishly disproportioned between their shoulder blades. But despite their appearance, the Crozins were intelligent and feared as ruthless warriors.

THREE Umdul battleships were en route with less than a two-day arrival time. Captain Pify reported a victorious crusade at a mining outpost where one Crozin flag ship was destroyed. The celebration was cut short when an intercepted transmission divulged at least five Tejat Rakta Crozin battleships were in pursuit, seeking retribution. Ship to ship, Victis transmitted to Captain Pify, "Do you have coordinates on the Crozins?"

Transmission received. Umdul C-9 Captain Pify, "Well, well, the tail we see ago the cargo ship. I'm pretty sure by the time the *caw* Crozins reach Palatu, distance we favor. If not, they'll watch the path abaft."

There were times Captain Pify drove Victis mad with his double talk. Clueless and no more informed than before, Victis thanked him for his allegiance and ended the transmission.

ATUE AND VOPAR MORPHED INTO body form at the dense, gas edge of the Helix Nebula. It had been a while since they last saw Vious and Duro, but it made sense they'd pursued Myosis in that direction. From there, they weren't sure where to go since no one would be foolish enough to enter the ominous Nebula. Even so, Atue felt compelled to share his concerns, "Do you think they would go in there?"

Vopar ignored the question. He was too busy flying alongside the gaseous border, trying to find a viable opening. It wasn't long before two familiar lights exited the Nebula and streaked towards them, spiraling into Duro and Vious.

"Keep up this time," demanded Duro.

Begrudgingly, the wayward Trekachaws streaked towards Palatu without the satisfaction of revenge.

Not far from the Nebula, five massive Crozin battleships flew in "V" formation with a Gystfin cargo ship trailing behind. Duro motioned for them to stop; he had a plan.

"I say we sabotage the battleship trailing on the right side of the 'V.' Atue, you and Vopar locate the main solar power grid and disable the ship. Atue, um… Einstein do you remember engineering?" Duro asked.

"Yeah, most everything," replied Atue.

"Good. Vious and I will target the bridge and the communication station. When you're finished, we'll wait for you on the bridge.

Keep your ears open for anything we can use later. Now that we're Trekachaws, we can do whatever we want."

"Wow Duro, I hope you're not serious?"

"You need to have some fun, Atue."

"Your fun is going to get us all killed," replied Atue.

Like it or not, everyone decided to follow Duro's grand plan. Atue and Vopar entered the Crozin's battleship through the main power grid station. To minimize detection, they flew in fast and dimmed their energy into concentrated orbs. By now, Duro and Vious should have breached the bridge. The Crozin crewmen were unaware of their presence and the ship's security system had not considered them a threat. To their advantage, the Crozin ship was almost a duplicate of a Ryquat ship. Of course, that was to be expected since most of the ships in the galaxy were designed by Ryquats and Umdul engineered.

Four, maybe five Crozins exited the power grid deck just moments after they floated through the wall. Their timing was perfect. Only two Crozins left to kill, and they were oblivious as to what was behind them. Vopar flashed red and waited for them to turn around. Both remained squatted on metal stools and fixated on a lit solar screen. Vopar flashed bright red again. That confirmed it, they were oblivious. Looking over the Crozins' shoulder, Atue could see a smaller schematic relay displaying where power was being regulated throughout the ship and, more importantly, to the bridge. From there, Atue knew how to disable the ship without destroying her. He signaled Vopar and morphed into body form to lock the hatch door, *"Clunk"*. In sync, the Crozins sat up and spun around on their stools. Vopar landed softly behind them on top of the power grid console ready to pounce.

The Crozins jumped to their hoofs, *"What is that? Kill it."*

Vopar grabbed their bulging heads and slammed the two together. *'THUNK'* …they sounded like watermelons being smashed. He held on to them until their bodies became limp. Thoroughly disgusted, he dropped the Crozins onto the floor and wiped his hands off on one of their uniforms. Atue didn't even notice. He was too busy disconnecting vital circuit relays from the power grid, causing a massive surge. The battleship violently pitched forward, spiraling into an accelerated descent before losing power. The two dead Crozins floated in the air for a second, then slid across the deck floor before slamming into each other. Vopar snapped his fingers to get Atue's attention, then pointed at the hatch. It was too late. Vopar had already unlocked the door.

Atue shoved the circuits he was holding into a small gap between the floor and the relay station, then flashed into energy to hide with Vopar inside the ceiling halo track. The hatch crashed open and a half-dozen Crozins rushed in. After a detailed inspection, they were baffled at what caused the damage and the ship's malfunction. Apparently, no one suspected foul play. Even more ironic, they assumed the two dead Crozins had died from injuries sustained during the ship's violent turbulence.

Throughout the ship, emergency lights were flashing, and back-up systems had activated. Crozin crewmen scurried about the decks trying to put out fires. On the bridge, the navigation crew had been thrown across the flight deck causing a multitude of injuries, and the Captain was preoccupied listening to overlapping exigency updates and intermittent static transmissions. Neither Vious nor Duro had linguistic chips to understand what was being said. However, Vious's Ryquat half could speak some Crozin. He was pretty sure the Crozin Captain was waiting for another battleship to rendezvous with his stranded ship. Soon after the transmission ended, a Crozin battleship locked in at a docking platform. The injured, along with most of the crew personnel, were transferred, leaving a skeleton crew behind. Given the new development, Vious and Duro concocted a new plan. As soon as Vopar and Atue were on the bridge, they'd take command of the Crozin battleship and fly it to Palatu.

CAVERN VILLAGE HAD GROWN EXPONENTIALLY with neighboring Quizans seeking refuge. The Gystfins were on a killing rampage, lashing out indiscriminately. Clearly, they were furious about the Ryquats' betrayal and their missing cargo ship. Making matters worse, they were short on supplies and had no weaponry. Azha called for an emergency briefing with Choan and Belton to discuss options for ending the Gystfin's carnage. For now, his search for Phera and Deneb would have to wait.

"The Gystfins need to be stopped. Today, we attack them at their campsite. Have your soldiers bring as many rocks and spears as they can carry. Instruct them to go in quietly and camouflage themselves amidst the trees above the campsite perimeter. Once everyone's in position, Choan and I will begin the attack."

Upon arrival, the campsite was exactly what Azha had imagined. The presumptuous Gystfins were gathered inside a dome modular building with no perimeter sensors or guards posted outside. A Quizan soldier crouched in an overhanging branch above the modular, waved at Azha to confirm they were in position. Azha whistled an Ayak bird call at Choan to get his attention.

"Shhh, follow me. Let's have some fun."

Choan thought it strange that Azha would think this situation fun. But, rather than question his request, Choan followed blindly, landing silently next to him on the roof above the doorway. Azha snickered, then jumped off the roof, landing on the ground in front of the door. Low and behold, he'd lost his mind. Azha started shaking his butt while dancing a little jig for all to see. He picked up a rock lying on the ground and began tossing it up and down in his hand. Choan's and the soldiers' mouths dropped, shocked by his outrageous behavior. It had to be Azha's Human-half making him act that way. Yes, that had to be it.

Azha wound his arm up and pitched the rock at the door hitting it with a *bang*.

Trying not to laugh out loud, he jumped onto the roof with Choan and waited for Gystfins to investigate the noise. One Gystfin cracked the door open just enough to stick his ugly head out. He took a quick look around, grunted, and shut the door. Azha snort-chuckled and jumped off the roof to search for another rock. He didn't have to go far. Next to the side of the modular was a boulder calling his name. Quietly, he rolled it in front of the door and picked it up with both hands. Raising it high above his head Azha launched the massive boulder hitting the door square in the middle. *'KA-BOOM.'* The same Gystfin swung the door wide open looking mad as hell. He fidgeted in the doorway scratching his head, then his hairy butt. Exasperated, he looked behind the door and noticed the huge dent, then slammed the door shut. Azha almost fell off the roof trying not to laugh out loud. By this time the soldiers understood the prank and were laughing hysterically. Choan waved his hands in the air, signaling the soldiers to quiet down while giving Azha a stern look.

"That felt so good. But you're right Choan, let's turn into energy and check out what the Gystfins are doing inside."

Azha didn't have to ask Choan twice. The metal building was nothing more than an open, long, corrugated room. He estimated approximately fifty Gystfins sleeping on stacked cots at the far end of the room, and at least ten more huddled together at the opposite end. The Beasts parted, revealing a *Leader Gystfin* lying on a padded bunk. It was the same vile Leader Azha had stabbed in the chest. He should've died, but there he was boasting to his pack of worshiping Gystfins.

Filled with rage, both his and Choan's energy flashed purple as they raced towards the traitor with one thought in mind; they were determined to kill him once and for all. Mid-air, they flashed into body form and landed on top of the Beast. Azha fought the worshiping Gystfins, while Choan gouged his thumbs into the Leader's eye sockets. Seeing they were no match for the Trekachaws, they ran away yelling for the others to wake up. Screeching in pain, the Leader clawed at Choan's arms trying to free himself from the Trekachaw's grip. Digging his thumbs deeper into his brain, Choan roared, "Die Quizan, rot inside this Beast, never to ascend!" Azha and Choan flashed into energy and streaked through the ceiling before hordes of slumbering Gystfins were able to fall from their cots and save their hero. Pandemonium ensued inside the dome, and the Beasts ran amok out the door into the open, searching for the Trekachaw assassins.

From above, Victis swooped in, landing on a large limb next to Azha and Choan. Their smug smiles were self-explanatory. "How are things on the ship?" Azha asked.

Victis wasn't amused, "Escort the soldiers to Cavern Village. Don't waste any more time here."

Azha took offense, "We just killed a Leader Gystfin. That's not wasting time."

Victis ignored Azha's insolence. "I'm sterilizing the area. The faster we vacate, the better the odds to vaporize the entire Gystfin camp. I can't afford to allow any of them to escape."

Azha stopped defending himself and signaled the soldiers to immediately mobilize and fly back to Cavern Village. As they flew away, the Gystfins howled, wagging their long tongues. Some gyrated their hips in vile humping movements while others urinated, directing the stream at them.

Azha knew something had gone wrong, but what, and why now? The reality was that Victis had no choice. The Gystfins had broken their ten-year raw material contract and had negotiated a new one with the Crozins for a higher price. Trying to reason with intoxicated, grey-death energy Gystfins was impossible. Therefore, every Gystfin on the planet had to be sterilized before the Crozin battleships reached Palatu. If it were possible to request Ryquat auxiliary support, life would be simple. Except life wasn't simple and that was out of the question. For now, he had to keep the new Trekachaws a secret from the Viceroy Counsel or be condemned for his flagrant disregard for Fidus Achates Decrees. His crew and the Trekachaws were on their own, aside from his old comrade Captain Pify.

Victis and Azha stayed behind to watch the pulsating blue beam sterilize the Gystfin's camp. At least that threat was gone. Upon their return, tired soldiers were sprawled out across the courtyard soaking up the bright Targus sun. Even though the threat was gone, Victis remained serious and anxious.

"Azha, find Choan *AFAP* and meet me at Belton's cavern."

"What's *AFAP?*"

"As fast as possible. What did you think it meant?"

"It's ASAP on Earth."

"No, it's not. 'S' is for slow, just go."

Azha sensed that Victis was about to unveil some seriously bad news. Choan was easy to find and equally curious as to why they were in such a hurry to get to Belton's cavern. Azha was still trying to remember whether ASAP or AFAP was correct. Victis's way did make more sense.

Belton's recovery was amazing. Other than a slight limp, he almost appeared normal. Before anyone was able to get comfortable, Victis stormed in and began the meeting by ordering everyone not to interrupt.

"I just spoke with an Umdul Captain who confirmed that five Crozin battleships will be in Palatu's orbit within two days. A Gystfin cargo ship is following them and will arrive in approximately three days. They believe I'm en route to Europa to reclaim the confiscated Gystfin cargo ship. What they don't know, is that I know our contract is void, and that they've contracted with the Crozins to purchase all the containers of raw materials on the planet. In exchange, the Gystfins demanded the eradication of Palatu, Azha, and all Quizans.

I destroyed the Gystfin's communications on Palatu before they had a chance to warn their superiors or the Crozins of our plans. Originally, there were three Umdul battleships en route for reinforcements. Unfortunately, that has changed. Two of the battleships were redirected to intercept a Crozin battleship in violation of Planet Opus air space. Therefore, Captain Pify and I came up with another plan. With that said, there must be no misunderstanding; we are outnumbered. Our only advantage is the element of surprise. If we fail, the Crozins will destroy Palatu.

Azha, I need you and Choan on the planet to defend the Quizans from a Crozin ground invasion. I had Tech Division resize the Neco glove to fit a Quizan soldier's hand. Twelve portable Laser Necos were just delivered outside Cavern Hall. Choan was a Neco instructor, he can show you how to operate them. Do what you can before the Crozins attack."

Outside, loud cheers and hurrahs disrupted the meeting. Everyone scurried pass Victis to see what all the ruckus was about. Bigger than life, Phera and Deneb strolled into the village. Azha's stripes turned brilliant green and he shoved through the crowd. Against all odds, she'd survived. Victis allowed the frivolous reunion for a few minutes, but they were running out of time to prepare for an impossible counter-attack. He could feel his blood pressure rising and a knot form in the pit of his stomach. Enough celebrating! Victis put his fingers in his mouth and let out an ear-piercing whistle.

"Now that I have everyone's attention... glad you're not dead, but I need to break up the festivities and continue our meeting. Belton, Choan, Azha and you two, *(pointing at Phera and Deneb)* let's go."

Belton apologized to the crowd for the interruption and encouraged the celebration to continue. Azha caught up with Victis, wondering why Deneb and Phera were invited?

Victis grumbled, "Get your head on straight and focus on what's important. Getting Quizans to move is like herding cats."

Azha stomped ahead, "You're an ass."

With all present, the meeting continued.

"Belton, Phera and Deneb, are you willing to merge with a Ryquat? If so, I handpicked Ryquats for each of you. Deneb, your Ryquat's name is Darcy. She's a weapons specialist assigned to Special-Ops. Phera I matched you with an Ops-female named Tara. She has several accommodations for bravery, excels in combat tactics and navigation. Belton, your Ryquat is called Larry. These three Special-Ops are some of my best soldiers."

Belton did not hesitate this time. His new goal in life was to kill Myosis and inflict as much pain as possible along the way. Deneb's only question was if Roon was alive.

"Yes, Roon is a Trekachaw on my ship. He merged with a Ryquat Science Officer named Simon," replied Victis.

Deneb agreed to join if Phera would. Phera raised her hand. "It's a yes for both of us."

"Whoa, whoa, whoa" ...Azha interrupted. "Phera will not merge with a Special-Ops female. Find a Science Officer or something else."

Victis was curt, "Tara is one of the females that you requested on ship... remember?"

"No, No, No, Phera I forbid this. It's too dangerous, wait for a female who is not Special-Ops."

Phera scowled, "Don't tell me what I can, or cannot do. I survived without you for a hundred years. Ryquat Victis I want this, do not listen to him."

Deneb seconded with, "Me, too."

Azha snapped at Phera, "I said, *NO.*"

Glaring at Azha, Victis cocked his head sideways, "You cannot forbid Phera. In my world, females are equal to males. Azha, you never listen to me, or anyone else for that matter. You will not dictate to her, nor will you order me to disrespect her decision. You can knock off the bad attitude and stop turning purple, I'm sick of it." Victis touched his wrist to contact the ship, "Confirmed, have Ops. Tara, Darcy, and Larry standby in the lounge."

"C-9, Uketotta."

Azha was regretting his swap with Roon. The whole purpose for returning to Palatu was for Phera.

"*Captain,* can I swap with Belton after the merge?"

Victis had already planned to make the swap; nonetheless, he'd keep that to himself. Azha's Human-side had a rebellious streak that liked to challenge his authority in front of others. Putting Azha in his place was necessary. Chuckling to himself, Victis thought it was hilarious when he told Azha to stop *'turning purple.'* In his mind, he pictured a bright purple balloon caricature blowing up until his head popped.

"No problem Azha. Belton and Choan can train the Quizan soldiers on the Neco Lasers."

Choan had no desire to remain on Palatu either. But being a disciplined Special-Ops Sgt., he knew better than to ask Victis for anything personal or self-serving. Plus, training soldiers with Belton was an important assignment.

It was settled, Belton, Phera, and Deneb turned into energy and flew out of the Caverns with Victis trailing close behind.

Outside the massive Ryquat battleship the three lights waited until Victis was inside the docking bay. From there, they followed him down the maze of corridors into a lounge. It was anyone's guess who was more frightened, the Ryquats or the Quizans. The tiny orbs of light flashed into silver fireflies buzzing a delightful dance around their hosts. Victis raised his arms, then lowered them, orchestrating the beginning of new lives with two souls and one voice.

Victis watched the Ryquat lives fade from their eyes and their bodies stiffen as they fell into a deep trance, no longer in control. The moments between the death and the creation of the Trekachaws were frightening to behold. Victis wasn't sure if a mortal was worthy of witnessing such a miracle. But unable to look away, he saw the tiny spark of light from their dead eyes reveal the first sign of life. Brighter and brighter the silver light grew, consuming their faces until the light exploded into bolts of silver. Victis tried not to stare, warning himself to look away. He'd lost his will; euphoria was consuming his soul. Screaming in his head, he told himself to move, run away, get out of the room.

Somehow, he found the strength to stagger out of the lounge and slam the door shut to cut off the burning desire to submit. Terrified, he slumped against the corridor wall to steady his trembling body and weak legs. Was it possible to join three souls or had he touched death and survived? A second later would have been forever one way or the other. Rubbing his burning face, Victis shook off his fears and lingering euphoria. Now more than ever, he understood the unspoken revelation and desperately wanted to become a Trekachaw.

Victis heard the lounge door open, but his burning eyes were still unable to focus. He blinked again and again, then squinted. A blurry silhouette came into view.

"Can you hear me, Captain?"

Victis could not discern who was talking. *Was it Belton?* If it were, his squeaky voice had transformed into a deep baritone.

"Shall I return to Palatu?"

Still fuzzy, Victis questioned everything including himself.

"Ah, yeah Belton? Yes, Palatu. Help with the Neco Weapons AFAP. There are only twelve, so be selective. One more thing, remind Azha that I need him on ship."

He must have sounded drunk. It would've been nice to have had a few more minutes to clear his head. Of course, that would be asking too much. Little did he know, Phera and Deneb had been standing in the corridor watching him the entire time. Rubbing his eyes again, Victis decided he could see well enough to walk down the corridor. *Wowzers,* was he caught off guard! Two female Trekachaws were standing right in front him! They were spectacular. Victis had always fancied himself a Casanova, a smooth operator. All that was about to change. When he opened his mouth, it was as if his tongue was tied, fat and dumb, *"Blah-ah, blah ay-ya."* What was he saying? This was incredibly embarrassing. His crude thoughts were disturbing, even to him. Damn, the more he tried to stop thinking about it, the worse they got. Such inappropriate raunchy acts that he'd love to do to them. Shit, could they read his mind? No, Azha couldn't read minds, so neither can they. *Holy-Toledo* their bodies were perfect, and they were naked, *completely naked.*

Before anyone caught him gawking at them, Victis directed his eyes upwards gazing at the ceiling. Well that looked stupid, so he looked down focusing on the patterns in the floor design. Damn it, he could still see them from his peripheral vision. Next impossible feat, how was he going to communicate with them? His heart was racing, and he could feel his face turning bright red.

This was out of control; he was out of control. Shit, I can't stop myself, don't think about it. *Not now, are you kidding, this was bad.* He was aroused, and it wasn't going away anytime soon. Seeing no other option, Victis quickly and awkwardly walked away.

Phera and Deneb were concerned about the Captain's bizarre behavior. They figured he was under a lot of stress and it would be best not to ask him to explain whatever it was he was saying. Instead, they waited until Victis disappeared around the corner to explore the ship. Deneb suggested they look for Azha first, believing Phera would jump at the chance. Her response surprised Deneb. Phera was flippant and declined the offer.

"Nope, let's find Roon. I'll run into Azha soon enough."

Towering above the crewmen, they gracefully strolled down the corridors, unaware of the commotion they were causing. Everyone stopped whatever they were doing to watch the magnificent female Trekachaws pass by.

Determined to resolve the naked female Trekachaw problem, Victis walked as fast as he could to his office. He requested the first available nurse. *Exactly four minutes and eight seconds later,* nurse Anna knocked on his door. Not that Victis was counting every second.

"Come in and close the door behind you."

Anna felt her hands trembling and hid them behind her back. Since the first day she was assigned to his battleship, she'd had a crush on the Captain. Anna kept her feelings to herself because the Captain never showed any interest and because of the strict rules regarding superiors fraternizing with subordinates.

"Sit down," Victis barked, pointing to a large leather chair across from his desk.

She promptly sat down and waited for the Captain to continue. Victis bit the inside of his lip trying to decide how he was going to phrase this unusual request. He took a deep breath and slowly exhaled, "Do you know about the Quizans and Ryquats merging?" Victis asked.

"Yes, they're scheduled for physical exams."

"That's perfect. Have you seen the females yet?"

Anna admitted that she had not seen them, but assumed they were somewhat like Pax. 'Good, he thought. She knew about the males being naked.'

"I need a discreet favor from you."

Direct orders or favors from a Captain were unorthodox. Confused, she told him absolutely and thanked him for the opportunity. Victis leaned back in his chair and smiled.

"All right then. Your assignment is to locate the two female Trekachaws, Phera and Deneb. Phera is the taller, prettier one. I want you to instruct them on how to wear clothes. If none of the garments fit, escort them to the couturier. Be discreet and stay with them until they're acclimated. Can you do this?"

Anna was disappointed. As always, the Captain showed no interest in her.

"Yes Sir, I promise to be discreet and make it my priority."

"Okay, keep me posted on their progress."

Victis was relieved to have that problem behind him. Communications squawked a transmission, interrupting his thoughts.

"Captain respond to the bridge, Crozin battleships detected."

On his way to the bridge, Victis mulled over in his head the strategy he'd been considering, *"I'll use Pify's Umdul ship as bait and camouflage my ship for an ambush. The Crozins still think I'm en route to Europa. Two to five aren't good odds, although the element of surprise could give us a fighting chance. Our battleships are far superior, polished from stem to stern. Crozin ships are neglected junk. Calculating the Crozins' speed and coordinates, their estimated arrival time should be in about three hours."*

Victis briskly walked onto the bridge and sat down in the Captain's chair. The crewmen were at their posts prepared for battle.

"The Crozins underestimate our resilience. Power up solar thrusters, check monitor codes, and ready the weapon systems. Akio… match the Crozin lead battleships' speed as they approach. Once we're in orbit, mirror its rotation around Palatu. To conceal our ship, I want the Crozin's sensors to think we are a reflection off the planet or a glitch on their radar."

"Yes Sir, no problem."

On a closed frequency, Captain Pify confirmed he was in position and prepared for battle.

fourteen

DIES IRAE

"A FOOL... IS TO NEVER RIGHT WHAT YOU KNOW IS WRONG"

ATUE and Vopar floated down the corridor towards the bridge. This Crozin ship was the exact same design as the older Ryquat X1-R Model Battleship, phased out over a decade ago. Somewhere along the way Atue's thoughts drifted off visualizing the days when his Human-half, Einstein, attended the United Achates Space Academy. Upon graduation, he received the distinguished award for Engineering and Aero-Space Technology because of numerous technical upgrades he invented for the X1-R. This solid old ship was familiar and steadfast, except for the antiquated weapon systems. He was confident the primary apparatus could be modified, thus increasing solar assimilation of geodesic and chiral molecules. With a couple of minor adjustments, he could boost propulsion and dramatically improve the weapon systems.

Vopar had taken a detour inside an armory. The temptation to snoop paid off. He'd discovered a cache of Laser Neco weapons stowed inside an unlocked cabinet. Vopar slipped a glove over his hand and waved at Atue floating above. After testing the laser indicators for efficiency, Vopar closed his fingers into a tight fist. The Neco glove was a perfect fit. Atue morphed into body form to search for his own glove. Faint sounds of approaching footsteps alerted them. Atue and Vopar ducked behind a cabinet and waited. Outside the doorway the footsteps grew louder then stopped. Whoever was standing outside rattled the locked doorknob before walking away. That was a close call. From now on they'd be more careful.

Discussing the pros and cons, they decided it best to leave their Neco Weapons behind. Carrying the weapons would make it impossible to scout the ship while in energy. For now, they needed to avoid detection. Taking a quick tour of the ship, they counted twenty-six Crozins, plus four still trying to figure out what caused the failure in the solar grid station, and an Ukaru sitting in his office adjacent to the bridge. Commandeering the ship was going to be easy. Fired up, Vopar and Atue streaked through the thick metal walls into the armory and morphed into body form. They slid their Neco gloves on and unlocked the door to step out into the corridor. Intruder alarms instantly sounded throughout the battleship. A bridge monitor displayed two armed aliens walking down the corridor leading to the bridge. Atue fired his Neco at a control box on the wall. The relays melted, freezing the last images of Vopar and Atue onto the screen of the bridge monitor. The Crozin Ukaru stormed out his office and sat at the helm. *"Car-duc. Gen!"*

A crewman secured the doors from the control station and awaited the Ukaru's next command. The bridge was alive with flashing lights blinking on and off. It was no wonder the two Trekachaws floating in energy above were unnoticed. Vious understood the Crozins enough to know that it was time to attack. Silently, their lights descended behind the helm where they morphed into body form. A muffled belch escaped from the Ukaru's mouth as Duro broke his neck.

A crewman watching a monitor was requesting instructions and clarification from his dead Ukaru.

"Do you want the decks eradicated? What are your orders?"

Vious crept over to the door and unlocked it, allowing Atue and Vopar access to the bridge with their Necos. The four Trekachaws rallied to the center of the room and waited for the crew to notice. Not one Crozin turned around. They were so glued to the monitors, they didn't notice that the aliens they were searching for were standing behind them. Atue found it strange how the Ukaru appeared tranquil sitting at the helm. His death came swiftly, leaving the smug grin on his repulsive face forever.

Exasperated by how oblivious the crewmen were, Vopar clapped his hands a couple of times to get their attention. And still they were clueless. No longer amused by their stupidity, Vopar pointed his Neco at the Crozin's head standing at the far-left side of the bridge. A thin, red, laser beam sliced through its skull and continued across the skulls of six more Crozins. It seemed much longer than expected before their bodies slumped to the floor. As they fell, the top half of their skulls slid off exposing the laser's clean slice and their brains. The Crozins' battleship was theirs.

fifteen

PALATU EXPOSED

AZHA and Choan gave up on the twelve modified Neco Lasers. They were never going to fit the soldiers' hands. How ludicrous, no one asked how many fingers they had? The Necos were worthless unless they fit properly. Worse case, the extra finger could cause a mal-function resulting in serious injuries or death. Back to the frickin rocks and spears for the Quizan soldiers.

Choan worked alongside the soldiers stacking rocks into neat pyramids, while Azha finished filling the last two vine totes. Racking his brain, he tried to think of anything else that could help prepare them for the invasion.

"Choan, what else can we do to get ready?"

Choan pretended not to hear Azha.

"Should we make more spears? Do you know what a Crozin looks like?"

Choan glared at Azha, irritated.

"What did I do? You've been like this all day. If you've got a problem with me, spit it out."

Tight-mouthed, Choan chucked the rock he was holding onto the ground and his stripes glowed bright red with a tinge of purple. Every soldier in sight flashed into energy and disappeared.

"What was that for? What's your problem?" Azha shouted.

"*You're my problem.* Why did you have us call rocks ...*Frickin Rocks?* And making Roon the Rangemaster of rocks and spears? Big joke on the stupid Quizans. Well, it's not funny, Azha."

"Whoa, I did not name *rocks* frickin rocks as a joke. When I returned from Earth, everything was confusing. My merge was not easy like yours. I stole Cole's body. I sincerely regret what I did, but I'm paying for it dearly. He constantly resists, and I can feel his wrath burning inside of me. And about the frickin rocks, I'm not the one who named them. If you remember, it started when I tried to explain how to bury the two Gystfins. You were there. They reeked, stinking up the whole village. None of you knew what bury was, or how to dig a hole. I came up with the ditch, remember? Zith led us to a ditch where we threw them in. All of us where throwing rocks into the ditch to cover them up. Roon asked me what kind of rocks to use. I said any damn frickin-rocks will do. Frickin came from Cole, I never heard of the word *frickin* until then. That's when Roon started calling any rock used for a weapon, a damn, frickin rock. Rather than correcting him, I figured at least everyone would know which rocks were being used for weapons."

BELTON FLEW INTO THE VILLAGE adjacent to the tree line. Choan and Azha didn't notice. They were in a heated discussion about frickin rocks. Determined to get their attention, he flew across the courtyard and landed in front of them. Since they were being rude, why not interrupt them? "Why are you arguing about frickin rocks?"

Azha stopped mid-sentence, "Is that you, Belton?"

Belton's stripes beamed brilliant green with pride, "Yep, it's me."

Curious Quizans buzzed in circles around the new Trekachaw. A few soldiers crept up to inspect the area where his leg had been injured. Belton squatted up and down, demonstrating his resilience. "Before I forget Azha, Cpt. Victis gave me orders for us to swap places."

For Azha, this was good news even though backstabber Victis had sided with Phera. He tried to imagine her as a Trekachaw and wondered if her personality had changed.

Choan refused to join in on the conversation and continued to stack rocks. Geez, Azha was in a bad mood and Choan was red. Belton was beginning to wish he'd stayed on board. Perhaps saying something positive would help?

"I can help train the soldiers on the Neco weapons."

Wham. Choan chucked the rock he was holding into the soft red dirt. And once again, frightened Quizans flashed into energy and scattered throughout the forest. Azha was fed up with Choan's constant grumbling and foul mood.

"Knock it off, you're scaring the soldiers. We're all worried."

Choan's fists were clenched and his stripes glowed purple. Azha stiffened and his yellow eyes narrowed. "That's it, you want to fight? Come on, one of us will die."

Choan squared off for a moment, then relaxed his hands. He looked defeated and sad, calling out to those hiding in fear, "Forgive me, I would never hurt any of you."

The tree tops sparkled with little bursts of light. One after another, the soldiers buzzed to the ground and morphed into body form.

Haunted by what he was about to reveal, Choan's stripes had faded to a pale tan. Azha felt bad for chastising him so severely, but maybe now he would talk about it. Choan sat on a tree stump and let the rock he was holding roll from his hand onto the ground. "Do you remember why Duro and I came to Cavern Village?" Azha nodded, *yes.*

"Remember how my Silwat Tribe was massacred by the bad Ryquat?"

"Yes, I remember."

Fighting his emotions, Choan closed his eyes. Azha assured him that whatever it was, he could be trusted. Choan opened his eyes filled with tears.

"The bad Ryquat who killed my entire village, Duro's family, my mom, dad, my wife and little quiey," He paused then spoke in a whisper, *"He's my Ryquat uncle.* You struggle with Cole's soul because you stole his body. My souls are ripping me apart."

Azha was truly speechless.

"My Ryquat-half loves and admires my Uncle Doug. My mom worships him. She believes he's a hero. After my father died in the war, he raised me like a son. That monster taught me everything since I was ten years old, and he was a key part in my acceptance at the Fidus Achates. He's a distinguished commander with formidable power and the fifth generation of a spotless military history. How can I tell Duro that I'm half-monster? No matter how much my Ryquat half fights me, *if I get the chance, I'll kill him."*

Azha understood Choan's misery. He faced five-hundred years of guilt and revenge unless somehow, he came to terms with the mutinous venom growing within himself. Choan had to prevail. Palatu, the Quizans, and their lives, depended on the outcome of this invasion.

Choan spoke first, "I promise no more distractions."

"Duro will understand when you're ready to tell him. You're not responsible for your uncle's crimes. I'm glad you confided in me."

Azha called out for Belton to join them. "My advice to both of you... show no mercy."

The three Trekachaws shook hands on it, and then Azha flashed into energy en route to the battleship.

THE SHIP WAS EERILY SILENT. Azha could tell that everyone was being careful not to make even the slightest noise. Victis was staring at an Umdul battleship bridge displayed on a large monitor screen. A shrewd, battle-scarred Umdul Captain was sitting at the helm, reigning with confidence. No doubt, that seasoned old guardian had seen many wars before this one. Azha descended and morphed into body form next to the helm. Victis briefly glanced over, then pointed to a chair, gesturing for him to sit down. Captain Pify was giving a detailed description of what he was viewing. Azha caught on that Victis was hiding behind Palatu until the Crozin battleships were close enough for an ambush.

This was the first time Azha had seen an Umdul. They were sort of cute and ugly at the same time and everything they said seemed to end in a question. He guessed them to be around four feet tall with squatty bodies and colorful, bushy, baby-fine hair that stood straight up on top of their heads. From the back, their hair either hung in a straight line to their waist or was attached to their spine. Either way, it was by far the most attractive feature of an Umdul. A second monitor switched over, displaying four Crozins battleships in view on the

Umdul's screen. Captain Pify scooted forward in his chair.
"Closer are they, nasty Crozins with four junk ships? Number five
we see, or not? Yah, serves you right scavengers. Twenty minutes
cold space if birds don't fail or fall. We meet once more for war."
Victis understood Captain Pify's cryptic message. He gave their
time of arrival and that the fifth ship was not within monitor range.
It was possible the fifth Crozin ship had been redirected from a
frontal-attack to a rear or side-assault. For now, the best strategy
was to stick with the original plan, so they waited.

Dead silence heightened the agonizing uncertainty aboard ship.
Only Azha welcomed it. For him it was a moment to reflect on how
far he'd come and how it could all end. If he were to die here, it
would be okay. He felt at home with Ryquats; they reminded him
of Humans on Earth. Cole, however, was never content. Every so
often he'd surface with a vengeance, making Azha sad with dark
thoughts and regrets. Tormenting memories brought back a disturbing longing for his mother and Ginger. How cruel and selfish of
the Quizan for not telling them the truth before leaving. Someday,
he'd return home to repent his sins.

Atue streaked onto the bridge, morphing into body form. Victis
jumped to his feet waving his arms in the air for Atue to be quiet. Atue
mouthed, "*Ok,*" then did a finger motion indicating that he needed
something to write on. A crewman grabbed a tabpad and handed it to
him. Atue frantically scribbled on the tabpad, then shoved it in front
of Victis's face. The spell-bound crew waited for the news. Victis got
a huge smile on his face as he read and mouthed, "*Oh, hell yeah.*"

Azha snatched the tabpad out of Victis's hand and silently read,
'*We killed the crew on the fifth Crozin battleship. I increased solar
power and weapons. We are just out of monitor range. Where do
you want us?*

Azha handed the tabpad back to Victis mouthing, *"Hell, yeah."*

Victis wrote back, *Wait until we break transmission silence. Then immediately destroy the flank ships."*

Atue snapped his fingers demanding the tabpad be returned. He read it, then wrote, *I know Captain Pify. Do you want me to streak over to his battleship and update him?*

Victis nodded, "Yes."

Atue turned into energy and flashed out of the ship. Azha and Victis smiled at each other, they knew the odds were now in their favor.

ATUE CIRCLED AROUND A COUPLE of times inside the Umdul's bridge before morphing into body form. Their ship was impressive, high-tech, and spotless. Captain Pify straightened up in his helm chair and whispered, "Appear here, how?"

"Captain Pify I'm a Trekachaw, half-Ryquat, half-Quizan. My Ryquat-half is your old friend Einstein, the Ryquat Engineer. There are several of us who have control of the fifth Crozin battleship. Captain Victis gave us orders that when he breaks communication silence, we are to destroy the Crozin flank ships."

"My, my stay there, out of monitor view will do."

Pify belly-rolled out of his chair and waddled closer to get a better look. At best, the squatty Captain stood at Atue's waist. Stumbling backwards, he motioned for Atue to bend over.

"A Trekachaw, you say? Captain Victis trumpet praise for kind."

Taking another step back, he motioned for Atue to bend over a little more. That was going to be difficult, if not impossible. Atue folded his legs and sat on the floor to lower himself to the Umduls height. The old Captain patted Atue's face with his stumpy fingers and whispered in his ear, "Later talk, you and me. Perhaps on a Crozin ship?"

In unison, the Umdul crewmen snorted with approval. Atue rose from the floor, turning into energy and streaked out of the bridge. The Umdul's battleship sensors alerted them to a barrage of incoming, pulsating, blue, laser blasts. The ship pitched hard starboard, dodging the impact and then accelerated at hikari speed towards Palatu. Four avenging Crozin battleships pursued the fleeing Umdul's while firing a relentless storm of blasts.

From Palatu, Choan and Belton watched the red sky turn white with laser strikes and beams of blue, light bolts. They knew they were as good as dead if their comrades failed.

The ship's stern-side was most vulnerable to laser damage. So far, Cpt. Pify had outmaneuvered the Crozins and dodged their lasers with barely a scratch. The old salt sensed he was running out of luck. Breaking radio silence Cpt. Pify transmitted, "Whammy mad birds, pluck out of space."

Victis transmitted, *"Engage, weapons intercept."*

The Crozin Captains heard the transmission and began scrambling their battleships in all directions. Victis fired on the lead ship with deadly accuracy. The sterilization beam vaporized every Crozin on board and the shock wave propelled the crewless ship into a spinning projectile, causing it to crash into another fleeing Crozin battleship. Both ships violently exploded, sending a firestorm of debris raining down on Palatu.

Victis transmitted, *"Take out the flanks."*

One of the last two Crozin ships was in Duro's line of sight. He fired a series of sterilization beams at the battleship, choosing not to destroy her. If he could intercept the vessel, the

Trekachaws would increase their fleet with another battleship. His aim was perfect. The crewless ship's speed decreased with the portside wing tilted down. It slowly began to roll, faster and faster, spiraling out of control towards Palatu. Atue shouted, *"Duro, cease fire!"*

In a flash of light, Atue streaked towards the plummeting battleship. Duro banked hard starboard and was gaining speed on the last fleeing Crozin battleship. For him, failure was not an option. He pushed the rickety war-torn ship to its limits and in a last-ditch effort, fired a long-distance hyperbaric shock wave.

Sensors alerted Victis that a Crozin battleship was spiraling towards Palatu, forcing him to re-direct his attention from Duro's pursuit to the imminent annihilation of life on Palatu.

Duro transmitted, *"Do not fire on the descending battleship, Atue's on board."*

Victis cancelled the destruct sequence, holding his breath as he watched the spiraling battleship disappear into Palatu's atmosphere. No sooner had he cancelled the order, Victis was furious that he'd listened to Duro. He should have disintegrated the Crozins' ship while it was still in orbit.

Duro and Atue's defiance was reprehensible. He'd ordered them to destroy the flank ships. Their insubordination allowed one Crozin ship to escape, and the fools crashed the other one into Palatu. Most likely, half the planet would be decimated, and the other half desolate. Sickened and outraged, he would be lucky to save a handful of Quizans. This was a catastrophe changing everything: the war, his plans, and the Trekachaws' future. Victis transmitted, "Duro, update the status of the Crozin ship?"

"In pursuit, gaining on it."

"Negative, stand down. Return immediately!"

The new Trekachaws were brazen; he could not trust them to obey orders. Until he got control of the situation, it was best to rein them in. Most of the Viceroys on the Fidus Achates Counsel were ambiguous regarding the merge of a Ryquat and Quizan. However, a few individuals on the counsel were appalled and protested profusely, insisting the merge was an immoral act with devastating consequences. Victis had one chance to prove their worthiness, loyalty, and superiority. Foolishly blinded by their charisma and physical superiority, he'd failed miserably. There was no reasonable justification for the loss of raw materials or the negligent destruction of the planet. To advocate saving the other Trekachaws, Victis had no other choice than to sterilize Duro and Atue. If the rest rebelled, he would be forced to sterilize them all.

Victis leaned back in his chair and closed his eyes visualizing the horrific impact and shock wave of the spiraling battleship as it crashed into Palatu. Ground zero... A crater six miles deep with a radius of three hundred miles, destroying everything in its path. The kinetic energy and solar radiation could easily spread over half of the planet, causing the climate to radically change. Nauseated by his thoughts, Victis sat quietly at the helm waiting for the impact. Poor judgment on his part resulted in an indiscriminate genocide. Soon the dark mushroom could be seen for all to view on the bridge monitor. And so, it began...

The atmosphere bulged from an immense billowing doom rising from the annihilation of Palatu.

Thick, swirling, red clouds cascaded from the black hull, revealing an unscathed Crozin battleship. Against all odds, Atue had navigated the battleship out of an impossible spiral descent. Victis felt a wave of relief and then jumped out of his chair shouting, *"Unbelievable, he did it!"*

The bridge came alive with cheers and hoorahs. Victis felt dizzy and his body was shaking, then the bridge seemed to darken, and voices sounded far away. He sat down trying to calm himself and concentrated on slowing his breathing. Before he spoke, Victis took a deep breath, "Duro, Atue, rendezvous and dock."

"Transmission received, confirm."

In flawless tandem they flew a victory lap with their trophies over Palatu. Assuming they were heroes, the ace pilots locked their Crozin battleships side-by-side with the Ryquat ship. The Umdul crew watched the show, then ascended, paralleling the Ryquat battleship. Cpt. Pify transmitted, "Permission, lock-in Captain."

Victis switched monitor screens and spoke face-to-face with his faithful comrade, "Welcome aboard."

He should've felt like celebrating. But, he did not. They were lucky this time; he could not allow a next time. Victis pointed at a crewman, "You, locate Trekachaws Phera, Deneb, Roon and Pax. Have them report to the bridge."

Atue, Vious, Vopar and Duro swaggered across the gangplank onto the Ryquat ship. On the way to the bridge, they almost collided with several Umduls and crewmen in their path. Cpt. Pify waddled behind them as fast as his short legs could go, yelling, "*Einstein, savior too blind?*"

Atue blatantly ignored him and continued to walk.

Cpt. Pify shouted, "*Einstein no halt, forthright refusal ricochet hereafter.*"

Atue spun around, "Do not address me as Einstein. My name is Atue."

Cpt. Pify pretended to quiver in his boots and then saluted with an equally rude response, "*Insolent Einstein disappoint. Divine Atue Trekachaw, lick my toes Prig.*"

Atue's stripes dulled to yellow and he bowed, "I apologize for my insolence."

After a brief tense silence, Cpt. Pify shrugged it off, "Acceptable regret. Curious, metamorphosis?"

Knowing his question would take much longer to answer than the short walk to the bridge would allow, Atue suggested they meet up later.

TO HELP CLEAR HIS HEAD, Victis paced the bridge until everyone arrived. Since nothing had gone according to their plans, it was necessary to close ranks and make new ones. Upon their arrival, he promptly escorted the group into his office and sharply told everyone to take a seat at the oval table. Azha was both excited and nervous to see if he recognized Phera after her merge with Ryquat Tara. She was sitting alone across the room. In his rush to sit next to her, Azha stubbed his big toe on a side table and had to hop the rest of the way. As he pulled out a chair, Roon jerked the chair out on the other side of Phera, sat down and whispered something in her ear. If that wasn't strange enough, Phera sneered at him and looked away.

"Phera, what's wrong? What did Roon say?" Azha asked.

Before she could answer him, Cpt. Victis ordered silence.

"The Fidus Achates Counsel contacted me regarding Palatu and the merging of Quizans with Ryquats and Humans. I'll update you on Palatu first. An incumbent order has been entrusted upon us to establish a Fidus Achates outpost on the planet. I recommended Trekachaws for the task. I have not heard back on their decision. The outpost's jurisdiction will be a one-light year radius. In addition to Palatu, we'll be responsible for Earth. With that said, there's a strict no-contact with Humans. Of course, we know the *no-contact order* is impossible, considering our circumstances. Anyone who disagrees with me, excuse yourself from this meeting with no consequences."

Heads turned looking at one another curious to see if anyone was going to leave.

"No one? Then let's continue. The Quizans will be protected at all costs and there shall be no further mining on Palatu. The existing mined materials will be transported by the Gystfin cargo ship Azha confiscated. Presently, that ship is orbiting Europa. Without Palatu's raw materials, there's talk Zaurak will be forced to succumb or destroyed by the Crozins. The two seized Crozin battleships will remain in Palatu's orbit. Captain Pify is in command until my return. Agreed?"

Captain Pify nodded his head in approval.

"Depending on what the Crozins know, we could be in a race with them to Europa. Most likely, Crozin battleships will return sometime soon to secure the raw materials and seek revenge. With that said, I have some good news. The Crozins need the raw materials as much as we do, and our alliances assured me they'll do everything in their power to keep the Crozins occupied on the front.

Next, the merging situation. To my surprise, they've approved Ryquat/Quizan merges to increase the Trekachaw species. Right now, that does not help us. Azha and I will return to Palatu in search of Quizan volunteers willing to merge with Humans. Once we've secured the cargo ship, we'll visit Earth to recruit Human volunteers. That's all for now. I'll take questions in order, starting with Cpt. Pify."

"Entertain Umdul Trekachaws? My, my, wouldn't that be something?"

Azha raised his hand alleging he knew the answer to Cpt. Pify's question. Victis gave him the go ahead.

"Before I say anything to offend you, I mean no disrespect. Long ago, Quizans made an oath never to merge with any species other than Humans. The Ryquat merges were out of desperation, and the Gystfin merges were from hate and vengeance. If given a choice, they'll merge with Humans. I believed in that oath with such resolve that I almost died trying to find Earth. Since then, I believe Ryquats have proven to be worthy. Quizans have no history or understanding of the Umdul species. Based on that, I doubt if you'll find anyone willing to merge."

Captain Pify puckered his lips and puffed-out air, "This, I accept. Can earn respect we find in time?"

Next around the table, Pax requested confirmation regarding his assignment as Chief Medical Officer.

"Good question. On ship, unless you're replaced with an equally qualified M.O. If you're thinking about a Human M.O., it's up to the Quizan to choose whomever they please. Plus, you would be responsible for making sure the Human Trekachaw is proficient."

Duro let out a bogus cough in protest. Victis was livid, but he kept his anger in check.

"Do you have something to say?" Victis asked.

"I'm staying on ship," demanded Duro.

Victis could feel his temper boil, so he took a moment to think about his next words. Atue and Duro were confrontational and defiant. They disobeyed his orders to destroy the Crozin flank ship, *and now this.* Victis touched his arm under the table to activate the laser to kill Duro, then rose from his chair.

"Have you forgotten who's Captain of this ship? I will say this only once, follow my orders and keep your mouth shut."

Victis glanced across the table at Atue, daring him to say anything in support of Duro. Atue spoke up in his own defense, "Captain I do not listen to Duro. I am loyal to you, I respect you and will follow your orders."

Duro sunk in his chair. "Captain, please accept my apology. I will not cause any more problems."

Victis scowled at Deneb, daring her to defy him, *"Question?"*

Deneb fired back, "No Sir."

In unison Vopar and Vious spoke, "No Sir."

Victis sat down and pointed to Azha, "Let's continue."

"Will I be going to Europa?" Azha asked.

"Yes," replied Victis.

"What is my assignment?"

"Advisor in the selection of suitable Humans and finding the best recruitment locations."

Deneb, Phera and Roon snickered, making light of his assignment. Azha's stripes flared purple and he clenched his teeth trying to restrain his wrath at their petty disrespect. Before he could stop himself, the chair he'd been sitting in was flung against the wall, shattering into kindling. Victis slammed his fists on the table and stood up, then stomped over to his desk mumbling, "Embarrassing childish imbeciles, this behavior cannot be tolerated."

Victis yanked open the desk top-drawer and grabbed a stack of papers from inside and threw them across the table onto the floor. After rambling through the drawer, he found what he was searching for. A shiny badge and a document. Victis barked at Azha, "Get over here and sign this."

Thinking he was going to die, Azha apologized for his outburst and trudged his way over to the desk. The document wasn't legible and Azha's linguistic chip did not provide him the ability to read

Ryquat. Grateful to be in one piece, he took the pen and signed it, **Azha Cole,** and handed it back to Victis. The badge lying on the desk resembled his Earth police badge. This wasn't a reprimand; this was a *promotion*. Victis picked up the badge and looked at Azha's chest.

"Uh, take the badge when I hand it to you, there's nowhere to pin it."

Not missing a beat, he placed the badge in Azha's hand, "I, Captain Victis allegiance of the Fidus Achates promote Azha to Senior Lieutenant, second in command. Azha has shown outstanding bravery and loyalty. Any disrespect or failure to follow his command will be punishable by Decretum Code 5-1."

No one dared to move or make a sound.

"Remain on board until I clarify your assignments. You're dismissed. Captain Pify and Lieutenant Azha, we have business to discuss."

Azha gripped the badge in his hand and stared at the document he had just signed. As soon as the door shut, and the room was safe to talk, Victis punched him in the arm.

"They had to stop disrespecting you. Rank is the only way to make a Ryquat listen. Between you and me, the document you signed is optional. What I need is for you to be at my side until Palatu and Earth are safe. Can I count on you?"

Victis had jeopardized everything to protect him, the Quizans, and Palatu. The least he could do in return was to promise his loyalty and support.

"I give you my word," vowed Azha.

Captain Pify belched to honor their special moment. "Embrace superb boon. Starved flying light, sapped on last leg. You too?"

Victis laughed, "I'm tired and hungry too, my friend."

Captain Pify's huge smile was dazzling. His gleaming white teeth were perfect and enchanting.

"Mutual serve, forever aye."

With a little jig, he swung the door open, skipped a few steps, then waddled out of the office. Shamelessly the old salt belted-out a jingle for all too hear, *"Umduls we do celebrate. Pluck those Crozins out of space. Can't run from yer fate, we will exterminate."*

Victis whispered to Azha, "Umduls are brilliant engineers, shrewd in combat, brave and loyal... very loyal. They are by far the quirkiest species in the Orion Belt, and my favorite."

Captain Victis looked tired. He hung on to the edge of the table and stooped awkwardly to gather up the papers he'd thrown on the floor. Showing no concern for order, he stuffed them back into the top desk drawer and flopped in his chair behind the desk. One long deep breath and then he exhaled slowly.

"Azha, please sit down. I need to discuss another matter with you."

Azha gladly sat down; he was still rattled and processing the formidable responsibilities of being second in command. Victis forced the desk drawer shut, tossed a couple of crumpled papers in the trash, then began rubbing his forehead. Apparently, it was very serious, Victis never took this long to say anything.

"What is it? Just tell me," asked Azha.

"You know paper is hard to come by and rarely used anymore, but I like the feel of it. Everything's recorded by code or tabpad."

Azha frowned, "Paper is not what you wanted to discuss."

"If we weren't friends, I wouldn't bother... well here goes. Do you know who Phera merged with? You don't have to answer that. She merged with Special Ops Tara. I was not privileged to this gossip until today."

Azha sat patiently waiting for Victis to get to the point.

"Tara and Simon are engaged and have plans to marry after this assignment. I'm prepared to devote as much as say... twenty minutes to deal with your anger or grief.

They sat staring at each other. It took a few seconds for the news to sink in, and then Azha smirked, "I did not see that coming. So that's why Phera has been acting so nasty."

Victis continued to stare at Azha, waiting for him to fall apart. Instead Azha cracked up laughing and his stripes lit up bright green. How odd. This was not the reaction Victis had anticipated. Did Azha understand what engaged and marriage meant? Victis had no idea how to respond, "Yeah, funny ha-ha. Real funny."

Azha stopped laughing just long enough to confess, "Phera's the only *Quizan or Human female* who has ever dumped me. Damn, she's dumped me twice now."

Victis relaxed, "I thought it a bit amusing, too. Glad you see it that way. What's dumped?"

The irony of his question, for whatever the reason, made Azha laugh so hard, he rolled out of his chair onto the floor. Shocked by his ridiculous behavior, Victis jumped a little in his chair and began to laugh, too. Both laughed so hard their sides hurt. He had not laughed like that since he was a young boy on Zaurak.

Twenty minutes had come and gone, and not once was Phera's name mentioned in the conversation. Victis opened the bottom desk drawer and pulled out an old flask, "Here's to love and war," then unscrewed the cap to take a swig of Coltaboone. "I take it you're not bothered by Phera's relationship with Simon."

"Nah, I have a wife on earth, it took me awhile to remember how I felt about her. Phera was my first wisp, that's what Quizans call a girlfriend. When I was a young quiey, my parents pre-arranged my bond with another Quizan. I would've challenged my parents and the village, but Phera wouldn't. For a hundred years, I secretly and foolishly lusted for her while being bonded with Rodia. I never appreciated how good Rodia was until she died. Besides, I lost my Phera when she merged with Tara. I'm relieved to have that fantasy out of my head."

"Well since we're admitting things to each other, I find Trekachaw females fascinating. When they're in my presence I have disturbing thoughts, I can't concentrate, and I embarrass myself. You must admit, Phera is mind-blowing. If I can't get control of myself, then I can't be around them. Seriously, what's wrong with me? Every time I'm around one of them, I get a boner. During briefing I won't look at them cuz I know what will happen."

"Victis, Victis, Victis, Trekachaw females could care less about your boner. The only way you're going to have sex with a female Trekachaw, is to become a Trekachaw."

"You're right, that makes sense. If that day ever happens, would you care if I had sex with Phera?"

"You have my blessing." Azha's chin dropped, "Oh shit, Deneb is bonded with Roon. Has anybody told Deneb?"

"No, I heard Deneb and Vious had sex, or whatever you call it when Trekachaws fornicate."

Azha smiled, "Good for Vious. He never bonded before the Gystfin attack and couldn't after. I bet he's one happy Trekachaw."

Lighthearted and with a lot off their chests, Azha and Victis went their separate ways.

Walking alone in the corridor Victis pondered the days' events in his head, finding it difficult to focus for very long. Exhausted, he gave up; an inviting bed was around the corner and he couldn't wait to crawl in. What did he forget? *Something important?* Whatever it was kept bugging him. His dark room made him even sleepier. Without thinking, he stripped off his clothes and laid down naked on his soft bed, feeling the cool sheets against his skin. Relaxed, he breathed in slowly, then yawned and closed his eyes.

Dammit, no one updated Choan and Belton on Palatu... that's what I forgot. For all they knew, everyone was dead and the Crozins were in orbit preparing to strike. His body was too tired to get up; it would have to wait.

sixteen

PALATU'S DESTINY

SCARED refugees poured into Cavern Village with no end in sight. Without fail, the grief-stricken Quizans told the same story. Three large Gystfins attacked their village, slaughtering everyone in their path. Thus far, they had not bothered to suck the grey-death energy from any of the bodies. The aberrant huge Gystfins were fast with wide stripes on their backs, and they could turn into energy. Belton and Choan told everyone about Myosis merging with a Gystfin and how he murdered Zith. In need of a formidable leader, the village unanimously delegated Belton to be interim King.

Choan's mission was to continue recruiting Quizans for his growing army. Because of their overwhelming respect for him, he was given the title, Papay of Soldiers. Sooner or later, Traitor Myosis and his Leaders would make a mistake. Belton and Choan would be ready to avenge the bloodshed caused by the butchers.

It was midday, and there was no word from above. If they didn't hear something from Victis or Azha by nightfall, Choan volunteered to search Palatu's orbit for shipwreck debris; Crozin or Ryquat.

Evening was approaching, their fears worsened, and hope was fading. Targus descended behind the red volcanoes and the moon's dark canopy revealed a burning sky. Falling shipwreck debris was proof they weren't alone. Rocks and spears along with twelve non-functional Neco lasers would be worthless against a Crozin invasion. Fear turned into dread.

seventeen

BON TON

"WARS DICTATE EVOLUTION"

VICTIS awoke rested, confident, and hungry. Enjoying a hot steamy shower and a clean uniform made him feel like a new Ryquat. Conversely, Azha endured a long, restless night. The news of Phera bothered him more than he wanted to admit. He grieved the loss of Quizan Phera and felt anger towards this new audacious Trekachaw Phera. Shaking it off, he stepped out of the Quizan quarters telling himself the past was the past.

For the crewmen, morning was the best time of the day. Odors of a hearty breakfast saturated the maze of corridors. Coffee, eggs, and bacon awaited Victis at the end of a long line. He didn't mind waiting his turn, listening to the loud, cheerful conversations coming from the jam-packed galley of hungry Ryquats was entertaining. Azha sat with Victis, listening to the boastful tales of yesterday's victory. He'd forgotten how long it took to eat. What a waste of time when he could be checking on Palatu's status. Victis sipped the last drop of coffee, then nonchalantly sat his cup down on the table. With breakfast finally finished, they were on their way.

Azha turned into energy and flew though the ship's hull. As always, Victis took forever to liquefy his Vexy spacesuit. Since he had no other choice, Azha passed the time watching a pebble float across the hull towards the misty, red planet. She was beautiful, as if suspended in space and framed by tiny, sparkling stars. Earth was beautiful too, though very different from Palatu. Cole's stubborn presence made it clear how much he missed Ginger, his mom, his friends, and everything about life on Earth. Cole was naïve to think he would be accepted on Earth now that his was a Trekachaw. Everyone he loved would see him as a ghastly, alien monster. The mission to Europa would be Cole's chance to contact his family and convince Ginger to merge.

Side by side, they flew over Palatu's silver ocean and soared above the red-hot volcanoes. In the distance, they saw Cavern Village nestled inside the lush, tropical forest. Now was a good time for Azha to ask permission, "I was hoping you'd consider recruiting my Human mother and wife?"

Victis didn't seem at all surprised, "Of course, if my first wife and mother were alive, I'd recruit them, too. With that said, it's not up to me. You need to remember it's your family's and the Quizans' decisions."

Azha didn't have a chance to agree. The cheers and hoorahs coming from the swarming myriad of Quizans and Soldiers greeting them were deafening. Cavern Village had practically tripled in size overnight. New cupola pods were springing up everywhere and every cavern was occupied.

Belton and Choan ran to the center of the courtyard, "You did it! We saw ships burning in the sky and thought you were dead when we didn't hear from you. How'd you do it? Come, we want to hear every detail."

Azha had never seen either Belton or Choan so cheerful. There was no way he was going to tell them they'd won the battle yesterday. Apparently Victis wasn't going to reveal that tidbit of information either. Instead, Victis directed his attention to the cheering Quizans.

"Yea, yea, the Crozins are dead. You're all welcome, now go home. All right, Belton, Azha, and Choan, let's continue our conversation inside the Hall."

Yep, same old Victis.

BELTON AND CHOAN CHASED EACH other across the dirt path in a tug-of-war until they reached the doorway where the two goofs refused to slow down and crashed into each other. Evidently unaffected, they scrambled to their feet, pushing and shoving each other to the other side of the cavern. Wide-eyed and anxious to hear *all about* the glorious battle, they briskly sat down on a low ledge.

Victis kept the details short and sweet. To skirt anymore questions, Victis changed the subject, asking why there were so many refugees. Belton's mood changed.

"Quizans are saying Traitor Myosis and his Leaders are killing everyone."

"Do you believe this to be true, or are they rumors created by frightened Quizans?" Victis asked.

"I believe them," Belton assured. "I've seen them a couple of times myself. They're in an encampment with normal Gystfins just beyond the volcanic ridge. We considered attacking them but thought it best to wait until we heard from you."

Choan's stripes flashed bright purple and his yellow eyes narrowed into thin slits, "I will raid their camp with my soldiers, now that we know the Crozins are gone."

"You're right. All of them need to be eliminated before they have a chance to escape Palatu, but not by you. I need you as an acting Captain on one of the two captured Crozin battleships in orbit."

Choan demanded that he should remain on Palatu with his soldiers.

Victis warned, "Need I remind you that you're half-Ryquat and a crewman of my ship? Your place is where I assign you."

Choan looked as if Victis had slapped him in the face, and his stripes faded from purple to orange.

Victis rolled his head sideways to relieve his stiff, achy neck. "Let's start over. Can Bruce engage a battleship?"

"Yes," Choan said in confidence.

"I hand-picked you from hundreds of special ops and promoted you to Sergeant because you were the best. And now to Captain of your own battleship because I still believe in you and in our trust for one another. Your ship is armed with a sterilization laser. Why endanger Quizan soldiers, unless it's necessary? Start thinking Ryquat if you want Palatu to survive."

Victis was right. Nonetheless, at heart Choan wished he could decline the offer and remain on Palatu with his soldiers. But if Palatu were to survive, he needed to think like Bruce, not Choan. In hindsight, Victis was a respected Captain who'd earned the reputation of being a cunning war hero even during grisly battles against the galaxy's most ruthless enemies. Anyone who served under him praised his resilience, honesty, and fairness.

"Forgive my insolence. I am grateful for the opportunity and your trust."

Victis scooted back on the ledge and leaned against the cavern rock wall before he continued.

"I named the two Crozin battleships, *Luxon* and *Paratus*. Choan, your ship is Luxon, with Duro second in-command. Phera is captain of Paratus, with Vopar second-in-command. Belton, you Deneb, and Vious will remain on Palatu. Azha, Pax, Roon and Atue will accompany me on my battleship to Europa. Once the cargo ship has been secured, Azha and I will fly the shuttle to Earth and recruit one-hundred Humans for Quizan merges. Right now, we need to recruit sixty male and forty female Quizans."

Choan and Belton were confident recruiting a hundred Quizans would be easy, seeing that most of the soldiers had already volunteered to merge.

Curious, Belton asked, "Why recruit Humans and not more Ryquats?"

Victis was tired of Ryquat defiance, but he felt the question deserved an answer.

"Ryquats are prejudiced. Humans have not been tainted by alien xenophobia. Plus, where would I get that many Ryquats?"

Azha moved his lips silently in a feeble attempt to repeat the word, *xenophobia.*

"What does xenophobia mean?"

With a flip of his hands, Victis responded, "This proves my point, Humans are the best candidates. Xenophobia means the *fear and hatred of another species.* Humans have no proof of aliens; they only hate and fear one another. Ryquats are far more advanced than Humans, but we're burdened with an unwavering hatred of many species."

Choan caught himself shaking his head up and down in full agreement with Victis' analogy. His merge with Bruce had created a disturbing rift between his two souls.

The meeting ended as abruptly as it began. Belton exited the Hall and asked the first couple of soldiers outside to notify the village of an urgent gathering. Waiting in the courtyard gave Victis the opportunity to appreciate the wreath of towering trees that encompassed the primitive village. He watched as the trees grew heavy with Quizans. When the trees could bear no more, the timid creatures stood atop their caves and swarmed the crowded courtyard far beyond the flat mesa. King Belton raised his arms, and all were silent.

"Heed Azha's words, follow his wisdom, and do not fear his allies."

Looking up towards the red sky, Azha summoned, "Our protector, *Victis of Ryquat* needs our help. I call upon forty brave females and sixty brave males to join us on our journey to Earth."

Clusters of Quizans perched in the trees, roared in unison with the masses on the ground. Soldiers turned into green energy and darted wildly about on the ground in a race with those scurrying down from the trees. How extraordinary; the once-scared species were now fearless and determined to be first in line to begin the epic journey. Victis was thankful his Vexy suit concealed his emotions. Tears would have shown weakness, and that he could not afford.

Suddenly, three energy lights streaked through the trees and spiraled into the courtyard. One of them morphed into a Gystfin just before crashing on top of Victis. Traitor Myosis stabbed his lethal claws into Victis's shoulder and jerked him off the ground into the air. Stunned, Azha watched in horror... a split second longer than forgivable.

High above them, Myosis screeched an eerie death cry. He flipped the limp body mid-air to bury his long fangs into Victis's back and slash the impervious Vexy suit, exposing Victis's unprotected flesh to Palatu's toxic atmosphere. Azha streaked towards the Beast to save Victis, but discovered Myosis was incredibly fast, faster than he was. He watched the ghastly attack as if everything was in slow motion. It was difficult to see what the Beast was doing until a piece of Victis's bloody spine hung outside the shredded suit. Myosis was chewing Victis in half as he spiraled in the air. Azha sped towards them and was almost within reach, but Myosis jetted straight up with Victis between his jaws. The Beast waited for Azha to get close for the sole purpose of provoking the almighty Trekachaw. Azha had underestimated Myosis's cunningness and his capabilities. Myosis and the Leaders streaked towards Azha, then flashed into a blinding energy and disappeared into the thick trees. Victis fell from the sky giving Azha seconds to break his fall. Azha screamed for help, *"Belton! Find a Quizan to merge with Victis! Anyone! Or he won't survive!"*

Azha cradled Victis's severed spine against his body in a feeble attempt not to cause further damage. His friend was difficult to look at; Myosis had chewed him almost in half. The only thing holding Victis together was a shredded piece of his Vexy suit. Terrified of losing him, Azha ran towards Cavern Hall leaving a trail of blood and severed chunks of tissue strewn across the ground. Unable to control his shaking, Azha stopped for a moment, questioning everything. He needed to accept that Victis was dead. Forcing himself to look, he could see the Vexy-suit was soaked with blood and shredded even worse than he'd thought. It was time to let go; he walked inside the cavern and carefully laid his friend on the ground. Azha tried to brush off the dirt stuck to Victis's severed spine and gave up. *Victis did not show any signs of life.*

Belton ran stumbling into the hall, "Zygo will merge. He's old and wise, perfect for Victis."

"Zygo merge now!" Screaming in desperation, Azha could feel his friend growing cold. He peeled off the head of the Vexy suit exposing

a ghostly face. Zygo turned into silver energy and disappeared into the top of Victis's head. Was it too late? Not a spark of light, not even a soft glow. He sat staring into his friend's hollow eyes, waiting for a sign. How strange his expression; acceptance was his last emotion? Azha's stripes faded to an ashy tan and he cried.

Belton and Choan lit up the walls with their raging purple stripes. "I will rip their hearts out!" roared Choan.

They streaked out of the hall in pursuit of Traitor Myosis and the two Leaders.

Azha's mind shut down and his body felt numb. It was as if he was looking at Victis through someone else's eyes. Powerless, he searched for answers from within. There had to be something. Victis would've never given up on him. Then it dawned on him, the Targus sun. Why had he not thought of that already. Azha carefully stood up with Victis cradled in his arms and headed for the nearest mesa. Along the way, he realized another chunk of bone or flesh had fallen onto the dirt. If he were to bend over and pick it up, more would fall. From there on, he'd slow down and be extra careful to support the dangling spine and ribs. Azha's thoughts were terrifying. If Victis died, no one would survive.

THE CROWD RESPECTFULLY PARTED AS Azha made his way towards the sunny mesa. Many circled above in energy as a gesture of sorrow and kindness. Slowly and so very gently, he laid Victis's lifeless body onto the smooth surface. With the utmost care, he removed what was left of the Vexy suit, allowing the warm sun to shine upon his naked friend. How frail Victis looked, so disfigured from the savage attack. Azha waited. Surely, Cole appeared dead after his merge in the old wine cellar. Even the slightest spark was enough to ignite a new life, a new Trekachaw. Azha looked away. Too much time had passed. How was he going to survive without Victis? Why would he want to survive without his friend?

A Quizan shouted, *"Look! A flicker, right here."*

Azha inspected every inch of Victis looking for a sign. The slightest light would be hope, something, anything. *There was nothing.*

"I don't see anything. If you see it again, show me."

The little Quizan giggled pointing at Victis's eye, "See, there it is."

Azha stooped over, casting a shadow across Victis. He stared, afraid to blink. *There it was, a tiny, silver spark deep within a vacant eye. A new life emerging from death's grip.*

A brilliant light exploded, knocking Azha backwards. Silver fire burned Victis's fingers and toes, spreading up his arms and legs. The inferno devoured his torso to his head, then danced in his eyes before bursting into flames. Victis the Ryquat was gone. Azha had never watched the birth of a Trekachaw before, but he remembered how his arms and legs faded away, leaving a silver hue in their place and then everything around him disappeared. Victis would be confused and disoriented, but very much alive. *His best friend in the universe was alive.*

Victis the Trekachaw laid motionless on the mesa. He searched the area with his eyes trying to grasp on to anything recognizable. Everything was a blur, and he could not remember how he got there.

"Is that you? Why am I lying down?" Victis asked Azha.

"Yes, it's me. Let me help you sit up. Do you remember what happened to you?"

Victis rubbed his eyes and squinted at the crowd of Quizans staring back at him.

"No, what happened?"

"Traitor Myosis attacked you and bit through your Vexy. I thought for sure you were dead. But an old Quizan named Zygo merged with you."

Victis's eyes opened wide, "I'm what, a Trekachaw?"

Azha chuckled, "Yes you are. Check yourself out."

Victis raised his head to look at his long, muscular legs with brilliant, orange stripes. He flexed his arms and held his hands out in front of his face, then slowly closed his fingers, making a fist.

"Damn, I'm really a Trekachaw. I feel... big, strong, powerful. Is that how you felt?"

"Yes, but that's nothing. Wait until you fly or turn into energy. I didn't want to rub it in, but everything is so much better."

Victis rolled onto his side feeling awkward and clumsy. When he tried to stand up, his legs wobbled out of control. Azha reached out to steady his friend and couldn't stop smiling.

ONCE AGAIN, MYOSIS ESCAPED INTO thin air, leaving Choan and Belton empty-handed. Upon their return, they noticed an unusually large gathering of Quizans around a mesa. What they discovered was anything but dismal. Victis wasn't dead; he was a Trekachaw getting his first taste of a new life. Belton high-stepped it over the Quizans' heads to the mesa, while Choan picked up and hugged every Quizan within arm's length.

Victis closed his eyes thinking about the countless times he'd tried to imagine what it would feel like to be a Trekachaw. Never would he have imagined this.

Choan and Belton were glowing green, and heckling, "Captain get up, turn into energy and fly."

He might as well. They weren't going stop until he tried. Victis turned to pure energy for a moment, then morphed back into body form. That was easy enough. Telling himself to float up, he hovered above the mesa, then flew to a tree limb, landing feet-first with perfect balance. After that, he couldn't wait to fly in space, in energy, what the hell, through anything or anywhere he wanted. Oh, yeah and sex. Yep, sex with Phera.

Azha was getting such a big kick out of watching Victis discover his new powers, he'd forgotten about the all-important mission and their brush with Armageddon. As always, pessimistic Choan was the first one to remind them.

"Probably already guessed Traitor Myosis and the Leaders escaped us. Shouldn't we get going?" Choan grumbled.

Reminded of the insurmountable burdens before them, and that time was growing shorter by the minute, Victis, Choan, and Azha bid their farewells to King Belton and streaked out of sight.

Free from the constraints of his Vexy suite, Victis soared in space. He clearly remembered his Ryquat life and likewise the tiniest detail of Zygo's two-hundred and ninety-seven years. More than ever, he was convinced the Fidus Achates Counsel would neither understand nor support what he had done or was about to do. United, the trio flew onto the bridge, landing in tandem. They were formidable adversaries and impressive to behold by any standards. Fate had brought Victis and Azha together, but this new life made them brothers. Together, they would win the war and find a new planet for their kindred Trekachaws.

PER CAPTAIN VICTIS'S ORDERS, FORTY females and sixty males buzzed in energy outside the battleship. To expedite their initiation, Pax was given permission to escort the group through the ship to their new home. After a quick presentation of the accommodations, the brave Quizans were left alone to settle in for the trek to Earth.

Victis's plan was finally in motion. He called for an emergency briefing with the Trekachaws and several Ryquat bridge officers to clarify changes, assignments, and time lines.

"If you do not recognize me, I am Captain Victis. So far, our journey has challenged all of us one way or the other. Together I am confident that we will prevail no matter what storm comes our way. If you haven't been counting, presently there are eleven Trekachaws. Soon, Earth will provide one hundred new Trekachaws and the promise of a viable future for all of us."

Phera raised her hand, "Who merged with you?"

"Zygo chose me. He was at the end of his time, and I was dying from injuries. I was very fortunate to have merged with such an extraordinary Quizan to guide me."

The Trekachaws were impressed. Zygo was admired and highly respected for his wisdom.

"Hold any more questions. We have a lot to cover. I promoted Choan to Captain, with Duro second in command. Their Crozin battleship is Ship #1, the Luxon. Phera is Captain on the other Crozin battleship with Vopar. Her ship is Paratus, Ship #2. Both battleships will remain in orbit around Palatu. Deneb, you and Vious will assist Belton at Cavern Village. Just so everyone knows, Belton was appointed King by the Quizans. Captain Pify is in command while I'm gone." *Victis pointed at the old, salty Captain standing at the back of the room.*

"Pax, Roon, Atue, and Azha will be on my ship en route to Europa. Let's go, we have a mission to complete."

This time there were no petty remarks or snide comments. The Trekachaws were adjusting to their new lives and roles that suited them best.

Captain Victis commanded, *"Akio, set a trajectory course for Europa."* The Battleship hummed. *"Check, solar thrusters' power-on-line,"* and the sleeping giant awoke. *"Commence,"* and excitement filled the bridge. A slight vibration... then the mighty battleship pitched forward, and in a flash of light was gone.

eighteen

DE NOVO

"IN THE END, A MEANINGLESS LIFE IS WORSE THAN DEATH."

AN estimated four days to Europa gave Victis the opportunity to spend time with Azha. He was antsy to share the wealth of information gained by his merge with Zygo, and he had questions about his new body. Eating rituals and sleeping long hours were no longer necessary. Even better, bathing was moot; a quick change into energy purified his body. If he knew then what he knew now, he would've taken Choan's offer. Even so, Zygo was a much better match for his destiny in life. For the first time in a very long time, he felt at ease sitting behind the old wooden desk inside the captains' office. He was at peace watching the asteroids and colorful gases rush pass the long port windows. Being in one place for too long was boring and being bored always seemed to create a maddening restlessness. As always, the best remedy was the next adventure. Today was a good day to reflect, especially on those things he could not control. Like the Fidus Achates Counsel, who should be praising his prominence, thus hailing him a hero.

Victis visualized himself standing before the counsel receiving the Gold Medallion at the renowned Alvorte Theater. Hundreds of peers and admirers were clapping wildly and cheering him on.

Azha barged into the office, interrupting his dreams of grandeur. Victis appeared rattled, as if he were embarrassed and irritated at the same time.

"Why do you look guilty? Are you thinking about Phera?" Azha asked.

Victis felt the need to defend himself against Azha's petty sarcasm, but refused to give him the satisfaction of knowing he was irritated. Instead, he ignored him, wishing that Phera was the distraction. In the real world, the Fidus Achates Counsel would most likely strip him of his rank and battleship, then court martial him for disobeying numerous fundamental laws. Like it or not, there was nothing he could do about it now.

"Where've you been, Azha? You're such an asshole," snapped Victis.

"Where have I been? And why am I the asshole? You need to be more creative if you're going to call me names. Check yourself. Neither one of us has an asshole anymore. And I came here on my own accord to find out if you're okay."

Victis's stripes had been gradually turning red since the minute Azha walked into his office.

"Silence! I'm the Captain of this ship. You'll show me respect!"

The office was now glowing purple from the two pissed-off, yellow-eyed Trekachaws. Without missing a beat, Azha spit-out, *"Screw you, Captain!"*

They locked eyes, staring at each other, as menacing as they could muster.

"Damn it Azha, enough is enough. Seriously, you can't talk to me that way in front of my crew."

Azha smiled and held up his middle finger. "There's no crew in here."

Since Victis had no idea what the middle finger represented, he figured it had to be silly Human salute.

"Why are you pointing your middle finger at me?"

Azha roared with laughter, "Geez, never mind. On Earth, it's a way to express one's anger. I thought you'd seen the middle finger thing watching Earth movies or TV. Just forget it, it doesn't matter. Since I'm here, do you want to talk, or should I leave?"

Indeed, he was dying to tell Azha all about Zygo's centuries of knowledge and Azha couldn't wait to hear the priceless secrets held by the wise, old Quizan.

"I shall start from the beginning. Wait...well, I'll start in a minute. Let's move to the table, my chair is too small. Remind me to requisition adequate chairs for the Trekachaws."

After a roundabout of musical chairs, Victis and Azha settled on those with no arms.

Victis started over, "Quizans are one of the original two-hundred and forty-three species to occupy the fifty-eight documented Universes within the Vastuscaelus. We were indigenous to a planet called Pala, located within another universe. Billions of years ago, Quizans were not as physically evolved. Like Humans, we required food, water, and shelter. Quizans explored the universes millions of years before Ryquats or Humans were capable of building fires. They were an advanced, compassionate species who engineered spaceships to rescue endangered life on compromised planets. Planet Pala orbited around a pair of White Dwarf Suns, providing the perfect environment for the Quizans. Tragically, a sudden shift in gravity pulled the two suns together, triggering the birth of a Super-nova. Disintegration of the planet was imminent, allowing very little time for the Quizans to escape. Pandemonium ensued, driven by the quest for individual survival. Sadly, only a small number of scientists, engineers and physicians were rescued on the first EXP-Science Spaceships. They barely escaped Pala's orbit before the Supernova left a path of destruction consuming their entire solar system that could be seen in space for eons. What saved our species were the hundreds of Quizans on spaceships scattered throughout the universes on missions. Eventually, the ships rendezvoused in search of a habitable planet. Perseverance prevailed. A perfect planet was discovered, providing the Quizans a new beginning. Our ancestors named this planet "*Palaone*." Today, Palaone is called Earth, *your Earth*. Back then, Earth was young and unstable. Active volcanos covered large areas of the surface, providing the Quizans with a perfect, carbon-dioxide-rich atmosphere. Over time, the Quizans became allies with a species living on a neighboring planet called Mars. That species was my ancestors, the *Ryquats*. During that period, Mars was a warm planet with oceans of water and rich in oxygen. The Quizans flourished on Palaone for millions of years, until the Crozins invaded Mars in their quest to destroy the Ryquats. The Ryquats had evolved into a thriving industrial species who made their presence known across the Milky Way Galaxy. Several aliens within the galaxy accused the Ryquats of aggressively entering and violating sacred space without permission. Instead of pleading ignorance or asking for a caucus to negotiate, the arrogant Ryquats vowed they would travel wherever and whenever they pleased. Their defiance split the Milky Way Galaxy and three neighboring galaxies into bloody territorial disputes. The boundaries have never been resolved and the war is ongoing.

One such enemy is the Crozins. They retaliated by disintegrating two of the four small moons that orbited Mars, thus causing a slight shift in all the planets orbiting the sun. Mars slowly lost her rich, oxygenated atmosphere, turning her into the red planet that you see today. Palaone gradually cooled and transformed into today's Earth.

It took centuries for the Ryquats to leave their dying planet and relocate to their new home, Zaurak. All the while, relentless Crozins continued to randomly attack the Ryquats as they fled Mars. One of the last Ryquat passenger cargo ships en route to Zaurak was attacked by a Crozin battleship, causing them to crash onto the harsh surface of Earth. A futile attempt to locate the lost ship was unsuccessful; therefore, she was classified as a *casualty of war.* Most of the Ryquats survived the crash on Palaone. The survivors found the planet to be hostile with a thin, oxygenated atmosphere and a blistering hot surface compared to their once-beautiful Mars. The stranded Ryquats prayed for months that a rescue ship would find them, to no avail. Years later, hope was gone, along with their depleted resources and food supplies. Sympathetic Quizans befriended the tattered Ryquats and willingly nurtured them during their acclimation on Earth. For decades, the Quizans provided them with an abundant source of giant beaver meat, vegetation, and salvaged containers filled with fresh water.

In time, the Ryquats adapted to the hostile environment enough to travel north where they found lush jungles and cooler temperatures. Regrettably, to survive they were forced to leave their beloved Quizans' habitat near the equator. Though apart, their admiration and loyalty were unwavering for each other. The Quizans and Ryquats often met at the edge of their neighboring climates to rejoice and exchange stories. Over thousands of years, planet

Palaone continued to cool into an Ice Age. The Quizans could no longer survive in the frigid terrain and were dying alongside the Teratorn, Wooly Mammoth, and the Sabre-toothed Cats. Preparing for the worst, they docked their spaceships inside deep craters and caves adjacent to active volcanoes. Ironically, the Ryquats were now thriving in the oxygen-rich atmosphere and had adapted to the colder climate while the Quizans grew weaker with each passing year. Eventually, they were unable to venture outside the warmth provided by the lava caves. Devoted Ryquats supplied them with food and essentials until the ice age should have passed. Years turned into decades and decades turned into centuries. Even though Palaone only grew colder, the Ryquats refused to abandon their frail, Quizan friends. Eventually, the Quizans were forced yet again to search for another planet. The Ryquats bid their sad farewells to the Quizans, promising that someday they would meet again.

A few idealist Ryquats refused to teach history or technology to their youth. This preposterous thinking by these misguided few was forced upon the others to preserve a transparent, mundane society. As a species, they severely digressed during the first thousand years. By the time the Zaurak Ryquats discovered them, they were considered an inferior species. Rather than destroying the savage Ryquats, the Council renamed them Humans. Other than random visits, they've been left to evolve at their own pace without interference. But now let's go back to the Quizans.

During the Quizans' long trek while searching for another habitable planet, a Quizan bio-chemist and a physician continued to work on a theory discovered while on Palaone. They perfected a process to bind, or what we call *merging*, using an extinct Phosphorus-Urodela Amphibian's DNA and a Quizan's DNA. These flying colorful amphibians we called Phobias, could change their body stripes into brilliant colors and absorb the sun's energy for nutrition. The merge was instant, and the results were amazing, making it possible to leave their ships and absorb solar energy. Without these advantages, the Quizans would never have survived the long, brutal journey to the new world.

Every Quizan physiology advantage that you see today is owed to those two scientists who miraculously mutated the Metamorphose Gene. The bio-chemist and physician are ancient ancestors of Zygo and you.

Their new planet, Palatu, and the Targus sun provided them with the perfect environmental conditions. Once settled, their Phobia DNA compelled them to remain close to home and bask in the sun. Quizan life was simple, and they blissfully multiplied, unfettered, until the Gystfins invaded Palatu. We being a passive species were unable to defend ourselves against the ruthless Beasts. As you well know, it didn't take long before the Gystfins discovered the addicting, euphoric high, as well as an incredible physical advantage, from our grey-death energy.

Zygo pleaded with King Myosis to allow Quizans the option of merging with Humans on Earth. He was certain the merge would create an invincible Quizan capable of defeating the Gystfins. Determined to prove his theory, Zygo traveled halfway to Earth only to discover that his will was much stronger than his body. He returned emaciated, discouraged, and far too old to attempt the trek again. Despite King Myosis forbidding a merge with any species, *especially a Human*, Zygo never gave up. He convinced several Quizans that a Human merge was their only chance for survival. Azha, you believed in me and were the only one brave enough to risk your own life. Before I forget to say it, thank you."

Azha was humbled by Zygo's words.

"While you were on Earth, the Gystfins continued to slaughter whole villages. Cavern Village was never directly attacked, not even by the bad Ryquat. Brazenly confident, King Myosis routinely ventured out into the dangerous woods for hours. I followed him one time to a large cave located on the other side of the forest. To my surprise, a Gystfin, the bad Ryquat, and an unfamiliar species *they called Crozin*, were waiting for him. It was obvious to me they'd met many times before. Scared to death, I stayed and eavesdropped on their conversation. It was sickening the way they talked about us and the devious alliance King Myosis had made with our enemies. The Gystfin and Ryquat were selling raw materials extracted from Palatu to the Crozins. They were skimming off a portion of the raw materials for their own profits.

Immediately upon your return as a Trekachaw, King Myosis warned them of your Human merge and how powerful you had become. He wanted them to kill you, but they laughed and refused to take him seriously. The bad Ryquat notified the Fidus Achates Council of the new hybrid species to stop any rumors or investigations. An unknown source contacted the council reporting a very different story. I still don't know who it was that exposed the truth about the Quizans being slaughtered. The Fidus Achates Council assigned me, *Captain Victis*, to investigate the rumors and report back. I thought Palatu was going to be quick assignment, a couple of days' tops. I was wrong. What changed everything for me was seeing you."

Victis sighed and gazed out the portal window.

"One more thing. Quizan lore and ancestral heredity are passed on by a select few. We are burdened with this honor for the next five hundred years."

Azha's mind raced. It was going to take some time to digest all the information. The tapping of Victis' foot on the floor made it clear to Azha that Victis wanted a quid-pro-quo regarding information relevant to Humans.

"What I'm about to tell you, is based solely on my biased opinions. Here goes nothing. Humans can either be really good or really bad, with the majority in the middle, and all of them are naïve about the complexity of the Universe. A select few might accept us, but the majority won't. I fear we'd create panic worldwide."

Azha's perception brought up valid concerns. How were they going to recruit a hundred Humans without revealing extraterrestrial life?

"What if we search for them at night? We can remain in energy until we've located worthy Humans, then morph to see how they react," suggested Victis.

Obviously, it was not that simple. But unless Azha had a better idea, this was the plan.

"I have one question. We can't land shuttles on Earth, so how will we transport them?" Azha asked.

That was a problem Victis had not considered. "Let's brainstorm the finer details later. I'm calling this mission, *The Kigen Selection.*"

Azha was glad the discussion had ended. He was distracted by an overwhelming urge to look out the window. From there, he could see a tiny, beautiful, blue orb beckoning him to come home. Cole's persistence was disturbing; he concentrated on suppressing his Human-half. Nothing worked. The closer they got to Earth, the worse he got. Vivid memories of Ginger and his mother were confusing and causing an overwhelming sadness. Victis tapped Azha on the shoulder. "Do you have anything else to add?"

Azha closed his eyes and collected himself before turning around. "Yes, I would like to contact Ginger and my mother."

"Why, of course. They'll be our first Human volunteers," assured Victis.

THE RYQUAT BATTLESHIP DROPPED INTO Europa's orbit adjacent to the cargo ship. Victis chose Azha and Roon to accompany him on the initial inspection, while leaving Akio in charge during his absence. Azha led the way through the vast cargo ship to the bridge where he'd stood before. Eerily, it seemed like a lifetime ago. Victis was busy touching everything in sight, reminding him of a kid on Christmas morning.

"This ship is nice. It's powerful enough to transport just about anything I want, and Atue can increase its speed with a few minor adjustments," Victis mused.

Roon was honored that he had been invited by the elite duo. This was a nice distraction from Quizan Phera or *evil Tara* dumping him. After their merge, the Tara he loved was gone and Phera was not at all interested. Lonely and heartbroken, he needed someone to confide in. Since Phera dumped Azha too, Roon was certain they could talk about the gut-wrenching pain she'd caused.

Roon let out long sighs waiting for Azha to notice his despair. Clearly, he was doing everything possible to get Azha's attention, and it worked.

"Roon, is there something you'd like to talk about?"

The dam broke. Roon was talking so loudly about his break up with Phera that Victis couldn't help but overhear the drama. Of course, he was interested. And why? Because it was Phera.

Azha vigorously shook his head *NO* at Victis, indicating that now was not the time to ask Roon if it was '*okay*' to have sex with Phera.

Victis mouthed, *"Fine," and made a face.* "Let's head back to the ship; it's time to put our Kigen mission in motion."

This was the first time Victis's stripes had turned into a brilliant green. *He was very happy.*

THIRTY-TWO CREWMEN WALKED ACROSS THE battleship platform to board the cargo ship. Most of them had been reassigned to the bridge and engineering deck. Victis approved the retro-solar grid intake and telerobotic upgrade that Atue recommended to increase speed and improve the overall efficiency. This was Atue's baby. He'd make sure every upgrade was installed with exact precision, including a weapons system that any battleship would be proud to have. Someday, every inch of the massive craft would be explored, but for now essential areas would have to do.

Azha and Victis buzzed into the Quizan quarters to announce the good news. "We've arrived at Europa." A deafening, high-pitched cheer rang out.

"May I have everyone's attention," Azha asked with a grin. The room grew silent and all eyes were on Azha.

"Victis and I will fly to earth first to recruit candidates. Once we've selected qualified Humans, we'll return to the ship. Your merges will take place on Earth. But I can't stress this enough, the atmosphere is oxygen-based, so remember to remain in energy until you've entered your Human's body."

Nothing was preventing Azha from leaving the battleship, yet he dreaded even the thought of leaving. Why now? He could feel his stripes turning from orange to a pale tan. What could be so bad on Earth to make him feel this way? Pushy Victis had already turned into energy and was flickering about like a firefly. Seeing Ginger again scared him. What if she rejected him? That's probably why he felt so stressed. No more thinking about what-ifs. Shaking it off, Azha turned into energy and followed Victis through the ship's hull.

The stars were spectacular. Flying weightless in this grandeur cleared his misguided thoughts. Doubt and anxiety were for Humans, not a Trekachaw. Besides, his future was with Victis. Together, they could lead their superior species to a new, uninhabited world. He just needed to stop listening to Cole.

nineteen

EARTH VADE MECUM

EARTH was beautiful. Too bad Humans were sheltered from their ancestry and isolated in the Universe. Now that he was closer to home, he wished desperately to stay. On second thought, Cole was the one home sick. Shit, he was angry, and not letting go. He was the reason for being hesitant to leave the ship. Cole needed to calm down and not interfere. Azha flew around the equator, over Hawaii and through the walls of the old, abandoned winery into the last cellar room. Cole flared with a vengeance, forcing his Quizan soul to see haunting memories. None of them were pleasant and none of them he wanted to remember. The rock walls glowed blue from Azha fighting desperately to gain control of his emotions. A thunderous *clap* in his ear awoke him from his trance. Victis was in his face yelling, "What's wrong? Azha, are you *okay*?"

"This is where I merged with Cole."

"Doesn't look like much to brag about," mumbled Victis. "Why are we here? I say, we meet the family."

More often, than not, Victis was impossible. But, he had a way of keeping things in perspective. The cellar room flashed and once more was black as night.

Azha's old backyard should have been the best location to spy on Ginger without being detected. But Victis was being so loud that all the dogs in the neighborhood were barking.

"What the *UNKO* are those? *DAMARE BAKA YAROU*," shouted Victis

Azha grabbed Victis by the arm and pulled him behind a tree. "Geez, shut up!"

An unfamiliar, elderly man and woman were pressed up against the living room window, peering out into the backyard at them. Victis could not control his fear, and his stripes were glowing bright red. Neighbors had turned on lights and were coming outside to see what all the commotion was about. Azha squeezed Victis's arm and pointed up, "Follow me."

Victis flew in circles, frustrated, admitting how much the beastly dogs had scared him. That was just about the most ludicrous thing Azha had ever heard in his Human or Quizan life. He'd witnessed Victis fight Gystfins with no fear in his eyes. How could he be afraid of a little dog and what was *UNKO, Blah, Blah, Blah*?

"What did you yell at the dogs?" Azha asked with a smile.

"Go ahead Azha, hope you're having a good laugh. Unko is a Japanese Earth word. If you're so smart, why don't you know what it means?"

"Why didn't my linguistic chip work?" Azha asked.

Victis stopped flying in circles. "I had the Japanese dialect removed so the crewman wouldn't know when I was swearing."

"Ah, you should know the crewman already figured out your bad words."

"I'll tell you what they mean, if you keep this dog thing between us."

"Deal," Azha agreed trying not to laugh.

Unko Damare Baka Yarou means *shit, shut up, stupid asshole.* Azha practiced saying the Japanese *swear words* over and over until Victis congratulated him on getting them right. All this time wasted, and nothing accomplished. Zilch. "Now that we've got that settled, I don't know the elderly couple. Can we check my mom's house?"

"I suppose, lead the way," Victis mused.

Azha floated in first, then Victis. His mom's house was dark and quiet. They dimmed their energy into a soft glow and searched the living room. Slowly, they drifted down the hallway into his mom's bedroom. Her bed had been replaced by a hospital bed with an IV bag hanging from a pole. The drip-line led to a frail, old woman sleeping in the dark shadows. The room smelled pungent, and a faint light emitted from a monitor hooked up to a stand adjacent to the bed. Even in the dark, Azha recognized the silhouette of her face. His mom was gaunt, and her breathing was labored. It appeared she had not been able to care for herself for a very long time. He morphed into body form and gently touched her face. Victis watched from above as his friend wept in sorrow.

The cover of night turned into dawn and the birds began to sing. Their familiar sweet songs soothed Azha. His mom had moaned several times during the night, but she never opened her eyes. From down the hallway, the sounds of another bedroom door opened. Footsteps were coming closer and closer towards his mom's room. Azha turned into energy and joined Victis floating against the ceiling. Ginger entered the bedroom and began caring for his mom. Azha watched as she checked the monitor and spoke lovingly to her.

"Morning Beverly. Today will be a good day. If you can open your eyes, I'll sit you up. Wouldn't that be nice?"

Azha morphed into body form behind Ginger. Silently, he watched her while searching for the right words to say. Ginger walked over to a dresser and saw the monster's reflection in the mirror. *Breathless, she froze.* One small step at a time, she shuffled backwards towards his mom's bedside.

Azha touched his chest, "I am Cole."

Ginger fell backwards, catching herself on the edge of the bed frame. Horrified, she gasped and covered her mouth with both hands to muffle her scream.

"Don't be afraid. I was a police officer. We were going to be married, but I disappeared. You and Mom saw me in the backyard out the kitchen window, remember?"

Azha heard footsteps scampering down the hallway. Ginger looked up at Azha, then her eyes darted over to the open doorway. She lunged to grab the boy as he scurried into the room and ran to the opposite side of the bed. Her hands were shaking as she draped her worn sweater around the child in a feeble attempt to hide him from view. With a voice filled with fear she stuttered, "Please stand over there," pointing to a corner in the room.

Azha stepped backwards into the corner. "I would never hurt you or my mom."

"What did you nickname Beverly?" She asked while trying to restrain they boy from peeking out from underneath her sweater.

"Beaver, because she likes to build things," replied Azha, relieved that he knew the answer.

Ginger appeared angry, "What happened to you?"

"So much has happened. I was feeling tired and decided to check out that old, abandoned winery where the kids hang out. No one was outside, but there was someone inside. Ginger, it wasn't a someone, it was an alien from a planet called Palatu. They're called

Quizans… I'm half Quizan. My name is Azha and I merged with Cole. Now we're a species called Trekachaw. I merged because Quizans are being slaughtered by vicious aliens. Forgive me, but we're running out of time and the rest will have to wait."

All the while Ginger was listening to Azha, the small boy on her lap was fidgeting trying to find a way to escape. Victis grew restless and morphed into body form at the opposite side of the room. *Ginger shrieked,* stood up, and then fell backwards onto the bed.

"That's not cool, Victis," snapped Azha. "Sorry, Ginger."

Victis smirked at Azha, then proceeded to introduce himself, "I am a Ryquat-Trekachaw and Captain of a Battleship."

"Oh my goodness, are there anymore aliens' in the house?" Ginger asked.

"We are the only two," Azha assured.

Beverly stirred in her bed and moaned in pain, "Do I hear Cole?"

Ginger leaned over and whispered into her ear, "You're dreaming, go back to sleep."

"What's wrong with my mom? How long has she been like this?"

"Mom doesn't have long to live, she has stage four cancer and is in a lot of pain."

Azha knelt down next to the bed, "She doesn't have to die. If a Quizan merges with her, she'll be young and healthy again."

Ginger kissed his mom's forehead, "If what you say is possible, do it now before it's too late."

"I'll pick out a Quizan for you," Victis grumbled, then flashed into a ball of light as he disappeared through the wall.

The boy was approximately four years old and surprisingly unaffected by the giant Trekachaws. He wiggled off Ginger's lap and ran over to Azha before she could catch him. "Are you a spaceman?"

Azha sat down on the floor next to him, "Why yes, young man. I guess I am a spaceman."

The boy climbed up on Azha's lap and pointed towards the bed, "Are you going to save my grandma, spaceman?"

'*What did the boy say?*' Azha asked himself. "Ginger... why does the boy call my mom *Grandma?*"

Ginger crossed her legs and curtly replied, "If you are Cole, then the boy is your son... Cole Jr."

While waiting for Victis, they spoke of the past and of the future as Ginger attended to her daily routine. Cole was pleased – thrilled – that he had a son and the opportunity to spend time with him.

Early that evening, two white lights flew through the bedroom wall. One morphed into Victis, the other floated next to Azha. Cole Jr. clapped his hands together and squealed in delight. She flashed red and darted to the far corner of the room flickering about.

"Do not fear the Human quiey, he's harmless," smiled Azha.

To Ginger, Azha's words sounded beautiful, like seagulls soaring over ocean waves.

Victis snapped, "Tic-toc Azha, get on with the merge, we've lost another day."

To his credit, Victis had been patient, but that was wearing thin.

Beverly moaned in agony as she twisted and turned in her bed trying to find comfort. Victis was right, no more distractions. Azha directed his attention to the Quizan, "What's your name?"

"Zeta, I am from the Kismet Ebb Tribe," flickering from red to white.

Zygo was close to Zeta's family for most of his two hundred and ninety-seven years. She was the sixth generation and the last survivor of a legacy that held great honor and respect. Victis chose wisely for Azha's mother.

Zeta insisted that everyone leave except for Victis. Azha picked up Cole Jr. and asked Ginger to leave the room. Ginger let go of Beverly's hand and scooted off the bed with tears in her eyes. "I'm praying for you."

Watching his mommy cry, Cole Jr. began to cry, too. Azha escorted them out, then shut the bedroom door behind him. Torn between opposing souls, Azha fought Cole who was demanding a presence and growing stronger by the minute. He held back a dire urge to leave that wretched house and Earth, along with all her bad memories.

"Are you ready?" Victis asked.

Zeta flickered *Yes* and turned into silver. She drifted across the bedroom and floated above the old woman. Her light sparkled as she slowly descended into the top of the Human's head. The cold, diseased body glowed beneath the thin white sheets. Beverly's face relaxed and she appeared peaceful. A calm euphoria filled the room and her body exploded into a blinding silver light igniting a fiery ball. No matter how much he wanted to witness the miracle, he looked away.

The old woman was gone and in her place sat a beautiful young Trekachaw. She appeared afraid, then scooted to the edge of the bed and tried to stand up. But her legs buckled, and she crumpled to the floor. Ginger flung the bedroom door open and froze, awestruck by the creature staring at Azha.

"Ginger, help me. I'm scared, what is that?" Beverly pleaded.

She ran to Beverly and wrapped her arms around the alien she had once called mom.

"That's Cole. He saved you."

Cole Jr. and Azha watched Ginger help Beverly back to her bed. It looked odd that she was still pampering the much larger

Trekachaw. Nonetheless, these were the roles to which they were accustomed.

Beverly sat up with a puzzled look on her face. "I remember who I am. Well, not exactly. I remember being here and on Palatu. Cole, is that you inside Azha?"

"Yes, mom."

"I knew it. People thought I was crazy. In my heart, I knew you weren't dead. Come here and give me a hug," insisted Beverly.

Azha walked over to Cole's mom feeling himself losing control. Beverly wrapped her arms around him and whispered, "I missed you, son."

Victis was tapping his foot, "We must go. Beverly, Zeta... Find Pax, and stay with him on the ship until I return."

Azha was relieved, he wanted out of there, whereas Cole was resistant and still worried about his family.

"Ginger, will you merge with a Quizan?" Azha asked.

"Yes. I'd follow you anywhere."

Victis intervened, "Azha, we'll return for Ginger and Cole Jr. after the other merges are completed."

Zeta, Azha, and Victis, streaked through the bedroom walls, finding the seclusion of night was upon them. This was perfect, fewer prying eyes to worry about. Cole was content for the time being, allowing Azha to be in control.

Victis followed Azha to a Veterans' hospital located in La Jolla, California. Most of the staff had gone home for the evening. It was easy to elude those few who worked the night shift. Floating from room to room, they found what seemed to be an endless number of beds filled with severely wounded soldiers who were physically and mentally broken. In one of the infirmaries, they found twenty-four men and fifteen women who were unable to consent due to horrific brain injuries. Victis morphed into body form, "We'll start here. These Humans deserve another chance." Azha wholeheartedly agreed; they were first in line for Quizan approval. The mission was back on track. Victis and Azha returned to the ship and informed the Quizans of the superb candidates. Every Quizan volunteered to merge with the Human Veteran Heroes. Azha noticed a very attractive female at the back of the room. He pointed at her to step forward. She stared blankly at him for a moment, then pointed at herself. Azha smiled and nodded yes. Quickly, she made her way through the crowd to the front. She was a perfect match for Ginger.

"What is your name?" Azha asked.

"Quetzal, from Cavern Village. We knew each other before you became a Trekachaw."

Once again, memory loss plagued him. Indeed, there were still plenty of blank pages to fill. He glanced around the room looking for Victis to get approval. Damn, he must have snuck out again. He hated when Victis disappeared like that. The ship was enormous. Perturbed, Azha excused himself and left the Quizan quarters to search for him. After asking at least twenty crewmen, he located Victis inside the captains' office having a serious private conversation with Akio. Judging by their gloomy faces, whatever they were talking about had to be bad news. Apprehensive to interrupt them, Azha lightly tapped on the door and waited for an invitation. Giving a thumbs-up, Victis waved him in.

It was worse than he'd thought. Victis looked visibly disturbed. He thanked Akio for his loyalty, reminding him that if he disobeyed the order, he too would be in violation of the Fidus Achates Decree. Akio stood firm on his decision to remain on board. They shook hands, then Akio left the office. The bridge crewmen stopped what they were doing to hear the verdict. "It's a go," announced Akio.

Clapping their hands to show support, they knew something Azha did not. But whatever it was, the crew was prepared for the worst-case scenario, or the best... *either way.*

"What happened?" Azha asked.

Victis could hide neither his despair nor his disappointment.

"While we were on Earth, a Viceroy Councilman viewed several of the Trekachaws performing crew assignments on an open channel. I should have told the Trekachaws they were not cleared for duty until the Viceroys gave approval. My officers tried to cover for me, but the Council did not listen. I've been relieved of duty with instructions to terminate all missions and immediately return to Zaurak. Akio accepted a promotion as interim Captain only to give me time to complete the merges. Once the Council realizes we've disobeyed their directives, my battleship will be classified as a Brigand-Ship. The officers and crewmen will be classified as criminals and guilty of treason, punishable by death. That's not all, there's more bad news. Akio was ordered to detain the Trekachaws and transfer them to the Science Investigation Division, S.I.D. I fear they'll categorize us as an unorthodox species creating a threat to the balance of nature within the Galaxy."

"Let them try," growled Azha.

"I have more bad news. They've reinstated the *bad Ryquat,* Doug Smyth as Captain of my ship and Administrator of Palatu's Mining Operations. That's the bad news. Do want to hear the good news?"

Azha was bright purple and spitting out profanities so fast, Victis could not understand a word he was saying.

Victis continued, "The Umduls offered us sanction and will defend our mission, even if it means separating from the Fidus

Achates. I can't see the Ryquats surviving this war without the Umduls' support. Cpt. Pify, Cpt. Phera, Cpt. Choan, Vopar, and Duro will continue to orbit Palatu. Belton, Deneb, and Vious will remain on Palatu."

What bothered Azha the most was Victis's punishment. If it weren't for him, the Quizans would have been slaughtered to extinction.

"I swear Victis, this is not over. We'll finish what we started."

Victis looked defeated, but he nodded.

Determined as ever, the two Trekachaws flew to Earth with thirty-nine Quizans at their side to begin the merges.

The V.A. infirmary came alive with sparkling lights dancing in anticipation. Victis landed next to Azha to orchestrate the sequence of silver lights above the forsaken souls lying dormant on their pillows. As the lights vanished into the comatose heads, a glow encompassed them, like the eclipse of a star. Silver lights exploded with each merge until darkness revealed the creation of thirty-nine new Trekachaws.

The courageous veterans turned into energy and, in a swirl of light, flew through the hospital walls en route to the battleship. Freed from their suffering Human bodies, they landed inside the Quizan quarters grateful to begin their new lives. The remaining sixty one Quizans marveled at their magnificent metamorphosis. Now more than ever, they yearned for their own.

Time was of the utmost importance. The mission had to be on a fast-track due to the looming threat of Fidus Achates Council retribution. To complete the merges before daybreak, Azha suggested asking the wounded Veterans. All things considered, they were a natural fit and accessible. The Quizans were briefed and warned to remain in energy until they merged. The battleship buzzed with flickering lights darting everywhere in anticipation. For now, one homesick Quizan was left behind awaiting her merge with Ginger.

The light show was entertaining, bringing smiles to the crew. All at once the swarm of lights were gone, then reappeared in space on the monitor screens. Like shimmering waves of sequins, they followed the curves of the sleek black hull. Liberated from fear, the Quizans orchestrated a synthesized dance. If day break had not been around the corner, Victis would have loved to dance with the Quizans in space.

The main wing of the V.A. Hospital was massive, towering far above the ground. Floating through walls from room to room, they found young and old wounded soldiers asleep in their beds. Azha had located an infirmary that housed patients with horrific physical injuries. Unlike the first thirty-nine merges, these Humans were mentally sound and painfully aware of their circumstances.

A swarm of Quizans poured into the infirmary covering the ceiling in swirling red flames. A young, dark-haired vet sat up in his bed and stared in silence at the ceiling. After coming to the realization that he was awake, he whispered loud enough to awaken the young man sleeping soundly in the adjacent bed. "Wake up, the ceilings on fire. We need to get out of here."

The sleepy young vet opened his eyes and became mesmerized by the swirling red flame.

"Yeah, I see it. I don't think its fire. It's not hot."

A seasoned old man sat up in his bed, "I see it, too. You're right, it's not fire."

By now all the sleeping men had awoken and were sitting up in their beds fixated on the spectacular, swirling, red flames. Azha and Victis descended from the ceiling and morphed into body form in the furthest corner of the infirmary. Azha expected the Humans to either attack in self-defense or fear; curiously they did not. Several Humans asked each other if what they were seeing was *real*, or a dream.

"I am real," answered Azha. "Please allow me to explain why we're here. We are an alien species called Trekachaws. I was a police officer on this planet. Now, I am half-Human, half-Quizan. We come here in need of soldiers to protect this region of space within the Orion Belt. If you wish to be whole again, we can make that possible. The red lights circling above are called Quizans. They can join bodies with you to create a new species like me. Life expectancy is five hundred years and you'll have powers beyond anything you can imagine. I am giving you a chance to join me on a remarkable adventure few will ever experience. With that said, this is a one-way ticket. Do not volunteer if you have loved ones that you do not wish to leave. You will remember both lives, Human and Quizan. We are running out of time, but I will try to answer as many questions as possible."

A weathered old vet spoke-up, stating that he had a couple of questions. He scooted himself to the edge of the bed revealing the stubs of both his legs; he was also missing his left hand. The old vet was gruff and direct, not wasting any breath on trivial questions.

"My name is Sergeant Swartwood, you can call me Clyde. What you're tellin us... is all we gotta do is let one of them sparkly lights go into us and we'll look like you? We'll live five hundred years with none of our missing legs or ailments?"

"Yes, that is exactly what I am saying," replied Azha.

"Well damn, sign me up son. I have no one here waiting for me."

This was encouraging; there had to be at least fifty Human males available for twenty-one male Quizans. The infirmary came alive with the red swirling flames flashing into sparkling silver. This was the chance for a new life, a new beginning for broken men who had sacrificed themselves in war.

Victis was saddened by the crippled, brave men who scrambled from their beds into wheelchairs, elated at the inconceivable opportunity. Through all the excitement, Victis heard a muffled voice from across the room crying out for help. His cries were mournful and difficult to hear, thus drawing Victis to his bedside. The soldier's voice was scarred and damaged from the tubes down his throat during countless surgeries to keep him alive. As he drew closer, Victis noticed that his cries had faded and now were not much louder than a whisper. The young man felt his heart pounding inside his chest, not knowing if anyone heard or cared. He struggled to move, and stared at the ceiling trapped in his bed. This had been his world for almost a year. This was not living. "Over here. Don't leave me. I'm over here. I volunteer."

Victis hovered directly above the young man, curious to put a face with the voice. He was thin and pale and couldn't have been more than twenty years old. His eyes appeared startled, then once again were filled with desperation to leave his shell of a body.

"Can you move?" Victis asked.

The young man's face relaxed and his voice calmed, "No, I can't move anything below my neck. An IED exploded while my squad was en route delivering supplies. Most of my squad died. I guess I'm lucky to be alive."

"What is your name?" Victis asked.

"Private McBride, Cody McBride."

"How old are you?"

"Twenty-two."

"Did you hear what you're volunteering for?"

"Yes Sir, I heard what you said about the lights. I'd be grateful for the chance and proud to be a soldier again."

"Then you shall be," smiled Victis.

Cody McBride and Clyde Swartwood were the first to merge. Soon after, the infirmary exploded into a blinding silver light. As the infirmary grew dim, shadows were cast revealing the Humans that remained. Azha was confident the Quizans had chosen wisely. He needed, *no*... he had to believe in their choices. Leaving the rest behind was gut wrenching. Proud men were begging to go. Although impossible, he wished he could've taken them all.

The new Trekachaws were disciplined and dedicated. First order: Fly in formation to the battleship and await further instructions. For Victis and Azha, the Kigen mission was not finished. Twenty-four buzzing female Quizans awaited their merge in the hallway outside the infirmary. Lucky for them, Clyde Swartwood seemed to know where everyone was and every corner of the hospital. He volunteered to guide them through the maze of hallways and floors where female veterans were housed. No one had to be reminded that the night was growing short. Any further delays would be disastrous. Clyde was the break they needed. He ushered Azha, Victis and the flickering red lights to an elevator shaft where they whooshed to the 14th floor.

There were fewer female patients, and most of them appeared young and weak. Azha and Victis morphed into body form. Scrutinizing the candidates, they decided to pick the *best* ones from a disappointing group.

"Wake up," clapping his hands, "I am Captain Victis. We've traveled to Earth in search of Human volunteers. Our mission is to create female Trekachaws. Volunteers will merge with one of those lights up there. They are female Quizans in energy form. I am a perfect example of a male Trekachaw. Enough said, I will consider some of you for volunteers."

Four females jumped out of bed. They looked around the room and began grabbing metal trays, IV poles and anything else not bolted down. How unpredictable and what strange behavior. The females sprinted towards them swinging the metal trays as weapons and were jumping in the air trying to stab them with their IV poles. Azha and Victis high-tailed it to the ceiling screaming, *"Put down your weapons!"*

A very tall, heavy-set female launched an IV Pole, hitting Victis's foot.

"Get out of here!" she screamed.

"Stop. Do that again and I'll throw it back. Trust me, I'm a better aim." howled Victis.

The violent female showed no fear. They were terrible creatures and worse, they started laughing. The loudmouthed female who had inaccurately thrown the IV Pole mocked, "What in the hell are you?"

"I told you, I am Victis and this is Azha. We are a superior species called Trekachaws recruiting Human female volunteers willing to merge with female Quizans."

"Why in hell would any of us want to do that? She yelled back. "Are you guys seeing, what I'm seeing?" she asked the other females.

All the commotion was heard down the hallway, awakening even the soundest sleepers. One after another, a steady stream of females crammed themselves into the infirmary. There had to be at least a hundred angry females packed inside the small room glaring up at them. Victis was rethinking his decision to merge Quizans with Human females. These women were vicious, violent creatures. Female Ryquats were a much better match.

A green light flashed across the ceiling and landed on the floor beneath Victis. A handsome, new Trekachaw snatched a bedpan from the vicious female and threw it down onto the floor.

"Niki stop, listen to them. It's me, Cody. I let them do this merge thing and now I can walk again. Walking is nothing, I can fly Niki. I can fly through walls, in space, anywhere I want. I'm free, my new body is incredible."

The female's mouths fell open and they dropped their weapons, *Clank, Clunk, Chink, Clank.*

"Are you really Cody?"

"Yeah, I'm Cody. They need soldiers to fight a war out in space. Do it, and we'll fight together."

Niki, along with most of the other females, raised their hands to volunteer. Several aggressive females began shoving one another demanding they be chosen. Alarmed by their display of continued poor behavior, Victis advised the Quizans to choose wisely. Human females were far more aggressive and undisciplined than the males.

Cody shouted, "*Soldiers att-n hut.* Captain Victis, do not underestimate these devoted veterans. They are courageous and capable soldiers. I have no right to ask, but may I request a merge for my wife, Niki? I give you my word she will not disappoint you."

"No, you may not. I will not choose a Human for a Quizan. From what I've seen, I wouldn't recommend any of them. What I will do, is honor the Quizans' choices."

Victis looked up at the swirling lights, "Quizans, choose whomever you please. If you do not accept any of these females, we will find others."

The infirmary exploded with silver lightning bolts, forcing Azha, Victis, Clyde, and Cody to close their eyes. When they were able to open them again, Niki was gone. In her place stood an exceptionally tall, robust Trekachaw. Standing behind her were twenty-four beautiful new female Trekachaws. Victis was pleased. The Quizans had chosen remarkably well. A flurry of lights drifted across the room and vanished.

Valiant women were pleading for Victis to take them. Knowing that he had no words to comfort their rejection, he and Azha turned into pure energy and disappeared into the wall. Outside the hospital, Victis said, "That was very difficult. I wish we could've taken them all."

Azha felt selfish for asking, but he had no other choice, "Ginger and Cole Jr., are still waiting for me."

Victis appeared thankful for the distraction, "Don't forget Quetzal and a Vita Brevis Suit for your son."

No words could ever express his gratitude for Victis. On second thought, too much was hanging in the balance; he shouldn't leave Victis's side. Besides, Ginger was safe on Earth. She could wait a little while longer.

"I'll follow you to the ship and stay on board in case you need me," he told Victis.

The battleship was engaged with all stations on high alert. Most of the new Trekachaws and Captain Atue were on the cargo ship en route to Palatu. Roon had intercepted several Crozin transmissions that gave them an accurate countdown of thirty-one minutes before three Crozin battleships reached Europa. The cargo ship would be out of sensor range before they could strike. Nonetheless, Earth remained in imminent danger. One way or the other, the Crozins had to be destroyed or forced to retreat. Victis would stay and fight even if it meant the demise of his battleship and all aboard. Even though Victis was consumed by last minute decisions and shouting orders on the bridge in preparation for battle, he paused for Azha. "Go. Get your family. I'll wait for you if I can."

Deserting Victis just before a bloody battle filled Azha with dread. If nothing went wrong, Quetzal could complete her merge with Ginger before the Crozins attacked. Azha thanked Victis, then sped off to the docking bay with Quetzal by his side. In all the turmoil, Victis had arranged for an engaged shuttle and one Vexy suit waiting for him in the docking bay. His Trekachaw brother was looking out for him.

Quetzal flickered about, nervous to enter the shuttle. Being the last to merge, she was scared and lonely without her tribe. Azha reminded her of all the reasons she volunteered, and she flew into the shuttle. The more he got to know her, the more he liked her. In fact, he was becoming fond of the brave little Quizan. The shuttle hummed and rose from the docking platform. Through a small portal window, he watched the battleship shrink. It felt wrong leaving them looming in space to face the Crozins' wrath.

EARTH'S NIGHT CONCEALED THE SHUTTLE landing next to the old winery. Azha and Quetzal turned into energy and quickly flew towards his mother's house. The well-lit rooms obscured their lights as they floated down the hallway. A strange man had his back to them and was gathering things in Cole Jr.'s bedroom. The man was Frank. *Why was Frank at his mother's house and where was Ginger?* Azha asked himself. There was no time for subtly. Azha morphed into body form on the opposite side of the bed. Frank pulled his gun from a side holster and pointed it at him.

"Get down, on the floor," he demanded.

"Frank it's me, Cole. Put the gun down," Azha remembered to raise his hands into the air.

Frank shuffled towards the door, "I said, get on the floor."

"Frank don't shoot, I'm Cole your friend. Let me prove it to you, ask me a question."

"Get on the floor, then we'll talk," Frank sounded afraid.

Quetzal zipped about the room in a red frenzy. Down the hallway, a little boy called out, "Daddy, where are you?"

Frank side-stepped towards the door while facing Azha. You could see it on his face. If Cole Jr. ran into the room, he was going to shoot. In the blink of an eye, Azha slapped the gun from Frank's hand sending it flying across the room. The gun hit the wall and discharged... *Boom,* an ear-splitting explosion. Frank fell to the floor and was scrambling on his hands and knees across the room. In front of him, Cole Jr. was jumping up and down in the hallway excited to see the *Spaceman.*

Azha streaked past Frank to block the doorway, "Cole Jr., stay there. Frank, stop."

Frank dove for his gun laying on the floor next to a toy box. Before he could reach it, Azha grabbed the gun, unloaded it and threw the bullets behind the headboard.

Frank screamed at Cole Jr., *"Run Cole, hide!"*

In a futile attempt to fight, Frank jumped on Azha's back and tried to choke him out. This was ridiculous, Frank was no stronger than a Quizan.

"Frank get off me, you're wasting your time. I do not breath oxygen, I absorb energy. You can't choke-out my whole body."

Azha reached around, gently pulled Frank off his back, and forced him to sit down on the bed. Believing they were play-wrestling, Cole Jr. crawled up on the bed and began jumping up and down giggling, *"Gerrrrr,* Daddy whack, ka-pow Spaceman."

Exhausted, Frank stopped resisting. "OK, ok, let go of me, shit-head. What are you?"

"Like I said, I'm Cole. The night I went missing an alien merged with me. I've told this story so many times I'm sick of it. I know this is a lot to take in, but I am Cole."

Frank took a deep breath, "If all this is true, not that I doubt the alien part, why are you here now? What exactly are you, alien or Human? That's a stupid question... duh. Obviously, you're not Human."

"I'm called a Trekachaw. My name is Azha and I'm half-Quizan. I can fly in body form, or energy, and travel in space without space-ships or suits. I'm here for Ginger and Cole Jr. See the flickering red light buzzing around the room, that's Quetzal. She's the Quizan that came here to merge with Ginger. Cole Jr. can't merge until he reaches maturity. Until then, he'll have either Ryquat or Umdul children to play with."

Frank was finding it difficult to believe anything he was seeing or hearing. For some reason, Cole Jr. didn't seem to be afraid of the creature. In fact, he liked him. Not having a choice in the matter, he figured why not listen to what the alien had to say.

"Fair enough. The night you went missing, the department searched everywhere. We searched for months with no leads. Everyone thought you had been murdered and dumped in a remote grave somewhere. Ginger was pregnant, and you were missing. I fell in love with her and your son. Judy got sick of the whole thing and divorced me. If you really are Cole, I apologize. But I thought you were dead. Ginger eventually married me, but it didn't last. I think she never stopped loving you. About a year ago, your mom was diagnosed with terminal cancer. Ginger moved in here and has been taking care of her ever since."

Azha interrupted, "My mom is fine, she's a Trekachaw on a Ryquat battleship."

"What the *fuooo* ... Oops," Frank glanced over at Cole Jr., who was staring back at him with two little eagle eyes. "*Fudge, what the fudge,*" Frank said clearly.

Frank spelled out, "G-I-N-G-E-R was taken into custody this morning. Detectives have concocted a case against her for a double homicide. I was told on the QT they have enough evidence for the D.A. to file charges. They're saying she's either involved or guilty in your disappearance and now, your mom's. I tried to reason with them, but I'm getting the feeling they suspect me, too. She asked me to take care of Cole Jr. until I can arrange for her bail. I'm not sure if that's even possible, or how much the bail is. I've called a couple of lawyers, but so far I haven't heard back."

Azha's stripes faded to a pale tan. Everything was going wrong. Victis couldn't wait for him and Quetzal was showing signs of listless vacuity. It was imperative she be allowed to rejuvenate in the sun or inside the Quizan chambers. Azha's best recourse was to return to the battleship and help Victis fight the Crozins. Afterwards, he and Quetzal could return to Earth and pick up where they'd left off. Frank obviously loved Cole Jr. Leaving the boy with him was the only logical thing to do. He hated leaving Ginger incarcerated at the county jail, but at least she was safe. Whereas, the Crozins were hell-bent on destroying Earth out of spite knowing Humans were ancestors of the Ryquats.

"Frank, I must go. I insist that you do not tell anyone of our encounter. If you do, everyone will think you've lost your mind and then who will take care of the boy?"

Cole Jr. was tugging Azha's leg, trying to pull him over to Frank sitting on the bed.

"Daddy, this is Spaceman."

Frank picked Cole Jr. up and sat him on his lap. "I'm the only dad he's known. Of course, I'll take care of him"

Azha couldn't hide how much those words hurt. So many moments missed, so many years gone.

"Take care of yourself and the boy. I'll come back as soon as I can."

"Wait, before you go. I'd like to go with Cole Jr. and Ginger. I have nothing keeping me here."

Azha considered Frank's request and realized jealousy would be the only reason to say no. This destructive emotion was a Human trait, beneath a Trekachaw.

"Okay, but I cannot promise that you'll be reborn as a Trekachaw. What I can promise is a position on a Ryquat or Umdul battleship."

Frank removed a cell phone from his shirt pocket. Would you mind if I took a couple photos of you? I promise not to show them to anyone. Once you leave, I won't believe it myself unless I have hard evidence."

"Promise not to show them to anyone and we have a deal?" Azha asked.

Frank agreed and held the phone up, *Click, click, click.* He handed the phone to Azha showing him the photos he'd just taken.

"Wow, I didn't realize how bright my stripes are. We're going back to the shuttle. Gingers' not here," Azha told Quetzal.

"What did you say to the light?" Frank asked.

"That she's not merging."

The dancing light circled Azha as he spiraled into a white light. Side by side they drifted towards the wall, then shot up and disappeared into the ceiling.

Frank sat quietly on the bed next to Cole Jr. thinking about what he'd just experienced. Had he dreamt the whole thing? The photos on his phone were proof that he wasn't crazy.

THE SHUTTLE WAS AS HE left it. Relieved, Azha morphed into body form with Quetzal flickering next to his shoulder. The shroud of night was gone and soon the grey sky would give way to morning. The shuttle hummed, and they sped off, leaving Earth behind. Quetzal was worn out from the trip and disappointed. Leaving his wife and son behind was not what Azha had hoped for, either. Open space made Azha feel relaxed and free for the moment. Of course, that did not last long. A relentless fire-fight of pulsating beams lit up the black space near Saturn's moon, Europa. The battle had already begun.

twenty

SINE DIE

VICTIS strategically selected a few Trekachaws to stay on board his battleship. Nikki, Cody, and Clyde were bold and aggressive; they'd be pivotal in warfare. Roon and Beverly were excellent bridge support for the Ryquat crewmen. And then there was Pax. He had his hands full prepping the Medical Station. He was by far the best trauma M.D. Victis had ever run across, and this could be a bloody battle. A twenty-five-minute count-down did not leave Victis much time for mistakes or procrastination. Roon called the Officers and Crewmen to attention, "Captain on the bridge!"

"Soon we will engage the Crozins in a battle for our survival and that of Earth.

Roon, Nikki, Cody, Beverly, Clyde and I will fly onto the trailing Crozin battleship. Our mission is to take possession of that ship before it reaches Europa. If we are successful, *Akio,* I want you to engage all weapons on the mothership. Do whatever it takes to destroy her. We will use the hijacked Crozin ship to disable or destroy the other battleship. If we fail and you do not see the trailing Crozin battleship firing on their other ships, then I am ordering you to disengage. With any luck, I'm counting on them pursuing you, instead of destroying Earth. Save my ship and crew if possible, and return to Palatu. Regroup with Cpt. Pify, and the ships Luxon and Paratus. They'll need all the help they can get to protect Palatu and the new Trekachaws. We'll stay behind and fight until either we destroy them, or they destroy us. Beverly, are you Zeta or Beverly?

"Zeta," she replied.

"Like I said, Zeta, Roon, Nikki, Cody and Clyde, you're with me. Kill every Crozin on board and do not hesitate. The most effective way to kill a Crozin is to smash their protruding skulls at the base. You can't miss the ugly thing, it hangs down between their shoulder blades. You have plenty of strength to crush their skulls with your fists. But don't let that fool you; Crozins do not die easily. Their bodies will continue to attack and fire weapons even after you think they're dead. Once we have control of the bridge, I want Zeta, Nikki, Cody, and Clyde to turn back into energy and search for any Crozins on board. If you find any, kill them. Be smart and work as a pack. It's much safer that way. If there are no questions, let's go get a Crozin battleship."

Six mighty Trekachaws blazed out of the bridge into space.

THREE CROZIN BATTLESHIPS WERE APPROACHING at a steady hikari speed; countdown fifteen minutes. Victis soared over the top of the trailing battleship with the five Trekachaws in tandem. Undetected by the ship sensors, they followed Victis into the ship's bridge where a dozen Crozins were scrambling to prepare for battle.

A crusty, old Ukaru reigned from a large metal pod located in the center of the bridge. The pod spun in circles as he coughed up commands to the nervous crewmen. The Crozins' skulls were grotesque, and the bridge stunk of a musty order that reminded Clyde of fish left to rot in the sun. It was difficult for the new Human Trekachaws not to stare at the sagging leathery eggs that hung between their shoulder blades.

The vile, old Crozin, Ukaru, continued to spin in his pod, while fixated on a blinking device attached to his arm. Victis signaled for the attack to begin. Midair, Victis morphed into body form and punched the side of the Ukaru's head as he spun by in his pod. His thin, leathery skull exploded spraying chunks of slimy brain tissue across the bridge. Nikki had a screaming Crozin pinned on the floor. She took a moment to smile at Victis before she bent him over her knee and snapped his spine. A shrewd, older Crozin was grabbing a Neco weapon from a slit hidden inside an interface display wall. Clyde wrestled the Neco from the Crozin's boney fingers and tossed it to Victis. Cody jumped in and punched the base of the Crozin's skull square between its shoulder blades. He felt his fist penetrate the leathery skull and bury deep into its mushy brain. Cody tried to flick the dead Crozin off his fist, but with each flick, the corpse flopped up and down in the air like a rag doll.

"Hang on Cody, I'll help yank that thing off you," shouted Clyde.

Cody tried flicking the Crozin one more time, then slammed the limp carcass onto the floor. Clyde stood on top of the dead carcass, "Alright, pull your hand out."

It sounded as if Cody was pulling his hand out of a jelly jar...
vuump, and he was free.

Zeta was injured; she'd been fighting two Crozins at the same time. One of the Crozins got off a laser blast that left a gash across her leg. Purple blood ran down her thigh, leaving a trail behind with each step. She had killed the Crozin who'd shot her and was decapitating the second Crozin with her hands. No one dared to intervene. Zeta raged on long after he was dead, and was now mutilating the carcass by ripping his legs and arms from his torso. Her stripes softened from purple to red, and her frenzy calmed. Exhausted, she slumped to the floor holding the gaping wound on her leg. Clyde tore a uniform shirt off a dead Crozin and ripped it into strips.

"I can dress that if you'll let me? I served in more than one war on Earth. When I was too old to be a Ranger, I retrained as a Field Medic."

She lifted her hands, revealing a deep open gash across her thigh muscle. Clyde wrapped the torn shirt around her leg, dressing it like a pro.

It was over in less than five minutes. The Crozins on the bridge were dead and the battleship was their sword to wield. They were minutes from Europa and not slowing down. Roon fired a hyperbaric wave at the Crozin Wing-battleship. The monitor screen flashed white, followed by a sonic boom pushing their ship backwards from the impact. Victis flipped head-first over a bridge railing. Roon, Nikki, Clyde and Cody slid across the deck and Zeta slammed into the corner of a step. The wound on her leg was bleeding a tannish color through the bandage and her back appeared disfigured.

"Who's hurt?" Victis called out.

Clyde was already on his feet running to Zeta's aide.

Roon hit his mark, the hyperbaric beam destroyed the Wing-Ship.

The Crozin mothership pitched forward and rolled. *They were preparing to return fire.* Akio's timing was perfect. Before they could complete the rotation, Akio fired a barrage of pulsating beams. The mothership exploded in space. It was a direct hit, taking out most of the starboard hull. Debris flew out in space as the crippled ship sped past Victis. Roon enabled their Crozin ship communications to transmit directly to Akio's coded systems. Ship to ship Victis concurred, "Akio success, we have another battleship in good shape. Do not pursue the Crozin mothership. I don't think they'll make it very far; let them die a cold death in space."

AZHA HAD CONSIDERED DOCKING THE shuttle on the Ryquat battleship during the siege. That thinking was foolhardy. Odds favored the shuttle being destroyed by crossfire, and leaving Quetzal behind was not an option. Best case scenario was to reduce the thrusters and hover in space outside the combat zone. In the distance, he caught a glimpse of three Trekachaw lights. They buzzed outside the shuttle, then flew into the cockpit. The lights morphed into Traitor Myosis and two Leader Gystfins. Quetzal dimmed herself into a small glow and hid inside a boot at the bottom of a foot locker. She wept, fearing Azha would not survive the attack. They had him backed into a tight corner and there was no room to maneuver.

Think fast... Azha thought to himself. Calculate their plan of attack to optimize a defense tactic.

His odds were grim. One advantage, Gystfins were predictable. They preferred to attack from behind, severing their prey's spine with their long claws and fangs. The narrow cockpit made it difficult for them to attack from behind or the side. This gave Azha a fighting chance. One of the Leaders was hesitant and showing signs of fear. Azha noticed a thick, metal rod used to open a control panel lying on the floor beneath him. He bent over and snatched the rod off the deck and stabbed it into the Leader's chest. The Leader's reaction was faster than Azha had anticipated; he had aimed for his head. The Beast stepped back, screeching in agony trying to pull the rod out. Quetzal floated out of the boot next to Myosis.

"No Quetzal!" screamed Azha.

She darted back into the safety of the boot. Myosis roared with laughter and snatched the boot from the footlocker. He tried to stick his enormous hand down it but was unable to, so instead he threw it across the cockpit. Azha grabbed the rod and pushed it out the other side of the Leader's chest. Traitor Myosis grabbed the end sticking out of the Leader's back and held on firm. A tug-of-war ensued until the howling Leader turned into energy and flew out of the shuttle. Traitor Myosis roared, "Let go and I kill you quick."

The second Leader Gystfin jumped up and down behind Myosis ranting, *"Kill, kill Azha. Bite his head, suck him dry."*

Myosis was strong, too strong to take the rod away from. Thick strings of drool hung from his mouth and were sticking to his fur. Myosis was rabid; his fangs were chattering in desperation to chew Azha's head off. They were deadlocked, pulling the rod back and forth and getting nowhere. Myosis dropped to his knees and yelled at the Leader behind him, "Go over top of me. Slice him... don't kill. Azha, you lose. Let go, the Quizan live."

The Leader behind Myosis had crawled onto the flight deck panel and was squeezing himself between it and the ceiling. Both he and Myosis were now wedged together and unable to move freely. Aroused by the violence, the Leader grabbed himself and began humping Myosis's shoulder. He threw his head back and hissed, showing his yellow fangs. Saliva dripped out of his contorted, stretched lips and down the side of his chin. His fangs chattered in excitement and his eyes rolled back into his head. He groaned, jerking himself wildly until thick urine sprayed in spurts across Azha and Myosis. Satisfied, he relaxed and let go of himself. Myosis was outraged but refused to let go of the rod. *"Slice Trekachaw, do it now!"*

The Leader stretched out as far as he could, swiping his claws back and forth. Azha was trapped while in body-form. If he turned into energy he'd have a good chance of outrunning them, whereas Quetzal would be as good as dead. Closer and closer, the Leader stretched his body, until his long claws sliced across Azha's chest. The pain was blinding, and he tried to press himself further into the corner. Again, the razor-sharp claws swiped past his head and sliced his stomach open down to the middle of his thigh. He could feel his flesh burn and blood gush from his body. Myosis let go of the metal rod and body-slammed Azha, forcing him out of the corner. He fell to his knees with Myosis clinging to his back. He couldn't stop his body from spasming out of control, and his mind was filled with flashbacks of his life with Rodia. Myosis buried his fangs into Azha's shoulder to hang on while using his long claws to shred the mighty Trekachaw into pieces. *Azha felt himself dying.*

He saw Quetzal's light leave the boot and fly into a grate on the floor. Azha turned into energy and escaped, leaving the shuttle and Quetzal behind. His pain was excruciating, beyond anything he had ever endured. Looking back, he saw two Gystfin lights on his tail. They had not given up; the chase was on.

THE TREKACHAWS DID ONE MORE sweep of the cargo ship to check for any wayward Crozins. Clyde, Cody, and Nikki discovered an injured Beast curled up in a ball sleeping beneath a dining hall table. It resembled a Gystfin, but different and much larger. Cody and Nikki gladly volunteered to keep an eye on the slumbering Beast while Clyde informed the Captain.

Clyde flew onto the bridge and described the strange Beast to Victis and that it was asleep in the dining hall. Victis jumped out of his chair and ran down the corridor towards the dining hall holding a Neco weapon.

Quietly they crouched down to get a better view of the foul-smelling thing. They snickered at how loud it snored with its long tongue flopped out sideways quivering on the floor. The Beast was disgusting, yet funny at the same time. Victis barged into the dining hall, all fired up with purple stripes.

"Move out of my way," ordered Victis.

He aimed and fired the Neco gun at the Beast. It uncurled and shook out of control, knocking dining tables over and chairs across the floor. He then laid flat on his back, stunned, with his eyes open.

"Stay on the floor, or next time I'll evaporate you," hissed Victis.

The Beast moaned and rolled onto his side in pain. It was nothing more than an act to hide its aura before flashing into energy. Victis wasn't fooled, he fired the Neco and a thin white beam sliced off a foot. The Beast shrilled in pain and thrashed about on the floor, cradling the stub of his bleeding ankle.

Victis's eyes glowed yellow, "Why did you betray us?"

Puzzled, the Beast howled, "Who are you?"

"I'm Zygo," said Victis.

"My brother? ... cut off my foot?" the Beast wailed.

"You stopped being my brother when you stole a Gystfin's body and joined our enemies to slaughter Quizans. Show remorse and tell me where Myosis is."

"We killed Azha," the Beast mocked.

Victis stumbled back, "No, you didn't. You're lying."

"Dead. Quizan, too. Trekachaw die in shuttle. Look, my shoulder. Azha try to kill me. You care Azha stabbed me, *brother?*"

Victis ran towards his traitor brother, flipping chairs and dining tables across the room to clear the way. Scrambling across the floor to the other side, the Leader braced himself against a wall. You could see the fear in his eyes as he postured in a feeble attempt to show strength. Victis pounced on top of him and smashed his face into the floor. Fighting with all his might, the Leader was able to flip over by flailing his arms and kicking his legs. Victis straddled the Leader's chest and stared into his eyes. Slowly he wrapped his hands around the Leader's neck and squeezed. The vile Beast fought back until he passed out. Before the Leader died, Victis released his hold, allowing him to breathe. When he was cognizant of his fate, Victis would slowly squeeze his neck again, listening to the Leader gasp for air. Whether or not he meant to, Victis finally choked the Leader until there was no life left in his bulgy eyes. Victis rolled off the Leader and sat on the floor, rocking back and forth in anguish. Sorrow... gut wrenching sorrow. The Leader had to have been lying. Victis cried out, *"Azha!"* His souls were dead, and he felt as cold as ice. Azha was his brother, not this wretched monster lying before him.

Nikki sat beside Victis and wrapped her arms around him. The fearless Captain began to sob. For Victis, nothing would ever be the same without Azha.

twenty one

EUROPA

"Death comes swift for those who wait."

MYOSIS and the Leader were steadily gaining on Azha, and he was too injured to fly any faster. Hiding in Jupiter's massive red cyclone gave him a slim chance to evade the relentless Gystfins. Out of options, Azha dove headfirst into the violent storm, leaving them behind. The cyclone was blinding with dense, swirling debris, and his energy was being ripped apart by razor sharp particles passing through him. When he could no longer bear it, Azha flew out of the cyclone expecting to face the Gystfins. But they were gone, and he'd survived for the time being.

Severely injured and drained of energy, Azha flew on instinct, in and out of consciousness. Evidently, the battle had gone well for Victis. There were no signs of debris from his ship. Though desperate to find the shuttle, he knew those odds were slim. Earth was the nearest safe-haven, and he could see her blue orb in space. Perhaps, he could find the strength to fly there and rest.

It wasn't long before he felt himself fading. Earth was too far away; he wasn't going to make it. His only regret was that he didn't want to die alone. But he took comfort in knowing that his life had made a difference.

A small speck in space caught a reflection from the distant sun. Was it an illusion, perhaps a figment of his imagination? No, it was not. Against all odds, he'd found the shuttle miles off course, drifting in space. To Azha's surprise, Quetzal had survived and was sitting on the hull soaking up the sun. He knew in his heart that she would've drifted in space forever waiting for him. Overjoyed, she streaked to his side and closely followed him into the shuttle. Azha morphed into body form and collapsed. His back was on fire and the slashes on his legs were so gruesome they were difficult for him to look at. When he tried to get up from the floor, the gash on his leg gaped opened and he could see his bone.

Quetzal buzzed around Azha's head telling him about her discovery. While searching for him, she found a cave on Europa where they could hide. Azha hung onto to the navigation station and pulled himself up to sit in the chair. His head was fuzzy, making the controls difficult to see. He set the auto-pilot to Europa and closed his eyes. Quetzal kept buzzing in his ear to keep him awake until they reached the surface. With her help, Azha navigated the shuttle to a moon-shaped cavern. He must have passed out after landing the shuttle because he could not remember doing it. Quizan was buzzing around his head shouting for him to get up. Azha drew his last strength from her determination to save his life. They turned into energy and flew far beneath the icy crust of Europa into an unexpectedly, large cave. It was beautiful inside, with high ceilings cast by shadows of soft, flowing colors of yellow and orange. The cave was soothing and provided energy as inviting as the Targus

Sun. She'd saved him from certain death and given him a fighting chance. Quetzal touched Azha's wounds and wept. Exhausted, they curled up together and drifted off into a peaceful sleep.

twenty two

REQUIESCAT IN PACE

SIX hours had passed since the knowledge of Azha's death. Old wounds resurfaced, opening painful forgotten memories of his wife and child. Victis tried not to think about them... it hurt far too much. Connie had given him a beautiful daughter while on the long trek to a new planet. His crew and family were the first to step foot on the blue planet he'd named Trinite. This virgin world was going to be their home for the next ten years. How long had it been since that horrible day? Five years? ...yes, almost five years. His dreams were uneventful now, unlike the chilling nightmares that haunted him constantly in the beginning. Still, from time to time, sleepless nights cruelly forced him to awaken in night sweats. He wondered if they would ever completely go away. Azha had given him a new life, a new beginning. But his friend was dead, and all those old feelings of loneliness and sadness were back. Everyone he loved had died a violent death by either the Crozins or the Gystfins. Thinking back, he would've done things differently. Such promise to have gone so wrong.

UPON HIS GRADUATION, THE FIDUS Achates offered Victis a cutting-edge battleship in the southern quadrant of the Orion Belt. He declined the offer in lieu of a vanguard research ship assigned to establish an outpost on a remote, newly-discovered planet located between Palatu and Earth. Connie would have supported Victis either way, but she was relieved to hear his choice.

His decision did not come without guilt; the war was not favoring the Ryquats. Young Officers were being promoted to Captain fresh out of the Fidus Academy due to shortages caused by war casualties. In addition, the Crozins were depleting the Ryquats' fleet and resources. He'd heard rumors that a previous silent ally called the Umduls had joined forces to defeat their common enemy. Collectively, the Ryquats' odds improved significantly.

Word spread quickly within the galaxy how the Umduls were collaborating with the Ryquats. This caused a wave of dissension among those species who before the coalition had been neutral. One such species was a vile, vicious race and distant descendants of the Crozins. The Gors evolved on a planet not far from their ancestors into smaller, thick-skinned beings with armored scales covering most of their backsides. If threatened by a superior opponent, the Gors curled into an impenetrable, tight ball. They were difficult to kill and multiplied quickly. One saving grace was that their life span was short; on average, they lived thirty Earth years.

Victis' mission was to establish Trinite into a viable outpost for Ryquat inhabitants. This new planet was fundamental as a safe refuge in case Zaurak was sieged or destroyed. Rather than being captured by the enemy, suicide by any means was by far the preferred method to insure a humane death. The Gors and Crozins were known to take great pleasure in torturing male adversaries. All male children and most of the female children under ten years were immediately slaughtered for food. Adult female Ryquats, or those close to puberty, were brutally violated and used as slaves by the Crozins until they became too old or ill. Fortunately for the female Ryquats, Crozins were unable to impregnate them, even though every vile method had been forced upon them. However, if ever a viable pregnancy was achieved, the father would be richly rewarded and held in the highest esteem.

TWO YEARS HAD COME AND gone since their arrival on Trinite. The war was in full force and favoring the Ryquats. To their credit, the Umduls had made a pivotal difference. Zaurak was safe for the first time in decades, and prosperity had returned. Several transport ships from the home planet were en route to Trinite carrying supplies and additional personnel to assist with new, sustainable industry and housing expansion. The Fidus Achates Council did not want history repeated with the same mistakes made on Mars. If it were to happen again, Trinite would be operational and established.

Trinite was a garden paradise. It was easy for the Ryquats to become complacent. Connie was pregnant again, and Heidi had grown into a happy, curious, little girl. Victis loved watching her play with the other children and run about the compound exploring everything in sight. Some of the indigenous animals and birds were friendly and made wonderful pets. The only real predators on the planet were carnivorous plants. Four of the larger, voracious, flesh-eating plants were exceptionally dangerous even to the Ryquats. Though strikingly beautiful with bold white flowers, the plants were destroyed around the compound as a precaution in case children happened to wonder outside the perimeter. One of the innovative chefs suggested testing the carnivorous plants for consumption. Low and behold, not only were they safe to eat, the stalk tasted like tender Chovo and the petals were a close match to Tuki fish. Life was good, but all that was about to end....

The deep-space tracking sensors did not detect anything. If they'd been warned, maybe it could have made a difference. A flash of light in the sky was the first sign of the invasion, and watching their research ship disintegrate into a thousand pieces was the next. Before leaving Zaurak, Victis had programed an auto-distress signal just in case his ship was destroyed. Trinite was at the edge of civilization; therefore, reinforcement would not arrive for days. The colony's only hope for survival was that the Crozins were satisfied with destroying the ship and wouldn't bother to invade the planet. The last thing Victis remembered was running towards his home to find Connie.

He awoke in pain, peering through blood-soaked eyes at the devastation. The Crozins were methodically stunning all life in the vicinity and feasting on young children. He heard fathers and mothers screaming for mercy, begging the Crozins to eat them, not their babies. Jacet and Bruce were bound together and tied to a fence post outside the commissary. Their faces were white, and in shock as they struggled desperately to free themselves. Victis's wrists and ankles were hog-tied together and staked to the ground not far from them. They were forced to watch the horror and could do nothing to stop it. They knew Crozins never showed mercy. The vile Beasts preferred raw livers, hearts and brains while they were still warm. Thus, many of the children were alive while their bodies were dissected, and their organs removed.

Bruce stiffened and pulled at his restraints screaming in agony, "No, stop I beg you. I'll do anything you ask," as the pack of Crozins dragged his wife and two small children across the walkway in front of him. He called out to his wife that he loved her and told his children to close their eyes. His wife heard him, despite their loud clicking and shrills, and was trying desperately to scream back that she loved him, too. A Crozin shoved her youngest daughter's severed foot down her throat to shut her up. They had yanked her pants down to her knees and she could feel a cold hand groping inside of her. Bruce cried out, begging for the Crozins to stop, but in his heart, he knew they were going to die. With every muscle in his body he tried to free himself, and when that didn't work he chewed the plastic bindings that held him prisoner. His wife's screams excited the Crozins and more of them swarmed to rape her. His children were being ripped apart and his wife was thrown to the ground making it difficult to see. Nonetheless, he knew by their screams the end was near.

When he could not stand to hear them any longer, he screamed to deafen the sounds of their torture. Jacet was moaning and had turned his head to look away from the carnage. Bruce slumped forward, gasping for air before he passed out. Victis felt dizzy and sickened by the savage attack and began concentrating on staring at the dirt between his legs. Nothing he did blocked the agonizing screams. It was a blessing that Bruce could not hear the end.

Victis had not seen Connie or Heidi, nor had he heard their screams. He shuddered to think they had died before he woke up. He kept telling himself that Connie was smart and resourceful. It was possible that she'd slipped out of the compound and was hiding with Heidi. His thinking was flawed in so many ways. Being in denial would not change the facts. He saw the carnage that had occurred while he was unconscious. Most of the adult Ryquats were already dead and were being laser-sliced into food containers.

A High Ukaru Crozin walked over to Victis, licking blood off his fingers. "Captain advise Fidus Achates this planet Galak territory. For this reason, I spare two lives as witness when Ryquats test us."

The Ukaru waved his hand at a group of Crozins standing in front of their shuttle. "Victis of Zaurak, I have not eaten."

A Crozin carrying Heidi stepped out of the shuttle and walked down the plank towards the Ukaru. She wasn't crying or struggling to escape, but he could see the fear in her blue eyes. Judging by her expression, it was clear that even at her young age she knew her father was unable to save her. Victis burst into tears, pleading with the Ukaru not to kill his daughter. This seemed to please the vile creature. Nothing Victis said was going to change the outcome. The Ukaru reached out to the Crozin holding Heidi, and gently took her away from him. Victis calmed himself before asking Heidi to look at him and then told her how much he loved her with all his heart. With those last words, the Crozin sliced open her chest and yanked out her heart. As she took her last breath, he dropped Victis' precious little girl in the dirt and walked over to him. From what he could see, there were four or five Crozins fighting each other as they ripped her body into pieces.

The Ukaru slowly opened his bloody hand, "You love her with all your heart. Here, I give you hers."

Before Victis thought to look away, the Ukaru's throat fluttered as he placed her small heart in his mouth and swallowed. His eyes were cold and pitch black. If Crozins possessed a soul, his was gone. He waited, wanting to enjoy Victis' grief. When there was none, he threw a knife into the ground within Victis's reach and walked away.

Victis quickly cut himself free and ran to Jacet and Bruce to free them of their restraints. By the time he found a Neco, the Crozins' shuttle was nothing more than a speck in the sky. The smell of death in the air and signs of devastation in the compound was overwhelming. Victis ran across the housing quarters screaming for Connie. What he discovered inside their home was painfully evident. Her shoes were in the entry way as if she'd stepped out of them while running. He saw her blouse and shorts she'd been wearing that day. They had been ripped from her body and were in bloody shreds strewn about on the floor. Behind the couch he found what was left of her bra and underwear. That's where she had lost the fight and was raped and murdered. He felt weak and the room seemed to darken and spin. Victis sat down on the couch holding the blouse he had given her on Mother's Day. Jacet and Bruce sat down on the couch next to Victis.

Far out in space, an Umdul Battleship sensor detected the signature of a ship being destroyed in Trinite's orbit. They cared enough to check on the Ryquats. Little did the Crozin Ukaru know, that someday Bruce would become the Special Ops Sergeant of Victis's battleship and upon Jacet finishing his medical training, he too would join the team. The Ukaru made a colossal mistake picking those three to live; they were destined to become Trekachaws.

IT DIDN'T TAKE LONG TO intercept the cargo ship. Cpt. Victis, Cody, Zeta, Nikki, and Clyde turned into energy and flew through the hull onto the bridge. Cpt. Atue couldn't wait to hear all about the battle. So far, all he knew was everything had gone according to plan, except that Azha had died. Seeing Victis in person, it was obviously too soon to ask. Instead he updated Victis with Palatu's status.

"Five hours ago, Cpt. Pify reported two Crozin and one Gor battleship en route to Palatu. I deployed twenty-four Trekachaws to intercept and take possession of them."

Victis's stripes turned red and his yellow eyes narrowed, "Captain's office, now." He followed Atue in and slammed the door.

"Why didn't you clear this with me first? Human Trekachaws are not ready to fight Crozins or Gors and they don't know how to navigate a battleship. Your stupidity will get them killed."

"No... I didn't think. What have I done?"

"How long ago did they leave?" Victis asked.

"About three hours ago. They're probably already there."

"Do any of them have transmitters? Does Cpt. Pify know you deployed the Trekachaws?" Victis asked.

"No, I didn't want the Crozins to intercept the transmission."

"From now on... do nothing unless you clear it with me first. Understood?" Victis ordered sharply.

"Yes Sir," Atue answered, ashamed.

Victis stormed out of the captain's office shouting orders for the cargo ship to disengage and remain at their coordinates until further instructions. There was no time for explanations. He ordered Nikki, Cody, Zeta, and Clyde to immediately return to the Battleship with him.

In a flash, they were standing on the bridge of Victis's ship with Akio.

"Atue deployed twenty-four Human Trekachaws to intercept two Crozin Battleships and one Gor Battleship. These are the last coordinates for their location," Victis advised Akio.

Victis gave Akio the cue and the ship disappeared at hikari speed to intercept the alien ships...

THE GOR AND CROZIN BATTLESHIPS appeared dead in space. Upon closer inspection, they could have been sterilized. There were no life signatures and no damage to any of them. Victis felt confident that if they were going to attack, they would've already done so. The Crozins and Gors were arrogant and had no patience.

"Roon, stay on ship with Akio and Pax. If things go bad, escort the cargo ship to Palatu. Zeta, you Clyde, Cody and Nikki are with me. We'll clear one ship at a time. You've killed a Crozin, but a Gor is different. They're much faster and they'll curl up in a ball that is as tough as a ship's hull. Set your lasers on maximum and hold the beam on one spot. That's the only way to penetrate their scales. Make sure they're dead. If not, they'll uncurl and return fire. One last thing, their Necos are not fitted like ours. Anyone can use them. We'll clear the two Crozin ships first and regroup before we breach the Gor ship."

The first ship's bridge had Crozin bodies piled on top of each other, reminding Victis of the frickin rocks the Quizan Soldiers used to stack. Wherever they found dead Crozins, they'd find them stacked in the same neat piles. Besides looking weird, he wondered why they bothered. Nonetheless, the Human Trekachaws were thorough. Not one live Crozin was on board.

The second ship was the same as the first. No Trekachaws, and the same stacked piles of dead Crozins. So far, so good, but they still had to clear the Gor battleship. He was nervous about that one and with good reason. Victis briefed the new Trekachaws before they left the Crozin ship.

"The last ship is the Gors. They are fast, relentless, and do not care if they die. Normally they keep their lasers in an armory next to the bridge. That's where we'll go first. Remain in energy until we are inside the armory or if I morph into body form."

Careful not to attract attention, they entered through the belly of the battleship. The docking platform was enormous, and there were far too many shuttles to count. Not one Gor was in the docking bay. That was unheard of, especially during an attack. Victis morphed into body form.

'Something's wrong,' Victis warned. "Follow me to the bridge and stay close."

They turned back into energy and floated through walls and layers of decks until they entered the bridge. Victis wished he'd been wrong, but he was not. Two of the Trekachaws had died from laser wounds. Several more were gravely injured and in need of emergency care. Victis remembered how good it felt to save the brave veterans from the hospital and how happy the Quizans were before they merged. Angry, he stood over them wanting to blame someone else. He'd saved them, only to have them die in space and cursed with *Aeon Devotio*. The Quizan soldiers had lost their eternal life needlessly.

"Unko, where are the Gors?" Victis whispered. He'd not seen one, dead or alive.

"Does anyone know where the Gors are?" Victis asked the Trekachaws.

A young Trekachaw tending a severely injured female Trekachaw stood up.

"We jammed the bridge door. They were trying to breach it just before you got here. I don't think we even grazed one of those things. The aliens on the other ships were easy. These things kicked our butts. We voted to take a stand in here."

What's your name?" Victis asked.

"Quizan or Human?"

"The one you want to be called."

"Human. I'm **Takeda**."

Victis heard movement behind the walls and in the vents. It wouldn't be long before the Gors breached the bridge.

"Good to meet you Takeda. Listen everyone, if you're unable to fight but can turn into energy, do it now and return to my ship. Those who can fight, stay."

Nine Trekachaws turned into energy and disappeared through a bulkhead. Thirteen remained. Victis transmitted a coded message for Pax. With any luck, the Gors would not decipher it.

Takeda had crossed the bridge and was kneeling over another Trekachaw.

"Captain, this one's dead, too." He sounded defeated. Victis could not soften the blow. The new Trekachaws needed to be tough if they were going survive.

"I must sterilize the ship. There's no time to transport their bodies."

An energy light floated onto the bridge and morphed into Pax.

"Captain, Akio scanned the ship. There's over two-hundred Gors on board and they've transmitted their location and status. The only reason they're not attacking is because they're waiting for reinforcements. Per Cpt. Pify, several more Gor and Crozin ships are en route with a Ryquat Battleship following them. Captain Pify believes the Ryquat Captain is Smyth. Choan recognized his uncle's voice. They need you back as soon as possible," advised Pax.

"I hear you. Help the three Trekachaws over there, they can't turn into energy. The other three Trekachaws by the display interface are dead."

"If they can't turn, they'll die. I'm out of my element. All I can do is first aid and try to stop the bleeding. Trekachaw physiology is nothing like Ryquat. What they need is energy from the sun or artificial sunlight on the ship," confessed Pax.

Clyde started tearing a weaved side-panel into strips. "I can wrap their wounds with this and slow down the bleeding. Five minutes might be enough for them to turn into energy."

Victis warned, "Five minutes, no more. The rest of you go now."

Pax, Zeta, Cody and Nikki asked if they could stay to help Clyde. He appreciated their loyalty to one another, but Victis knew better than to endanger them needlessly.

"No, go now," order Victis. "We won't be long."

Clyde was able to slow down the bleeding. The Trekachaws were showing significant signs of improvement, but they were out of time.

"Clyde, I can't jeopardize my ship. Tell them to turn now, or they'll die," demanded Victis.

Two of the Trekachaws heard Victis and turned into dull-blue lights and floated through the bulkhead. The bloody bandages Clyde had so carefully wrapped, fell onto the deck floor into a tangled mess. One Trekachaw remained. She looked scared and wouldn't let go of Clyde's hand.

"Captain, she's almost ready. Can I stay just a little longer? A couple of minutes, if not, I'll leave her," pleaded Clyde.

"If you wait too long, I'll be forced to sterilize the ship with you on it," warned Victis.

"What does sterilization mean?" Clyde asked.

"All you need to know, is that you'll die."

En route to his ship, Victis questioned his decision. For both their sakes, he hoped he was wrong. He liked Clyde and didn't want him to sacrifice himself trying to save her.

Akio had intercepted a Gor transmission and was advising Capt. Pify via the bridge monitor. It seemed the Gors were no longer waiting for reinforcements and were close to re-routing the bridge controls to the main interface. Hearing this made his decision easy. The Gor ship had to be sterilized immediately.

Clyde caught the faint sound of a laser on the other side of the bridge door, then a red-hot line slicing across the top. He had an idea. Not a great one, but it was worth a try. He turned into energy and entered her dying body. He could feel his life force being drained and hers gaining strength. She turned into energy and together they floated through the ship into space. Slow and steady they flew towards Victis's battleship. Half-way home a blue-beam shot out from the bow and began rotating back and forth across the Gors' battleship. He wondered if the blue-beam was the sterilization Cpt. Victis had warned him about. She was in pain and fading away, and he was growing weaker by the minute. He flew directly into the Quizans' chambers and separated from her. They morphed into body form and collapsed on the floor. The artificial sun felt good and he could feel himself gaining strength. Her stripes were blue, and she was unconscious, but very much alive. Clyde absorbed enough energy to carry her to a cot and laid down beside her to rest. He wanted to be there when she awoke.

CLYDE WOKE UP REFRESHED, BUT he'd completely lost track of time. He raised his head off the cot to look at her face. She looked peaceful and no longer in pain. He rubbed his eyes and sat up. While he was asleep, she had died. Clyde laid back down and held her in his arms, "I'm sorry."

He prayed for her, then let go of her cold body. Clyde trudged down the corridor towards the bridge. Along the way, several Ryquats patted him on the shoulder and told him that Cpt. Victis would be pleased that he'd survived. This was not the first time he'd lost a comrade in battle. Nonetheless, it was the first time a woman had died fighting beside him. He found this to be incredibly disturbing and was angry at himself for going to sleep. Directly in front of him was the bridge. He needed to get control of his emotions before entering. Clyde was old school. He believed a good soldier was a strong soldier and showed no weakness.

Indeed, Victis was pleased. He wanted to ask Clyde what happened after he'd left, but right now was not a good time. Akio had sterilized the Gor ship twice. The first Crozin ship was sterilized, and the second ship was in progress. Victis assigned Akio and Zeta to board the three sterilized battleships and program the auto-pilot to Palatu.

In less than fifteen minutes Akio transmitted, "Gor ship completed, en route to assignment two."

Victis watched as the Gor battleship disappeared on the monitor. A few minutes later, one of the Crozin battleships disappeared. Akio and Zeta were amazingly fast. The tiny shuttle flew around the last Crozin ship just before it disappeared on the monitor. Victis clapped his hands, "That's how it's done. Wish you could've been here to see that, Azha."

With everyone back on board, Akio set coordinates to the Cargo ship at Hikari speed.

twenty three

EUROPA SOLIST ANTRO

AZHA guessed they'd been in the cave for a couple of days. His wounds were barely visible anymore, and he was getting antsy to rescue Ginger. However, spending time with Quetzal had been a pleasant surprise. She was fun, interesting, and intelligent. Azha couldn't have asked for a better match for Ginger.

"Quetzal, I'm strong enough to go. That is, if you're ready?"

"I'm ready, but I was thinking we could have our ceremonial Owari bond before we leave?"

"Ah, now?" Azha stammered.

"I think it's important that we keep our Quizan tradition sacred," she said nervously.

"I understand, but I'm worried that Ginger will think I cheated on her if we bond."

"That makes no sense. I thought you liked me? What's wrong?" Quetzal asked.

"Nothing's wrong. I just want to wait until you're merged with Ginger or she'll know I cheated."

"What about Rodia?" Quetzal countered.

"Rodia and I never bonded after I became a Trekachaw. I was afraid I'd hurt her."

"What about Phera? I know you and Phera had lots of bonding. Everyone talked about it."

"Phera doesn't count."

"Why doesn't Phera count?" Quetzal snapped.

"I was confused," replied Azha.

"That's ridiculous. If Ginger believes that... she's a *Bodo.*"

"She's not a Bodo. Quetzal, that's not nice. Can we please wait? I've made so many mistakes, I just want to do this one right."

"When you put it that way, okay," she said with a fake smile.

"Thank you." Azha was glad that was over.

Azha kissed the top of Quetzal's head. She giggled and pinched his stomach.

The shuttle was docked inside the entrance just where he'd left it. Quetzal was buzzing next to his shoulder, excited that today she was to become a Trekachaw. It felt strange returning to Earth with just himself and the little Quizan. For the moment, he'd found peace between his two souls. Since his encounter with Zeta and proving his determination to rescue Ginger, Cole was content to leave him alone.

Earth was growing larger on the monitor along with his anxiety. He didn't want to hurt Quetzal's feelings, but he cringed at the thought of being Owari bonded again. The old winery was in view and the coast was clear to dock. Azha turned into energy and headed towards his mom's house with Quetzal by his side.

It was just past midnight and the house was quiet as they floated down the hallway towards his son's bedroom. Azha could see the top of Cole Jr.'s fuzzy little head. His hair was sticking straight up from static electricity. The queen bed was far too big for the little bump beneath the race car blanket. Amused, Azha had lit up the house before he realized it. Frank came storming out of the master bedroom yelling, "Who's there?!"

Azha morphed into body form, "Frank, it's me Azha, I mean Cole. We're back for Ginger."

"Good, great. Shit you scared the crap out of me. Let me get some pants on. Who's the light up there with you?"

"Quetzal, she's here for Ginger."

"Man, I was beginning to think you weren't coming back. Ginger's still incarcerated in the county jail. I've tried everything to get her out. A friend in Detectives told me a top-secret agency took jurisdiction of her and are scheduled to pick her up on Monday for transport to who-knows-where."

"What's today?" Azha asked.

"Monday morning? Let me look, yeah, it's 12:15 am. You'd better hurry while she's still there. Can Cole Jr. and I go with you?" Frank asked.

"Sorry Frank, not this time," shaking his head.

"My lawyer is handling your mom's estate. According to law, Cole Jr. is the rightful heir. I'm not sure where we'll go."

"Are you able to care of Cole Jr.?" Azha asked.

"Legally I'm his father. Don't worry, Cole Jr.'s safe with me. I love him just as much as you do."

"I know Frank, and I'm grateful for that. How will I find you if you move?"

"I'll keep the same cell phone number until you return," assured Frank.

Frank wrote down his cell number on a piece of paper and handed it to Azha.

"I'll memorize it, can't carry anything while in energy. I'll never forget this number or what you've done for me."

Azha turned into energy and disappeared with Quetzal. Frank stood in the hallway thinking there was no way he could sleep now, wondering how long it would be before Cole came back, and hoping it would be soon. Frank headed for the kitchen to start a pot of coffee.

COLE KNEW THE COUNTY JAIL like the back of his hand. He guided Azha to an area where prisoners were housed in a single-cell before transport. This was good. Ginger was alone. Outside the cell, a camera was monitoring every move she made. Ginger's head moved ever so slight when she saw the floating lights. She smiled at them and closed her eyes. Quetzal's light turned to silver and disappeared into the top of Ginger's head. The concrete cell flashed into a blinding silver light. When the light faded, the cell was empty, and another mysterious missing persons' report had to be filed.

twenty four

SERVO QUAD NAVIS

"INNOVATION MAKES UP FOR EDUCATION"

FOR Atue, waiting was worse than being punished. He never asked to be a Battleship Captain. He was an Engineer Officer and a darn good one. Being responsible for the Human Trekachaws wasn't something he wanted, either. They were curious to the point of being exhausting. Maybe this was a Human trait, their nature, or perhaps it was simply bad manners. In any case, he'd given them strict orders not to touch anything and not to explore the cargo ship without permission. Of course, two of the Trekachaws' curiosity got the best of them and they wandered off into the belly of the ship. Hours passed and neither one wanted to admit they were lost. Every corridor looked alike and every corridor led to the same thing… enormous, empty, dark, cargo bunkers.

Duroc talked too much and rambled on about nothing. **Ajax**, on the other hand, said almost nothing and communicated with grunts. He stopped listening to Duroc and figured grunts were safe, whether a yes or no response was correct. After a few more hours of wandering aimlessly around the ship, Ajax decided to have an actual conversation with Duroc as he'd started asking more than a grunt could answer.

"We could turn into energy and fly out," suggested Duroc.

"That'd be no fun. Let's not give up," replied Ajax.

"I'm from Arkansas. How'd you get a name like Ajax?" Duroc asked.

"I'm from southern California. My parents are computer geeks. Brother's name is Fax. The word Ajax is a method of building interactive applications for the web. Never heard the name Duroc, either."

"Yep, me neither. My parents run a big pig farm. Duroc's a red pig, good bacon and ham. Guess we're from different parts of the country. No matter. I like ya anyway," smiled Duroc.

A loud thud followed by a crash came from inside a closed door down the corridor. Something large had fallen and was rolling across a floor. Duroc ran to the door and pulled down on a handle to open it. The door must have been spring-loaded because it slammed shut.

"That was weird. None of the other doors did that," said Duroc.

Ajax stepped to the right side of the door, "Get on the other side. I'm gonna try to open it again."

Duroc stepped to the left side of the door and gave the 'Ok' sign. Ajax reached out and pulled the handle down, then pushed on the door. It opened a few inches than slammed shut again. Of course, whatever had rolled across the floor must be blocking the other side.

"Help me push it open. Something blocked it," said Ajax.

Duroc and Ajax put their shoulders to the door and shoved it open. A large bulky silhouette ran across the room and disappeared behind a stack of crates.

"Did you see that?" Ajax asked.

"What do ya think it is?"

"I have no idea. Did you get a look at it?"

"No. If I didn't know better, I'd say it looked like a Grizzly Bear," said Duroc.

"Have you ever seen a real Grizzly Bear?" asked Ajax.

"You're asking a country boy if I've ever seen a Grizzly Bear?"

"What would raising pigs have to do with knowing what a Grizzly Bear looks like?" Ajax quipped.

"You'd know if you were a country boy. How bout we check this thing out?"

Ajax found a small crate to prop the door open, providing some corridor light into the bunker. Hundreds of crates filled the dark room. Some were at least twenty-feet tall and roughly as wide. Ajax was beginning to believe they'd seen nothing more than a shadow, but that didn't explain why the door keep shutting. Another minute and they would've given up. Something moved, and a scratching noise came from within one of the huge crates. Duroc searched the edge of the crate with his hands for a way to pry it open. Ajax knocked on the crate to determine if it was empty or full. Something inside returned the knock. Duroc and Ajax jumped back and ran to another crate for cover.

"Did you hear that?" Duroc asked.

"How could you not hear it? What do you want to do?"

"If we leave we'll look like lily-livers," said Duroc.

"What is a lily-liver?" Ajax asked.

"You know a coward," replied Duroc. "Right. How are we going to open it?" Ajax asked.

"Captain Atue ordered us not to be down here," said Duroc.

"We can't just leave. If both of us grab the edge of the crate; we might be able to pull it open," suggested Ajax.

They tiptoed over to the crate and pulled on an edge until a side-wall broke away and crashed onto the floor. Inside, a brown, furry animal with black spots was hiding in a corner. Whatever it was, it was big, and had its backside towards them with its head tucked between its knees. It whimpered and was shivering, scared to death. Duroc, being a farm boy, figured he could sooth the animal by talking to it, "Hey boy, it's okay. We're not going to hurt you."

Ajax had an epiphany from his Quizan-half and remembered *it* was a Gystfin.

"Duroc get back, that's a Gystfin. They'll bite your head off and suck out your grey-death energy."

The word *Gystfin* was like a slap to Duroc's face. "Holy cow, you're right. It is a Gystfin. What's it doin down here?"

"I don't know. But we need to kill it," said Ajax.

The Gystfin started crying and pleaded for mercy.

"I think he's harmless. Maybe some of them are friendly. I don't want to kill him if he's friendly. Do you?" Duroc asked.

"No, I don't either, but what if he's playing us?" Ajax questioned.

"Na... I think he's really scared, I can tell," said Duroc.

"You stay then, I never even had a pet cat. I'll ask if we can get linguistic chips, so we can speak Gystfin. Atue said whoever wanted one, could have one."

"You want me to stay by myself with a Gystfin?" Duroc asked surprised.

"You're tough. Don't Arkansas people ride cows?" Ajax said with sarcasm.

"Bulls, stupid, we ride bulls. You think you're smart, but to me you're an ignorant city boy. I told you, my parents are pig farmers. Geez, just go."

Ajax turned into energy and flew the through cargo ship into space. Outside, he made a mental reference to a portal and reentered near the bridge. Atue was repairing a computer *thing.* Ajax thought he was smart on Earth; being here, not so much.

"Excuse me, Captain Atue, I was wondering if the linguistic chips are still available?"

"Over there, inside the top drawer next to my chair. The injector looks like a pen."

"I found the pens. Now what?" Ajax asked.

Atue laid his instruments down on a cart. "Give it to me and stick out your arm."

Ajax balked at Atues bluntness. *'Stick out your arm'* to do what?

"Give me your arm, I'm busy." Atue grabbed Ajax's wrist and injected the chip.

"Done. Now go away unless there's something else."

"No sir," replied Ajax.

Ajax turned into energy and sped outside the ship. After a quick check to get his bearings, he found the portal and reentered. Nothing had changed. The Gystfin was still sobbing in the corner and Duroc was squatted on the floor watching the Gystfin cry. The crate was well lit from Duroc's glowing orange stripes, making it easier to see the Gystfin.

"You know, all we had to do was make our stripes glow to see in the dark. I've been practicing while you were gone." Duroc boasted dimming his stripes, then making them bright again.

"If you're finished, I couldn't bring you a chip. Let's find out if mine works?

"Gystfin, what are you doing down here?" Ajax asked.

The Gystfin was afraid to face the mighty Trekachaws. His words were muffled from his face being tucked between his legs.

"No diieeey. Transmit Ryquats, save Quizans... not bad."

Ajax and Duroc had no idea what he meant about transmitting the Ryquats. However, that justified their excuse not to kill him. Besides, Captain Atue would want to interrogate the Gystfin for information.

"What's your name?" Ajax asked.

"Boo," said the Gystfin.

"Boo, like when a ghost jumps out to scare you, *Boo*?"

"Don't know ghost. Boo is my name."

"Why are you on the ship, Boo?"

"Azha Trekachaw stole ship. Hiding here. Kogbor search Palatu to kill me. Kogbor knew Boo transmit to Zaurak tell them many Quizans die for grey-energy. Other Ryquat lie for Kogbor."

"Who's Kogbor? Why did he want to kill you?" Ajax asked.

"Kogbor is Dux Ducis, rule Palatu. Ryquat Captain Smyth told Kogbor, Boo transmit Ryquat Counsel Fidus Achates explain lies told about Quizan deaths. Captain Smyth is a Crozin ally."

"What about Smyth?" Ajax asked.

"Captain Smyth kill more Quizans than Gystfins. Kogbor exiled me to cargo ship long ago, Boo refused to kill Quizan. Boo hide from Kogbor."

"My name is Ajax, and this is Duroc. We won't hurt you."

"Scared to die. Can never return to Gardux."

"What is Gardux?" Ajax asked.

"Boo's home."

"Duroc, this Gystfin is the reason Victis was sent to Palatu. I'll go explain everything to Atue, if you'll stay here with Boo. If I'm not back in twenty minutes, it's because Atue plans on hurting Boo. Leave Boo here and meet me in the corridor outside the bridge."

Ajax flashed into energy and was gone. Duroc sat across from Boo, unable to communicate. His Human-half saw Boo as a magnificent Beast, beautiful and strong, like a Hyena crossed with a Grizzly Bear. His Quizan-half wanted to turn into red-energy and hide. Gystfins were evil monsters. Protecting one was ludicrous.

HE GUESSED IT HAD BEEN thirty minutes since Ajax left. Boo rotated his head sideways and peeked out from underneath his fury arm at Duroc. Slowly, he inched his way out of the corner and twisted just enough to see the Trekachaw. The mighty Trekachaw stood up. Boo's eyes widened with fear and he crawled back into the corner. Duroc raised both his hands into the air showing that he meant no harm. For Boo, the Trekachaw was challenging him to fight. Boo sprung to his feet looking for an escape. There was none, and the crate opening was blocked by the devious Trekachaw. Boo hissed and peeled back his lips revealing yellow-stained fangs. This was a Gystfin's true nature. Duroc's Quizan-half screamed inside his head to turn into energy and hide.

Two lights flew between them and morphed into Ajax and Atue.

Atue screamed, "Stop, or I'll kill you where you stand. Did you contact the Fidus Achates and report the slaughter of Quizans?"

Boo retreated into the corner and squatted against the crate.

"Did you contact the Fidus Achates?" Atue demanded.

"Yes!" cried Boo.

"What happened? Why was Boo going to attack you?" Ajax asked.

"I don't know. You saw him, he went crazy," replied Duroc.

Boo snarled, "No, Trekachaw lie."

"Then you tell me what happened?" Atue asked.

"Trekachaw raised arms. Challenged Boo to fight."

"Duroc was not challenging you. That's how Humans demon-strate compliance," explained Ajax.

"Chip for Duroc necessary. Boo learn Human traditions."

"Did you contact the Fidus Achates regarding Gystfins killing Quizans?" Atue asked.

"Yes, Boo contact. Refuse to bite off Quizan head for grey-death energy. Kogbor exiled Boo to cargo ship. Boo premier engi-neer reason Kogbor spare life. While Boo alone on ship, Boo contact Fidus Achates. Kogbor hunt Boo to kill. Hide on ship. Trekachaw Azha stole ship from Kogbor."

"I believe you. We were wondering who notified the Fidus Achates. I am Atue, Captain of this ship. Anything you can tell me about this Cargo Ship would be greatly appreciated."

Boo smiled and took a couple of steps forward leaving his stronghold. "Boo honored. Know ship well."

"Guide us to the bridge. We're lost in this maze of corridors," admitted Atue.

"Boo guide Trekachaw Captain Atue."

The corridors echoed with laughter as they made their way to the bridge. Boo was funny how he told the stories of others being lost in the belly of the cargo ship. Captain Atue promised to keep Boo safe and that every Trekachaw on board would be injected with a linguistic chip. Boo's selfless act helped save the Quizan species from extermination. Word spread quickly about the hero Gystfin called Boo.

FOR FIFTEEN DAYS, THE UMDUL Regents and Ryquat Counsel had been in a heated disagreement regarding the Trekachaws' acceptance as a viable new species. Negotiations were exhausting, and they were no closer to a resolution than day one. Captain Pify was given full support by the Umdul Regents to protect the Trekachaws by any means necessary. The Fidus Achates threatened to intervene until the Umduls advised their intent to secede if they interfered with the negotiations. The Ryquat Counsel were split in their decision, therefore making no official recommendations. Captain Pify was given command and a new agenda to redirect the Umdul fleet, from Zaurak to Palatu. The Ryquat Counsel refused to reconsider even when it meant jeopardizing the safety of their own planet.

The Umdul fleet en route from Zaurak intercepted several transmissions revealing vital information. Approximately twenty Gor and Crozin battleships had joined forces to invade Palatu. According to the latest intercepted transmission, their E.T.A was thirty-six hours. The Gor and Crozin campaign was flawed. They believed Palatu was protected by a handful of battleships. Little did they know, they were outnumbered three to one. Thirty-two Umdul battleships were in orbit around Palatu and nine more were within a days' arrival from outposts. Captain Pify sent a coded message to the twenty battleships en route from Zaurak to standby. Their new orders were to allow the Gor and Crozin ships to pass their coordinates, then pursue undetected to Palatu for an astern attack.

Captain Pify transmitted ship to ship on a coded frequency to Captain Victis, "Heard good mission, true not so good Azha? Future find positive will grow strong again... to the end, you and me. Patience before we meet again, protect our interests. I send you Phera and one of my best, Yagi. Two will make three in case you find Crozin birds to pluck. Maybe blinded Gor will try to wangle what is ours, chance to step on parasite. Aevitas my friend, be diligent to see the end unscathed, accept?"

"Accept. Be safe old friend, we will meet again soon." Victis ended the transmission.

He wished he could fight alongside the old salt that he worshiped. Waiting in space was not his idea of being useful. As always, Pify was right, and every move perfectly calculated. Protecting the cargo ship was crucial and the Human Trekachaws were vulnerable until they received basic training. If Azha was alive, he would have guided the Human Trekachaws. Such a waste. Who would be best suited for the task now? He'd get back to that problem later. If he could go back and do things differently, Azha's wife would have merged before they left Earth. Would've, could've, and should've was not helping. The cargo ship was in monitor range and he couldn't allow himself to be distracted. But that didn't last long. Having nothing to do but think, Victis reexamined his anger towards Atue. He should never have appointed Atue as Captain. He was too compassionate, and sensitive to a fault. Atue would never forgive himself for the Trekachaw casualties. He should have paired Clyde with Atue. Together they would've made a well-balanced team. Azha would have advised against Atue being a Captain. But Azha was dead. He should have known better than to force Atue into a position he was not suited for or trained to do. Victis was just as much at fault for the Trekachaws' deaths. From now on Atue would do what he did best, a valued Chief Engineer.

THE BATTLE WAS OVER BEFORE IT began. The Gors and Crozins divided into two collectives and retreated at Hikari speed. It seemed last-minute they knew about Captain Pify's ambush. Even so, not all was lost. A wing Umdul ship disabled two of the fleeing

Crozin battleships. Pify wanted prisoners, preferably Ruks or a Ukaru. He would interrogate them to confirm if a Ryquat traitor was leaking information. Prior to the Umdul Sentries boarding, most of the Crozin crew had committed suicide by ingesting poison. Quick action prevented a Crozin Ukaru and a handful of bridge Ruks from completing a battleship self-destruction count down. The prisoners were transported, and Umdul engineers boarded the Crozin ship for repairs. What came next was a gruesome discovery.

"Captain Pify, three female Ryquats in the belly of this ship. Sad, they are. One old, one young and one not. Ryquat doctor in need for one not, suffer she has," transmitted an Umdul Sentry.

"Comfort, you shall. Transport when stable," advised Pify.

Ship to ship, Captain Pify briefed Victis and Phera regarding the Crozin and Gors status and of commandeering two of their ships. Pify added, "Three Ryquat females discover in belly of Crozin bird. Toogus physician request Ryquat physician dire need says he."

Victis acknowledged and assigned Phera to transport Pax to the Crozin ship hikari speed.

Now that the threat was gone, Victis was given confirmation for the cargo ship to proceed to Palatu. A couple of changes in crew assignments needed to be addressed before giving orders to set course. Roon and Clyde were to replace Atue on the cargo ship. Atue would return with him to his battleship where he could inform him of the Human Trekachaw casualties in private.

Pax couldn't wait any longer. He needed to tell Victis something in confidence before Phera arrived. Not wanting to create a problem, he'd kept the nagging information to himself because it was nothing more than a gut-feeling. Plus, ever since Azha's death, Victis had been distant, distracted, and short tempered. Nonetheless, Victis needed to know.

"Victis, we need to talk about two of the Trekachaws Atue deployed. Their Human names are Joshua and Nick. They were two of the first Human Trekachaws that came back. When I examined the group, everyone was severely injured, except for them. They were covered in blood and acting as if they were in pain, except I didn't find a single scratch on either one of them. To me, the blood covering them looked smeared. I think they rubbed another Trekachaw's blood on themselves and played dead or hid so they wouldn't have to fight."

"Did you confront them?" Victis asked.

"No," admitted Pax.

"I met a Human Trekachaw called Takeda while on the Gor ship. I'll ask him if he knows anything about Joshua or Nick. If you find out anything else, let me know. Update me when you know something about the female Ryquats," Victis added.

"No problem," said Pax.

Captain Phera came into view at the end of the docking gateway. She was magnificent. Even Pax commented on how beautiful she was.

"What are you two staring at?" Phera asked.

"We're not staring at you," Victis said looking away.

"Right. Pify wants to know if you need another battleship to assist with the cargo ship escort? Umdul Captain Yagi is here and available. And since you thought it so important to name the ships, what's your ship's name?"

"My ship's name is Trinite. And *No*, I don't need Yagi. Pax, let me know about the female Ryquats."

Pax was so distracted by Phera walking down the corridor in front of him, he didn't hear Victis the first time.

"Pax, let me know about the female Ryquats."

"I got it. As soon as I know, you'll know," Pax said, not turning around.

The docking station closed, leaving Victis to watch their departure out a portal window. In a flash, the two battleships were gone. Like it or not, he was stuck escorting the cargo ship back to Palatu.

Akio sounded excited and out of breath, "Captain, report to the bridge."

That was strange, Akio never showed his emotions. Victis turned into energy and flew through the bulkhead onto the bridge. As he morphed into body form, Akio was yelling, "I think that's our shuttle out there. Look Captain, it is our shuttle. Who's flying it?"

twenty five

HOMEWARD BOUND

NOW that Azha knew what a battleship was capable of, the shuttle flight seemed as if it were going to take forever to navigate home. But, then again, where was home? Palatu was not home anymore, and certainly not Earth. Was he a galaxy nomad? No, home was with the Trekachaws, where ever that may be. Most of the flight had been restful. Cole seemed content now that Ginger was in his life. On the flip side, Azha's Quizan-half missed Quetzal. She often reminded him of Rodia. This time, he would honor and appreciate his Owari bond with a faithful, supportive female. It was necessary to remind himself of his good fortune during the first couple of days after leaving Earth. Azha flew out of the shuttle more than once for some peace and quiet. Quetzal and Ginger were butting heads, both adamant about keeping their name. They argued non-stop until they finally agreed on a compatible Trekachaw name; *Ginzal.* Azha liked the new name. Very creative how they combined both names to create a new one. He was pleased when they decided to cooperate with one another. Not only for his sanity, but for theirs, too. Eventually, one would dominate the other. He didn't care who, though he hoped the decision would be made sooner than later.

Over the next couple of days, Azha had the opportunity to bond with his Trekachaw wife. He liked bonding with her, though not as much as he'd hoped. Rodia didn't deserve his betrayal and neither did Quetzal. Knowing it was wrong, he'd think of Phera to make his bonding with Ginzal more energizing. Even worse, after about twenty times he wasn't all that interested in her. Him comparing the two was not fair. Phera was exotic, exciting, and dangerous. Ginzal was none of those. For everyone's sake, he had to convince himself that true love was better than lust. No matter what, he'd never admit to anyone how he felt. Checking the shuttle navigation, Palatu was within four days. That is, bearing no complications.

A battleship crossed his path. Azha thought about diverting, but most likely their sensors had already detected him.

"Ginzal, if the battleship's Crozin, we can't return to the shuttle. Palatu's not that far, we'll fly the rest of the way in energy. Are you ready?" Azha asked.

Ginzal look scared. Then he saw a familiar expression appear on her face. Quetzal had taken over.

"Ready. This isn't the first time we've outwitted monsters," smiled Ginzal.

Azha cut the power, leaving the shuttle adrift. The tiny craft faded in space as the battleship came closer.

Azha and Ginzal flew through the portside. The battleship did not stink of Crozin or Gystfin. Azha saw a Ryquat crewman walking in the corridor underneath him. He was home, "Ginzal, we're on Victis's ship." Azha streaked through the walls onto the bridge. There stood Victis in the flesh staring at a monitor, telling Akio to contact with the shuttle. Roon looked the same, but a new Trekachaw was standing next to Victis. He was probably one of the new, Human Trekachaws. Azha flickered to Ginzal asking her to remain in energy. She flickered back, excited for Azha. This was perfect, no one noticed when he morphed into body form behind Victis.

"Did ya miss me?" Azha asked.

Victis spun around and his stripes turned so pale they were almost white.

"It's me, Azha. Are you okay?"

Roon screamed and Victis fell to the floor.

"Holy shit" yelled Roon.

"Is he dead?" asked Akio.

"No. I think he fainted," said Azha.

"Someone do something!" yelled Roon.

"Go get Pax!" shouted Azha.

"Phera transported Pax to Palatu," said Akio.

"Look he's moving," said Clyde.

"What happened? Help me to my chair," commanded Victis.

While Azha, Roon, and Clyde were helping Victis stand up, Ginzal morphed into body form behind them.

"Roon, when did Victis start doing this?" Azha asked.

"This is the first time I've seen him do it. We thought you were dead. We found an injured Gystfin Leader on a Crozin battleships we commandeered. Before Victis killed him, he told us Traitor Myosis killed you on the shuttle. That Leader was Zygo's brother."

"Traitor Myosis and two Leaders almost did kill me. I flew into Jupiter's Red Cyclone or they would have. When I flew out, Traitor Myosis and the other Leader were gone. I stabbed the Leader you found with a metal pole. He turned into energy and left the shuttle before Myosis and the other Leader chased me to the red cyclone."

Ginzal flashed her stripes.

"Allow me to introduce my wife, Ginzal. Quetzal merged with my Human wife, Ginger. Is Beverly on board?"

Slurring his words, Victis sat up in his chair, "Welcome home Azha. Yeah, your mom's on board. She's called Zeta now. Somebody let her know that Azha's on the bridge. What happened to me?"

Azha squatted down in front of Victis, "Well, I think you passed out."

"Unko damare," swore Victis.

"Saying 'shit shut up' in Japanese won't change a thing. Everyone saw you do it," smiled Azha.

"Never did that before. Hope I never do it again," Victis said worried.

"Me, too. You kinda scared all of us," said Akio.

"I'm fine. Probably need to absorb some sunlight, that's all."

"Would you like to meet my wife?" Azha asked.

"Absolutely," replied Victis.

"Ginzal, this is my Trekachaw brother, the greatest battleship Captain that ever lived. Victis this is my new wife Ginzal."

The bridge crew clapped their hands and the Trekachaws' stripes glowed a brilliant green. Three more lights entered the bridge and spiraled above Azha before morphing into Zeta, Cody, and Nikki.

Zeta screamed her son's name, "Cole! We thought you were dead."

Azha succumbed, allowing Cole to rise, "See mom, I'm fine. Ginger's here, she merged with a Quizan named Quetzal."

Zeta let go of Azha and threw her arms around Ginzal. "Thank you for taking such good care of me, Ginger. How can I ever repay you for all your kindness?"

"Zeta, ah, Beverly, you're like a mother to me. I took care of you because I love you."

Ginzal took a couple of steps back, "Beverly, you look fantastic. So, beautiful."

"I'm so thankful for what Cole did for me. Are you happy merged?" Beverly asked.

"Yes, I think so. I'm still working out the kinks with my Quizan half."

"Where is Cole Jr.?" Beverly asked.

"The police thought I was somehow responsible for your and Cole's disappearances. When I was arrested, Frank took custody of Cole Jr. When we return to Earth for Cole Jr., Frank wants to go with us. It would be wrong to leave him behind," said Ginger.

Victis told Beverly and Ginger to say goodbye to Cole. He needed Azha for the new Trekachaw training. Of course, that wasn't the real reason. Victis had missed Azha. They needed to catch up. Allowing this to continue was out of the question.

twenty six

DEO VOLENTE

"ARE YOU FREE TO DO WHATEVER YOU WANT TO DO?"

VICTIS adjusted his schedule to meet with Azha in the Quizan chambers where they could soak up artificial rays and he could hear all about Azha's near death experience. Zeta and Ginzal were joined at the hip talking about earth. Azha was grateful for Victis's invitation. He was tired of hearing about Human good old times.

Neither Azha nor Victis said more than a couple of words. They nodded off almost immediately under the warm artificial sunrays. Victis awoke startled. As always, he was under pressure and loose ends needed his attention before departing to Palatu. Clyde and Roon were on standby waiting to trade places with Atue on the cargo ship, and Azha's shuttle was still floating in space.

Nikki and Cody had been boasting to the Ryquat navigators about their Earth fixed-winged pilots license. Therefore, in their astute opinion they should be considered candidates to assist with the retrieval of the shuttle. Akio was intrigued by their enthusiasm and decided to take the eager new Trekachaws under his wing.

Navigating the abandoned shuttle floating in space was the perfect opportunity for the new pilots. Per Victis's approval, they were good to go.

Next on Victis's agenda, the cargo ship. He requested, Roon, Clyde, and Azha to the bridge.

"Roon, you'll be acting Captain of the cargo ship with Clyde second in command. Azha, do you want to go with us?"

"Yes, it seems like a life time ago since I stole it," replied Azha.

The four Trekachaws turned into energy and in tandem flew through space towards the massive cargo ship.

Entering from the bow made it much easier to locate the bridge. Atue's nervous habit of rubbing his ear along with his tan stripes were a dead giveaway he was dreading the news. Victis did not wish to make him suffer needlessly, so he got right to the point.

"Four Human Trekachaws died fighting the Gors. We're both responsible for their deaths. Having no previous training, you acted in good faith. From now on, I will respect your position as a Master Engineer. Do you have any questions for me?"

Atue slumped over in his chair and covered his face with his hands. "No, Captain."

Akio's voice came over the intercom.

"Captain I have Pax on com-4 waiting to speak with you. He says it's an emergency and will only relay the information directly to you. Do you want me to transmit?"

"Yes, we're still figuring out the system over here. I don't want to lose him by changing coms," advised Victis.

"Copy, standby."

The monitor blacked-out for a second, then it lit up with Pax on the screen.

"Is that Azha?" Pax asked.

"Yep, I've returned from the dead. Traitor Myosis missed his mark," replied Azha.

"I don't know if you can see me, but I'm glowing green," said Pax.

"We can see you. Thanks, glad to be home. I have my Human wife with me. She merged with Quetzal."

"Congratulations can't wait to meet her," smiled Pax.

"Pax, Azha, are you finished? I don't want to be a party popper, but what's the emergency?" Victis asked.

"The expression is *party pooper*," replied Azha.

"No. I clearly remember the idiom to be *party popper*. *Pooper* doesn't make any sense," argued Victis.

"Don't be such an *ass*. It doesn't have to make sense," protested Azha.

"You're bad. Why do you feel the need to use foul words?" Victis scolded.

"You say foul words all the time in Japanese," replied Azha.

"Ha, you're bad and I'm an ass. Together we're *bad asses*," smiled Victis.

"Unko, I missed us doing this," Victis chuckled. "So, Pax what's the emergency?"

"Ah, three female Ryquats were found in a holding area. The older woman has been caring for an adult female and a little girl. I do not recognize the older female. But I recognized the adult female. She's your wife Connie, and the girl's probably your daughter. She's the right age for Connie being pregnant when she was captured. The girl is healthy and has been well cared for by the older woman. The girl's name is Tilly and the older woman's name is Marilyn. I'm sorry to inform you that Connie has suffered great physical harm and is psychotic."

"Connie? Are you sure she's Connie?"

"I'm positive," assured Pax.

Victis looked as if he were about ready to faint again. Rather than taking a chance, Azha helped him over to a chair and told him to sit down.

"Connie died on Trinite. I found her blouse on the floor ripped to pieces... soaked with blood. Azha, if this is true, if I had known... Pax, I didn't know. She must hate me for not rescuing her from those monsters. Azha, can you take over here? I need to go."

"Yes, Victis. Don't worry, Akio can manage your ship just fine and I can stay here on the cargo ship. Do you want Roon and Clyde back on your ship to help Akio?"

"Yes."

"Go, we'll be fine," insisted Azha.

Victis turned into energy and disappeared.

"Akio, are you listening in on the com? Did you hear what Pax told Victis?" Azha asked.

"Yes, I will match your speed. Can the cargo ship Hikari?" Akio asked.

"I don't know? Atue are you listening? Do you know?"

"Yes, I had help from a friend that knows this ship. He's also the one who told the Fidus Achates about the Gystfins and the bad Ryquat slaughtering us. I'd like to introduce him, but you must promise me you won't hurt him?"

"Why would I hurt him? He saved us," asked Azha.

"Promise me," replied Atue.

"I'm going to hurt you, if you ask me again," warned Azha.

"His name is Boo and he's a Gystfin," said Atue.

"Are you out of your mind? A Gystfin? You're protecting a Gystfin?"

"Azha, you promised. If you try to hurt him, I'll stop you."

"How do you know he's not a spy? Who else knows about this Gystfin?" Azha demanded.

"He's not a spy. All the Human Trekachaws like him. Two of the Trekachaws found him living inside a crate."

"How long has he been on the ship?" Azha asked.

"He was on board when you stole it. Kogbor exiled Boo from Palatu because he refused to kill or suck grey-death energy from us. Boo was Kogbor's Chief Engineer. That's the only reason he's alive. I can understand why Kogbor didn't kill Boo; he is an excellent Engineer. He's not like any Gystfin we've ever met. Boo is good, not a monster."

"We'll see. I want to meet Boo first, then I'll make the decision whether he is or is not of value," Azha said in anger. "Where are you?"

"In the cargo bay next to the bridge. I've never asked you for anything. Boo is my friend. I'm asking you not to hurt him."

"I'll be right there," barked Azha.

Azha morphed into body form next to Atue.

"Victis trusted your judgement and you got five Trekachaws killed. Why should I trust your judgement?"

Atue's stripes flared purple and his eyes turned yellow, "Take that back Azha. *No*, don't even try. I don't care what you think of me anymore. I have six Trekachaws who will stand with me to protect Boo," Atue warned, preparing himself to fight. "Boo risked his life to save Quizans. Kogbor tried to kill him when he found out that he was the one who told the Ryquats. Boo hid in the ship to stay alive."

The weary Gystfin shuffled out from behind a monitor and surrendered himself.

"Atue, Boo die now. Do not fight."

Boo lowered his head, "Azha, kill Boo fast. Not suffer."

Six Trekachaws stepped between Azha and Boo.

"Stop! You've made your point. Gystfin, look at me and remember my words," threatened Azha.

Boo raised his head and shivered.

"I will not kill you now. When I have proof of what you say, be it truth or lie, that's when we'll speak again. Have I made myself clear?" Azha demanded.

"Yes," Boo nodded.

"Akio, are you still listening?"

"Yes, Azha."

"Send the Trekachaws on the battleship to the cargo ship with instructions to meet me on the bridge. Do you want Roon, Clyde, Nikki, and Cody to remain on your ship?"

"That would please me," replied Akio.

"Is Roon on the Bridge?" Azha asked.

"Yep, standing next to Akio. How can I help?"

"Our mission is to fly these two ships safely to Palatu. Assist Akio with monitoring any anomalies or threats en route. If either of you suspect anything, no matter how trivial, contact me immediately."

"Understood. Zeta, Clyde, Takeda, and nineteen Trekachaws are energized and ready to go."

"Send them now," Azha confirmed.

"Anzen'na tabi."

"Akio, I didn't copy your last transmission?" Azha asked.

"Anzen'na tabi. *Safe journey.*"

"You too, Akio."

VICTIS REFUSED TO BELIEVE CONNIE was alive; Pax had to be wrong. Crozin captives rarely survived for very long. Personally, he had never met one. Rumors told, it was better not to survive. Painful memories flooded his mind, none of them pleasant, none of them he wanted to remember. Heidi would have been eight years old.

What would he say to her, if she was Connie? How could she ever forgive him for assuming she was dead? There was no excuse for his unforgivable mistake. Nothing he said now was going to change the hell she endured. Pify's battleship came into view.

The bridge was bustling with colorful Umduls. Right away, Pify noticed his energy light and waved. Victis morphed into body form next to the old Captain.

"Welcome. Pax meet family thought gone. Daughter delight, not so your wife. Together we go, Connie afraid. Have patience today, tomorrow we'll see."

Victis knew it was bad if Pify felt the need to escort him. The corridors were closing in on him and he was lost for words. Pax greeted them at the door. His worst fears had been confirmed, the look on Pax's face said it all.

"Before you see her Victis, sit down. I need to explain a couple of things. After you visit Connie, I'll introduce you to your daughter and the woman who cared for her."

Victis felt dizzy and his legs were weak. Pax shoved a chair underneath him and told him to sit down.

"We can do this later," suggested Pax.

"No. I want to see her."

"Connie's improving, but she's extremely psychotic. She's disfigured and has quite a few physical scars. And she doesn't trust anyone except for Marilyn, the older woman. So, don't be offended. Do you want me to continue?" Pax asked.

"Yes," replied Victis.

"When the Crozins attacked Trinite they took Connie as a breeder. Marilyn told me Heidi died on Trinite."

"I know she's dead Pax. I watched the Crozin Ukaru rip her heart out. Don't you remember?" Azha snapped.

"No, forgive me. I passed out when they killed Bruce's family. We've never talked about it since that day," replied Pax.

"I'm glad you forgot. I wish I could forget," Victis said with remorse.

Pax grabbed a chair and scooted it over next to Victis. Unable to talk, he sat down and covered his face with his hands. Pify shuffled over to them and grunted. He patted their cheeks with his fat little hands trying his best to comfort them.

"Better I say to Victis, Connie not well. Connie afraid of dark. Connie's mind is haunted, sees monsters where there's none. I go too, when ready," offered Pify.

"I'm ready," said Victis.

Victis lied. He was never going to be ready.

Pax stood up and waited. Victis stood up slowly. Pify grunted, "We all go," and shuffled towards the door. Pax wiped the tears from his eyes and followed Pify. Victis concentrated on Pax and Pify walking in front of him, trying not to overthink what he was about to see.

At the end of a corridor was a locked metal door with a small window at eye level. Pax unlocked the door and stepped to the side. Inside, the lights were dimmed, and the room was barren of conventional furniture. Connie was sitting in a chair that was bolted to the floor. Next to the wall, a small bed with restraints validated the severity of her paranoia. She looked disoriented and old, much older than her years. Pax and Pify entered the room and stood against the wall adjacent to the door. She recognized Pax by her willingness to look at him. As Victis entered the room, Pax pointed at him and spoke softly, "Connie, this is the other Trekachaw I was telling you about. Remember I was Jacet. This Trekachaw was Victis."

It was painfully clear Victis was not welcomed. Her eyes turned crazy with fear and she hissed at Pax.

"You liar. That's not Victis. Get him out of here," she screamed.

Connie squirmed out of her chair and slithered on her stomach across the floor to hide beneath the bed. One of her legs was horribly disfigured. It looked as if it had been broken and healed on its own. When she was screaming at them, Victis noticed that her face was swollen and most of her front teeth were either cracked or missing. Her cheek bone was dented in, causing her eye on that side to droop, and her nose was crooked from being broken more than once. She was far worse than he'd imagined. Pify grabbed Victis by the arm and pulled him out of the room.

"Connie special care, Pax knows best for sure. Tilly waits for father."

"Pify, what did they do to her?" cried Victis.

"Pax care for Connie. You meet Tilly. We go," said Pify pulling on Azha's arm.

Two Umdul Toogus aids ran past them into the room and shut the door. Victis followed and looked through the window in the doorway. Connie had crawled out from underneath the bed and was throwing herself against a wall, trying to hurt herself. She screamed profanities at Pax accusing him of being a lying Crozin. Connie's eyes got wild, and she clawed at her face causing herself to bleed. In her head, someone was there. She began running across the room in circles dodging the monster that haunted her mind. Turning to face the beast, she ripped her gown off. Hissing for everyone to stay back, she scrambled onto her bed, jumping up and down.

"Come on; I'll kill you; you can't hurt me anymore."

Victis looked away. Seeing her like this was more than he could take. He heard sounds of cloth ripping and a scuffle. Connie was screaming over and over, *"Victis not here, Crozin Bastards. Victis not here, Crozin Bastards."*

Pax spoke to her in a calm monotone voice, but Victis could hear a hint of urgency in his words.

"Connie, I'm not a Crozin. If you'll calm down, I won't have to sedate you again."

He warned the Umdul aids to be careful, that she had bitten him and other medical staff. Victis listened to the struggle as they held her down. Pax had no other choice than to sedate her.

Victis slid down the wall and sat on the floor. That was not Connie. This was far worse than death. She was completely insane and disfigured from years of abuse. What did the Crozins do to her and why would they keep her alive? Connie was right, he was not her Victis. No wonder she saw him as another monster. Unless a Quizan was willing to merge with her, their life together died on Trinite.

Pax and the Umdul aides walked out of the room and locked the door behind them.

"She's better now. This will take a lot of patience and reha- bilitation. Would you like to meet your daughter? She's not afraid of me, anymore."

"Anymore? Was she afraid of us, too?" Victis asked.

"Very afraid. Marilyn is like her grandmother, so she listens to her. Without Marilyn, Tilly would've been an hors d'oeuvre at a Crozins dinner years ago. I don't know how she did it, but she protected her, "said Pax. "Do you want to know any more about Connie?"

"Might as well. I don't see how it could get any worse," said Azha.

"We can stop if it's too much. Connie believes you're on Zaurak or Trinite. She keeps asking to go there. I had hoped when she saw you, something would've clicked. We can try it again while she's sedated, if you want?"

"Maybe. Whatever's best for her," said Azha.

"On a different note, I spoke with Vexy about transporting them to Zaurak. For now, that's impossible. The Crozins and Gors are trying to occupy Zaurak while the Umduls are at an impasse," advised Pax.

"You spoke with Vexy?" Victis asked.

"Yes, yesterday. She told me as soon as the Umduls left Zaurak space, the Crozins were waiting to attack. If you ask me, they were tipped off. Zaurak is going to lose this war. I can't understand why they won't negotiate with the Umduls. None of this makes any sense," said Pax.

"Is Vexy safe?" Victis asked.

"For the time being. She claims to have an escape contingency plan if necessary. The Fidus Achates are reviewing the proposal and are entertaining a re-vote to side with the Umduls. In the last couple of days, she was able to sway some of the Ryquat Council members. Vexy's afraid that if she continues to speak out on your behalf, she could be in danger. We both know she's a cunning and resourceful woman. When it's not safe, she'll find a way out. Vexy's worried about you. She told me to tell you, good luck and if you need anything she'd do her best to help."

"She's always had my back, even when I pushed her away. She gave our marriage her all. I never gave her the credit she deserved," said Victis.

"I think she knew you weren't ready for a relationship. She pushed you into a marriage thinking her love was enough for both of you. Believe me, she doesn't blame you," assured Pax.

"I was not a good Ryquat and I'm not a good Trekachaw. Look at what I've done. Connie, and now I feel guilty about Vexy. Pax if I spend too much time on this, I'll compromise everything the Trekachaws have accomplished. I can't allow myself to be distracted by them or anything. Can you take care of Connie and Tilly?" Victis asked.

"Of course, I will," replied Pax.

"You must think I'm incredibly selfish."

"Victis, it's impossible to please everyone. You are a Trekachaw, not a Ryquat or a Quizan. We are fighting for our very existence in the galaxy with more enemies than we have friends. Before this is over, you'll be forced to compromise yourself time and time again. Stay strong for us. We need to find a new planet we can call home."

"You're right, I can't allow myself to be distracted from what we've started. There's too much at stake."

Tilly was waiting with Marilyn to meet her father. Victis knew he was no more a father than he was a husband. For her sake, Tilly would remain with Marilyn on Opus or Zaurak where they'd be safe. Victis continued walking down the corridor with Pax to a conference room questioning, why? If he wasn't going to be a part of her life, why confuse her? Outside the room, Victis stopped. He saw his past, that other life that existed only in his dreams. Sorrow, an overwhelming burden of grief, made him want to block the images of Heidi playing outside their home on Trinite. They were vivid, as if he could reach out and touch her. Sounds of Connie laughing reminded him of the love he once felt for her. Those precious memories were replaced by screams and the Ukaru Crozin ripping out Heidi's heart. He wanted to forget the pain, the helplessness, the lives he could not save. Pax was saying something. Victis felt himself wanting to fly away.

"Victis, do you want to do this some other time?" Pax asked.

"No, I should meet my daughter at least once," replied Victis.

Pax opened the door. She looked exactly like Heidi, same smile, same perfect little girl. To his surprise, she let go of the woman's hand and boldly walked up to him. She reached up to grab his finger and pulled him over to a chair next to the old woman. Victis sat down and waited for Marilyn to speak.

"I am honored to meet you, Captain Victis. This is Tilly, your daughter. Would you like to hear about her?"

"Yes, I would, very much so," replied Victis.

"The Crozins assigned me to Connie when she was bastilled on Galak. I helped Connie with her delivery and tended to her needs until she was strong. Tilly has been with me since she was born. My hope is that you'll allow me to remain with them," asked Marilyn.

"You have my promise. Can you tell me what happened to Connie?" Victis asked.

"Of course. Connie was pregnant with Tilly when she arrived on Galak. The Ukaru who captured her wanted Connie for his own breeding. Why he didn't immediately terminate Connie's pregnancy is a mystery. I believe in the beginning the Ukaru kept Tilly alive because he knew she was your daughter. After Tilly was born, he became attached to her in his own way. He assigned me to Tilly and protected both of us from Crozins who wished us harm. From the time she could crawl, Tilly was free to roam his ship. We were genuinely liked by most of the Crozins, the Ruks, and especially the Ukaru. Tilly adores the Ukaru and has no fear of them. Connie was detained in a bastille by herself and for the most part isolated from Tilly. Every so often, I was given permission to escort Tilly to the bastille where she'd visit her mother. The Ukaru used Tilly to control Connie. When she fought him, he would threaten to hurt Tilly unless she cooperated."

"What did he make her do?" Victis asked.

"A Crozin and a Ryquat's reproductive genitals are very similar. The Ukaru tried to impregnate her for years. During that time, he kept Connie for himself and protected her from the Ruks. The breeding was unsuccessful, so another Ryquat female was gifted to him. Normally, when a Ukaru discards a breeder, he kills her, then eats her to demonstrate his dislike for her failure to reproduce."

"Why do they want to create a Ryquat-Crozin hybrid?" Victis asked.

"Besides Crozins being very attracted to female Ryquats, they believe a hybrid would be physically stronger and the skull would be reduced. The Ukaru should have eaten Connie. Instead, he gave her to the Ruks for pleasure, never to be killed. This was the only way to keep her alive without compromising his position. The Ruks rarely have an opportunity to breed a female Ryquat. Unlike the Ukaru, they took pleasure in torturing Connie before, during, and after breeding. For a while, they tried to remove her eggs for an artificial reproduction program. When that failed, she was given back to the Ruks. Eventually she stopped fighting them.

The Ruks grew tired of her and bred her less often. But when they did, it was vile and sadistic. I overheard some of the Ruks talking before the attack. It sounded to me like they were planning on using Connie and Tilly as a trade. Several of the Ruks spoke of a Ryquat Captain conspiring with them to invade Zaurak and Palatu. The Ruks obey and honor this Ryquat as if he were a Ukaru. A Gystfin called Myosis was contracted by the Ryquat Captain to kill you and a Trekachaw called Azha. Myosis's price was to watch Connie being bred by the Ruks in lieu of payment. He tried to negotiate for Tilly, but the Ukaru warned him never to ask again. I was present in a view container as the Ukaru's witness to insure no one killed Connie. During the breeding, Myosis took his own pleasure as the Ruks took turns forcing themselves upon her. When the Ruks finished, they threw Connie to the floor and ordered her to crawl on her hands and knees across the room. When she tried to stand up, they'd laugh and push her down demanding she kneel before them and kiss their genitals. Myosis took great joy in watching and requested permission to punish the wife of Victis. A Ruk denied Myosis's request, reminding him that a Gystfin is not worthy of touching a female Ryquat. Myosis waited until the Ruks left, but I was still there. That monster hit Connie in the face so hard he knocked out most of her front teeth.

I thought he had killed her, there was so much blood. The Ukaru was livid when I told him what Myosis did. The Ukaru warned Myosis that he'd feel his wrath if he ever disobeyed him again. Not more than a day before the Umduls raided this ship, the Ukaru and Myosis took a shuttle to rendezvous with the Ryquat Captain. Lucky for me, the Crozins never consider me a threat. If they knew what I know, I'd be dead."

"There are no words to express my gratitude. I am forever in your debt. We need to discuss where you, Tilly, and Connie can live and not be in danger."

Pax and Pify had been waiting quietly inside the room, listening to Marilyn. Pify snorted and waddled over to Victis, "Pax confirm, plan good for all. Tilly likes Umduls, Marilyn too, right?"

"Yes, Captain Pify, I like Umduls," smiled Marilyn.

"Entertain, Umduls Opus best for all. Toogus superior, Pax agrees perfect for Connie. Pax on battleship, shall we agree twice on important future. Toogus escort family on ships you plucked from Crozin and Gors. Soon depart for Opus to start this new and better life. Umdul engineers gussy-up birds and expel stink. Friction Energy, we do, then old ships return new. My gifts Captain Victis for war and victories to come."

"What can I say?" Victis agreed.

"All but you knew plan to come," replied Pify.

"OK then, it's a plan my old friend. May I ask, what is Friction Energy?"

"Should you? Friction Energy future infinity. Umduls comprehend to assimilate into new. Raw materials obsolete, not important Umduls destiny to be."

"When did the Umduls discover Friction Energy?" Victis asked.

"Secret till sure we were. Secret for now. Secret of Umduls till secret no more. This I will tell. Phera is clever, has her ways. Shows me ways to better self. You too, want to know? Go now, awaits dwell-8, mezzanine zone."

"She has her own living quarters on your ship?" Victis looked surprised.

"Close we are as one. Phera makes you call old salt, happy." Cpt. Pify smiled wide showing his big white teeth and Victis couldn't help but notice a twinkle in his eye.

"*NOOO*, you and Phera?" Victis gawked.

"Not so strange, are we? Care for each other, me and Phera. I agree knowledge you need. Phera teach old salt many new ways. Smart you are to learn from Phera, fool if not. Teach communication possible for Ryquat wife beyond the walls of fear. Phera show you trick or two same for me."

"I'm not sure what you just said, but I trust you, Pify," laughed Victis.

"Phera waits, otherwise you lose. Learn skills, if not, soon Toogus ship leave with regrets," said Pify.

Victis turned into energy and circled the ship before landing outside dwell-8. He was having second thoughts about what he was getting himself into. Too late, Phera was buzzing in energy next to him.

"Are you coming in or what?" Phera asked.

Victis flew through the door and morphed into body form. Phera landed far too close for comfort and morphed into body form standing face to face.

"Why are your stripes blue? Are you sick?" Phera asked.

"No, Pify told me to meet you. I'm a little confused, that's all," replied Victis.

"Well, allow me to clear thing up for you. Pify and I have owaried, married or whatever you want to call it. We are committed to each other," replied Phera.

"I know bonding with Pify is impossible, Phera. I'm not in the mood for games," snapped Victis.

"Hear me out before you give me grief. I *tried* to bond with Pify the normal way and yes, you're right it was impossible. There are other ways, if you want to know. We experimented and discovered that when I enter his body while in bonding energy, I can make him feel like we do when Quizans or Trekachaws bond."

"Do you feel anything?" Victis asked.

"Nothing. Pify makes me happy in other ways. He gives me power and status among the Umduls that is greater than any bonding. Umduls do not restrict their mates from the pleasure of others. What they do demand is a mate they can trust."

"I thought being faithful was part of trust," Victis said, doubtful.

"Umduls have many partners and wives. They do not think the way Ryquats do. None of that is important. What is important is this... when I enter his brain, I can communicate with his thoughts. We talk to each other when I'm inside of him," explained Phera.

"You two talk while bonding?" Victis asked.

"No. When I enter his body to talk, I do not stimulate his libido. I concentrate my energy in his left frontal lobe and left temporal lobe. If you learn this skill, it would be possible for you to enter Connie's brain and speak to her without fear and chaos."

"How do you do it?" Victis asked.

"If you'll allow me, I'll show you how," replied Phera.

"Does Pify know what we're doing?"

"This was Pify's idea," assured Phera.

"Alright then, show me how."

"Do not turn into energy. I must enter you while you're in body form," instructed Phera.

Phera turned into white energy and entered his body.

"Can you hear me?" Phera asked.

"Yes," replied Victis.

"You know Victis, I can hear your thoughts. So, you find me hard to resist? Victis, you have a dirty, dirty mind," teased Phera.

"*Stop reading my mind, Phera.* Just tell me how to do this," Victis said embarrassed.

"Ha, I knew you wanted me. Don't be so serious, I'm just having some fun with you. Did you feel me when I entered your brain?"

"Yes, you felt warm," said Victis.

"I'm leaving your body now."

Phera slipped out of his mind, leaving behind a cold rush. Victis hadn't realized that his eyes were closed until she told him to open them.

"Are you alright?" Phera asked.

"I'm not sure. That was exhilarating. Phera you are... well, you are hard to forget," admitted Victis.

"That I am. Would you like to enter me?"

"I'm having a hard time not thinking about, well, you know," Victis confessed.

"Oh, flatter me some more. I can take care of that desire, too."

"Do I enter your brain?" Victis asked.

"That is exactly what you do, from the top of my head. It's easier that way. Listen for my voice, then follow it until you can hear me clearly. Don't be afraid of hurting me; I'll tell you how to do that later."

"Well, that's disturbing. Are you going to hurt me?" Victis asked concerned.

"No silly. Just go with it."

"Here goes nothing," replied Victis.

He turned into white energy and entered Phera through the top of her head.

"Hello Phera, can you hear me." Victis heard a faint voice as if he were in a tunnel.

"Come towards my voice. Say something Victis, follow my voice," advised Phera.

"I can hear you, Phera. Can you hear me better now?"

"Yes. Don't move. You're there," replied Phera.

"This is so weird. If you hadn't bonded with Pify, or whatever you'd call this, no one would've ever figured this out."

"Told you it was incredible. Now you can talk to your wife. Are you ready for lesson two?"

"Yes," replied Victis.

"Move towards the back of my brain and down almost to my spinal cord. There's an area called the medulla and just above the medulla is the pons. That's where I stimulate Pify's libido. When you're there, I will not be able to talk to you. Don't stay there long, because you'll get me excited. Move back up to where I can talk to you and I'll let you know if you found my libido spot," instructed Phera.

Victis couldn't control his lust listening to Phera talk about her libido.

"Victis, you are a dirty Trekachaw. We need to concentrate. Stop thinking that way and move down."

"This is killing me, I've never bonded as a Trekachaw. A little patience would be appreciated," Victis said frustrated.

"Never? That's too bad. You're an attractive Trekachaw," charmed Phera.

"Phera, that's not helping," questioning if he should continue and if she was seducing him for her own benefit.

Victis moved his energy to the lower part of Phera's brain next to her spinal cord. He moved around, hoping he was in the correct area and then returned until he could hear her voice again.

"Did I do it?" asked Victis.

"Give me a minute. Ah yes, you found it. I've always done this to Pify, but I've never had it done to me. Do it again," coaxed Phera.

"What about Pify?"

"Pify told me to have ou-dim-fa with you."

"What is ou-dim-fa?" Victis asked.

"Umdul sex. Pify cares about both of us. He understands that we need ou-dim-fa. To share me is an act of love for him. Pify is very happy. Stop overthinking this. Umduls are not a one-partner ou-dim-fa species. They believe it's healthy to have bonding relationships with whomever one desires, and I agree. No one is being betrayed," said Phera losing her patience.

"Not true. I have a wife that I thought was dead, a daughter that I don't know, and an ex-wife risking her life to spy for me. Oh yeah, and I'm about to have sex, ou-dim-fa, or whatever you call it with another Trekachaw whom I've lusted after ever since you became one. I've even betrayed myself. How arrogant, justifying my reckless decisions by convincing myself I'm always right. Who's right? I feel guilty and responsible for an entire new species. What have I done?" Victis said in anger.

"Gag me, you sound just like Azha when he was on Palatu trying to save the Quizans. You did what you had to do. Victis, you saved the Quizans and most likely Earth. I don't understand the Ryquats blatant dislike for us. Personally, I don't care what they think. The Umduls have our backs, and I'm positive others in the Galaxy will, too. Vexy sounds like a Ryquat I'd like to meet. Your daughter will be fine, and your wife is a casualty that you had no control over. Don't beat yourself up. Do what you must do and move on. *Do you know why?* Because you can make a difference for all of us," replied Phera.

"What if I could arrange a Quizan merge with Connie before she's transported to Opus?" Victis asked.

"Victis, who knows if you'll ever find a Quizan willing to merge with her. I've asked Belton to help me find a Quizan for Pify. Zilch, nothing."

"Why won't a Quizan merge with Pify?" Victis asked.

"Between you and me, no one wants to be the first to merge with an Umdul. Look what happened when Myosis merged with a Gystfin. Making matters even worse, Pax spread a rumor that when Trekachaws die, their grey-death energy won't ascend to Aeon Devotio."

Victis nodded, "Pax told the truth. We don't ascend."

"Damn it, there's no telling if another Quizan will ever merge knowing that. Pify is getting old, he needs to merge soon, or he'll die."

"How long does an Umdul live?" Victis asked.

"Around two-hundred years," replied Phera.

"How old is Pify?"

"A hundred and eighty-one."

"He still has time; someone will merge with him. Pify deserves to be a Trekachaw. Do you want me to ask Belton?"

"Don't bother, he's trying," replied Phera.

"Phera, do you want me to find your spot again? No pressure, you've been very gracious. We can talk or not, whatever you'd like."

"Yes and no. Let's stop talking about sad things," said Phera.

"Okay," Victis was not sure what to say.

"Victis, this is what I'd like. Let's bond the Trekachaw way."

He felt her warm energy joining him in pure ecstasy. Victis could have stayed there forever. He was not strong enough to leave. Phera morphed into body form laying on the floor.

"Victis, come join me," she whispered.

He floated next to her and morphed into body form.

"Do you think Pify would allow us to do this again?" Victis asked.

"Victis it's up to me, not Pify."

"I'm available anywhere and anytime," replied Victis.

Phera laughed, "I'm sure this won't be the last time."

Victis and Phera lay on the floor for hours. They were surprised that no one came knocking at her door or requested her over the intercom. Pify probably ran interference for them.

"Before we leave Victis, I need to explain one more thing," said Phera.

"All right."

"The brain stem starts behind the medulla and pons, then continues down the back of the neck. I believe if we were to concentrate our energy in the brain stem, we could kill an alien by restricting their breathing, causing cerebral hypoxia death."

"How do you know this?" Victis asked.

"My Ryquat-half, Tara, graduated from a medical academy before she became Special-Ops."

"Shit, nothing about medical training was documented on your Ops background," said Victis.

"I requested my medical training be expunged from my file before submitting a précis profile of qualifications required for a Special Ops position on your battleship."

"Why?" Victis asked.

"You would've assigned me to Pax instead of Special-Ops."

"You're probably right. Did you ever think you'd be a Captain of your own battleship?"

"Not this soon. Did you ever think you'd be a Trekachaw?" Phera asked.

"Not in a million years."

"I'm going to find Pify," said Phera.

"Sounds good to me," smiled Victis.

twenty seven

PECCAVI

THE Trekachaws protected the Quizans, allowing them to do what they did best...soak up the sun and bother no one. Belton was busy being King and liaison for those who visited Palatu. Deneb and Vious had grown restless and were anxious to leave upon Victis's return. There was one small addition that needed the Captain's approval. They had bonded in silver and were the proud parents of the first Trekachaw purebred. Vious insisted on addressing him by the Ryquat term, baby. Whereas, Deneb profusely protested wanting to call him a quiey. Tomato, *Tomãto,* he was the first. Eventually the baby was named after the Earth mission...*Kigen.*

Unlike a Ryquat baby, Kigen inherited the attributes of a Quiey, and walked within minutes after his silver-light morphed into body form. By the time he was a week old, Kigen had the dexterity and speed of his parents. Until now, Trekachaw eyes were yellow. Kigen's eyes were as blue as Zaurak' shimmering snow. It was anyone's guess when the boy would reach maturity or his life expectancy.

Kigen was exactly two weeks old and pestering them relentlessly to visit the ships in space. Bored to death, Vious and Deneb were happy to accommodate their son's curiosity. Besides, they wanted Captain Pify and Pax to meet Kigen. Belton was invited but he declined, claiming he had *many things to address* before Victis returned. They were neither surprised nor insulted. Belton preferred to soak up the Targus sun all day on a flat boulder outside his cavern. Every night when the sun set, he'd socialize with his crony Quizan Soldiers in the courtyard. Belton preferred his life as a Quizan.

Kigen was impossible to control. They discovered a new skill that only their baby Trekachaw could perform. He was on the bridge one minute, and then gone the next. Panic ensued when he disappeared. Everyone searched high and low, even in outer space. It was Phera who first spotted two blue eyes following her as she walked past a control panel. The eyes faded when she stopped and then gradually disappeared as she moved towards them to get a closer look. The metal on the panel was slightly different, as if a thin layer of clear plastic was covering it. Phera opened and closed her eyes several times to test her own vision. She wasn't sure what she'd seen, but whatever it was, had vanished. Maybe an extra pair of eyes could decipher the anomaly.

"Pify, take a look at this." Phera pointed at the spot where she last saw the eyes. "Vious and Deneb should come over here and look at this. I saw blue eyes watching me, or at least I think they were," Phera explained.

"Bridge navigation panel. Blue eyes not see. Not sure you are, ask me?"

"Pify, I saw something," said Phera.

"Blue eyes strange, I go. Vious, maybe Deneb then we'll see," said Pify.

Pify waddled back to the bridge with Deneb and Vious trailing behind. Phera pointed to the spot where she first saw the blue eyes. "I think I saw them again. I swear there's something there."

As if in a trance, the four of them fixated on the spot where Phera had pointed. Not a word was said between them, not even a blink of an eye. The blue eyes appeared then flashed red. Phera jumped back and tripped over Deneb. Deneb moaned in pain and fell on her derriere. Vious stumbled over Deneb and hit his head on the rail and Pify yelled out, "Too funny, almost pee on self."

Kigen stepped out of the control panel giggling at the silly foursome. The boy Trekachaw was a chameleon. He could permeate and change his colors to perfectly blend with any object or background.

What else could Kigen do? Only time would tell. Phera turned into energy and flew into the control panel, then flew out and morphed into body form. "How does he do that? I can't morph while in a solid object."

Vious and Deneb tried to morph inside the control panel and failed. "Kigen is the only Trekachaw I know of who can do that," said Deneb.

Pify watched the boy change colors and disappear several times while the adults were testing themselves. When the indicators on the panel flashed red, Kigen's blue eyes turned red and flashed in sequence with the lights.

"Kigen special, wild is he. Danger hide good not find. Show Victis pleased I'm sure," said Pify.

Deneb and Vious spoke at the same time, "Victis is here? When did he get back?"

"One day past. Victis captive kinetic to detail before social spirit," explained Pify.

"What? Phera do you understand what Pify said?" Vious asked.

"Victis needs to take care of something, then we'll meet him," replied Phera.

"Oh. When do you think he'll be finished with... whatever Pify said?" Deneb asked.

"Spirit says when," replied Pify.

Deneb and Vious looked at each other, then started to speak at the same time again.

Phera threw her hands up in the air. "This is so stupid, it's funny. Deneb go first."

"I'm flying to Palatu to get Belton. He should be here when Captain Victis finishes his spirit captive kinetic detail thing. Vious said he'd stay here with Kigen."

"Try to keep Kigen from morphing into anything else," Phera asked Vious in a snarky tone.

Pify waddled with a skip and a hop over to his captain's chair and sat down. Phera followed Pify; she'd had enough of the Trekachaw boy for one day.

In a hushed voice Pify asked, "Phera come close, Victis good? Libido brain, teach communicate with wife?"

Phera leaned over Pify's shoulder and whispered into his ear, "We did. Victis feels much better. He says thank you. Victis was worried that you'd get mad. Didn't want to betray you."

"Phera explain not Umduls' way. Ataraxia Victis' pain. We care, we share?" Pify asked.

"All the same Pify, you should talk to him," advised Phera.

"Pify explain Umdul way," replied Pify.

Phera kissed Pify's cheek and stood up. On the top of Pify's head something wiggled in his hair. Phera screamed, "*Shit, Pify don't move there's something in your hair.*"

Pify ducked and fell out of his chair as Phera slapped the top of his head.

"*Phera, NO,*" yelled Pify.

"Hold still Pify. *Gross*, it's moving around on your head. Yuck, what is it?"

A tiny dazed head with wiggly eyes popped up and looked at Phera.

"*NO* Phera, my Tit," yelled Pify.

"Your what? Your Tit? *You have a Tit on your head?*" Phera gasped.

"Fizz pet Tit. Don't violate my Tit." Pify blocked Phera from hitting his head again.

"Oh, I'm so grossed out. What's a Tit? How long has that... been in your hair?"

"Years, Umduls keep Tit companions," explained Pify.

Pify yelled out to his crewmen, "Display Umdul Tits."

Indeed, there were colorful Tits on every Umdul's head. What she could see of the Tits were a perfect color match to their respective Umdul's vibrant hair. If she didn't know better, she'd have thought they were hair accessories. Phera's face looked shocked, disgusted, and curious all at the same time.

"Does that thing sleep with you?" Phera asked.

"Tit home Umduls hair. Tit die if not. Cute Tit friendly. Phera fizz not gross," refuted Pify.

"I guess, if she means that much to you. Did I hurt her?" Phera asked.

Pify baby-talked to Fizz, "Fizz, ooh Fizzy. Phera hurt, not know."

Two tiny black eyes popped up, peeking out from Pify's orange hair.

"I won't hurt you again, Fizz. Sorry I slapped you," said Phera.

The little Tit crawled up on a tuff of Pify's hair and reached its hands out to Phera. Pify was right, Phera was smitten by Fizz's charm.

"Her body is adorable and so tiny. How big is she, an inch?" Phera asked.

"Pify love Fizz and Phera. Inch less or more, Fizz three centimeters." He was relieved his secret was out and they had officially met.

"I'm going to feel really bad if I hurt her. Her fuzzy, tiny, orange body is the cutest thing I've ever seen. She's the same color as your hair. Was she that color when you picked her out, or did she change colors?

"No hurt, Tits tough. Come in all colors," replied Pify.

"Sorry Fizz. I promise to never hurt you again, little cutie patootie," Phera cooed.

Fizz looked up at Phera and winked. She reached out again, wanting Phera to pick her up. Pify encouraged her, demonstrating how to hold her hand flat next to Fizz. Phera understood why Pify loved Fizz the moment she crawled onto her hand and curled up.

"Phera, Fizz share. You care Fizz in hair," suggested Pify.

He placed her hand on top of her head and waited for Fizz to crawl off.

"We'll share her, until I get my own," replied Phera.

Three monitors switched screens to Azha and Atue requesting a ship to ship transmission from the cargo ship. They had entered Palatu's orbit and were eager to dock with Pify's battleship. Captain Pify waddled to the center of the bridge. "Open com for ears to hear. Azha good are you, Atue same?

"Yes, we are. I have urgent information to discuss with you and Captain Victis," advised Azha.

"Urgent you say? Not ship to ship? Captain Yagi best for cargo ship for now?" Pify asked.

"Affirm. Akio is escorting a Gystfin in a shuttle to your ship with your permission. Is there someone who can replace Akio on Victis's battleship? He should be at the briefing to answer questions," said Azha.

"My, my, a Gystfin you say? Briefing interesting will reveal," said Pify.

Phera spoke up, "You captured a Gystfin?"

"It's not what you think. The Gystfin is an ally called Boo. He was the source of the leak to the Fidus Achates regarding the Quizans being slaughtered by Captain Smyth, Kogbor, and the Gystfins. Pify, I must have your word that Boo will be safe on your ship."

"*Guarantee,* Boo safe he is," promised Pify.

"Thank you Pify. Roon, Zeta, Nikki, Clyde, Cody, Takeda, Duroc, Ajax, and my wife Ginzal are flying over in energy to be at the briefing. The other Human Trekachaws will not be attending. If possible, Phera, Choan, Vopar, Vious, Deneb, Pax, and Duro should attend," said Azha.

"Pify make possible. Brief in Mezzanine three... Welcome home."

"Glad to be home my friend," replied Azha.

Pify asked Phera to take charge of assembling the attendees at the Mezzanine. Victis did not return to the bridge with Phera. Instead, Victis thought it best to spend what little time he had left with his daughter before she departed to Opus. Pify walked as fast as his short legs permitted down the corridors to Tilly and Marilyn quarters. The door was shut, but he could hear Victis talking inside. A couple of tap-tap-taps were enough to get his attention. Victis opened the door and looked down at Pify.

"Hey Pify, come in. Marilyn and Tilly are telling me some incredible stories."

"Must ask end stories, follow me. Azha present Palatu space, important data he shares. You convey."

"Okay? Give me a minute to say goodbye."

Pify skipped a few steps, "I wait, go soon."

Pify stood outside the door whistling then he broke into a song, "*Coo-coo to-da-da. Coo-coo*
ou-dim-fa-da. Victis and Phera do da coo-coo ou-fa-la."

Victis heard what he was singing and panicked, "*Gotta go.* I'll come back as soon as I can."

Red faced with green stripes, he ran out the door and shut it. "Pify, *shhh-shush.*"

"Funny, Victis outré bright stripes. Good, with daughter. Ah-ha, green stripes funny song sings too? Phera report superb for ou-dim-fa. Make Pify happy."

"Well, I guess? I take it Phera told you everything?" Victis asked.

"Oh, detail. Victis good?" Pify asked.

"Very good. I'm glad you're an understanding Umdul," replied Victis.

"Umdul way, good way. Sing now?"

"How about we sing after the convey or whatever this is you're taking me to?"

"Perfect, we go," said Pify.

The Trekachaws had arrived and were assembled inside the Mezzanine, with one exception. Atue stayed behind to accompany the shuttle, fearing for Boo's safety. Azha walked up to Victis and gave him a bear hug that would've crushed a Ryquat. They both looked down at Pify with devilish grins.

"No hug me, too small. *Get away.*" Pify started to waddle under the table, but not fast enough.

Victis picked him up and sat him on top of Azha's shoulders. They walked through the crowded Mezzanine, then careful lifted Pify from Azha's shoulders and set him down on a table. Looking out into the crowded Mezzanine, Pify needed to be higher if he were to be seen. Azha found a sturdy chair and placed it on top of the table. He then stood Pify on top of the chair. Pify smiled and clapped his hands.

"Tall am I, a view not known. Trekachaws, loyal Ryquats, Umduls unite, strong we are. Speak Azha, want to hear," announced Pify.

Atue, Akio, and Boo entered the back of the Mezzanine and stood against the wall. Heads spun, and the Mezzanine glowed red with yellow eyes fixed upon the Gystfin.

Pify shouted, "Gystfin guest, my ship, my rule. Azha speak, hear or leave not to return. Umdul gave promise."

More than a few Trekachaws were angry. Azha ordered sharply, "Stop staring at the Gystfin. Shall we continue? Alright, now that I have your attention. As you know, three Trekachaws did not survive the journey. For those who knew them, I am deeply sorry for your loss. We shall honor their sacrifice. Ryquat Trekachaws, I would like you to welcome the new Human Trekachaws. They will need your guidance and support. They are our future and family. Captain Victis, do you have anything to address?"

"Yes. This is mandatory. Everyone be here tomorrow, same time. The Human Trekachaws will attend tomorrow's meeting. Until then, there will be no contact of any kind with any of them unless I approve it first. Phera, Pax, Roon, Nikki, Cody, Zeta, Clyde, Takeda, Atue, Akio, and Boo, do not leave. Everyone else is dismissed."

Pify sat down on his table top chair and waited for the Trekachaws to exit the Mezzanine. Azha dreaded what came next. He wondered how Victis would take the news.

Victis didn't wait, "Who's responsible for this Gystfin?"

After looking back and forth at each other, Azha raised his hand.

"Boo reported the Quizans being slaughtered. He's the reason you were sent to Palatu."

"So that's how it got leaked. Nice to meet you, Boo. As far as I'm concerned, your part of this mess we're all in. You're welcome on my ship, too. Is there anything else we need to discuss?" Victis asked.

Azha raised his hand again.

"Two Human Trekachaws are conspiring to dominate Earth as Gods, and they're trying to recruit other Trekachaws to join them."

"Who are they and who have they tried to recruit?" Victis asked.

Pax stepped forward, "Those are the same two that claimed to be injured on the Gor Battleship. I analyzed the blood covering their bodies. It was not theirs. Neither one of them had a scratch. When I confronted them, they refused to answer and walked away."

"Has anyone here been approached by them regarding an Earth invasion?" Victis asked.

Everyone raised their hands and began talking at the same time.

"Whoa, Azha you go first. I'll listen to the rest of you in order."

"They never came to me directly. However, several Human Trekachaws told me in confidence what they're planning," replied Azha.

"Do you know the names of the two conspiring?"

"Joshua and Nick," replied Azha.

"Akio, what do you know?"

"They never came to me directly, either. Although, Nikki, and Cody told me plenty. It concerned me enough that I changed the security code for the shuttles and the battleship to an encrypted code. The old code was entered on five separate shuttles on two separate occasions. Someone was tampering with them trying to figure out how to engage the launch systems, cockpit displays and the weapon systems. I entered a second code required to unlock the systems when Myosis became a threat. That's why they couldn't figure it out. Cody and Nikki have more information."

"All right Akio, Nikki, and Cody tell me the rest. Nikki, you go first."

"Cody and I were the only two Human Trekachaws that had permission to remain on the battleship. Everyone else was assigned to the cargo ship. Joshua and Nick snuck over here five times that I know of. They wanted Cody and me to teach them how to fly a shuttle. I asked them why and they told me because they were planning on flying it back to Earth. We reported them to Akio as soon as they left. Akio told us if they approached us again, we were to act like we were interested. Well, they did, and they spilled the beans."

Victis looked puzzled, "Explain beans?"

"That means they told us what they were planning," replied Nikki.

"Okay. I still don't get what that has to do with beans. What else did they say?" Victis asked.

"They wanted us to help them recruit more Trekachaws to take over your battleship and return to Earth as Gods. When they couldn't get anyone else to join them, they tried to steal a shuttle."

"Who else heard this?" Victis asked.

Zeta, Clyde, and Takeda raised their hands.

"Roon, did they say anything to you?"

"No, but Zeta and Clyde told me the same thing Nikki just told you."

"Atue, did they approach you?"

"No, not directly, but I heard the same thing."

"Zeta, is this what you heard too?"

"Spot on. They were even pushy about it and when I told them no, they got angry."

"Clyde, do have anything else to add?"

"Nope, they're a couple of scoundrels with no honor or gratitude. No one wanted to be a part of their mutiny."

"Good. Boo, do you have anything to say?"

"No Captain, happy here."

"I will deal with Joshua and Nick. Do not discuss what we have talked about to anyone. You're dismissed. Pify and Azha, we have additional matters to discuss."

The Mezzanine echoed with the sounds of Trekachaws leaving and the door closing behind them.

"Pify, you and Azha inform every Captain to add encrypted security codes on their shuttles and battleships. Pify, when do you think our Crozin and Gor ships will depart for Opus?" Victis asked.

"Sooner better, tomorrow best. Improve on Opus, friction-energy to fracas Crozin, Gor dirty birds."

"Very well. Tonight, I would like to visit Connie and Tilly before they leave. Azha, I'd appreciate it if you'd arrange for all the Trekachaws to meet on the Cargo ship tomorrow at 1400 hrs. Have Akio and Boo attend, as well. Pify, do you have navigators to manage Choan and Phera's battleships while they're at the meeting?"

"Navigators plenty."

"Great. Pify, I'll be on your ship for a while if you need to find me."

"Victis, ou-dim-fa with Connie?"

"No."

"You do fa da Phera? Mind rest. Body, too."

"We'll see," smiled Victis.

Victis questioned himself if he should attempt to visit Connie again. The last time was disastrous. Ou-dim-fa was completely inappropriate, and communicating inside her brain could make matters worse. He promised Tilly they'd spend more time together, and that promise he was going to keep. Victis met with Marilyn in the corridor outside their room.

"Has Pax spoken with you yet?" Marilyn asked.

"No. Why?"

Marilyn had been crying. Victis followed her back into the room and waited for her to sit down. Tilly was busy playing a game with a Toogus.

"What's wrong?" Victis asked

"Tilly shouldn't hear this again. Could you have Pax explain to you what happened? He's probably with Connie."

"Of course. Are you okay?"

"No," cried Marilyn.

Victis flew through the ship landing outside Connie's room. He peered through the small window in the door and saw what he thought was blood splatter across the walls. He realized it was, when he saw the sheets soaked with blood. Sickening memories of Trinite flashed in his head and the feeling of utter helplessness overwhelmed him. He opened the door and the same smell of death was in the air. How could this happen? He failed to protect her again.

Pax walked in with a Toogus. He had planned on cleaning the room before Victis was told. "I'm sorry you had to see this. I'm worried about Tilly. She may be in danger."

"Why is Tilly in danger? What happened?" Victis demanded.

"I'm having Marilyn and Tilly escorted to the bridge for their safety. Nurse Anna shuttled over from your battleship to assist us with Connie's transport. Anna found Traitor Myosis and a Leader scalping the Umdul Aid with a mediatric laser. I heard Anna screaming and ran into the room. Myosis and the Leader turned into energy and flew through the wall. Anna and the Umdul were injured …or I would've chased them. Connie was already dead. If the Umdul makes it through surgery, he'll have a fighting chance. Myosis slashed Anna across her stomach with his claws. I'm told she'll be okay. Myosis could still be on board for all we know."

"Did Myosis rape Connie?" Victis's voice cracked.

"Do you really want to know what Myosis did?" Pax asked.

"I'm not going to ask you again. Did Myosis rape her?" Victis demanded.

"No. Myosis did what every Gystfin does. He bit her head off."

"Have Zeta and Clyde stay with Tilly and Marilyn. Tell them not to let them out of their sight. Where's Azha?"

"I told Pify and Azha what happened. There're on the telerobotic solar deck looking for energy anomalies."

"Find out if they're still there and let them know I'll be on the bridge," ordered Victis.

The bridge monitors were receiving multiple distress messages from the Cargo Ship. Takeda was requesting either Azha or Victis to return, and for emergency medical assistance. Victis switched coms and spoke with Takeda.

"Who's hurt and how bad are they?" Victis asked.

"Atue and Boo are hurt bad. They have deep bite wounds and cuts from fighting Myosis and a Leader. They were killing Boo when Atue found them. Atue pulled Myosis off Boo, but then the Leader and Myosis ganged up on Atue. They were killing Atue when Duroc and Ajax came in. Myosis and the Leader let go of Atue and disappeared into a crate. We searched all the crates, the entire bay, and most of the ship. So far, nothing," advised Takeda.

"I'm dispatching Pax with emergency medical staff. Where do you want them?" Victis asked.

"We were afraid to move Atue or Boo; they're still in the cargo bay."

"Have Duroc meet us outside the ship. He can guide us in," ordered Victis.

Pax, Azha, and Pify landed on the bridge just in time to hear the end of the transmission.

Victis gave them a brief recap and sent Pax on his way. He then directed his attention to Azha.

"Find Phera and have her meet me outside the cargo ship. You stay here with Pify in case Myosis attacks this ship again. Akio, you take charge of Phera's ship and notify all the other ships to be on 'Keijo-alert'."

Clyde spoke up, "Captain Victis, I know how to transfer my energy. Can I try to help Atue?"

"Yes, go Clyde. Do what you can. Azha, when you get to the Cargo ship, assign five Human Trekachaws to Pify's ship, five to Choan's ship, and five to Phera's ship to assist Vopar. Have all of them report to the bridges. Roon, you're coming with me to my ship. Azha, can you manage the cargo ship?"

"Yes," replied Azha.

"Everyone to your assigned ships. Belton and Vious, take ten Human Trekachaws with you," ordered Victis.

Coms and monitors lit up with distress calls from Palatu. Myosis and the Leader were on a killing spree and there were no signs of them slowing down. Last count, over a hundred Quizans were dead.

"Change of plans, I'm going with Belton to the Planet. Roon, take care of my battleship," ordered Victis.

Azha, Phera, and Clyde flew out of Pify's ship en route to the Cargo ship. Not far behind them, Pax navigated the medical shuttle to the Cargo ship. Captain Pify ordered his thirty Umdul Battleships to activate 'Bogtu Urp' lock down and for the engineers on the Gor and two Crozin battleships to enter cryptic security codes, disable all weapon systems and extract the magnetic cores. The Engineers were to return to Pify's battleship until told otherwise.

Belton, Victis, and Vious streaked towards Palatu. Akio flew a shuttle to Phera's ship to assist Vopar. Zeta, Clyde, and Deneb remained on Pify's battleship to protect Kigen, Tilly, and Marilyn. And Roon was en route to Victis's battleship by himself.

GINZAL AWOKE FROM HER NAP and strolled onto the bridge. "Zeta, where is everyone?"

"Gone. A lot happened while you were asleep. Myosis and a Leader killed Victis's wife, scalped an Umdul Aid, and hurt a Ryquat nurse. Also, they almost killed Boo and Atue. Right now, Myosis and the Leader are slaughtering Quizans on Palatu."

"Where's Azha?"

"He went with Pax, Phera, and some other Trekachaws to the Cargo Ship."

"How long ago?" Ginzal asked.

"About five minutes," replied Zeta.

"If anyone cares, I'll be on the cargo ship with Azha," Ginzal said with attitude.

Azha selected the Human Trekachaws per Victis's instructions and sent them on their way. Joshua and Nick asked to remain on the cargo ship because they felt ill. Azha knew they were lying, but he didn't care. They were worthless anyway.

Atue's stripes were white and his eyes were hollow. Boo was torn apart, covered in blood, and his breathing was labored. Clyde bent over and felt Atue's chest with his hand.

"Phera, I transferred my energy to an injured female Trekachaw and it helped her. If I can't transfer enough energy, are you willing to give yours, too?"

"Absolutely, do it."

Clyde entered Atue's chest and a soft glow appeared in his hollow eyes. Phera entered the top of Atue's head. She knew her skills would ease his fears. Slowly she moved towards his cries for help.

"Atue, I'm Phera. Clyde is transferring his energy to you. Can you feel him?"

"Yes. Phera I'm scared, I'm dying and there is no Aeon Devotio waiting for me. I will not ascend to join the others," cried Atue.

"We won't let you die. Absorb Clyde's energy. Concentrate on living, not dying."

"Phera, I can feel him. How's he doing this?"

"Clyde knows how. I'm going to leave you to help him. Do not be afraid. Between the two of us we can save you."

"If you can't, promise you'll come back. I don't want to die alone," begged Atue.

"We won't let you down."

Phera exited Atue's head, clueless as what to do next. Clyde was still inside his chest. She wondered how long he could transfer his energy without risking his own life. Atue's eyes glowed brighter and his stripes had a slight tan color to them. This was crazy. Clyde had been inside far too long.

Phera screamed, "Clyde stop, get out of there!"

A dull glow exited Atue's chest and morphed into Clyde. He was almost completely drained.

"Phera, he's not strong enough yet to survive. Can you transfer some of your energy?"

"Tell me how," asked Phera.

"Enter through his chest and release your energy into his heart. You'll know when you've given all you can."

Phera turned into energy and entered Atue's chest.

Boo moaned, "Aut diey?"

Clyde placed his hand on Boo's forehead, "No, Atue is alive. We're getting you help real soon, save your strength."

Pax barged through the door with his medical team and began working on Boo. Phera's energy was enough to save Atue and Boo was in stable condition and expected to live. Their deaths had been thwarted despite Myosis and the Leader's best effort to end them.

Azha entered the cargo bay and morphed into body form. He felt such a relief to see Atue alive, and then he saw Phera. She looked pale, and when she tried to stand she stumbled. Azha grabbed her around the waist and held her close for the first time since she became a Trekachaw. Phera wrapped her arms around his neck and listened as he whispered into her ear, "I have always loved you and I always will."

Phera kissed his cheek and whispered back, "I believe we are destined. Not now and not tomorrow, but someday we will find our way back to one another."

A small light hovered above, watching and listening to her unfaithful husband. Ginzal was furious. His betrayal was unforgiveable. Her light flickered red with sparks of purple. It wasn't her imagination after all. Azha had been attracted to Phera from the very beginning. How could she have been so gullible. Azha was a fool. Everyone knew Phera wasn't faithful to anyone. What was wrong with Azha? Ginger is the mother of his Human child and she gave up Aeon Devotio to bond with the *great Azha*. Where was Phera when he was being attacked in the shuttle? She had waited for Azha, scared and alone in space. Myosis could have come back and bitten her head off. She had even found a cavern on that moon just in case he wasn't dead. What an ungrateful lying loser. 'He doesn't deserve me,' Ginzal thought. 'If he wants to be with Phera, fine, she can have him.'

Ginzal couldn't stand to watch them any longer, and shot out into space.

Belton scrambled together what was left of the Quizan soldiers. Myosis was long gone, leaving a path of destruction and carnage behind. Victis was as frustrated as ever. Myosis was always one step ahead. This had to stop. For now, it was best to leave the Human Trekachaws on Palatu with Belton. Victis had no business staying on Palatu any longer than necessary. He let out an ear-piercing whistle demanding everyone's attention in the courtyard. "Belton prepare your Quizan Soldiers, and Vious, train the Trekachaws for combat. I'll be available on com six if you need me."

Little did Victis know that while he was on Palatu, a catastrophe had unfolded on the Cargo Ship.

PHERA NOTICED A RED-LIGHT HOVERING in the far corner of the cargo bay. She stiffened and slowly moved her head back to look into Azha's eyes with a cold sobering stare. Azha blinked slightly, questioning her intent. Phera rolled her eyes up towards the red light and back down at Azha. Not a sound came from her mouth as he watched her lips move, *Myosis*. Steps away lay two Neco weapon within reach on the floor. At last, a chance to kill Myosis. Clyde caught on and was sheepishly moving towards the Neco Weapons. He acted as if he tripped, landing on top of them, then rolled over keeping one for himself and threw the other to Azha. The red light flashed and disappeared behind a stack of crates. Myosis was not going to get away this time.

Clyde was the first to fire on the crate and Azha followed with repeated lasers blasts, blowing it apart into a thousand pieces. They continued to fire their lasers into burning flames of debris. This time Myosis would not escape. A scorched body screamed in agony. The scream was not that of Myosis. Before them lay a scorched black body curled-up into a ball. No one could save Ginzal. She had returned to confront Azha.

Azha dropped to his knees. Clyde cried out that he was sorry, and Phera looked away from Ginzal's smoldering body. Ajax kneeled over her, "Why was she up there? Why was she red?"

Pax's hands shook as he checked her for any signs of life. "Phera, can you go in her to find out if she dead? I don't know how to help a Trekachaw."

Phera gasped. She wasn't sure if she could bring herself to enter the brain of a dead Trekachaw. Clyde volunteered to try with Phera's guidance.

"Are you sure you want to do this?" Azha asked.

"Gotta say we tried," said Clyde.

"I'm sorry, I just can't do it," said Phera as she turned away.

Clyde took Phera's hand, "Tell me how."

"Enter through the top of her head. Listen for her voice ...her thoughts. Move slowly downward and around. If you cannot feel or hear anything, then she is gone."

Clyde turned into energy and slowly disappeared into the top of Ginzal's head. He waited for her thoughts, but there were none. Methodically he moved, searching her brain for a sign. A hint of life was desperate to escape. A soul searching to escape this world. Clyde moved toward the essence, "It's Clyde, what can I do?"

"Find a way for us to escape this body and ascend in *Aeon Devotio*. Cut off my head. Ginger's soul is waiting with me. Hurry, we must go now if we're to continue our journey."

"Hold on, Ginzal."

Clyde's energy flew out the top of Ginzal's head and morphed into body form next to Phera.

"Their Aeon Devotio is alive. I must cut her head off for them to ascend."

Azha grabbed a Neco weapon off the floor and sliced Ginzal's neck, decapitating her. Two grey-death energies ascended and spiraled above, free and at peace. Azha reached up begging for forgiveness. They refused to allow him to touch them and steadily rose, then disappeared before his eyes. He could only pray they were in a better place, safe from this dismal world. Someday, he would ascend and tell them how ashamed he was for not being able to cherish their love.

twenty eight

INTER NOS

"THE BODY HEALS, YOUR SOUL REMEMBERS"

COLE rose from the depths, screaming in pain and venom surged through his body, making them deathly ill. He was trying to kill Azha to avenge the death of Ginger. Azha had underestimated Cole's strength and determination. He was using an exhausting amount of energy to fight suicide. If Cole won, Azha knew he would kill them both. Phera sensed Azha was in agony.

"This was not your fault. All of us thought she was Myosis," said Phera.

Clyde and Pax were sliding Boo onto another gurney.

Clyde spoke louder than normal on purpose, "Under the same circumstances, I would've done the same thing. Phera's right, we all thought she was Myosis. Don't blame yourself for her death."

"She was my wife and the mother of my Human child. My God, I killed her, and now Cole wants to kill us. What I've done is unforgivable."

Phera was afraid for Azha. She had never seen him in such despair, accepting defeat. Willing or not, she would fight his Human-half to save him.

"Azha, you need to listen to me. I can speak with Cole and explain what happened. He needs know how important you are for the survival of Earth and what you've sacrificed for all of us. Will you let me try?"

"If you fail, I will succumb to Cole. His hatred for me is debilitating and I deserve his wrath."

Clyde rolled a gurney over to Azha and gently nudged him to lay down. Given a moment to reflect, Phera regretted boasting how confident she was about interpreting Azha's regrets to Cole. Phera's energy disappeared into Azha to search for Cole. "Can anyone hear me?"

"Phera, it's Azha. I don't know how you do it, but I feel relaxed."

"I must leave you to find Cole. I won't be long, try to rest until I return."

"I trust you Phera."

"I will do my best," she said lovingly.

Azha felt her warmth leave and the darkness and despair returned. It seemed as if she was gone forever and then he heard faint voices. Voices that brought back memories of the caverns that echoed when he was a Quiey. They were soothing voices, soft as a song disguising the words into melodies. Phera was speaking with Cole. They were not arguing, nor was Cole angry. He listened, trying to understand them, to no avail.

Azha awoke lying on the gurney alone. Apparently, he had fallen asleep. The question was, for how long? Cole was no longer present, and his despair was not clouding Azha's mind. Out of the shadows Phera appeared. "How are you feeling?"

"I'm good. How long have I been asleep?" Azha asked.

"A couple of hours."

"What happened? What did Cole say to you?"

"Mostly we talked about your past and why you journeyed to Earth alone. Cole was angry because you stole his soul. I asked him for forgiveness so that you may continue to save us all. I explained how his Human sacrifice saved the Quizans, Earth, and you from dying. I spoke of our lost Quizan love and of Rodia's death because of Kogbor's vengeance. I reminded Cole that you never gave up on rescuing his mother and Ginger. We spoke of heroes and of their sacrifices with impossible expectations. Lastly, we talked about Ginzal's death. He saw what happened in the cargo bay and understands that it was a horrible accident. Knowing however, does not lessen the agony he's enduring. Together you have become a living legend who has earned respect from both friend and foe. He accepts his role and forgives you for what you have done and for what you must do."

"Thank you, Phera. We are at peace for the first time. You made this possible. Confessing my love for you was inappropriate, but I'm not sorry I said it."

"I love you too, but not the same. I am committed to Pify. We Owari bonded. The Umduls call it Pali-Otos. If you love me, be happy for me."

"Like you said, maybe someday," Azha said with hope.

Azha, when I said that to you, I meant it might be possible in maybe two-hundred years. No one can predict the future. Right now, you and I are not a good fit. We butt heads and disagree more often than we agree. Pify makes me laugh and I'm his equal, or at least he made me his equal. On Opus, I am a Regent. Umduls are one of the most powerful and respected species in this Universe.

He doesn't get jealous or angry and he trusts me unconditionally, as I do him."

"But how do you bond or have sex with Pify? I know that's important to you," asked Azha.

"You're right. It is none of your business, but I'll explain it to you anyway. I can satisfy Pify. He is unable to satisfy my needs. And for that reason, Pify supports my choice of having casual bonding with whomever I please. Umduls do not think of sex the same way Humans or Ryquats do, and definitely not the same as a Quizan. I find the Umdul way invigorating."

"How could Pify not care? That's hard to believe," argued Azha.

"Knowing you Azha, I'm sure that is hard for you to believe. Nonetheless, it is the Umdul's way."

"You're telling me that you and I could bond and Pify would not care?" Azha said with a snide voice.

"Yes Azha, that is exactly what I am saying. He would support me in my selection and not be jealous. Pify knows I will be with him for as long as he lives. I could teach you techniques that would enrich your life and soothe your uptight disposition, that is, if you can accept what I've told you. Maybe then, we could partake in pleasure and pick up where we left off at the Cupola Pod."

Azha was turning several shades of green with red and silver mixed in. Phera was heartless, taunting him with sex. He didn't want to share her.

Phera whispered, "You were my first as a Quizan. You were exhausting and erotic. I can't imagine the fiery passion we'd have as Trekachaws. If you can accept my terms, I'm willing. If not, at least we have an understanding."

Azha couldn't stop thinking about Phera, and he couldn't stop feeling guilty. One thing was for sure, Azha had a lot to think about.

PER PIFY'S REQUEST, VICTIS, PAX, Nikki, Cody, and Takeda rendezvoused with Azha, Phera, and Clyde on the cargo ship. Boo and Atue had been transported to Pify's battleship for medical care and recovery. Duroc and Ajax were assigned to assist the Umdul Medical Toogus caring for Boo and Atue. The Human Trekachaws assigned to the battleships and those on Palatu were to remain on post until advised otherwise. The remaining sixty-one Human Trekachaws on board were summoned to attend a meeting inside the tier-one deck adjacent to the bridge.

Victis abruptly began the meeting by ordering the Human Trekachaws to sit on the floor. He directed Azha, Pify, Phera, Nikki, Cody, Clyde, Pax, and Takeda to stand behind him during the meeting. Once everyone moved to their locations, Victis stood on top of a bench and spoke in a loud monotone voice.

"It has been brought to my attention that some of you do not wish to remain with us. Who wants to return to Earth?"

Two Trekachaws raised their hands. Victis told them to stand up.

"What are your names?"

"I'm Nick and this is Joshua."

"Nick, do you always speak on Joshua's behalf?" Victis asked.

Joshua took a step forward, "No, he does not. I can speak for myself."

"Do you want to return to Earth, Joshua?"

"Yes."

"And why do you want to return to Earth?"

"To rule."

"Rule who?" Victis asked.

"Rule the Humans on Earth to make it a better world," said Nick interrupting.

"Why do you believe that you're better suited to rule Earth?"

"Didn't you hear me?" Nick snapped.

"Oh, I heard you. Nick, do you feel the same way as Joshua?"

"Why shouldn't we rule Earth. Humans are inferior and igno-rant," Joshua boasted.

"You are half-Human," said Victis.

"What's your point?" Nick countered in a snide voice.

Azha was red and his eyes glowed yellow, he stepped forward and stood next to Victis. Without looking away from Nick and Joshua, Victis stretched his arm out to stop Azha from moving any closer.

"Your intentions are clear to me. What do you believe should happen here?" Victis asked.

"Who are you asking, me or Nick?" Joshua asked in a pompous tone.

"You go first," replied Victis.

"Give us a shuttle and we'll be on our way."

"Nick, do you agree with Joshua?"

"Yeah. One shuttle isn't going to make a difference," argued Nick.

"Neither will two Trekachaws."

Victis raised his arm and pointed his hand at them. A red beam crossed their bodies. Before they fell, Victis sliced the beam through them again. The Human Trekachaws sitting on the floor flashed into red energy and flew to the ceiling.

Victis lowered his arm and spoke, "I take no pleasure in what I was forced to do."

One by one the Trekachaws morphed into body form and slowly sat back down on the floor.

Azha leaned into Victis and whispered, "Phera and I discovered if you cut a Trekachaw's head off, their grey-death energy can ascend to *Aeon Devotio.*"

"Is that right? Don't cut their heads off, they're evil," Victis said with a sharp tongue.

Clyde's eyes questioned Victis's decision. He looked at Azha for answers. Azha looked back with conviction. Victis could see the fear on the Trekachaws' faces. This was not the first time, nor would it be the last, that fear was instrumental in ensuring respect. If there was any question before, chain of command was established. Victis was in charge and comfortable in making the difficult decisions.

Pify spoke up, "Captain Victis, end malice Trekachaws. Undeniable awry disposed to acclimate. Celebrate *tabula rasa.* Umduls concur for future, agree?"

The Human Trekachaw faces changed from fear to confusion. Azha asked Pify to explain Tabula Rasa.

"Captain Victis make clean slate, *Tabula Rasa.* Agree?" Pify said slowly and over pronounced his words.

The Human Trekachaws looked pleased while nodding their heads up and down in agreement. Victis raised his arm up to get their attention and chaos erupted. The Trekachaws flashed into red energy and scattered trying to find hiding places.

Azha yelled, "Victis, put your arm down. Damn, they're scared shitless. They're flickering so fast they look like fireworks. I'm surprised they didn't fly out of here."

Victis lowered his arm and clasped his hands together behind his back. "Talk them down so I can finish the meeting."

"Trekachaws, I give you my word, it's over. What had to be done is done," shouted Azha.

Red swirling lights faded to white and descended to the floor, morphing into Trekachaws.

Being conscious of keeping his hands behind his back, Victis continued, "Azha is my second in command. He will train you for the upcoming war. Be here tomorrow at eight o'clock sharp. You're dismissed."

The cargo deck emptied leaving Victis, Azha, and Pify behind. Pify danced a little skip and chuckled, "Harsh, Victis no nonsense. You, Phera, ou-dim-fa."

Azha perked up when he heard Phera's name. "What's ou-dim-fa?"

Victis grinned and looked down at Pify. "My salty old friend takes care of me. Phera has taught me glorious things."

Pify and Victis danced in a circle singing, "Ou-dim-fa, ou-dim-fa, ou-dim-fa." Around and around they spun irritating the crap out of Azha.

"Okay, you've got my attention. What's ou-dim-fa?" Azha snapped.

Victis jumped up into the air and landed next to Azha. "Ou-dim-fa is sex. I had sex with Phera!"

Azha turned bright purple and looked as if he were going to pop. "You and Phera had *SEX?*"

"Yep, the best sex I've ever had," bragged Victis.

Pify spun in a circle and began singing ou-dim-fa again.

Victis laughed, "Azha don't be so skinny-minded."

Azha screamed, "YOU'RE SO STUPID. It's not skinny-minded, it's narrow-minded."

Victis and Pify were laughing so hard they were leaning on the wall to keep from falling to the floor.

Pify snorted and took a deep breath, "Forget bodies? Messy to leave boorish bygones."

Victis walked over to the dead Trekachaws. "No, I didn't forget. There'll be no funeral, they will simply disappear."

Victis raised his arm and evaporated them with a beautiful blue light that swept across their bodies.

TWO DAYS HAD COME AND gone since the departure of five battleships to Opus. Captain Yagi would be relieved when the journey was over. He was responsible for the children and the raw materials. Opus was the only safe planet to raise the children, at least until Trinite was colonized. Kigen loved being on the Umdul ship and playing with Tilly. He didn't seem to mind being estranged from his parents. Whereas, Deneb and Vious were emotional wrecks. Barring any unexpected delays, the ships were scheduled to return within the week.

Pify spent his free time singing ditties and non-stop talking about the new secret Umdul technology. The first eight battleships would far exceed any existing ships in the galaxy. The new weapon systems were stream-lined, efficient, and incredibly lethal. Long range sensors were improved by eighteen percent and acceleration by a whopping twelve percent. Friction Energy made it possible to support the power necessary for the new technology. These battleships would be put to the test soon enough. For everyone's sake, it was imperative they lived up to the hype.

Rumor was, Belton had met several times with Boo, Atue, and Pax on Pify's ship to discuss an unbelievable request. A Quizan asked to merge with Boo. The Quizan was the lone survivor of Myosis and the Leader's latest rampage on Palatu. Before the merge could transpire, they needed Victis's approval. Questions and comments were thrown back and forth in favor and in opposition concerning Boo's loyalty after the merge. When it was all said and done, they agreed to allow the merge. Pify was disappointed that he was not chosen but supported the Quizan's request. Phera was livid, she had begged for a Quizan to merge with the love of her life. Pify asked her not to voice her disdain for the Quizan, fearing it would further repel those considering a merge with an Umdul.

A small, private gathering waited nervously outside the room during the merge. Boo was well-liked by the Trekachaws, the Ryquats, and the Umduls. It would be a shame for him to turn into a mangy monster like Myosis. But that was not the case. Despite all their skepticisms, Boo surprised them all. His body looked completely different from Myosis or the Leader. Boo was quite attractive with sleek fur, and he was incredibly large. He was as graceful as a cat and strong, stronger than any Trekachaw. Best of all, his personality remained gentle yet fearless, as before. He would be a formidable adversary in combat. They were lucky to have him on their side.

THE UPGRADED BATTLESHIPS HAD ARRIVED and were lining up to dock with Captain Pify's ship. Atue was healing quite nicely and impatient to get his hands on the new Friction technology. Like always, Boo could be found following Atue where ever the call for service sent them. Today was no different. Boo was on Atue's heels through the maze of corridors leading into the docking port for the grand presentation of arriving battleships. Indeed, they were marvelous. The exterior design had been modified to accommodate speed. Pify waddled onto the docking bay alongside the Umdul and

Trekachaw Captains. The new battleships would be awarded to them first. Pify pointed to a battleship with silver lines running the entire length of the ship. Grinning from ear to ear, "Bird I take," he then pointed to Victis.

"Victis of Trekachaws, new bird carries to victory."

Victis marveled at the magnificent battleships, "That one. Third from the end," he smiled.

"Phera, choose bird," said Pify.

"The one with the red wing tip," smiled Phera.

"Choan, choose bird," said Pify.

"The first one. Thank you, Pify," replied Choan.

"Yagi," said Pify. Before Pify could finish, Yagi snorted and was jumping up and down. "Bird," pointing at the second battleship.

"Umdul Captains, Teltoo, Oyee, and Poipu choose homeless birds."

The Umdul Captains waddled over the port window and pressed their faces against it. It was impossible to understand who chose what. Pify clapped his hands congratulating them.

"Old birds, new Captains," said Pify.

After a serious debate, Choan's old ship, the Luxon, would be assigned to Vious and Deneb as co-captains with Duroc and Ajax second in command. Apparently, Kigen was impossible to control without his parents. He played innocent tricks on Marilyn and the Umduls by morphing into objects on the battleship and flying into space whenever he pleased. What they found amazing, was that Kigen could match the Battleships' speed. No Trekachaw could do that.

Roon was assigned to Phera's old ship, the Paratus, with Zeta and Clyde by his side. Victis's old ship, Trinite, was awarded to Nikki as Captain with Cody second in command and Takeda the navigator.

Last, but not least, Pify awarded his old polished battleship to Boo
with Atue second in command. Per Boo's request, Duroc and Ajax
joined his ship as bridge crewmen. The wise old salt had ulterior
motives assigning Boo to his battleship. He had kept it to himself
that a Gystfin Dux Ducis and a Kogbor had contacted him requesting
a confidential tryst. Boo was the perfect liaison for negotiations
between the Umduls, Ryquats, Trekachaws, and Gystfins. So, it
was done. The Trekachaws were stretching their wings with the
help of the Umduls. No telling how far they could fly, or how high.

WITH MINIMAL CONFUSION, THE SHUFFLING of ships and
crew personnel were completed. For the Captains, naming their
new Friction Battleship was as important as naming their first
born. Pify dedicated his ship to Phera's Ryquat-half, Tara. Phera
named her new battleship Kismet Ebb in memory of her village
on Palatu. For the other Captains, it was going to take some
time to decide.

Pify made up some lame excuse how he was taking his new
ship, Tara out for a spin. One thing for sure, Pify was a terrible liar.
His exact words were, "Spin with Tara, me alone. Reason none,
soon return."

Victis and Azha couldn't help from tracking him to see what he
was up to. What came next was strange and perhaps sneaky. They
saw Boo's unmistakable energy signature fly into Pify's ship moments
before take-off. Sure enough, the Friction Battleships were faster
than the old ships. They were impossible to keep up with.

Not far from Palatu, Pify's battleship came to a dead stop in
space.

"What is he up to?" Victis asked.

"We shouldn't be spying on him. How would you like it if he did this to you? Azha replied.

"What are you getting at?" Victis said annoyed.

"Think about it," Azha said condescendingly.

"If you want me to understand what your implying, say it intelligently," mocked Victis.

"Screw you Victis," swore Azha.

"Well that was eloquent," quipped Victis.

"Look, do you see what I'm seeing?" asked Azha, pointing at the monitor.

A Gystfin battleship approached out of nowhere and was docking portside with Pify's ship. Azha let out a *'no-way'* and Victis mumbled, *"Unko, Nanda?"*

Azha's curiosity got the best of him. "I know Unko means *shit*. What does *nanda* mean?"

"What the hell," answered Victis.

"Yeah, what the hell is Pify doing?" Azha agreed.

"Is that why Boo's on board? What are they up to? Should we ask?" Victis said aloud.

"Too late, Pify's trying to contact us," said Azha. "Now what. Are you going to answer them, Victis?"

"Unko. Yeah, don't say anything, Azha. This is going to be difficult enough to explain."

"Don't explain anything. Your big mouth is why you always get caught with your pants down," snapped Azha.

"What pants, I don't have pants on," said Victis.

"Forget it," replied Azha.

"And how am I supposed to forget it? You already said it," asked Victis.

"I wish I hadn't," replied Azha.

"Azha stop talking. Unko, here goes."

Victis switched the monitor, ship to ship. "What can I do for you Pify?"

Boo and Pify were so close to the monitor, their faces covered the screen. What looked even more ridiculous was their blank expressions and their mouths hanging open. Both were perturbed at such a stupid question.

Pify snorted, "No do for me. Victis mind yourself to behave with own business?"

Victis stepped out of view of the monitor. "Shit, he caught us," he whispered, then stepped back into view.

"My apologies Pify, I should've waited for you to tell me."

"Accepted, Ryquat nature. Ask, future curiosity. Tell you, not in business or feed Ryquat nature. Join if you wish, interesting tryst you see."

"We'll be there in a flash," advised Victis.

THE DUX DUCIS AND KOGBOR straightened up in their chairs when Victis and Azha morphed into body form. Pify quickly wiggled out of his seat and pulled out two chairs between his and Boo's chairs.

"This side. Not too close, better for all," requested Pify.

Victis and Azha sat glaring at the Gystfins who were glaring back at them. Pify banged the table with his cup and snorted, "Continue, progress negative Trekachaws differ from goals. Brief I will to convey knowledge."

Victis leaned forward in his chair, "Pardon my insolence."

The old scared Dux Ducis voice was deep and gravely, "Gystfins regret what transpired on Palatu. Our path is with the Umduls if acceptable terms are agreed. Umduls support new species Trekachaws, as coadjutor, so do we. Gystfins no longer serve the will of Crozins. They have aligned with Gors. Gors enslave Gystfins rather than exchange services and compensation. Gors hunt Gystfins as preferred meat to supplement organic commodities."

Pify could barely see over the table. The chairs that accommodated his guests were not comfortable for him. Tired of stretching his neck, Pify climbed up on the table and sat down with his legs crossed.

"Must agree. Gystfin cargo ship returned post-delivery raw material on Opus. Umduls compensate for Gystfin post labor on Palatu. No more, no less, fair enough, agree?" Pify asked.

The old Gystfin grinned, revealing mustard-stained fangs that reminded Azha of his near-death experience. It was going to be difficult to trust a Gystfin other than Boo.

"Speak for Gardux. I agree, Captain Pify. Give you information to benefit Umdul strife."

"Benefit good," replied Pify.

"I have coordinates of Ryquat saboteur with battleship. Ryquat ship provides asylum for Myosis, a Leader, and Crozin Ruks. They report to a Crozin Ukaru. Captain Doug Smyth has spied for Crozins many years. The Ukaru promised planet Zaurak to Smyth for loyalty. Without Umduls, Smyth will rule what's left of planet."

Pify unfolded his legs and stood up, "Umduls shield Gystfins from Gors, agree. Return, Gystfins taboo planet Palatu and Trekachaws. Honor must."

"We honor and agree to these terms. Myosis and Leader rouge aberrant. They are neither Gystfins, nor Trekachaws," said the Dux Ducis.

The Dux Ducis looked at Boo and snarled.

"Umduls exterminate Myosis plus Leader. Boo-Trekachaw protected by all, no confusion," demanded Pify.

Boo showed no expression but was watching and listening as they spoke back and forth.

The old Gystfin snarled, "Boo Gystfin traitor, contacted Ryquat Counsel, caused many Gystfin deaths."

Azha and Victis pushed their chairs back and stood up.

Pify took a deep breath and spoke loud and direct, "Boo is Umdul. Boo is Trekachaw. Boo not negotiable. Dux Ducis of Gardux take heed. Gors hunt Gystfins, same Gystfins hunt Quizans. No agree. No cargo ship, no labor, no trust. Umduls protect Boo. Challenge say you, war it is."

Pify shook his fist at them and scooted off the table onto a chair. Unable to jump off, Pify asked Azha to help him get down from the chair onto the floor.

The Dux Ducis pleaded for Pify to stop, "My mistake, start over. Agree Boo is Trekachaw, not Gystfin."

Victis scowled. "I do not trust these Gystfins."

Azha shook his head in agreement. Pify waddled over to Boo and leaned against his chair, "Boo decide future, trust or not."

"I'm honored Captain Pify. Gors do not see Gystfins as an intelligent species. They see them as food and strong Beasts used for labor. Gystfins will flip to whomever suits their needs best. Trust is not advisable; necessity is what's important. For now, the Gystfins are afraid of the Gors and will say or do whatever it takes to survive."

The Dux Ducis twisted in his chair, acting as if he were offended. Before he could voice his defense, Boo snapped, "Don't insult me. We both know it's the truth."

That's when the true Gystfin showed its ugly self, "Boo brave, the Umduls and Trekachaws protect you. If not, I'd gift you to the Gors with one condition... cut you into pieces alive," hissed the Dux Ducis.

"Do not trust this Gystfin-Trekachaw. He is a traitor to his own kind. Show good faith, keep the cargo ship and labor as my gift. Traitor Boo will not succumb from Gystfin revenge. Do we have your allegiance?" The Dux Ducis asked Pify.

"Acceptable. Trekachaw Boo liaison for Umduls. No threats appoint virtuous amidst representative. Unite Boo and union forthcoming," confirmed Pify.

The Dux Ducis sat back in his chair, "I don't understand what you said?"

Victis's stripes turned red, "Captain Pify requests a Gystfin that can be professional, unbiased, and productive when consulting with Boo, not you. Like it or not, he's the Umduls' liaison. Enough antics, *yes or no*?" Victis demanded.

"Yes," growled Dux Ducis.

Pify was moving slower than normal and appeared ill. He stretched out his stubby arms, "Victis, help up table, view better."

Victis carefully scooped Pify into his arms and sat him gently on the table.

"Agree differences. Transaction fair, labor, cargo ship compensated agreed prior to Boo bashing. Dux Ducis reveal our enemies," asked Pify.

The Dux Ducis leaned back and crossed his arms, "Captain Doug Smyth is orbiting in the Targus asteroid belt. Battleship shadows asteroid to fool your sensors. Crozins and Gors entered Ryquat orbit defeating escutcheon shield and communications. Ground invasion has already begun. Our monitors intercepted Crozin transmissions.

Ryquat Counsel has been captured or killed. Gystfin planet Gardux is being invaded by Gors. Gors took control of our airspace. Will you send battleships?" Dux Ducis asked.

Pify scratched his head and fluffed his hair to hide Fizz. The little Tit was sensing Pify's fatigue.

"One-hundred Battleships, two days Gardux. Agree Secret, Umduls one Gystfin ship spy. Choose virtuous Gystfin unite Boo," replied Pify.

"On behalf of all Gystfins, I honor and pay homage to your generosity. May Jaaku protect you and your battleship." The Dux Ducis stood up and bowed to Pify.

Victis waited until the Gystfins left the room before helping the old Umdul scoot onto a chair. Pify sat for a while before speaking. "Age catch old salt. Sleep soon, battleships discuss now Zaurak? Trekachaws make final. Yes, or no?" Pify asked.

In all the years, this was the first time Victis saw his tough, old friend show signs of vulnerability.

"Pify, are you feeling well?" Victis asked.

"Malignant years inevitable. Quizan accept, embrace anew to thwart death. Not over, end dignity, remain useful."

It took a few moments for Pify's words to sink in. Tears filled Victis's eyes when he realized what his friend was saying. How long had Pify felt this way and how bad was the pain that he could no longer mask it?

Pify's time was growing short and clearly the great Umdul warrior was accepting his death.

Victis hugged his old friend, "You will always be useful to me. I swear, Phera and I will find you a Quizan to merge with."

"Promise not Quizans sacrifice. Sailed Galaxy, privileged life ample." Pify said with remorse.

Pify snorted and buried his face in Victis's shoulder rather than showing his sorrow.

"Adore wife Phera. Pify not worthy. Regret depart world. Victis, Azha must decide fate of Zaurak."

Azha voiced that since he was not a Ryquat, Victis should have the final word on helping Zaurak.

Pify pressed his face against Victis's shoulder and mumbled, "Azha not Human, Azha Trekachaw. Council defy Trekachaws, aberrant pariah. Azha word necessary."

"Yes, then I vote for saving Zaurak," said Azha.

"Victis vote?" Pify asked.

"Yes Pify, we should save Zaurak. What would we say to our loyal Ryquat crewmen?"

"Save agree. Gor, Crozin many. Comrades across Galaxy afar bolster unify strength. Kiki species wise, virtuous. Honor alliance good match Trekachaws. Gors, Crozins shiver at Kiki greatness," explained Pify.

"Then it is settled, we will join forces with the Kikis. I will be honored to meet your comrades," replied Victis.

Victis carried Pify down the corridor to his quarters with Azha following close behind. The room was stark and small, not that of a Captain's expected grandeur. The tired, old, salt kicked off his boots and got undressed. His head had barely hit the pillow when a loud snore rumbled past his lips. Victis and Azha tiptoed out of the room and shut the door behind them. Though not of blood, Victis and Pify could not have been closer than father and son. He wouldn't rest until he found Pify a Quizan.

twenty nine

CASUS BELLI

"THE COSMOS EXISTANCE HAS NO BEGINNING,
THUS HAS NO END.ENTERNAL LIFE IS THE COSMOS"

PIFY awoke bright-eyed and rested. He was frustrated that his age hindered his *raison d' être* during the tryst. Umduls lived to excel in innovation and achieve the highest standard of productivity. It was his nature to push everyone, including himself, to finish the task at hand before relaxing. Refusing to accept the facts of growing old, Pify often pushed himself to exhaustion. If he continued, his stubbornness would put him in an early grave.

Phera thought about joining Pify in his quarters, for no other reason than to check on him. Learning from Victis and Azha that he wasn't feeling well shook her to the core. Like it or not, it was best not to disturb his sleep; therefore, she waited with them on the bridge. Victis and Azha were searching the asteroid belt for Cpt. Smyth's battleship on long-range sensors. Seeing how worried she was, they asked Phera if she wished to join them, knowing it would be a distraction.

The new technology paid off. The coordinates given by the Dux Ducis were spot-on. A Crozin battleship was docked with Smyth's ship in a slow orbit. Deciding how best to proceed was imperative. Whether they should destroy the ships or spy on them was the question. No one could decide. Finding them was simply too good to be true.

Phera wanted to enter a Ukaru's brain for information and then test her theory of killing the vile alien with an energy surge. That was one way. The other way was to blow them out of space and end the threat. Phera won the debate. Choan would go with her since Smyth was Choan's uncle. If he declined, Victis was next in line, then Azha. Phera requested ship to ship on a coded com.

"Choan, your presence is requested on Pify's battleship regarding an urgent matter," Victis transmitted.

"Acknowledged, one moment to advise Duro. May I ask the nature of this urgent matter?"

"Negative."

"Copy that."

Seconds later, Choan morphed into body form next to Phera, "What's the urgency?"

Victis spoke up, "We have your Uncle Smyth's Battleship coordinates on long-range sensor. A Crozin Battleship is docked with his ship in a slow orbit. They're oblivious to our new technology and that we can detect them at this distance. We recently learned that Smyth is conspiring with the Crozins and Gors to defeat Zaurak. He was promised dictatorship of Zaurak. Phera wants to infiltrate the Crozin's battleship to test her skills of mind manipulation on the Ukaru. We thought it fair that you get first dibs to go with her. If not, we understand," said Victis.

"Refusal? Oh, there will be no refusal. I've been waiting for this. What do you want me to do?" Choan asked.

"Eavesdrop. Find out what you can and who's on board," advised Victis.

"When do we leave? Where's Captain Pify?" Choan asked.

"You're leaving now, and I want you back in one hour. Find out what you can and protect Phera. Pify is getting some much-needed sleep."

"Who knows about this?" Choan asked.

"Just us and those on the bridge," Replied Victis.

"Smart. We should keep it that way. Phera, lead the way."

In a flash, they disappeared through the bulkhead into space. Victis looked over at Azha, "Do you think we did the right thing by sending only two?"

"Yeah. They'll be gone one hour and the Crozins will never know they were there. This was the best way."

Pify stepped onto the bridge with a big smile on his face. "Good sleep. Update who speak?"

Victis looked at Azha, then over at the monitor, "Step over here. As you can see, a Crozin and Smyth's battleship are in view."

"Clearly join, Crozin bird," said Pify.

"Phera wanted to eavesdrop on the Crozin ship and to test her theory on manipulating a Crozin brain while in energy. Choan's with her. They've been gone ten minutes with a one-hour window to return," advised Victis.

Pify frowned and his big smile dropped. "Phera gone? This bad, Pify scared Phera hurt. Victis approve foray, not wake?" Pify scowled.

"She told me not to wake you. Pify, you know better than anyone she'll do whatever she wants to do. Phera is smart and tough; if anyone can do this, she can," Victis said, trying not to show his concern.

EN ROUTE, CHOAN ASKED PHERA if he could have ten minutes to check his Uncle's ship first, then meet her on the Crozin bridge. This was not the original plan. However, Phera figured ten minutes would not make a difference. Not so. The moment Choan entered the bridge a magnetic charge stunned him, forcing him into body form. Unable to move or speak, he could see that he was being transported through a corridor into a room crowded with Crozins. The last thing he saw was his Uncle Smyth leaning over him and asking a Crozin if the Trekachaw would survive the charge.

Phera entered the Crozin battleship through the shuttle bay bulkhead. Beneath her, a young Crozin was nervously connecting hoses to the exterior of a shuttle. Standing at the far end of the bay, a huge Ruk was shouting orders to Crozins running back and forth preparing the ship for a magnetic charge. She dimmed her light and descended into the young Crozin's head for a safe place to stay until she understood more. Finding it amusing, it was difficult not to laugh when he slapped his own forehead several times and then tried to shake off the bizarre, tingling sensation by blowing his nose.

Phera remained silent and drifted over to his eyes, curious if she could see what he saw. The images were blurry with no color, and from that location she was unable to hear his thoughts. Maybe, if she condensed her energy into one eye the images would improve. Sure enough, she could see clear images from there. Now that she had that problem solved, she would speak to him as if a little voice in his head was giving invaluable advice. Phera drifted away from his eye into the center of his brain, listening for his thoughts. There, she could hear him. What was he saying? The more she heard, the worse it got.

"Jipvoy, Ukaru alert decks Trekachaw gaffed. Engage one through fifteen. Check sensors, no tolerance, failure is death."

"*Uyea,*" answered Jipvoy.

She could sense his fear and heard his thoughts, "Am I losing my mind? Ruk Drocca will blame me if anything goes wrong. He'll kill me."

Phera whispered in his head, *"Drocca wants you to fail. He'll blame you if the Ukaru demands a sacrifice. Go to the bridge and warn the Ukaru of his treacherous lies. Ukaru will reward you for your bravery and punish the Ruk for his deception."*

Drocca slapped Jipvoy across the back of his head screaming, "Do what I told you!"

Phera shouted, "Don't let him bully you. The voice you're hearing is a Trekachaw in your head. Grab his arm and I'll punish the Ruk."

"NO, I won't," yelled Jipvoy.

Drocca spun around and back-handed Jipvoy so hard, he almost lost consciousness as he fell to the floor.

"What did you say to me?" Drocca demanded.

Drocca made a colossal mistake when he reached down and grabbed the young Crozin around his neck. That gave Phera the opportunity to transfer her energy into the Ruk. She wasted no time in finding Drocca's thoughts.

"Pay attention ignoble. I am a Trekachaw inside your brain. Do as I say, or you will die a painful death," threatened Phera.

Drocca kicked Jipvoy in the head. "You had a Trekachaw inside you and said nothing?"

Phera surged, sending a blast of energy into his brain. Drocca screamed a high-pitched shrill and grabbed his head. Phera sensed his excruciating pain and fear of dying.

"Do I have your attention?" Phera shouted.

"What do you want from me, Trekachaw?"

"Go to the bridge and touch the Ukaru. I'll leave you and enter him. Refuse and I'll make you suffer until I find another host" warned Phera.

"The Ukaru will kill me," Drocca said aloud.

"No, he won't. I will not reveal myself to him. Besides if you don't, I'll kill you and transfer into whomever touches you. Do you need to be reminded of the pain I can cause?"

"Jipvoy knows, what about him?"

"The Ukaru would kill both of you. If Jipvoy wants to live, he will keep his mouth shut. Stop talking out-loud and think what you want to say from now on. We can communicate without others hearing us."

Phera listened to his thoughts. They were sick demented acts of what he wanted to do to her. Unlike Jipvoy, Drocca's purpose in life was taking pleasure in torturing any living thing. A glimpse of him throwing a Ryquat woman appeared in his mind. She tried to run into a corner of the room to get away. Phera could sense his joy when he punched her so hard, blood spewed from her mouth. Given the chance, this is what he would do to her. Drocca moved quickly down the corridor towards the bridge. Several Crozins who were unable to get out of his way fast enough felt his wrath. The moment he had no one to knock down or backhand, images of children's dying faces popped in his head. He tried blocking out what he was plotting by concentrating on one child he was eviscerating with his teeth, while starring into her eyes. Even so, he couldn't keep his darkest secrets from Phera. He had every intention on telling the Ukaru that she was hiding in his head. Phera flashed her energy in the center of his cortex. She could feel his brain spasm and his thoughts were gone. As he collapsed to the floor Phera concentrated herself behind one of his eyes. She saw the Ukaru bend over and place his hand on Drocca's neck. This was her chance, Phera entered the Ukaru, leaving the Drocca's corpse behind. She remained silent until the disorder and confusion of Drocca's sudden death was over. How strange were the Ukaru's thoughts, suspecting other Crozins for Drocca's unusual death? Paranoid of everyone, he wondered if poison was the cause and if he were next.

Phera answered his question, "No, he did not die of poison. I'm a Trekachaw and I fried his brain. Do what I tell you or I'll fry your brain slowly until there's nothing left of you. Do not speak out loud, think what you want to say."

"What do you want?" The Ukaru asked.

"Excellent, we have an understanding. Tell your crew you're taking a shuttle. Make sure no one follows you. Do that, then we'll talk again," ordered Phera.

"How do I know you won't kill me anyway?"

"You don't. I could burn your brain up and take over your body. Would you prefer I do that?" Phera asked.

"No."

The Ukaru barked orders to the crew, then marched out of the bridge, advising that he was taking a shuttle. Phera had bluffed, claiming that she could take control of a body. That he couldn't hear her thoughts was extremely fortunate and unexpected. It seemed the only time he could hear her was when she directed her thoughts to him.

EN ROUTE TO THE SHUTTLE, the Ukaru considered his options. They were grim at best. He hesitated before entering a shuttle, wondering if that would be the last time he'd set foot on his battleship. The Ukaru took a deep breath and sat down in the navigation chair. His nerves were shot, and he feared for his life. When he spoke, Phera could hear the strain in his voice. "I did what you asked. Now what?"

"Set your coordinates for mark 28 and advise your ship that you are checking on something they'll believe."

"By advising my intentions I would raise suspicion. That is not the way of a Ukaru."

"Did you mark 28?"

"Yes."

At last, she could relax a little now that she was free from the Crozin battleship. The shuttle sped through space, headed for home. Phera surged her energy just enough to cause the Ukaru to black-out. What a relief to exit his body and morph into a Trekachaw. It must have been hours since her last contact with Victis and Azha. By now, Pify would be awake and be worried sick about her. As soon as the shuttle was within range of Pify's battleship, she requested ship to shuttle communications.

"Don't disintegrate me. Cover me for a long range Crozin hyperbaric wave," Phera transmitted.

Pify shouted and waddled in a circle, "Phera safe I hear. My, my, caught little Crozin bird."

"Hi Pify. That's not all I caught. I have a Ukaru on board that I brained-zapped. He'll be waking up in a few minutes. Victis, I have some information I think will please you. Is Choan back yet?" Phera asked.

"We thought Choan was with you?" Victis replied.

"He's not with me. I flew into a nest of Crozins. Choan was on the Ryquat ship. This Ukaru has some weird thoughts in his head. If I'm not mistaken, he's the one who took Connie and killed your other daughter on Trinite. Crazy as it may sound, I think he loved her. He kept wondering if Connie was safe on your ship. Even more bizarre, I could feel his sadness that Tilly was out of his life."

Victis flashed bright purple. "I'll meet you in the shuttle bay."

By the time Phera had docked, the Ukaru was sitting up on his own. Still groggy, he was rubbing his eyes and complaining that his head was throbbing. He looked out the port window to get his bearings.

"You tricked me. I would have rather died than this," he said glaring at her.

"Forgive me Crozin for not having sympathy for you," Phera replied dryly.

Victis was waiting outside the shuttle with Azha and Pify. As the door opened, she could hear Pify asking Victis to give his word not to kill the Ukaru. Whether Victis heard what Pify asked was anyone's guess. He must have, because he allowed the Ukaru to walk past them. Victis followed them to a fortified holding cell near the bridge. No sooner had the door slammed shut, then Pify was summoned to the bridge for an urgent message from Vexy. The Ukaru would have to wait for now. Victis, Azha, and Pify ran to the bridge. Azha took a few steps and stopped, then looked back at Phera standing outside the cell. When she was late getting back, he was panic-stricken. Phera's stripes were pale and her hands were trembling.

"Phera, the last thing I want is to disrespect Pify or make you uncomfortable. Just know, if there's anything you ever need, I'm here for you. And don't do such crazy things anymore, Okay?" Azha pleaded.

"Okay, I'll try not to. I feel the same way about you. Let's get out of here and find out what's so important. Thank you for being understanding," smiled Phera.

"You are welcome."

PIFY AND VICTIS COULD SEE images of Vexy running alongside Ryquats screaming for her to move and take cover. Sounds of crashing debris muffled her cries, and clouds of dust and ashes filled the screen. Vexy spoke fast and she was out of breath. "Victis, can you hear me?"

"Affirmative," Victis yelled.

"The Chancellor Towers are being incinerated on Zaurak. Most of the battleships protecting our airspace are destroyed. We are at the mercy of the Gors and Crozins. They've landed and are harvesting us for food, and taking younger women for slaves. We're trying to find a way to the underground shuttle bay. My Special Ops. assigned to me is still alive. Rohan thinks he knows another way that will bypass the Gors. Please send help now. If I make it to the shuttle, mark coordinates 2-14. Victis, it's in the asteroid belt. We'll hide there. I have a spy on Smyth's ship. Last transmission intercepted inferred that a Trekachaw has been captured. A Gystfin called Myosis is..." *The transmission was lost, and the screen went black.*

A BLAST OF HOT AIR slammed Vexy to the ground. The air was thick with smoke, making it impossible to breathe. She could hear Rohan calling her name. If she were to die, let it be now and not by the Gors ripping her to shreds. Everything went dark.

"Vexy, can you hear me?"

She could hear Rohan and knew he was running with her in his arms. Was he bleeding, or was it her? He stopped and laid her down to shoot behind them.

"Vexy, can you hear me? Wake up," Rohan's voice sounded desperate.

She felt him wiping her face and picking her up again. "Rohan I'm..." the pain was excruciating. Rohan stumbled, and they crashed to the ground. She watched Rohan scramble to his feet while firing his Neco behind him. Sounds of Gors were echoing off the walls. The scrapping of their claws on the pavement was unmistakable.

"Vexy get up, move!" his voice was strained.

She crawled onto her hands and knees. Rohan grabbed her around the waist and stood her up.

"Run Vexy, there's too many of them."

She could see enough to know they were in a familiar, underground garage. She must have fainted again, Rohan had carried her for over a mile. His face was blackened with smoke and he was limping badly. His clothes were soaked with blood down one side of his body, and he was breathing heavily.

"Rohan, I'm sorry I couldn't run," she cried.

"The shuttle's on top of this building. Can you walk on your own? I don't see any more Gors behind us."

Rohan leaned Vexy against the wall and took a few steps forward.

"I don't see any Gors ahead of us. We'll have to go above ground to get to the shuttles. Ops hid them in case of an emergency. The Gors won't know about them," he whispered looking back again.

Her legs felt weak. She used the wall to steady herself to step over the half-eaten bodies lying across the steps and the landings.

"The smoke should give us cover. When we get to the top if I tell you to drop, get down and act dead. The Gors prefer to eat Ryquats when they're alive."

Twice they laid on the stairs listening to hordes of Gors running past them. On one of the landings, a double door had been propped open to a lobby. She opened her eyes and watched in horror as a group of Crozins lined up at least twenty young girls to inspect them. A Crozin walked to the end of the line and sniffed a girl up and down. For some reason, she did not pass the test. Two other Crozins picked her up and tossed her into a metal container used to store food. When full, the container would be shot into space where everyone inside would die of suffocation and freeze for later consumption. The next girl he sniffed passed the test. What he did next was unconscionable. The same two Crozins began ripping her clothes off her body. Another Crozin dragged the girl out of Vexy's line of sight. The other girls in line were crying and holding hands waiting for their turn. Vexy played dead and watched one girl after the other learn her fate.

The last two girls were sisters. The older girl refused to let go of her younger sister's hand. A Ruk Crozin grabbed the older sister by her hair and threw her down on the floor. The younger sister was screaming hysterically and begging the Ruk to stop all the while being forced to watch the entire, brutal assault. After raping the older sister, he cut her throat and walked away. Vexy laid perfectly still. Their cries for mercy and the gruesome images would forever haunt her.

Rohan reached out for Vexy's hand. "We couldn't save them. When I squeeze your hand, we'll move again."

Vexy turned her head to face him and blinked her wet eyes.

Falling buildings crashed all around them, making it difficult for her to hear Rohan. One thing was certain, it was time to move. He was squeezing her hand. She had regained some strength and was able to run slowly. Rohan pulled her along with one hand and in the other he had his Neco weapon ready to fire. So much blood was running down Rohan's leg, she was afraid he'd pass out. Sunlight filtered through black smoke and dust as they climbed the stairs to the next landing.

Gors and Crozins were everywhere in the building. They were too busy eating babies and young children to care about Vexy and Rohan. Vexy saw several bodies fall from the floors above and glanced over the edge of the rail. On the ground, hordes of Gors were packing broken bodies into the food containers. On the next floor, fathers and mothers were fighting the Crozins in a last-ditch effort to protect their children. Vexy stopped looking and concentrated on the ground and the wall adjacent to where she was running. Rohan grabbed her around the waist to help her up the last set of stairs. Rohan opened a large steel door and they ran through it into darkness. She didn't realize her ears were ringing until there was silence. Rohan leaned his back against the wall and slid down, holding his leg. He pushed on a gaping wound trying to stop the bleeding. Even in the dark she could see the concern on his face. Vexy removed her blouse and tore off one of the sleeves.

"Lift up your leg a little so I can wrap it. It'll help slow down the bleeding."

She tore off the other sleeve and wrapped a second bandage over the first. She picked up her tattered blouse and redressed herself. Her hands were shaking out of control, making it impossible to fasten the buttons. Rohan pushed against the wall and stood up.

"Here let me help you with your blouse. We gotta go. The shuttles are in a bay at the end of the hall."

Vexy's heart was pounding so hard as they ran in the dark; she wondered if Rohan could hear it. He opened another door into a lit hanger. They made it; four shuttles were unscathed waiting to save them from certain death. They moved quickly to the first shuttle and boarded as quietly as possible. Rohan groaned when he sat down in the navigation seat. He adjusted his hurt leg, then rotated the chair to engage the systems. The shuttle was equipped with a minimal defense system against small arms. With any luck, there were no battleships directly above them.

The moment the hanger doors opened, Gors and Crozins fired a barrage of Neco lasers at their shuttle. Rohan mowed them down with the shuttle on his way out. Looking down on the city, Vexy saw the devastation. The Counsel Towers were gone. A hole in the ground was the only evidence they were ever there. Buildings were on fire and containers holding Ryquats were stacked in endless rows waiting for transport. She prayed for those on Zaurak, and then she prayed for herself that Victis could save her and Rohan in the asteroid belt.

VICTIS SCREAMED, *"Get her back, get her back now."*

Panicked crewmen waved their hands over controls and reset emergency keys. Zaurak was off the grid. Phera and Azha walked onto the bridge as the screen reset, revealing clusters of stars in space. No one moved, and no one spoke. The crew was in shock, fixated on the screen that had unveiled the horrors on Zaurak.

Pify shouted, "Victis, Vexy tough survive. Contact Kiki's, imperative."

"Captain Pify, I have Captain Smyth on com requesting to speak with you," advised Akio.

"Open com," shouted Victis.

Smyth came into view on the screen sitting next to a Crozin. "Do you have Ukaru Narthex aboard your ship?"

"Smyth know Narthex? Indeed, a Ukaru. Quid-pro-quo, Choan?" Pify asked.

"Yes. Return Narthex, or I'll kill Choan," demanded Smyth.

"Threats empty, Narthex alive. Kill Choan? Narthex, Choan fate same," Pify warned.

Pify gave hand signals to his crewmen to send five Umdul Battleships to surround Smyth's and the Crozin ship. Smyth's expression changed, "Call your ships back or I'll kill him now."

"Kill Choan, kill yourself. Umdul ships faster, escape not. Think, options Umdul bad to test."

Pify cut the transmission to speak with the Mikado of the Kikis.

"Ah, good Umduls join, Thude Kiki Pashas. Zaurak infested Crozins and Gors ugly it is," said Pify.

"Glad to see your still in one piece, old friend. I don't get out much since elevated to Mikado status. Wouldn't mind joining you one last time. We have four hundred battleships and Zaurak is in monitor view. My Pasha's are the best in the fleet. Better hurry or we'll conquer the nasty pests without you. *No...* I take back what I said, there are thousands of Gor and Crozin battleships," said Thude worried.

"Kiki pause, together fight," said Pify.

"We may not have that luxury..." The transmission ended.

Pify jumped down from his chair, "Trekachaws convene battleships. Five Umdul ships beleaguer Smyth and Crozin battleship. Escape attempt, destroy. Add five, Umdul birds sixty-one, two, three, four, five, shield Palatu. Align formation, hikari Zaurak engage."

White laser strikes, and beams of blue, lighting bolts flashed across the dark space above Zaurak.

The war had begun...

THE END

The saga continues...

TREKACHAW

The

CROZIN WAR

Trekachaw Glossary

Earth, our home. Not long-ago, astronomers believed she was flat and that the stars circled around us. We are far from those dark ages. But understanding and exploring vast space with all its wonders and secrets is a journey yet to unfold. Now is the apex of an evolution. The next generation of seekers who dare to take chances. Those who dream of what could be and are willing to explore the impossible. This is the story of a man who sacrificed his soul to another willing to risk everything. New worlds and those who have been protecting us will be revealed. This is a journey into our past and future. We are not alone.

QUIZAN SPECIES:

Quizans are one of the original two-hundred and forty-three species to occupy the fifty-eight documented universes within the Vastuscaelus. They explored the universes millions of years before Ryquats or Humans were capable of building fires. Originally, Quizans were indigenous to a planet called Pala located within another universe. Billions of years ago, Quizans were not as physically evolved. Like Humans, they required food, water, and shelter. They were an advanced, compassionate species who engineered spaceships to rescue endangered life on compromised planets.

Planet Pala orbited a pair of White Dwarf Suns, providing the perfect environment for the Quizans. Tragically, a sudden shift in gravity pulled the two suns together, triggering the birth of a Supernova. Disintegration of the planet was imminent, allowing very little time for the Quizans to escape. Eventually, the ships rendezvoused in search of a new habitable planet. Perseverance prevailed. A new planet was discovered, providing the Quizans a new beginning. Our ancestors named this planet "*Palaone.*" Today, Palaone is called Earth, *your Earth.*

Due to an Ice Age on Earth, the Quizan's were forced to search for another habitable planet. During the Quizans' long trek, a Quizan bio-chemist and a physician continued to work on a theory discovered while on Palaone. They perfected a process to bind, or *merging*, using an extinct Phosphorus-Urodela Amphibian's DNA and a Quizan's DNA. These flying colorful amphibians we called Phobias could change their body stripes into brilliant colors and absorb the sun's energy for nutrition. The merge was instant, and the results were amazing, making it possible to leave their ships and absorb solar energy. Without these advantages, the Quizans would never have survived the long brutal journey to the new world, Palatu, and the ability to create the Trekachaw.

Planet.	Palatu.
Sun:	Targus.
Life span:	300 years.
King/Leader:	Rulers of Palatu.
Fathers/Mothers:	Papay/Manany.
Marriage:	Owari Bond.
Quiey:	Quizan babies or children.
Ayak:	Palatu bird.
Grut:	Rat-like creature.
House:	Caverns at Cavern Village.
	Cupola Pod/Odeum Pod at Kismet Ebb.
Bodo:	Gas bubbles released from the bottom of Quizans' feet when they absorb to much energy.
Vox Populi:	Unanimous Vote.
Ola:	Three feet.
Pavo:	One hundred.
Aeon Devotio:	Life after death/Grey-Death Energy (Latin).
Atmosphere:	Combination of Carbon dioxide/Sulfur dioxide/ Carbon Monoxide/Helium/H20.

Phosphorus-Urodela: Extinct Earth lizard DNA used for creation of
Quizan hybrid.
Sopa tree: Palatu tree.
Jacko tree: Palatu tree.
Villages Cavern Village, Kismet Ebb Village,
Silwat Village

QUIZANS

Zith: Palatu prince. Son of Myosis.
Rodia: Azha's Quizan Wife. From Cavern Village.

Quizan/Ryquat Merges

Zygo/Victis: Ryquat Battleship Captain.
He merged with Zygo from Cavern Village.
Phera/Tara Azha's first love. From Kismet Ebb.
She merged with Special Ops. Tara.
Roon/Simon: Friend of Azha. From Kismet Ebb.
He merged with Science Ofc. Simon.
Atue/Einstein: Friend of Azha. From Kismet Ebb.
He merged with Engineering Ofc. Einstein.
Pax/Jacet: Saved by Victis. From Kismet Ebb.
He merged with Battleships' M.D. Jacet.
Choan/Bruce: From Silwat Village.
He merged with Sgt. of Special Ops Bruce.
Vopar/Eric: From Cavern Village. Brother to Vious.
He merged with Special Ops. Eric.
Vious/Dillon: From Cavern Village. Brother to Vopar.
He merged with Special Ops. Dillon.
Duro/Washington: From Silwat Village.
He merged with Special Ops. Washington.

Belton/Larry: Friend of Azha from Cavern Village.
                          He merged with Special Ops. Larry.
Deneb/Darcy: From Cavern Village.
                          She merged with Special Ops. Darcy.

Quizan/Human Merges

Azha/Cole: Azha traveled to Earth.
                          First Trekachaw hybrid with a Human.
Quetzal/Ginger: Cole's human wife Ginger merged with Quetzal.
                          Renamed themselves, Ginzal.
Zeta/Beverly: Cole's Human mother (Beverly) merged
                          with Zeta.
Human Duroc: Veteran from earth/Quizan merge.
                          Human parents were pig farmers.
Human Ajax: Veteran from earth/Quizan merge.
                          Human parents were computer
                          specialist from California.
Human Clyde: Veteran from Earth/Quizan merge.
Human Nikki: Veteran from Earth/Quizan merge.
Human Cody: Veteran from Earth/Quizan merge.
Human Takeda: Veteran from Earth/Quizan merge.
Human Joshua: Veteran from Earth/Quizan merge.
Human Nick: Veteran from Earth/Quizan merge.

HUMANS:
Cole: The first human with whom a Quizan merges,
                          he becomes Azha.
Frank: Cole's childhood friend/Married Ginger
                          after Cole's disappearance.
Cole Jr.:   Cole's human son with Ginger.
Judy: Frank's ex-wife.
Andrew: Ginger's blind date after Cole disappeared/Bioengineering.

RYQUAT SPECIES:

Ancestors of Humans. Were once inhabitants of Mars. During that period, Mars was a warm planet with oceans of water and rich in oxygen. The Ryquats had evolved into a thriving industrial species who made their presence known across the Milky Way Galaxy.

Several aliens within the galaxy accused the Ryquats of aggressively entering and violating sacred space without permission. Instead of pleading ignorance or asking for a caucus to negotiate, the arrogant Ryquats vowed they would travel wherever and whenever they pleased.

Their defiance split the Milky Way Galaxy and three neighboring galaxies into bloody territorial disputes. The boundaries have never been resolved and the war is ongoing.

One such enemy is the Crozins. They retaliated by disintegrating two of the four small moons that orbited Mars, thus causing a slight shift in all the planets orbiting the sun. Mars slowly lost her rich oxygenated atmosphere, turning her into the red planet that you see today.

It took centuries for the Ryquats to leave their dying planet and relocate to their new home, Zaurak. All the while, relentless Crozins continued to randomly attack the Ryquats as they fled Mars. One of the last Ryquat passenger cargo ships enroute to Zaurak was attacked by a Crozin battleship, causing them to crash onto the harsh surface of Earth. A futile attempt to locate the lost ship was unsuccessful; therefore, she was classified as a *casualty of war.* Most of the Ryquats survived the crash on Palaone.

The survivors found the planet to be hostile with a thin oxygenated atmosphere and a blistering hot surface compared to their once beautiful Mars. Palaone gradually cooled and transformed into today's Earth.

The stranded Ryquats prayed for months that a rescue ship would find them, to no avail. Years later, hope was gone along with their depleted resources and food supplies. Sympathetic Quizans befriended the tattered Ryquats and willingly nurtured them during their acclimation on Earth. As a species, they severely digressed during the first thousand years. By the time the Zaurak Ryquats discovered them, they were considered an inferior species. Rather than destroying the savage Ryquats, the Council renamed them Humans.

Planet:	Zaurak.
Sun:	Hoshi.
Life span:	150 years/Human Ancestors.

Ryquats

Akio:	Battleship Navigator/Battleship.
Anna:	Nurse assigned to Battleship.
Connie:	Captain Victis's first wife.
Heidi:	Captain Victis's first child with Connie. Murdered via Crozin Ukaru, Narthex.
Marylin:	Ryquat who cared for Connie's/Victis second child while captive via the Crozins.
Tilly:	Connie/Victis's second child, born while captives of Crozins.
Vexy:	Captain Victis's second wife/Ryquat Counsel.
Doug Smyth:	Evil Ryquat Battleship Captain.
Fidus Achates:	The coalition of Species within the Orion Belt to protect planets threatened by hostile aliens (Crozins and Gors).
Decree:	Fidus Achates laws.
Decretum code 5-1	Prison or Death sentence.
Viceroy:	Government Officials.
Counsel:	Titles of Viceroy Officials.
Neco Weapon:	Laser handgun. Capable of lifting, moving, and holding items up to 45 kg. Multi-levels of lasers. Worn as a glove.
Vita Brevis:	Ryquat custom space suit. Vita Brevis: Latin (Life is short).

Hikari speed:	Maximum Battleship speed.
Linguistic Chip:	Microchip imbedded under skin.
	Provides translations of alien languages.
Chovo:	Ryquat-bird. Hybrid Ostrich/Chicken/Vulture.
Xenophobia:	Hatred, distrust or contempt of each other species.
Vastuscaelus:	Fifty-eight charted Universes.
Caltaboone:	Ryquat Whiskey.
Mito Drink:	Liquid nourishment.

Japanese words:

Endo Dens:	End transmission.
Anzen' na Tabi:	Safe journey.
Keijo:	Breach/Battleship lockdown.
Baka Yarou:	Stupid asshole.
Damare:	Shut up.
Unko:	Shit.
Nanda:	Hell.

TREKACHAW SPECIES:

Quizans who merged with Ryquats or Humans.

Life span: 500+ years.

Kigen: First purebred male Trekachaw. Parents: Vious/Deneb.

Trinite: Planet once established via Ryquats as a safe haven.

UMDUL SPECIES:

The Umduls are prominent members of the Fidus Achates Territory and close Ryquat allies. Throughout the galaxy, they have a reputation of being formidable warriors and respected spacecraft engineers.

They are sort of cute and ugly at the same time and everything they say seems to end in a question.

Umdul's are approximately four feet tall with squatty bodies and colorful, bushy, baby-fine hair that stands straight up on top of their heads. From the back, their hair either falls in a straight line to their waist or is attached to their spine. Either way, it is by far the most attractive feature of an Umdul.

For thousands of years, the Ryquats provided avian-nautical blue prints and raw materials to the Umduls. In return, the Umduls provided the Ryquats with reliable high-tech battleships, cargo ships, transports, and shuttles. Umduls are brilliant engineers, shrewd in combat, brave and loyal. They are by far the quirkiest species in the Orion Belt.

Planet:	Opus.
Sun:	Uta.
Life span:	200 hundred years.
Government:	Regents.
Advisors:	Chancellors.
Physicians:	Toogus.
Cpt. Pify's Toogus:	Oiba.
Pify:	Battleship Captain and old friend of Victis.
Yagi:	Battleship Captain.
Teltoo:	Battleship Captain.
Oyee:	Battleship Captain.
Poipu:	Battleship Captain.
Marriage:	Pali-Otos.
Tabula Rash:	Clean slate/fresh start.
Inter Nos:	Just between us.
Umdul sex:	Ou-Dim-Fa.
Bailiwick:	Umdul Captains Office.
Bogtu-Urp:	Battleship on high alert.
Raison d' être:	Reason or justification/being or existence.

Uketotta:	Affirmative.
Fizz Tit:	Umdul pets that live in hair.

KIKI SPECIES:

They come from a galaxy called Coma Berenices, about thirty million light years from Zaurak. The Kiki's planet Kowok has about a third of Earth's gravity.

The Kikis are highly sophisticated, virtuous, and courageous beautiful creatures. They walk gracefully upright on two legs and are covered with colorful, iridescent, short feathers except for long, brilliant tail feathers. They are fast and have very slender, sleek bodies. Adult Kiki's stand approximately five to six feet tall. Though they resemble birds on Earth, the Kiki's have arms instead of wings and are unable to fly. Kiki battleships are iridescent like the feathers of the Kiki. For millions of years the Kiki's have been allies of the Umduls.

Planet:	Kowok.
Sun:	Jiju.
Galaxy:	Berenices.
Life span:	175 years.
Pasha:	A Battleship.
Bevy:	A fleet of Battleships.
Jagnar:	Name of Kiki Government Officials.
Mikado:	Title of Battleship Captain.
Thude:	Battleship Captain. Captain Pify's comrade.
Watoto:	Thude's Adjutant.
Hai:	One hour.

Quizan/Gystfin Merges

Myosis: Quizan King. Later deposed, who becomes fixated
                     on destroying his former species.
                     Stole a Gystfin's body/soul for revenge.

Noyac: Myosis' chosen Heir.

Leaders: Noble Quizans of Myosis' cadre. Stole Gystfin souls.

Boo: The Gystfin who reported the genocide of Quizans
                     to the Ryquat Counsel. A Quizan requested
                     to merge with Boo.

GYSTFIN SPECIES:

Enemy of the Quizans. The Gystfins have a reputation of being mercenaries and are not to be trusted. They are known for dangerous manual labor contracts within the Galaxy. The Ryquats and the Gystfins formed a coalition to occupy Palatu and construct enormous mining camps designed to strip the planet of precious ores. The Ryquats supplied the technology and the Gystfins received a percentage for their manual labor. Upon arrival almost a decade ago, the thick-headed brawny Gystfins hunted the frail Quizans simply for the thrill of killing. During one of their many brutal attacks, a Gystfin bit off a Quizan's head and discovered something extraordinary, grey-death energy. The death energy made it possible for the Gystfins to breathe the hostile atmosphere and fly without the aid of an apparatus. This discovery triggered mass executions across the planet.

Gystfins resemble Earth's hyenas, except they're much larger. They have broad shoulders, with long muscular arms and short legs. Their hands look more like paws with three fingers and a short thumb. When the paw is squeezed, the pad extends out revealing six-inch claws like that of a cat. A Gystfin's face is broad and ugly with a wide muzzle baring long, baboon-like yellow fangs. Merged with a Quizan, a Gystfin is stronger and faster than a Trekachaw.

Planet:	Gardux.
Sun:	Mushfig.
Life span:	100 years.
Dux Ducis:	Dignitary.
Kogbor:	Battleship Captain.
Jaaku:	Gystfin God.
Cargo ship:	Used for large inter-space transports.

CROZINS SPECIES:

Ryquats despise Crozins, and they consider them a vile, ugly species. Likewise, and for good reasons, that same sentiment is felt by most Galaxy inhabitants. Crozins walk upright on three-toed hooves, but often run slumped overusing their forearms to gain speed. Their faces are long and narrow with a split nose that can separate. Even from a distance they are easy to recognize by an oversized skull that hangs freakishly disproportioned between their shoulder blades. But despite their appearance, the Crozins are intelligent and feared as ruthless warriors. The Ryquats have been and will be at war with the Crozins until one species is exterminated.

Planet:	Galak.
Sun:	Akuma.
Life span:	150 years.
Ukaru:	Battleship Captain.
Ruk:	Officer.
Tajat Rakta:	Crozin Battleship.
Car-duc. Gen:	Battleship on alert.
Narthex:	Crozin Ukaru who imprisoned Connie (Victis' first wife).

GOR SPECIES:

This species is a vile, vicious race and distant descendants of the Crozins. The Gors evolved on a planet not far from their ancestors into smaller, thick-skinned beings with armored scales that cover most of their backside. If threatened by a superior opponent, the Gors curl into an impenetrable, tight ball. They are difficult to kill and multiply quickly. One saving grace, is their life span is short; on average thirty Earth years.

The Gors and Crozins are known to take great pleasure in torturing Ryquat male adversaries. All male children and most of the female children under ten years are immediately slaughtered for food. Adult female Ryquats, or those close to puberty, are brutally violated and used as slaves by the Crozins until they became too old or ill. Gors hunt the Gystfins for food and use them for slave labor.

Planet: Storsa.
Sun: Zon.
Life span: 30 years.
Jarb: Battleship Captain.

PRO TEMPORE EARTH	Lat., For the time being
IN ABSENTA	Lat., Absence
MALUM	Lat., Evil/Wrong
ANTE BELLUM	Lat., Before the war
VIS - a'- VIS RYQUAT	Fr., Face to Face.
PASSIM	Lat., Here and there.
SEMPER PARATUS	Lat., Preparation
EX TEMPORE	Lat., Out of time
VAE VICTIS	Lat., Woe to the vanquished
DIES IRAE	Lat., Day of wrath, Judgement Day
BON TON	Fr., Good breeding manners
DE NOVO	Lat., From the beginning.
EARTH VADE MECUM	Lat., Summons, go with me
SINE DIE	Lat., Late, without a day to meet again
REQUIESCAT in PACE	Lat., May he rest in peace
EUROPA SOLIST ANTRO	Lat./Sp. One collective
SERVO QUAD NAVIS	Lat., Protect the ship
DEO VOLENTE	Lat., God be willing
PECCAVI	Lat., I have sinned
INTER NOS	Lat., Just beyond us
CASUS BELLI	Lat., Event Provoking war

Acknowledgments

My world changed the day I attended the La Jolla Writers Conference. Jared Kuritz along with a cast of expert speakers lectured on specific topics that gave me a new perspective on the publishing industry. Everything I thought I knew or was guessing became evident and transparent. How can anyone thank another for the gift of a lifetime? My special thanks to Antoinette Kuritz, my mentor, my guiding light. Without her knowledge my book would have never been published.

Thank you.

From the beginning of my career, Galt Police Department Chief Robert S. Fuller took a chance and hired me as a CETA employee. After I graduated from the Sacramento County Sheriff's Academy, Assistant Chief Bill Essex was instrumental in hiring me as a fully sworn police officer at the University of California Davis. Soon after, Chief Calvin Handy supported me and the Police K-9 division at U.C. Davis far and above what I could have ever hoped for. Chief Calvin Handy was and is a friend to this day. Eighteen years later, Chief Victoria Harrison promoted me to Sergeant at the University of California Berkeley. Chief Harrison was a role model for me and an inspiration for all women in law enforcement.

A very special thanks goes to those officers and leaders who encouraged and supported me even when I was insatiable in my quest to explore new adventures in law enforcement.

Lieutenant Earl Tomlinson (E.T.) In the shadows you were my advocate.

Kevin Andrews, the most intelligent and kind person one could know. And, though few people had the privilege of hearing him sing, I can still remember the echoes of his beautiful voice on the Putah Creek path as we walked our police dogs on patrol.

Lynn Matranga, the voice of reason. She treated me like family and gave me advice that kept me safe, even when I resisted.

Dave Orth, my friend. You were incredible fun to work with and a stellar K-9 handler. You introduced me to Travis Air Force Base, where I met Sgt. Kevin Kirkland who trained me to be an Explosive Ordinance Dog Handler.

What can I say about Frank Cioli? My long-time friend and buddy. Love ya.

To Darcy Smith, my adopted daughter. Thank you for everything.

To my niece Anna Schroeder, you have been a diamond in my life ever since sharing a bedroom with you when you were a baby. I'll never forget waking up to that little smile. I cherish our time together.

Writing a book was an incredible journey and more rewarding than I could have ever imagined. None of this would have been possible without all the people I crossed paths with while in Law Enforcement. I want to thank EVERYONE who ever said anything positive to me or taught me something. I heard it all, and it meant something.

About the Author

POLICE SGT. BRENDA FLORES was a pioneer. One of the first women in law enforcement assigned to patrol, she also created the canine police program for U.C. Davis, training canines in police work and bomb detection. A gifted artist, she served as a composite artist for her department. And she was at the forefront of handling domestic violence and abuse issues while on the force.

A wife, mother, and grandmother who is now retired, when not writing Brenda stays active by working out, spending time with family and friends, traveling, and by enjoying all the activities the southern California sunshine has to offer.

While Brenda now finally considers herself a writer, she dreams of someday venturing out into space.

Learn more about Brenda at www.brflores.com

Made in United States
North Haven, CT
01 August 2023

39794609R10236